CRIMSON
LEGACY

THE CRIMSON LEGACY
BOOK ONE

CRIMSON LEGACY

MICHELLE BRYAN

Published by Aelurus Publishing, February 2020

ISBN 13: 978-1-912775-42-2

www.aeluruspublishing.com

For my boys. Thank you for all your support.

CHAPTER 1

Rivercross

It's still dark outside, not quite morning, but I lay wide awake. The sun has yet to rise and start heating up the day. Today is my born day. My eighteenth year. I am, as Miz Emma would say, officially a grown woman. I don't feel any different. I get out of bed, pull on my tunic and trousers, braid my hair, and wash my face in the basin of water beside my bed. My morning ritual. Born day or not, I still have traps to check.

My worn, leather boots are lying under the bed where I dropped them last evening. I pull them on and lace them up real tight. Grada's snoring filters through from the other side of the tin wall that separates my bed from the rest of the shanty like claps of thunder. I grin to myself. With that god-awful racket, it's no wonder I can't sleep. Quietly, so as not to disturb him, I tiptoe around him sleeping on his cot in front of the cold hearth. I don't want to wake him. He's been having troubles sleeping as of late.

On the wooden table next to my water skin and hunting knife waits a surprise. A small bowl of sweet bush berries and a faded blue neck wrapper. My born day gift. A smile tilts my lips. Grada never forgets. The calico cloth looks real familiar. I think maybe it was once a piece of Miz Emma's apron, but it doesn't matter. I know he would've made her a fair trade for the cloth, maybe some jerky or dried taters, something from the cellar. Slim pickings though since the cellar is running mighty low.

I wonder how he'd gotten the berries. You had to walk a fair way now for berries, and ever since Grada fell off the shanty while fixing the roof, his leg's been bothering him something fierce. My guess is he talked Ben into fetching them. However he got them, they look mighty tasty. I pop one into my mouth and bite, and the sweet flavor bursts across my tongue. I cover the rest in the biscuit cloth, saving them for later tonight, but the wrapper I tie around my neck. It'll definitely come in handy today out in the sand lands. The cloth is real soft and smells like washing soap. I hold it up to my nose and take a deep breath before realizing Grada is watching me, smiling under his bushy gray whiskers. I didn't even notice the snoring had stopped.

His hair sticks up in white tufts and his eyes are heavy with sleep.

"You found your gift all right then," he says, and I smile.

"Aye. It's lovely, Grada, truly is. Thank you."

I go to him, kiss his wrinkled cheek, and pull his blanket over his shoulders.

"Sleep now," I say. "It's still barely mornin' yet."

"You takin' the bow?" he asks at my back as I head back to the table.

I nod as I put the knife and water skin in my slingbag and hook the bow and quiver over my shoulder.

"Just in case. You never know when you're gonna sight a wild rabbit or such," I say.

"Well, don't stray too far. There's been sightin's of a couple of wild wolflings roamin' to the north. You don't wanna run into them."

I nod again at his words. "Yeah, I heard about that."

"Be careful, girlie," he says.

I grin at his worry. He says the same words every time. I've been doing our hunting for years now. I think it's time he got over the worrying part already.

"I will, Grada. I'll be back before noon."

I cover my head with my hat, pick up my slingbag, and head out. The sun is just starting to crest the horizon, but the morning's already warm. It's going to be another scorcher.

There's another early riser up along with me. Shelly is already at the well in the center of the shanties, filling her cooking pot. She smiles at me as I join her to fill my water skin.

"Mornin' Tara," she says, and I nod a greeting. "Happy born day."

"Thank you," I say.

"Eighteenth if I recall. Gods, the time does fly by. Seems

like it's only been a few years since your Grada brought you home." She shakes her head like she can't believe her own words.

"It's gonna be a grand celebration tonight for certain. It's not every day you become a woman, now is it? Thomas was already out and found a nice big hunk of prickly wood for tonight's fire. He says the secret to a good celebration is a slow-burning fire and a fast-burning whiskey." She laughs at herself. I laugh too, though I don't think it's funny at all, but I don't wanna be ill-mannered.

"Why, I remember for my eighteenth born day we—"

"Ma … hurry up with the water. I'm starvin'." Young Thomas, one of Shelly's two young'uns, yells at her from their shanty door. *Thank gods*, I think. Shelly is a fine woman but once she starts talking, she doesn't know when to shut up.

"I'm a comin'," she yells back, and I wince. The screech sounds more like some cat that got its tail stuck in a shanty door. Smiling back at me, she says, "I'll see you tonight, child."

"Aye, you will." I cap my water skin and watch her hauling the heavy, black, metal pot towards the shanty, thinking maybe I should help. But then young Thomas runs out to meet her. He grins at me and waves as he takes the pot from his ma. I wave back. I like him; he's a good boy.

I don't meet nobody else. The rest of the shanties are quiet and still. Everybody's either still sleeping or already out trying to garner some kind of offering from this barren land. I don't even meet Lou, which I think is a bit peculiar. He's always up before dawn, working on his copper still, shining and cleaning. I truly believe he thinks more of that still than he does his own shanty. Then again, I guess you can't get whiskey from a shanty, and Lou ... well, he likes his whiskey.

I trudge over the dry earth heading out of the village, each step sending up a puff of dust into the air. Haven't seen rain for quite some time now, the brown, muddy well water a true testament to that. But we keep hoping. Sometimes we get teased with dark clouds on the horizon, and we pray to the gods that they make it this far. But they don't. They just break up and disappear before they get anywhere near us. Grada believes the rain will come. He says it always does, that the gods wouldn't be so cruel. I can't understand why he thinks this because if the old folks' stories are to be believed, the gods have always been cruel.

The old folk say that the land wasn't always dry and barren. I grew up hearing stories of how once, long ago, the land had been green and alive. How every kind of plant imaginable had grown wild and that crops had covered fields as far as your eye could see, just waiting for the harvest. It was said that rivers ran swift and clear and were so full of fish they looked like shadows moving in the water. They would tell us young'uns of how the settlers long before us had built huge buildings called shop markets filled with food and supplies, and you could just walk right in and take what you wanted. And that those same settlers could travel over the sand lands—in a day no less—in moving machines called "veacals" and fly through the air.

Those stories were passed down through the years, and I heard them over and over again. And like every other young'un, I listened to them all wide-eyed and reckoned every word to be the gods' honest truth.

I don't really know if I believe them anymore. It's my eighteenth born day. I shouldn't believe in the children's tales even if Grada swears they're all true. He says when he was a boy he saw one of their flying veacals. Or what was left of it anyways. There wasn't much left of anything from before the Shift.

The Shift. That's what the old folk called … well, whatever it was that happened to the lands a long time ago. Grada was full of fanciful stories, but I know there's some truth to the tales. There has to be since I've seen for myself ruins of old settler buildings, rotted away and half-buried by the sands. And just about two leagues from Rivercross, there's an old relic field that we call the pickin' grounds. Found things there I can't rightly explain, but they come in real handy.

What happened to the settlers that owned all that stuff? I really can't say for sure. The old folk have their version. They say it was a terrible sickness. A man-made plague that killed off most of the people or changed them into muties. They say the plague was the consequence of the third great world war. Third. As in number three. I guess they didn't learn their lesson from the first two? But the story goes this third war destroyed the land and made it the way we know it: a dry, dusty, barren land scorched by the sun and cruel to every living creature that now walked upon it. If this was all true and the gods allowed for that to happen, then I don't believe they really care if the rains come or not.

I pull the brim of my hat down a bit lower to shield my eyes. The sun is climbing now in the cloudless, blue sky. A blazing and merciless ball of fire. I look out over the landscape that lies before me, shimmering already in the morning heat.

The hard-baked, cracked ground I'm walking on with its sparse brush and stunted prickly trees that only grow to your waist is so unlike the green wetlands of the stories that it's kind of hard to believe they truly existed at all. Don't even know why the stories are knocking around in my head this morning. Maybe because it's my born day, and I'm thinking about tonight's celebration.

My stomach quivers in anticipation. Born days are real special in Rivercross. We don't usually have much cause for celebrating, so the whole village gets involved when we do. There would be food, storytelling, and music. Grada or Thomas usually did the storytelling, and Shelly, well even though that woman's voice hurt your ears from her talking, her singing could bring you to tears it was so lovely. Lou would break out his brewed whiskey. That always made the old folk smile. And just thinking about Miz Emma's sweet berry bread made my mouth water. She always made berry bread for everybody's born day—if we could get berries that is—and it was the best I ever tasted. Well, it's the only one I ever tasted, but doesn't mean it wasn't the best. Grada always said there was none better in the world, but I reckon he hasn't been more than two day's travel from Rivercross anymore than I have.

Rivercross is my home. Lived here my whole life. Not much to look at. Ten shanties built out of whatever could be scavenged from the pickin' grounds. Mostly plastic and metal, a bit of rock, and some wood if you were lucky enough to find it. About twenty-five of us or so live here, mainly old folk. Besides myself, there's only three other young'uns. There used to be more, but sickness came about five years ago and took some of the folk, old and young alike. Even Grada fell mighty sickly. I tended to him for days, wiping down his fevered face, holding his hand, and willing him to live. He'd been the only lucky one. He had fought it off. The others … they weren't so lucky. It didn't affect me at all though. I can't remember ever being sickly a day in my life, but I do remember that. It had been a real bad time.

Rivercross is just as good a place to live as any I reckon, and better than some. We're family. We look out for one another. We grow what we're able in the tired soil. Sometimes, if we're real lucky, we get enough rain for a fine harvest of taters or yellow corn. It's always a good year when that happens. We forage for berries, hunt and trap what game we can find. Hunting used to be a lot easier with Grada's iron shooter, but we haven't had lead slugs for it going on two years now, so I do my hunting with my crossbow. Grada says I'm a natural with the bow and the snare wires we got off a trader some time back. Can't remember what we traded for them, but it was the best trade we ever did. Dirt dog meat is the main source of food for the folk of Rivercross now, and my snare wires do most of the supplying. I don't mind. I look forward to checking my trap line every morning, up and out before the sun gets too hot and the day so dry so that all you can taste are sand grits. It's quiet and peaceful and allows me time to think. And sometimes when I'm just standing and watching the sun rise, I swear the land speaks to me. Nothing like real words. Nah, that would be bat shite crazy. But I swear I can hear it waking from its nightly slumber and welcoming the sun. I can even tell sometimes when the rain is coming since I feel the land's eagerness for the water.

I tried to explain this to my friend, Ben, but he just tells me to keep my mouth shut about it else people might think I belong out in the sand lands with the muties. So I don't mention it to anyone. It's a secret between me and the land.

I move up the trail a bit more and hunker down by a scraggly bush to check on my next trap. Unlike the ones before, this one has snared a dirt dog. Good. I'd promised fresh meat for tonight's stew, and I didn't want to disappoint. I hook the furry carcass onto the strap of my slingbag and say a quiet "thank you" to the critter for its sacrifice. Ben scoffs at me when I do this. He calls it superstitious shite, but I believe in thanking the land for providing. And I won't admit it to him, but I truly believe the land hears me when I do.

Shizen, it's hot. Lifting my hat, I wipe the dust and sweat from my face with my neck wrapper. A warm, southerly wind picks up and feels real good blowing through my sweat-soaked hair. The day is heating up real quick. I'd best be finished before the sun sits too high in the sky.

I keep moving up the trap line, humming a tune that pops into my head. I try to remember what song it's from, but I draw a blank. I don't recall ever hearing Shelly or Grada sing it before, but they must have. I hum it a bit more, and it scratches at my brain. *Maybe*, I think, *it's something my ma used to sing to me when I was a baby*. Wouldn't that be something?

I don't remember my ma, or my pa for that matter. Never knew them, but I reckon I must have had them at some point. Nobody in Rivercross ever knew them. Don't exactly know where I come from. Grada says he found me one day while he was out scavenging. All he was looking to find was some medicinal herbs or at least some good trading trinkets, but instead he stumbled upon me. He says I was just laying in a building husk, crying my fool head off and as dirty as the day was long. He reckoned I'd been there a couple of days at least and that no one was going to come looking anytime soon. There was no sign of my folks. He didn't know if I was left there on purpose like or if something awful bad happened to my ma and pa.

As low as it sounds, I like to think they were eaten by devil cats or taken by a dust storm. It kind of makes me feel better than thinking they had just left me on my own to die. Grada, now saddled with a bawling, hungry baby, figured he may as well take me home and he reared me ever since. For eighteen years now, so today is really my "found" day. I always laugh when he says that.

He's been real good to me, taught me everything I know. He's a mighty fine shot with the crossbow and the iron shooter, but he says there are days when I'm a hell of a lot better. He taught me to plant for harvest and to find and brew the medicinal herbs needed to treat sickness and infection. He showed me how to make stew and corn biscuits, though mine always turn out awful bad tasting. He also taught me to read and write some. Even though I didn't see the point of that, he kept saying it would come in handy someday, so I didn't argue the learning … much. I just went along with it. Can't say an opportunity has ever arisen out in the sand lands for me to use my word learning, but as long as it made Grada happy. He loves me like a real grada. Though some days when I rattle his nerves, he says he should have traded me instead of keeping me, but I know he doesn't mean it.

The hot wind blows stronger now, and dust fills my mouth. I pull the neck wrapper up for cover and turn into the wind towards Rivercross. The sun is getting a bit high in the sky. Ben's late this morning. Then, as if my thoughts conjure him up, I see him running across the sandy ground like a bunch of devil cats are nipping at his heels. I smile underneath the wrapper. That boy is always rushing to get nowhere.

The familiar "Hey, Tar-Tar," reaches my ears shortly before I'm lifted up in a bone-crushing hug.

"Happy born day."

I punch him in the shoulder. "Put me down, you mule turd."

He does as I say, and I look up into his face, amazed again that I have to do so. Growing up, I was always the bigger and taller one being as I was a few months older. But this year, he's grown so much. He must be a good head above me now. It's a bit unsettling. He's covered in a layer of dust from his boots to the top of his sun yellow hair, but his brown eyes are shining bright with laughter.

"And how does it feel to be an old folk now?"

"What? Who you callin' old?" I snap. "I can still kick your butt, boy, like always, so show some respect."

He laughs. A loud, belly-busting sound. That laugh always brings a smile to my face.

"Aye, no doubt you could," he says. "I brought you something."

I grab eagerly for the cloth he takes from his slingbag, but he pulls it out of my reach and holds it high above his head.

"Hey, not yet. We gotta eat first. Me and Pa were out

before dawn, and I'm starvin'."

His words irritate me some, and I don't try to hide it, but it just makes him smile more. He truly enjoys teasing me.

A shallow cave of rock with a small overhang sits in the middle of the trap line, giving us protection from the wind and dust. Our usual place to rest up when we're out hunting. We settle down in our little nook, and Ben pulls from his slingbag a water skin and two round wedges of sweet berry bread.

"Here. Ma said 'cause it's your special womanly born day, you can have an early treat."

I ignore his snicker of amusement at my expense, and eagerly take the offering. It's still warm. I hold it up to my nose and sniff, and the smell makes my mouth water in anticipation. Not able to wait any longer, I take a huge bite. The sweet berry flavor floods my mouth, and I close my eyes. It's so good.

"Shizen, this is delicious," I say around the hunk of bread in my mouth, but I don't think Ben understands. He looks at me in confusion, then shakes his head and laughs.

"Just close your mouth and chew, Tara."

I do as he says. Taking a swig from the water skin, I wipe my mouth with my sleeve.

"Your ma is the best cook ever," I say.

"Aye, that she is," he agrees.

We eat in silence for a bit, just enjoying the rare treat and listening to the wind howl as it raises and swirls little dust devils outside our shelter. I keep eyeing the gift Ben has left sitting between us the whole time. He knows it's bothering me, but he ignores my burning curiosity.

"Found a good patch of berry bushes yesterday out past the old swimmin' hole," he says, breaking our comfortable silence.

"Oh yeah?" I ask. The swimming hole has been dried up for years now. I haven't been there in a while.

"Got us a good bucket full, me and Pa. Ma was real pleased."

I nod. "I reckoned the berries this mornin' had been your doing."

"Aye. I snuck 'em in real early. Your Grada asked me to. You were still sleepin' and snorin' like Lou's old hound used to do."

"What?" My eyes open wide with indignation. "I was not. I don't snore."

"Now, how do you know if you're asleep?" he says. "I ain't lyin'. You nearly busted my eardrum."

But he's laughing, so I know he's just pulling my leg again.

"You're an asshole," I say.

He raises an eyebrow at me. "Oh, is that so?" He picks up the gift and starts stuffing it back in his slingbag. "If I remember correctly, Ma's got a born day comin' up soon. I'm pretty sure she don't think I'm an asshole."

"No." I lunge at the gift. "I'm sorry, Ben, truly."

He holds it above my head again. "Truly?" he asks.

I nod. "Cross my heart."

"Okay, here."

I yank it from his hands, and once it's safe in my possession, I mutter, "Sorry you're an asshole." He snorts with laughter.

Gently, I place the cloth on my lap and start to unfold

the layers. Lying inside is a flower, but not like any flower I've ever seen around Rivercross. Couldn't put a name to it, or what it's made from. Maybe some kind of settler plastic. The flower's center is pure white, but the petals surrounding it are all shiny black. One of the petals has a leather thong laced through it to wear around my neck. Despite the couple of chipped edges, it's one of the most beautiful things I've ever seen. But all I can manage is a stupid, "Oh."

Ben lifts a brow, worry creasing his forehead. "That's it? Oh? You don't like it?"

"No, it ain't that." I hurry to reassure him. "It's just … I've never owned anything so pretty before."

I guess it's the right thing to say since he's smiling again.

"Well go ahead … put it on."

I untie my neck wrapper and start to place the leather strand around my neck, but Ben scoots over and takes it out of my hands to do it for me. I lift my long braid out of his way.

"Found it last week when me and Pa were out at the pickin' grounds. The bucket it was stuck to was full of these things, but this one … this one was special. Had a hell of a time gettin' it offa the bucket, but I knew it had to be this one 'cause the black and white was just like your hair. Made me think of you."

He stops talking, but right away my hands move instinctively to cover my hair. My hair is as black as crow feathers, but it has these two gods-awful white stripes on both sides of my face that run from the top of my head straight to the ends. It's always been like that for as long as I can remember.

I can't recall how many times the old folk would say "how strange" it was or joke about how I must be a mutie or something. I always tried to hide them in braids or under my hat, but they were a real sore spot with me. Hearing Ben mention them makes me selfconscious. He pushes my hands back to my lap and goes right on talking.

"It reminded me of how darn pretty your hair is, so I says to myself, 'Ben, this has got to be Tara's born day gift.'" His hands brush the back of my neck, making me shiver. "There, nice and tight so you won't lose it."

I glance down at it lying against my dingy tunic. I'm quiet for a bit. I've never been good at putting my soft feelings into words. Ben has always been better at that sort of stuff. But I want him to know what it means to me.

"Thank you, Ben. It truly is the best born day gift ever," I say quietly.

He shrugs and then grins at me, the laughter back in his eyes.

"Weren't nuthin'. Would have given you the bucket too, but Pa figured it would come in real handy for takin' out the slop."

I laugh at this. I laugh so hard I get a shooting pain in my gut. Trust Ben to turn our conversation to slop.

"You're an—"

"Asshole. I know, I know," he says and ducks the punch I throw at his shoulder. "Hey, if you want help checkin' the trap line, you better stop with the hittin'."

"Lot of good you are to me … ain't much of it left to check," I say, but I'm just teasing.

My words halt his laughter, and he glances at my slingbag.

"You're almost finished checkin', and that's all you got? Two dirt dogs?" he says in disbelief.

"Yeah," I say. "Not much, I know. Was hopin' for a couple more at least. If I don't find any then I think I might head out a bit further into the sand lands, see if I can catch a wild rabbit or maybe even a wild hog."

He looks at me, eyes wide in disbelief, before bursting into laughter again. But this laugh is tinged with a touch of sarcasm.

"Wild hog? Ain't been no wild hog around these parts goin' on two years now, Tara. You're talkin' foolishness."

I know he's right. There hasn't been any decent game spotted anywhere near Rivercross in a long time. But his laughing at me only irritates my snarky self.

"Who are you to say I won't find no wild hog? You a seer now like old Molly?" I snap.

"No, but I'm not a fool either." The smile drops from his face, and his look turns serious all of a sudden. Not the look I'm used to seeing. "I know what's happenin' even though none of the old folk will say so. Rivercross is a dyin' place, Tara. I cain't remember the last time we caught us a fish, or rabbit, or hog … can you?"

I want to argue. I don't want to admit he's right, but I finally concede with a slight shrug. "It's been a long time."

"Exactly. And we ain't ever gonna see them things again, mark my words. We ain't ever gonna see that river run no more either. Might as well call the place Muddy Cross since it's all that's left of that damn river."

He's angry. His face flushes a deep red and his brow furrows. I've never seen him look like that and it truly surprises me. Ben is never angry. He's always joking, or laughing, or downright irritating, but never angry. My surprise must be evident because he glances away in shame.

"I'm sorry, Tara," he sighs. "I shouldn't have snapped at you like that and on your born day and all. It's just …," he looks back at me, and his eyes remind me more of some old man than his true seventeen years. "Don't you ever worry about what's gonna happen to Rivercross? To us?"

"What are you sayin', Ben?" I don't like how he's talking.

He scratches his head, mussing his hair even more so and loosening some dust that floats lazily in a stray sunbeam sneaking through the cracks above our heads. "I cain't understand why the old folk don't do nuthin'. Every year is worse than the one before. Every year, we have less, and it gets harder to find. And what do they say? 'Oh, the gods will provide. The gods will bring rain.' It's a load of shite. We ain't had rain in months. The well is all but dried up along with the river. All the animals have practically died off. And the harvest … well, there ain't no way in dirt dog hell we're gonna have a harvest this year or the next."

I know he's speaking the truth, but like the old folk, I guess I don't want to admit it either.

"Then we go look for water," I say. "There's gotta be another river or spring somewhere. We find it, and we bring water back. We dig another well maybe, whatever we have to do. If we gotta travel further into the sand lands to find game, then we do that, too. And the rain will come, you'll see, and there will be a harvest next year."

"Tara," he stops me from talking. "Open your eyes. You sound worse than the old folk, than Pa. Rivercross is dead."

"No," I argue.

"Yes, Tara."

"No, you're wrong." His words fuel my anger.

"Why you bein' so mule-headed about this?" he asks.

"Because. This is our home. To say Rivercross is dead is to give up on our home, and I ain't no quitter and neither are you." I poke him in the chest so hard it hurts my finger.

He just sighs at me. "I'm not sayin' we should give up, hell no. What I'm sayin' is we should move on elsewhere. And if the old folk weren't so stubborn, they would know that's the right thing to do. There's gotta be a better place out there," he jerks his hand toward the sand lands, "somewhere."

I tamp my anger down and stare at him. "You talked to your pa about this then?"

He nods. "Aye. He's too stubborn to see it though, just like the rest of them. He keeps sayin' it will turn around, and that a boy my age shouldn't be concerned about things of that nature. It's just frustratin'."

"You ever think maybe he's right?" My words are hard. "Maybe we ain't got no reason to be concerned. The old folk have been around a long time. They're not gonna let Rivercross perish. You gotta know that. Grada and your pa and the others, they know what they're doin'. And as for *out there*," I use his words, "there ain't nuthin' out there except ruins and dead lands. And beyond that, what? Muties and raiders and critters that'll just rip us into pieces, gobble us up, and shite us out."

I'm not expecting the laughter.

"We ain't ever been more than a day's travel from Rivercross. How the hell do you know what's out there?

Muties? Raiders? Have you ever seen such things, Tara, or you just lettin' the old folk scare you with such nonsense?"

In all the years I've known Ben, I've never heard him talk like this. Something sure has got him riled up. "It's not just the old folk. The traders that pass through Rivercross sometimes speak of such things, too. You've heard 'em same as me," I say.

"Aye, I've heard their stories around the campfires. I've also heard 'em speak of magic and witches and monsters. Does that make it all true? It's just tales, Tara, meant for scarin' young'uns. Don't try to tell me you don't believe the same."

He knows me too well. But unlike Ben, I don't want to say those thoughts out loud. To speak ill of the old folk seems wrong and disrespectful somehow. He takes my silence as agreement.

"Look, we know there's other places out there somewhere. Other villages. The traders prove that much. They have to come from somewhere. They ain't just blown to life by the dust and the wind. All I'm sayin' is maybe where they come from is better than here. Don't you think we should at least find out for ourselves?"

I finally understand what he's trying to say, and it scares me. "You want to leave Rivercross?" I'm shocked. I can't imagine living here without Ben. We grew up together. Did everything together. We were kin.

He shrugs. "Dunno ... maybe. Been thinkin' about it for a while now. Who knows what I could find? The world's a big place, Tara. Bigger than you or I can imagine, I reckon. Maybe I'd find some magical place where there's always fresh water, always a good harvest, and always clean beds with not a single damn grain of sand in 'em."

I consider his words in silence for a moment. "Yeah, maybe you will," I agree finally. "And then again, maybe I'll shoot a wild hog today, too."

I know he's trying to stay somber, but he can't keep a straight face and he laughs. A big, honkin' belly laugh.

"Okay, you win this one," he snorts.

"I win always." I toss his water skin at him in victory. "Come on. Enough talkin' already. We still got work to do. That trap line ain't gonna check itself."

He scowls at me, but his eyes are still twinkling as he packs up like I ask. I follow him back out into the heat of the day, glad we're not arguing no more. It would have ruined my born day gift with all that talk about leaving Rivercross. I know he isn't serious about that … he'll come around. He never was one to stay somber for long.

I hitch my bag over my shoulder and glance down at my flower, admiring how it sparkles in the sun. I'm so busy studying it I don't see Ben stop in his tracks right in front of me. I ram into his back, almost knocking me off my feet.

"What the …?" I right myself and follow his gaze to the horizon. A huge cloud of dust, about two leagues away, is rolling towards Rivercross.

"What is it?" I ask, anxiously. "A rider?"

He squints into the sun. "No, too big."

"A dust storm?"

"Dunno … maybe."

We watch in silence as it draws closer.

"Whatever it is, it's movin' fast," I say.

Then we feel it. Vibrations under our feet like thunder, only unlike thunder, it doesn't stop. I've never felt the ground shake like this, and a knot of fear starts growing in my belly. I stare at Ben and the worry on his face makes the knot tighten.

"Maybe we should head back," he says.

"Yeah," I agree.

We start running full out as the vibrations grow stronger. Even the land is disturbed by the dust cloud since I can sense its distress and its whispers of *danger*.

———•◦•———

Every villager is out watching the dust cloud move in. Some are holding their axes or bows, some pitchforks, but every single one looks mighty scared. Their fear hangs heavy in the air, almost like you can reach out and touch it. I've never experienced this kind of shared worry before, not even from the lightning storms or massive sand-devils that spring up sometimes without warning. Doesn't take a genius to figure out something real bad is happening.

Shelly runs up to us as soon as she spots us, panic etched in her face. "Have you seen Jane and young Thomas?" She's nearly screaming at us she's so scared. I shake my head no, and she wrings her hands. "Oh gods, they were out playing. I gotta find 'em. Help me find 'em!"

She don't wait for us to help though. She just takes off, yelling their names, her worry making her voice high and shrill. I look over at Ben. His dark eyes are clouded with panic.

"Go get your crossbow," I order him. "This ain't good. And tell your pa to get his ax. I gotta find Grada."

Used to my gut instincts, he don't question me. He just gives me a curt nod and runs off. I head for the shanty, the vibrations in the ground so strong now they jar my bones.

Grada comes limping around the shanty, his look of relief evident as he spots me. He calls to me, but I can't hear his shout over Shelly's yelling. I run to him, struck by the panic in his face. I've never seen him look like that. Grada is a big man, a brave man. I've never seen him scared of anything. It terrifies me something fierce.

"Tara! You have to come with me right now. You need to get to the storm cellar." He reaches for me, not giving me time to respond. Grabbing my wrist in his beefy hand, he starts hauling me around the shanty toward the back.

"Grada, no. It ain't a dust storm," I say, thinking he must be confused. As if to confirm my words, the rumbling vibrations from the cloud are made much worse by a high-pitched screeching. No. Screaming. I look over my shoulder. The massive dust plume is almost upon Rivercross now, and every villager can plainly see what it was hiding. I stop in my tracks, frozen.

Shizen. I've never seen anything like it in my life. Black metal monsters crawl over the land, gobbling it up and spitting out the dust. There's three from what I can see, rolling on huge wheels taller than any man. They're like something straight out of a night terror. I can't even begin to comprehend what they are.

"Tara, no."

I don't even realize I'm gravitating towards them and the

screaming villagers until Grada grabs me around the waist, nearly lifting me off my feet.

"There's no time. You have to get to the cellar."

Old Molly runs by us screaming, her eyes bulging with fear. I vaguely notice she's only wearing one boot, but she doesn't seem to pay heed to the sharp rocks cutting into her bare foot.

"They found us! Death is here!"

She trips and goes sprawling in the dirt.

I should help her, I think. But I can't move. I can't breathe.

Everybody's running and screaming, but it's muffled like I'm back at the swimming hole listening to it all from under the water. Like none of it is happening for real.

Molly scrambles back to her feet and runs straight for us. She gets so close in my face I can see the beads of sweat lining her upper lip.

"Hide from 'em, girl," she whispers, her eyes wild and crazy as she stares into mine. "Don't let 'em get ya."

Then a visible shiver wracks her body before she tears her eyes from me and runs in the opposite direction.

"I have to find Ben," I croak as Molly's fear soaks through my skin. I try to pull away from Grada's grip, but he just holds me tighter and shakes me, making my teeth rattle.

"Listen to me, Tara, and mind what I'm saying. You have to hide in the storm cellar. I'll cover it well enough. They won't find you. You stay in there nice and quiet until they're gone."

I hear his words. I see his lips moving, but what he's saying doesn't making sense.

"I'm sorry. I thought we woulda had more time …"

He looks over my shoulder, and the despair in his face makes me want to cry. But he keeps talking.

"When they've gone, you follow the riverbed east to a place called Littlepass. You find a healer there by the name of Lily. You find her and tell her who you are. You tell her … tell her she was right. Tell her I'm sorry, and I should have sent word long ago but … I was being a selfish old man. You mindin' me, girl?"

He shakes me again and his words finally sink in.

"No!" I scream in his face. "I ain't hidin'. I ain't leavin' y'all out here. We need to fight, Grada. Whatever those … things are, we gotta fight 'em. We gotta protect everybody."

He shakes his head at my words, and his hands leave my shoulders to fall at his side.

"No, girlie, we cain't stop 'em."

The rumbling is so loud now it's hurting my ears. I stare into Grada's face. His eyes look empty. Dead. And I know he's already accepted what's about to happen.

"No!" The denial bursts out of me; I can't hold it in. There's a strange burning flowing through me, like my blood is on fire. "We will fight. We have to."

I tear the crossbow from my shoulder, thread my arrow and turn to face the oncoming threat. I know in my soul that I have to protect Grada, Ben, everyone. I have to at least try.

"I'm sorry, child, but you must stay alive."

Grada's voice, strangely calm in the face of all this chaos, disturbs me right to my core. I turn to him just in time to see the cooking pot from our fire pit aiming straight for my head.

Blackness surrounds me like a cloak. I think my eyes are open, but I can't see. I'm lying on my stomach. The cold ground presses into my cheek and I roll over. Where am I? I try to stand, but a shooting pain in my temple sends me back down to my knees. My stomach flips and churns like I'm about to retch up Miz Emma's berry bread.

I remain on my knees, take a few deep breaths and the bread thankfully stays in my stomach. My head throbs something fierce. I reach up, probing gingerly above my left eye where it hurts the most. There's a lump about the size of an egg and real tender to the touch. I'm bleeding, too, the sticky liquid covering the side of my face. How'd this happen? I can't think straight. But then I remember. I remember Grada hitting me with the cooking pot, the metal monsters, everything. It all comes flooding back into my head, and panic starts clawing at my throat.

I need to get out of here. I have to find Grada and Ben. I try to gather my wits. My muddled brain tells me I'm in the storm cellar because I can smell the familiar scent of damp earth mixed with dried herbs. My steps are tentative as I reach out with my hands, feeling my way through the darkness and the stairs to the hatch. I keep moving, scuffing my feet in the dirt until finally my boot hits something solid. The stairs. I crawl up on my hands and knees, bringing up in the hatch and creating a whole new wave of pain. I ignore it, pushing on the wood cover blocking my way. It won't open. I push again, harder this time.

Nothing. There must be something lying on top of it and weighing it down. I try to keep my panic under control, but the blackness is pressing in on me and making it hard to breathe. I push on it again with all my might and then start ramming it with my shoulder, putting all my weight behind it. Each jolt is causing me so much pain I think I just might black out again. But finally, I hear something shift and the hatch flies open. I'm instantly blinded by light, and my arms go up to cover my eyes.

Smoke is the first thing I notice, followed by the deafening silence. Blinking away tears, I peer through the haze covering the village like a dense fog.

Crawling out of the cellar, I move the overturned water barrel blocking my way. That must have been what was covering the hatch and keeping it down. I push to my knees, then stand upright, swaying a little as I try to get my bearings. The smoke is all around me, burning my eyes and my throat. I suddenly realize it's the shanties that are smouldering, some even starting to fall in on themselves. Oh gods. Our homes are burning.

I start coughing and pull my wrapper over my nose and mouth, still searching for any movement in the dense smoke. I don't see anybody. Where are they?

"Grada? Ben? Hey?" My voice shatters the quiet. "Shelly? Molly?"

I receive no answer. I take a couple of steps through the ghostly tendrils surrounding me, but I can't find a soul.

"Ben? Grada … Can anybody hear me?" I'm screaming now, but I can't help it. I'm scared. Why isn't anyone answering me? I stumble to our shanty. The roof has already fallen in and there's smoke billowing out the open door. No, Grada's not in there, I tell myself. He can't be.

He and the others, they must have gone somewhere safe. I just have to find them.

I run to the next shanty and the next, still calling out their names.

The smoke is overpowering. It's hard to see, to breathe, but I don't stop. I'm desperate to find somebody.

Making my way to Lou's shanty at the edge of the riverbed, I notice the copper still knocked over, all broken and twisted.

Lou's gonna be pissed, I think dully.

There's still flames burning inside his shanty, but I run right up to it anyways, calling out his name and hoping for an answer.

That's when I see them.

They're spread along the edge of the riverbed like everyone of them lay down to take a rest at the same time. All in a line so neat that maybe, I'm thinking, maybe they are sleeping, even though the pain blossoming in my chest is saying elsewise. I don't want to go any closer, but my feet move on their own accord.

"No, no, no, no."

A miserable wailing reaches my ears, and it takes me a moment to realize the sound is coming from me.

Lou is the first I see. His arm is lying across his chest, and his sightless eyes are staring up at the sky like he's just cloud watching. There's a dark red stain spread out underneath his arm. My chest tightens, and I start gasping for air, but I keep looking.

Shelly is lying where she fell, all bloody and still. Thomas is crumpled over her, like he was trying to protect her. Ben's ma and pa are next. They're holding hands, but their eyes are open. Lifeless. Dead. At the sight of them my legs go out from under me, and I fall to my knees.

I can't look anymore. I want to scratch my eyes out so I won't have to look at them. But my eyes don't listen to my brain, and they keep searching until they find the familiar face.

Grada.

I crawl to him on my hands and knees, ignoring the sharp rocks biting painfully into my palms. The pain in my chest is far more excruciating. Sobbing his name now as if expecting an answer, I grab his hands. They're still warm. *Maybe he's okay*, I think, even though he's got the same bloody hole in his chest like the others. I cover the wound with my hand, willing him to be okay just like when he was real sick. I willed him better then; I can do it again. Come on Grada, wake up. Wake up. Wake up, damn it!

He doesn't wake up.

Feels like there's a knife twisting in my chest, ripping me open. I've never felt such anguish. Surely, my heart will burst apart from this pain.

"No, Grada," I whisper. I rub his face. His whiskers are rough against my hand. His blue eyes are open and staring. I close them gently and kiss his forehead. I don't even realize I'm crying until my tears splash onto his cheek.

The pain overtakes me. It hurts so bad. I wrap my arms around him and lay beside him, wishing for the pain to take me too. I close my eyes. I don't want to look anymore. I don't want to see any more dead faces of the people I love. I don't want to see Ben's brown eyes with the light all snuffed out.

Some time passes. I don't know how long I laid there. I

can't rightly say I would have ever got back up, but through the mist of grief, I hear my name. It's all low and choky like somebody was trying to talk through a mouth full of root wad, but I hear it.

"Tara …"

I sit up, listening. I start to think my mind is playing tricks on me when I hear it again. Then I see a slight movement out of the corner of my eye. Somebody is moving.

Molly!

I crawl to her, reaching for her like she's a lifeline. I grab her hand, bawling again, so overcome that somebody's still alive. She has the same chest wound as Grada and the others. I know it's an iron shooter that's caused it. I also know chances aren't good she'll make it, but for now she's alive.

"They didn't get … you girl … good …," she says.

"Shhhh," I whisper to her. "Don't try to talk … save your strength."

She pats the hand holding hers as if she's trying to comfort me.

"Don't fret … 'bout me, child … my time … is passed …" She gasps for air, and her chest makes this awful gurgling sound. I shake my head and try to shush her again, but she's not done.

"They took … the young'uns … but not you …," she says. She takes a coughing fit then, and blood sprays from her mouth down the front of my tunic. I wipe the blood from her mouth with my sleeve.

"Molly … just stay with me … please." I beg desperately.

She grips my hand so tight it hurts me. I can't understand how she has such strength. There's so much blood. Her eyes burn into mine something fierce.

"I seen it, aye I did … I knew you … was special, child … they're gonna need you … to show 'em the way …"

That's all. She doesn't say another word. She sighs, and I watch as the light in her eyes fades away. Her hand, so strong earlier, goes limp and I shake it with a desperate need.

"Molly," I cry. "Molly … please."

It doesn't do any good. She's already gone.

I kiss her calloused palm and lay her hand by her side. A sob escapes me. I hurt all over. I'm so full of pain and fear that I want to scream so as to release the overwhelming pressure in my chest. I run my hands through my hair, look around … alone … lost. I don't know what I should do now. I don't know.

Then slowly Molly's words break through my paralyzing grief.

"They took the young'uns."

They took them.

I force myself to stand, to make my way through the line of death. I look at every loved face lying there. Everybody I'd ever known my whole life is there, but not young Thomas. Not Jane. Not Ben.

My legs go numb again, but this time from relief. They're still alive! A strangled laugh escapes at the thought, but right away I cover my mouth with my hand, stifling the sound and feeling ashamed for the spark of happiness. How dare I be happy when everybody else is gone? Dead.

Staggering away from the carnage, I focus on the horizon and the sinking sun. Anything but the dead.

It's gonna be dark soon, I think. The day is almost done.

My born day. I'd forgotten. I look down at my tunic. At my gift from Ben, hoping that somehow to see its beauty would erase some of the horror burned into my brain. Instead all I see is blood. Grada's and Molly's. I'm covered in it.

I bend over, grab my knees to keep from falling, and retch on the ground. I retch until there's nothing left, and the dry heaves take over. Finally, I spit and wipe a shaky hand cross my mouth. A sudden urge to run tears its way through my gut. To get away from the bloodshed, the death. But I know I can't.

I can't leave them like that, I think.

It's not right to leave them all out in the open so the crows and vultures can shite on them, and pick out their eyes, and worse. The thought of it makes my stomach heave again. But I know there's no way I'm going to be able to dig graves for them all and bury them by myself.

I mull it over in my head. I look to the shanties. They're still smoking some, but the flames have all died out. It was only the things inside that could burn anyway, and none of them contained much. Then I realize that one doesn't seem to be smoking at all. In all the haze and confusion earlier, I hadn't noticed. It isn't smouldering like the others. Why not?

The door of the shanty is hanging by a hinge, and I can see the torch that had been tossed in lying on the wooden table. It had scorched the table somewhat, but the torch had snuffed out. Nothing but luck that this one didn't burn like the rest.

It's Shelly and Thomas' shanty. I step slowly inside, and right away my eyes are pulled to the cold hearth. I swear I can see us young'uns sitting there, listening all wide-eyed while Thomas tells us spook stories, making us squeal in fright.

He sure could tell a good story.

Angry at myself, I shake my head to clear the images away. I don't have time for that, not now. I stride straight to the hearth where I know a candle and flint are kept, and I take them both. I need to go down into the storm cellar, and I'm going to need these to light my way.

My slingbag is lying on the cellar floor like I hoped, as is my crossbow and even my hat. Everything I had on me when Grada put me down here. I check to make sure my water skin and knife are still in the bag. They are. I start packing the bag with the little supplies left in the cellar. Enough jerky and dried taters to last me a couple of weeks maybe if I ration it. A few medicinal herbs—there's not much. I haul it all out of the cellar then go back for the last two jugs of "medicinal" whiskey Lou kept here for emergencies, brewed from a good corn harvest a few years back. I take them, one in each hand. I'm going to need them for what I'm planning.

I drag everything back to the shanty and apologize in my head to Thomas and Shelly for what I'm about to do. I strip the beds in the shanty, roll up the two heaviest of the blankets and tie them to my slingbag. Next, I root through the clothes chest. I find a couple of Shelly's worn dresses and some of Jane's and young Thomas' things. Those I put aside with the other blankets. I find a clean tunic of Thomas' and exchange it for the one I'm wearing. I can't stand having their blood on me anymore. I take his worn, rawhide jacket too, but this I pack in my slingbag.

Done with the chest, I move on to the hearth. I find four

root biscuits just sitting there as if Shelly was planning on warming them for their evening meal. The sight of them makes me want to bawl again, but instead I grab the biscuits and throw them in my slingbag before I change my mind. Another water skin and Thomas' hunting knife are lying there too. It's a big knife, bigger than mine, nice and sharp. Thomas took real good care of it. I use the big knife to cut all the clothes and blankets I had gathered into strips. I hack at the cloth with a simmering anger, but it doesn't help lessen my hurt none. All it does is make me feel guiltier about what I was doing to Shelly and Thomas' things. But then I remember they're not going to need them. Not anymore. Not ever. Annoyed at the tears that are threatening to fall again, I push on my eyelids with enough force to make me see black spots. It works. I don't cry.

I take some of the strips and tie the knife sheath to my thigh, nice and tight. I want to keep this knife handy. The rest I soak in the whiskey brew. Now for the hard part.

The moon sits high in the night sky by the time I'm done with my gruesome task. I'd moved all my kin. I didn't want to think of them as bodies. I'd moved them all as close together the best I could manage and stuffed the spaces between them with twigs and kindling from the wood pile and the strips of soaked cloth. Some of the bigger strips I'd used to cover their eyes. I couldn't stand to have to look at their eyes while I was doing what I was doing. I take the leftover whiskey and pour it all over their clothes, glad for the darkness hiding the worst of their wounds from me. Finally, I'm done.

I stand back and wipe the sweat out of my eyes, just stare at the moon. I know what I have to do now; I just can't bring myself to do it. The moon is in its shrinking stage, a waning moon. I smile a bit as Grada's voice fills my head.

"Now when the moon is waning, Tara, it's the best time for plantin' the taters, and when it's a waxing moon, then it's time for the corn. You gotta remember that if you want a good harvest."

"I'll remember, Grada," I whisper at the moon.

"Good girl," it says back in Grada's raspy voice. "Now, finish what you started."

"Aye, I will," I say.

I stand alone in the dark. It's quiet. So quiet I can hear my own heart thumping. These past few hours I been occupied, so busy with what I was doing I haven't had time to think. But now with the quiet all around me, things are just jumping into my head.

Why Grada? I think. *Why did you just save me? Why didn't you at least try and save the others or yourself? Why did you hide me and nobody else?*

Grada's last words to me echo in my head. "You must stay alive."

Why? Just to feel all this pain and grief? The ache in my chest wells up again, and I take a few deep breaths to stop it. *The time for crying is over, Tara,* I scold myself. *Do what you gotta do.*

I strike my flint and light the torch I'd made earlier from Shelly's wood table leg and some of the whiskey-soaked cloth strips. The flame burns bright in the dark and I shade my eyes, but I hesitate before I light the kindling.

There's something I should be saying, but nothing comes to mind. If Ben were here, he would know what to say. But

Ben isn't here. It's just me. Why I should be standing here while everybody else is gone … it's not right.

"I'm sorry," I say finally. My voice is scratchy and raw from my crying. "I'm sorry that I couldn't help save y'all. I'm sorry those things came from the sand lands and killed you, and I don't even know what for. You were good people. Proper people. Grada … you were a fine grada. The best a girl coulda ever wanted. And I'm sorry I cain't give you a proper burial. I'm gonna miss you real bad."

I stop talking because my throat hurts again. I start setting aflame the pockets of kindling.

"May the gods show you mercy and grant you peace."

I stay just long enough to make sure the fire catches. I throw the torch into the flames. The moon will be bright enough for walking, and a lit flame out in the sand lands would just draw unwanted attention. From what, I'm not sure, but I don't want to take any chances. Waiting for morning isn't an option. There's no way in dirt dog hell I'm going to stay another moment in this place of death.

I pick up my slingbag, heave my bow and quiver over my shoulder, and start walking. East, along the riverbank like Grada had told me to do. I'd never heard of Littlepass, but if he said I'd best go there, then that's what I do. If I'm going to stand a chance of finding Ben and the others, then I'm going to need help. Lily, he'd said. Find a healer named Lily. How hard could it be?

I keep walking a steady pace, one foot in front of the other. I don't look back. There's no point. Ben was right after all. Rivercross is dead.

CHAPTER 2

The Sand Lands

———◆———

I've been walking for days. Eight to be exact. Eight days of sand and wind and the burning, cruel sun, with nothing to distract me from the awful thoughts running through my head. Replaying the deaths of my kin over and over again, wondering if there was something … anything I could have done to save them. Worrying about Ben and the young'uns. If they're okay. If I was ever going to see them again. If they were even still alive. Sometimes, the despair is so overwhelming that I don't want to take another step. Just want to lay down, right where I'm standing and let the critters have at me. But I don't. I keep moving. I keep walking the flat, desolate lands. Sometimes, I come across the occasional husk of a settler's ruin, but I don't bother to look in them. They're nothing but skeletons already picked clean long ago by scavengers. I haven't seen another living soul.

I stop only long enough to sleep, praying to the gods for an evening of rest free from the night terrors, but they come every night. Every night I see their faces and hear their screams. Some nights the metal monsters in my dreams have teeth, and they eat up every one of my kin, even Ben. I hear their bones crunching from the metal jaws, and I wake myself up with my cries, my face damp with tears. I lay there shivering and afraid, listening to the howling of the devil cats and wolflings being carried on the wind and sleep don't come no more. So I walk.

It's taking a toll on me, all the walking. Yesterday, I had to cut the tail off my tunic and use it to wrap my feet. They're cut up real bad. The wrappings helped though; my feet aren't hurting so bad today. And my head isn't hurting anymore either. It had healed up real nice. Even the cut had closed up, not even a scab. I always was a real fast healer.

I keep walking.

———

Twelve days into the sand lands. Least I suspect it's been that long. I'm losing track. This is my second day of traveling on no sleep. I did make camp last evening, but just as I was settling down, I heard a noise from the other side of the boulder I was sleeping under. I snuck a peek, trying not to make any sound. The moon had been bright enough for me to see the shadow of something about ten or twelve paces from where

I was set up. Couldn't say if it was human or critter, though it appeared to be walking on two legs, all hunched over and shuffling its feet. My heart was beating so loud I figured for sure the thing would hear it, and although it paused for a moment it thankfully moved on, heading gods only knew where in the empty wastelands. I waited for a time, wanting to make sure it was well gone before I packed up and moved out. I didn't know if it was a mutie or raider or such, but I knew I didn't want to run into it. And I surely wasn't sleeping any tonight. So, I walked again. I walked until the sun came up. Only then did I stop to rest.

The food I'd brought with me is almost gone, and one of the water skins is bone dry. The other is half-empty even with my rationing. I'd come across watering holes along the way, but they'd either been dried up or gone foul. I keep checking the riverbed, hoping for one of the flash floods of water the old folk would talk about, but it's as dry as always. The bottom of it nothing but baked, cracked mud. Another story I no longer believe in.

I'm going to have to hunt soon, I think. It'll slow me down some, but I have to eat. I've seen the occasional wild bird and crow. Haven't spotted any dirt dog but no matter. I left my snare wires back in Rivercross, and dirt dog is almost impossible to catch with an arrow. They never stuck their heads out of their burrows long enough to get a good target on them. No, food isn't going to be a problem, but water … that's worrying me a lot.

—◦—

Day… something. The land I'm walking on is altering. I've been noticing it for a while now. The empty, hard-baked ground I'm used to seeing is turning to sparse grasslands and sloping hills way off in the hazy distance. I can even see what I believe to be a tree line on the horizon. A good sign. Where there are trees growing, there's water. Just in time, too. I reckon the water I have left won't last the day.

I stare at the tree line, trying to work out in my head how long a walk it'll take me, but I'm not sure. My thinking is getting a bit muddled. I need to drink more water soon; I know that for a fact.

Hunching my shoulders, I head for the tree line when suddenly I'm nearly blinded by a flash of light. What the hell? I squint into the glare as awareness slowly filters into my jumbled brain. It's the sun hitting something off in the distance to my left and reflecting it back to me. Is that? No … can't be. But it is, sure enough. Shanties, about half a league from where I'm standing. Between the blowing dust and heat shimmers, I hadn't noticed them before.

I turn direction, heading right for them. The only thoughts in my head are water, food, people. But I don't get no more than five paces when my mind goes clear again. What if I find something there I don't want to find? Like muties? Or raiders? I hesitate, my steps faltering. Then again, maybe it's just normal people like me, with fresh water and maybe even a bed for me to sleep in for a night. Shizen, the thought of sleeping in a soft bed instead of on the hard ground crawling with sand biters … well, I figure it's worth taking the risk. Decision made, I head for the shanties.

I approach them slowly. I don't see or hear anything, but I

keep my eyes open for movement. For any sign of something not right, because if it is muties or raiders living here, then they probably won't be out greeting me with open arms.

There are three shanties in all, facing each other in a kind of triangle formation. They look a bit different than the shanties of Rivercross; these are mostly built of wood. Comes from living so close to a tree line, I reckon. But they still have the tin roofs and doors I'm used to seeing. Two of the doors are torn off, and the third is just hanging by a hinge, swaying in the breeze. I stop walking and look around. It's real quiet. The silence spooks me. It reminds me of the ghost villages from Thomas' scare stories. I take a couple of steps toward the closest shanty, the rocks crunching under my boots the only sound in the dead calm. I poke my head in through the doorless entry, but I don't go inside. I keep my attention on my surroundings. I don't want to be stupid enough to let somebody creep up on me.

The shanty is just a small, one-room building, and it doesn't take me long to see it's empty. The place is messed up though, belongings scattered everywhere. Somebody searched it, but it hasn't been scavenged or set aflame. Strange. I find the next two shanties in the same condition, both of them empty as well.

Where are the people who live here? What happened to them?

I stand in the middle of the three buildings looking around. My gaze falls on a stone well on a little rise just past one of the shanties and my curiosity is quickly replaced by one single thought. Water! Hoping in my heart that the water isn't tainted, I sprint for it.

The wooden cover is knocked off and laying on the

ground in pieces, but the rope and bucket are undamaged. I lower the bucket down, hear the splash, and pull it back up. Please, please, please, let it be drinkable.

I peer into the bucket. Looks clean enough. Doesn't smell foul. I taste it and smile for the first time in weeks. My parched lips crack open and bleed from the effort, but I don't care. I can't stop smiling. The water tastes like gods' brew. I want to drink until I burst, but I know if I do that I'll just retch it back up, so I take my time and sip it slow. I drink my fill, the cool liquid easing my dry throat. Finally, my thirst quenched, I take off my hat and pour the rest of the water over my head, not even bothered that it's soaking my clothes. It feels real good, and I know I'll dry quick enough in the heat of the day. I lay down my slingbag and bow, rub my shoulder to ease the tension. Reckon I may as well take a rest, fill my water skins. The place appears harmless enough.

I'm busy looking through my slingbag for the second water skin when I hear it. A low, deep, guttural growling. I freeze. Slowly I raise my head, my hand reaching for the knife strapped at my thigh. A pair of blood-red eyes stare into mine, no more than five paces from where I stand. A devil cat.

My heart beats furiously against my ribs, and I can taste the bile in the back of my throat.

I'm gonna get eaten alive.

I stare at the beast, trying hard not to pass out. I've never seen one up so close … not a live one anyways. The creature is freaking huge. Sweat beads my upper lip as we keep eyeing each other. I'm afraid to break the contact lest the beast takes it as a sign of weakness and attacks. By now, I'm holding the big knife out in front of me, holding on so tight my knuckles turn white. The beast growls again, showing me its dagger-sharp teeth. Its pointy ears flatten against its broad head.

It doesn't make a move. Neither do I. The hand holding the knife is so slick with sweat I'm afraid I'm going to lose my grip on it. Finally, I can't take it anymore.

"Gods dammit, whadda you waitin' for?"

It's either scream at it or black out. It moves then, and I tense, expecting any moment to feel the sharp claws tearing through my skin and ripping it off my bones. It moves at me … and sits down on its haunches. It keeps staring me down, but it don't attack.

"It's okay. She ain't gonna hurt you."

My nerves already wound tight from the stare down with the devil cat, the voice makes me jump. The cat goes back on all fours at my movement, eyeballing me again.

"Cat. Down, girl."

A young boy, no more than twelve born years to be sure, walks up to the massive black beast. He goes right up to it and unbelievably starts rubbing its head. And if that's not strange enough, this beast, this killing machine from the campfire spook stories, just falls to the ground and rolls over so the boy can scratch its underbelly. I can only stare, openmouthed.

"You can put your knife away," he says.

Didn't even realize I was still holding it. I hesitate, look from the knife to the devil cat, and then put it back in its sheath. I reckon if the beast wanted to eat me, it would have done so by now. The boy continues to scratch the animal's belly, but his eyes don't leave my face. He's on the losing side of scrawny with unkempt, matted red hair hanging to his shoulders and a smattering of freckles cross his nose and cheeks. Least I think it's freckles, could be just dirt. He looks like he hasn't had a proper washing in months. Or a decent meal for that matter. His tunic and trousers are mud-caked and hanging from his tiny frame like they aren't even his. I realize I must look just as strange to him with my own clothes so dirty they could probably stand on their own, and my wet hair hanging in strings about my face. We stand in awkward silence, just sizing each other up. Finally, my curiosity gets the better of me, and I nod at the beast.

"How come it lets you do that and don't bite your hand off?" I say.

He smiles then, a big ol' gap-toothed grin and scratches the beast's belly even harder. The damn critter actually starts to purr.

"I reared Cat since she was a cub, going on four years now. She would never hurt me."

"You reared up a devil cat?" I ask, still not believing what I'm seeing.

"Already told you that," he says in disdain.

"And you named it Cat?"

"Aye, was a fittin' name as any," he says.

Can't argue that.

"What's your name?" I ask.

He stops scratching, and the black beast nimbly gets to its feet. It's just as tall as the boy, could probably snap him in half in one bite if it had a mind to. I still can't help but be terrified by it.

"Finn," he answers.

"Nice to meet you, Finn. I'm Tara … of Rivercross." I look around. "What's the name of this place?"

He looks at me strangely.

"Ain't got no name … just the homestead, I guess. At least that's all Ma and Pa ever called it," he says.

"Oh," I say. "And where are your ma and pa?"

I regret asking right away. His face scrunches up like he's trying real hard not to cry. I watch him struggle, but he's tough. The tears don't fall.

"Dead," he finally answers, but his voice quivers. "About four weeks now since the monsters on wheels came and killed 'em. All of 'em. I buried 'em over yonder."

He points with his chin out past the rise we're standing on. I can see disturbed ground marked by cairns. There are five of them from what I can tell. That familiar pain starts blossoming in my own chest.

"I'm real sorry," I say quietly. "They came to Rivercross and killed my kin, too."

He nods, as if talking about your dead kin is normal conversation. We both fall quiet again, each lost in our own painful memories. Then a thought strikes me.

"How did you bury them by yourself?" I ask, looking him up and down again. He's no bigger than a twig.

He shrugs his skinny shoulders at me. "I done the digging and Cat helped me drag 'em. She's real smart, does what I tell her to," he says.

About two weeks ago, I would have thought that to be a crock of shite and reckoned the boy was lying to me. But between the metal monsters on wheels and a tame devil cat, well, I guess anything could be possible. Ben would be tickled pink by my new beliefs.

The beast, Cat, is getting restless now and starts moving towards me. Its head is level with my chest, and it comes so close I can see the dirt stuck in its black, matted fur and feel the heat rising off of it. It starts sniffing my hand; its nose is cold and wet. It keeps sniffing, moving up my arm to my neck. Too terrified to move, I watch as a long, blue tongue escapes from its mouth and slowly licks my face, leaving a slimy trail cross my cheek and my lips.

Shizen. It's gonna eat me, I think. I look to the boy, my eyes pleading for help, but he's just laughing his fool head off.

"I think she likes you," he says, bent over with laughter.

"Call … her … off," I say through clenched teeth. I don't want to open my mouth for fear that blue tongue will find its way inside. He's still laughing but calls her name, and she backs off.

Right away I start wiping my face with my sleeve. Ugh. Disgusting.

"Don't worry, Cat don't eat people," he says as if he's reading my mind. The beast is now back sitting meekly at his side, licking its paws and cleaning its whiskers like it's just some tame village cat and not a killing machine. I keep eyeballing it. I don't trust it.

"Well, except for the bad man from the metal monsters. She caught him before he could escape back into his machine. The rest of 'em, they got away, but he never. Aye, she caught him and ate him up real good. There weren't nuthin' left except his weapon and boots."

Finn sounds pleased as anything by this, but it makes my stomach heave, and I scrub my face even harder. Ugh. The boy doesn't seem to notice my disgust.

"I kept his weapon, but I never seen nuthin' like it before. I ain't got no idea what it is. You wanna see it?" he asks.

I wipe the remaining foul traces of the cat's slobber off my face before I shrug. Why not? I'm real surprised to hear from the boy that there were actual men in those metal monsters. Maybe seeing this weapon will help me understand better what they are. He grins at my acceptance and scurries off to the shanty with the hanging door. I follow behind, making sure to keep distance between me and the beast. I can't help but feel it's going to pounce on me when I least expect it.

The shanty is still the same as when I first inspected it, but now I notice the signs of the boy living here. The wood stacked in the hearth ready for the evening fire, the full water jug, and cooking pot. I should've seen all that earlier. I'm going to have to pay attention from now on, so I don't get caught unaware again. I might not be as lucky the next time.

The boy goes to the wood chest at the foot of the only bed in the one-roomed shanty. He opens it and pulls out a long metal and wood object, and I recognize it right away. An iron shooter. He turns and starts waving it at me, and my heart jumps into my throat.

"Shizen! Give me that," I say and yank it out of his hand before he can shoot it at me. "You gotta be careful with these things, boy. Don't you know anything?"

"What is it?" he asks, ignoring my harsh words.

"It's called an iron shooter." I glance over it. It's in much better shape than Grada's. It's oiled up real nice and not a bit of rust on it. I check to see if there are any slugs. It's missing just one.

"See here, these are lead slugs. They're what come out of the shooter and do gods-awful damage to critters … and people."

He nods solemnly. "Aye, I seen what it done, to my ma and pa and the others."

His eyes drop down to stare at the floor, and I can feel his pain in my own heart. Judging from my past couple of weeks, I reckon Finn's had his share of night terrors too.

"So, the man you said Cat killed, you sure it was a real man? For sure?"

He nods at my question. "I seen 'em. They were men all right. Was only luck me and Cat weren't here when they showed. We were out explorin'. I heard what I figured to be a storm comin'. Next thing, I hear yellin' and … well, funny poppin' sounds. Cat knew something was wrong. She started hightailing it back here. I ran after her, I did! But then I saw the metal monsters and I … "

He goes real quiet and hangs his head in shame. "I hid. I could see my pa and Unk fightin' 'em. Ma, she was screamin'. I wanted to help. I did … but … "

He doesn't even try to stop his tears this time. They run down his face, leaving twin streaks through the dirt and drip from his chin. I feel real bad for his hurt, and I fight against the lump building in my throat. I lay my hand on his shoulder.

"Hey, it's okay. Don't be ashamed because you hid. There wasn't anything you could have done. You would have been killed or taken. You did right by hidin'. That's what your folks would have wanted you to do," I say.

He looks up at me through his tears. His eyes are red and

swollen, and his pale skin speckled with rosy blotches. "You being truthful?" he asks.

"Yeah," I say. "Cross my heart. And if it makes you feel any better, I hid from 'em, too."

I figured I wouldn't mention it was because of Grada knocking me out with the cooking pot and throwing me in the cellar. He didn't need to know that much. He sniffs for a bit and wipes his nose with his sleeve. He sniffs again but doesn't cry anymore.

"Cat tried to stop 'em. She chased 'em, but we were too late," he says, his voice filled with guilt. Poor kid. No doubt he's been beating himself up over it ever since it happened, thinking what he could have done to stop it. Like me. For the first time since it all happened, I don't feel so alone in my grief or my anger. It's comforting somehow to know that they were just men and not monsters like I'd first feared. And that they could be killed—had been killed—by the beast. Maybe I had misjudged the devil cat. Maybe she isn't so bad after all.

I lay the shooter back in the chest. I don't want to look at it or touch it anymore. Just holding it is making me queasy, thinking about what it did to Finn's kin and what others like it had done to mine. Even the touch of it makes me feel strange. The boy watches me, his cheeks still wet from his crying.

"Are you gonna camp here tonight?" he asks unexpectedly, and his question is tinged with hope.

"If you like," I shrug. "I mean, I wouldn't mind stayin'. I gotta hunt though. My food's all gone."

He brightens instantly. "No need for huntin'. Cat's real

good at catchin' rabbits and dirt dogs. We were out huntin' before you showed up. Got us a nice, fat rabbit. Only thing is though you got to give her the innards … that's her favorite part."

I look over at the black beast now lying halfway in the shanty door to keep a watchful eye on Finn, her head resting on her massive paws.

"Cat can have whatever she wants," I reply. I'm not stupid enough to argue with the she-devil.

After stuffing ourselves on boiled rabbit, we talk long into the evening. I tell Finn all about Rivercross. About Grada and Ben and everybody. Feels real good to talk about them, like somehow they're still with me. I talk and talk and talk … I can't stop. I talk about me and Ben as young'uns and growing up together and all the trouble we caused. I tell him about Grada finding and rearing me and how he was so good to me. I talk about Thomas' spook stories and Miz Emma's berry bread. I don't know why, but the words just pour out of me. I talk about everything and anything. Finn just listens and laughs at times, but he doesn't interrupt. It's as if he's just happy to be hearing another person's voice. Finally, I tell him about the monster men coming and how they took Ben and Jane and young Thomas and how I need to find them. He hasn't heard of Littlepass either. I reckoned as much—him being a young'un and all.

When I'm all talked out, it's Finn's turn. He tells me all about his kin that he lost … his ma and pa, his pa's brother and wife, and his grada. They all lived here together. Unlike my village, the monster men didn't take anybody because Finn had been the only young'un here, but they had still killed the rest. He asks me why they did it.

"I dunno why," I say. "Some men are just born with darkness in their hearts, I guess."

It's the only reason I can give him, but he appears to accept it. He goes on to tell me about how he remembers once living in a bigger village with lots of other young folk to play with, but for some reason his kin up and left that place and settled out here in the sand lands. He doesn't know why; he was never told the reason. He said he remembers being real lonely until one day, his pa was out hunting and found a dead devil cat. It was beat up real bad. His pa couldn't say what had done it, but he heard some gods-awful bawling coming from under it. Sure enough, the she-cat had a cub, all curled up underneath her and trying to feed from its dead mama. Finn said his pa had too kind a heart to kill it or leave it to die, so he brought it home. His grada had taken one look at it and wanted to kill it, but Finn had a fit, he says, and of course he got his way. The cub was his and, well, he reared it ever since.

"Me and Cat's family now, ain't we, Cat?" he says.

The beast looks up at her name but just yawns, showing her wicked-looking teeth. She still makes me shiver, but Finn assures me I got nothing to fret about. He says Cat is the best protection, better than any crossbow or iron shooter. For him, maybe. For me, well, I'm not so sure. I still didn't want to be alone with her. I'm in no hurry to find out how good of a meal I would make.

The boy yawns too, and I'm surprised to see how low the fire is. Nothing left but glowing embers … must be real late. I feel kind of bad, but I take Finn up on his offer of the bed while he takes to sleeping in front of the hearth. He doesn't mind, he says. Cat makes for a real soft pillow.

After weeks of sleeping on the hard ground, the bed feels like laying on a cloud. It doesn't take long for my mind to shut down, and I drift off. I'm not sure if it's the soft bed, the boy's company, or the protection offered from the devil cat, but for the first time since leaving Rivercross the night terrors don't come, and I sleep.

— • —

"Finn, you ain't comin' with me, and that's that."

We've been arguing since the sun come up. For some reason, the boy has decided he's to go with me to Littlepass, and I can't get him to change his mind. I'm not even sure when he made up his mind about this, but he's like a hound with a bone. He's not giving up on it.

"Why would you want to leave here? You have food, shelter, water, Cat to keep you safe. You're just bein' foolish," I say for about the fifth time.

"I'm goin' with you, and you cain't stop me," he says. He's standing in front of me, his feet planted apart on the ground, and his hands on his hips. His face is about as red as his hair, but it's got nothing to do with the heat of the day. And the look on it … well, it kind of makes me want to laugh, but I don't dare. It's a real stubborn, mule-headed look, and for some reason it kind of reminds me of Ben, though they don't look the least bit alike.

"And I'm tellin' you *again*, it's too dangerous. I dunno what I'm gonna find in Littlepass. Shizen, I don't even know if I'm gonna make it to Littlepass. I could get killed by raiders or eaten by critters today, tomorrow. Anything could happen."

I'm losing patience with the boy. I just want to get back on the road. After my night's rest, I feel full of energy and renewed. Even my feet have healed up good; calloused and hardened. I just want to fill my water skins and head out. Feels like I've wasted enough time already, and I need to move quickly to make up for it. I believe the longer I stay here, the further and further Ben is moving away from me. But Finn's not giving up.

"Then that's why we should go with you, to protect you. Cat's real good at protectin'. She'll keep you safe from any old raiders or critters."

"Yeah, she probably could," I say. "But then what? Say we make it to Littlepass. What then? We just gonna walk right on in with a full-grown devil cat trailin' behind us? 'Oh, don't run and get your axes or bows, folks; she's a real nice devil cat. She only ever ate one person, and he well deserved it.' Is that what you're gonna say to 'em? They'll kill her before you get two words in, they will."

I know I'm being mean, but I'm trying to make the boy understand.

"You don't know that," he argues stubbornly.

"Yes, I do," I say, putting the cap back on the water skin. I'm done with the conversation. I concentrate on checking my slingbag to make sure I'm not forgetting anything.

"No, you don't," he yells and knocks the water skin right

out of my hand. I look at him, surprised by this outburst. He crosses his arms over his skinny chest and sticks his chin out in defiance. I feel the anger churning in my gut. That certainly wasn't called for. But before I can say anything, his chin starts to quiver, and he chokes out, "Please, Tara, don't leave me here. I don't wanna be alone anymore. I cain't stand it. Let me go with you, please. Please, Tara?"

Oh gods. My heart twists at his plea. I don't need this. I don't need or want to be looking after some skinny little runt who will undoubtedly slow me down. And traveling with a devil cat … well, nothing like drawing attention to yourself.

No, absolutely not.

"Please," it comes out as a whisper, and one single tear escapes and rolls down his cheek. He wipes it away angrily. I look at his pleading face. I mull his words over in my head. I sigh, pick up my water skin, and dust it off.

"I'll be leavin' shortly," I say. "You best be ready. I ain't waitin'."

That stupid grin nearly splits his face. He starts to scamper off but changes his mind and runs for me instead, wrapping his scrawny arms around my waist.

"We'll be a real good help, you'll see. Me and Cat. We'll hunt and protect you real good," he says and then runs off again, to collect his things I reckon.

I watch him go, shaking my head. What have I just agreed to? Letting the boy and beast go with me is just asking for trouble. I can feel it. I glance over at the cat. The whole time we'd been arguing, the critter had lain real content in the shade of the shanty, not the least bit interested. Now, she's watching me intently with her red eyes as if she knows what decision has been made. I stare back at her.

"Don't make me sorry for this," I say. She blinks at me. "And for gods' sake, if you get hungry durin' the night, don't eat me."

In response, Cat snorts at me, shakes her head, and the blue tongue I remember so disgustingly well pokes out to lick her lips as if saying, "I ain't making no promises."

Gods help me, I think.

We set out: the boy, the beast, and me. I couldn't have imagined more unlikely traveling companions if I tried. But Finn is true to his word. The critter does all the hunting and provides for us every meal. We never go hungry. Whether it's rabbit, dirt dog, or some crow unlucky enough to have landed when it shouldn't have, Cat supplies us with food. And I'll never admit it to Finn, but it's real nice not having to worry about hunting. As for the boy, he doesn't complain about all the walking, not once. He doesn't shut up either though. He talks so much it finally just sounds like buzzing in my ears. Funny thing is I find I don't mind. It keeps me from thinking about other things and worrying about stuff I have no control over. As far as traveling companions go, they're all right.

We'd reached the tree line about six days past and had been walking in the woods since. Didn't have much of a choice but to go through them. The tree line is massive, as spread out as far as the eye could see. Would have been foolish and a waste of time to try and go around. Plus, our easterly course is straight through, and I'm not willing to veer off course.

I'm not used to trees this size. It was a little overwhelming at first. The biggest trees in Rivercross only grew to your waist, but these trees tower over us. The canopy of gnarled branches blocks out the sun and keeps some of its heat off us. Would have been kind of nice if it wasn't for the smell of death and rot coming from the wood. Only easy to see most of the trees are sickly; their bark gray as ash and their leaves dry and withered. A lot of them are just snag trees: dead, half-fallen over into each other, and blocking our way. Slowing us down. We try not to stray too much off our path, but sometimes it can't be helped. Cat scouts ahead of us at times. We lose track of her for a bit but never for too long. All it takes is for Finn to give two short whistles, and she's back, checking on him. She brings an occasional tree rat or crow, but there's not a lot of game in these dead woods. There's not a lot of anything but stillness and quiet. It rattles our nerves. Even Finn, who hasn't shut up for days, talks a bit quieter now and less often the deeper into the woods we get. It's as if he doesn't want to disturb any ghost or demon that might call this wood home. It spooks me something fierce.

The evening dusk is coming on us fast. It always comes earlier in here. The shadows are getting longer and darker, making our minds play tricks on us. Making us see shapes and things we know aren't really there. We'll have to make camp soon. There's no way either of us wants to be walking these woods after dark. At least we don't have to worry about a fire. The one good thing these dead woods did have to offer was plenty of fire kindling.

Stumbling into a small clearing that appears big enough for a campfire and for us to stretch out our bed rolls, I stop walking and glance around. Finn stops beside me.

"Here?" he asks.

"Aye," I say. "This'll do."

We have it down to a routine now. While I get the makings of our fire together, he clears the ground for our beds, lays out our blankets, and gets the water skins out. He even lays out the iron shooter. I didn't know he'd brought it along at first. Can't rightly say I would have let him bring it had I known. To me, it's just a reminder of the evil men it had come from. But now, after being in these damn frightening woods for days, it's almost comforting to have it so handy.

We work in silence, and it's not long before I have a nice flame burning, chasing away some of the shadows and keeping them at bay. Finn joins me at the fire and hands me a water skin. It's almost empty. With the three of us drinking now, the water is being used up a lot faster, but there's no way I'm tapping any of those trees for water. The thought of drinking from something so sickly doesn't feel right. We can't chance getting sick. We'll just keep looking for a water supply. I figure there has to be something here.

I pull the remaining crow we cooked last evening from my slingbag and share it between us. Cat's nowhere to be seen. I reckon she can fend for herself tonight. Finn takes his and starts chewing, staring into the flames.

"How much longer you think these woods will last, Tara?" he asks eventually.

"Dunno," I say, biting into my own crow meat. It's tough and hard to chew, but it's all we have.

Finn keeps eating, all quiet like, then he asks, "How long you think it's gonna take us to get to Littlepass?"

"I dunno that either," I say.

Why's he asking me questions I don't know the answers to?

"What do you think we're gonna find when we get there?"

"Do I look like some kind of seer?" I snap at him. "I dunno. Maybe we won't find nuthin' or nobody because sickness done took 'em all. Or maybe the monster men came and killed all of them, too."

Don't know why his questions are bothering me so. Maybe it's the frustrating, endless walking, the endless heat, the little food, and the even less water. The not knowing. Everything I guess. But his questions are getting to me, and I don't know how to answer them.

Then I look at his face. His eyes have gone all big and round at my cruel words, and his mouth is hanging open so I can see his half-chewed food. Shame washes over me, and I think to myself, *He's just a little boy, Tara. A scared little boy just looking for some comfort.*

"Or maybe," I say, a little gentler this time, "we'll find a magical place where food grows on the trees and the animals all talk and … and the people live in buildin's that touch the sky. And they keep their mouths closed when eatin' crow."

I poke him in the ribs, and he giggles.

"Now, you're just bein' foolish," he says, but I feel much better at hearing him laugh. I poke him again, and then start tickling his ribs, making him shriek in glee. "Stop, Tara! Stop!"

I don't see Cat approaching until she's almost on top of us. She's so black she blends right in with the night shadows.

Silent as the wind, she pads up to Finn and drops whatever she's caught tonight between us.

Shizen!

I fall backwards on my elbows and shimmy away in fright at the rather large and still-moving critter.

"What is that?" I shriek as the critter starts to slither toward me. Finn, unlike me, is beyond excited and grabs the creature's head—no wait, heads. There's two of them attached to the long, writhing body. He gets to his feet and the critter is about as tall as he is.

"Ain't you ever seen a tree snake before?" he asks, grinning like he's got the moon in his hands.

Feeling a little foolish now for showing the boy my fright, my answer is tinged with annoyance. "If I did, then I wouldn't have to ask, now would I?"

Sniffing and wiping my hands on my trousers, I try to hide my embarrassment. "Don't look like something we should be eating."

The boy shakes his head. "Nah, tree snakes are good to eat and real tender, too. I cain't believe you never seen one before."

He's truly tickled to be one up on me. I give him my best exasperated look.

"Aye. Well, if you're such an expert, then you can clean it and cook it," I say, holding out my knife.

He just shrugs and takes it from me. "Okay. I'd be better at it anyways since you don't even know what it is," he says and cracks up laughing at his own words.

"Mule turd," I growl, but my lips twitch in amusement.

I watch in interest as he chops off both heads with one

swing of the knife, then a part of the tail. The snake looks huge lying on the ground, almost two arm spans I reckon. He slits it from the tail end up, then makes a couple of notches with the knife and pulls off the skin all in one piece. I've never seen anything like that done before.

"Snakeskin is real good for tradin'," he says and lays it aside. He tosses the heads, tail, and innards to Cat waiting patiently by the fire, then spits it on a long twig and hangs it over the low flames.

"Oh gods, my mouth is waterin' already. I cain't wait." He's hopping like a wild rabbit back and forth from one foot to the other, looking all of his twelve years. I can't help but laugh.

"Well, you're gonna have to wait. And you're gonna have to clean up," I chide. "Your hands are a mess. Go see if you can find some wet leaves or moss or such."

"Okay," he says, agreeing with me and grinning slyly. "Besides, it's time for my nightly droppin's anyway."

I screw my face up at him. "Ugh, really? You're disgustin'."

His laughter follows him into the trees. He disappears from sight with my warning of not to go too far trailing after him. I lay back and close my eyes. Here in the woods the nights run cooler, so the warmth of the fire feels good against my skin. The smell of the cooking snake fills the air, blocking out the stench of the rotting trees. It's making my mouth water as well.

If it tastes as good as it smells, then we're in for a real treat. I yawn, the day's travel catching up to me. Maybe just a quick nap while I'm waiting.

"Tara!"

The scream makes my blood run cold and I bolt to my feet in an instant, but Cat is much quicker than me. She's already gone. I grab the iron shooter and run in what I hope is the right direction.

"Finn?" I yell, crashing through the trees. I can't see anything; it's too dark, and my eyes aren't adjusted from the firelight.

"Finn?" I yell again, panic gripping me because he's not answering. I trip over something, a root maybe, and I stagger but don't fall. Why isn't he answering?

"Over here," he finally says, and at the sound of his voice the ice-cold fear in my belly starts to thaw.

I stumble onto him standing on a little bank, looking perfectly fine, and Cat calmly sitting at his side. No sign of danger, or attack, or critters like I was fearing. There's nothing. He was screaming his fool head off over nothing. My fear starts escalating to anger until I notice what he's staring at. A creek, no less. A nice, big watering hole.

"You scared the hell outta me," I say, but my anger is quickly waning by what I'm looking at.

"Sorry," he says, but he don't look it. He looks excited and hopeful. He points to the water. "You think it's good for drinkin'?"

Even as I shrug in uncertainty, Cat makes her way down the small slope. She sticks her head into the creek, her slurping sounds drifting back to us. She's real thirsty. We glance at each other, silly grins etched on both our faces.

"I suspect so," I finally answer, and Finn's excited whoops echo loudly in the still night air.

"I found us a waterin' hole. I found us a waterin' hole."

His chanting is followed by some two-step dance that makes him look more like a hog in its death throes than anything, and I bust out laughing at his antics.

"Okay, okay mister hero, you found us water. Now make yourself useful and go fetch the water skins."

———

After we filled the water skins and drank our share, we laid back on the creek bank, just staring at the moon's reflection on the dark water and reluctant to leave our little haven. Being around the water was comforting.

"Tara." Finn breaks our companionable silence.

I look over to see him watching me with the oddest expression on his face.

"What?" I ask, wondering what's going through that head of his.

He shrugs. "I was just thinkin'."

I nod at him. "Yup, thought I could smell wood burnin'."

"Huh?" He looks at me in confusion.

I shake my head and sigh sadly. "Nuthin'. Just something Grada used to say."

"Oh," he drawls. "Well anyway, I was thinkin' it would be real nice to wash up. Ain't had a good wash since … well before …"

I know what he means by "before," and I don't want him thinking about that, so I punch him lightly in the arm. "Yeah, I know what you mean. You smell worse than Cat."

"Hey." He looks at me all offended. "I ain't that bad." Cat raises her head and snorts like she's disagreeing.

"Besides, you don't smell no better."

I don't take offense since I know it to be true. I shrug. "So let's take a wash then."

"But ..."

"But what?" I say.

"Well ...," he sounds real uncomfortable as he sits up, dropping his gaze from mine. "You're a girl and I'm a boy." He trails off in embarrassment.

I try not to laugh at him, and I'm glad he's not looking at me so he doesn't see my grin.

"Tell you what, you can go wash up that end, and I'll go over there." I point to where a low-hanging tree is growing sideways over the creek as if it's reaching for the water, its branches forming a wall. "Besides, it's real dark, and I promise not to peek."

He mulls it over, but the draw of the water overtakes his shyness. Jumping to his feet, he runs for the creek, yanking his tunic off as he goes. "Last one in is a mule turd!"

The water feels really good. I wash off the dirt and dust and maybe even some of the misery of the past few weeks. I loosen my hair from its braid and duck underneath the water, wishing I had some of Grada's mint soap, but instead I make do with just running my fingers through my hair. I come back up sputtering and just let myself float. Finn's laughter echoes from the other end since by now Cat is in the water too, and she's thinking it's play time. I listen to their splashing and laughing, and my mind starts conjuring up memories of me and Ben back when we were young'uns at the swimming hole. I think about how Ben used to challenge me for everything. He always wanted to be the fastest swimmer, the deepest diver, the highest climber. Most times, I would beat him with little effort, but sometimes I would let him win just so I could watch his stupid victory dance. I can't help but smile as I relive the memories one by one. But then that familiar pain starts blossoming in my chest again, so I shut them off. I don't want to deal with it right now. Angry at myself and my weakness, I climb out of the creek and busy myself with squeezing the water from my dripping hair. Takes me a while to get dressed since I don't have a drying cloth, but finally clothed, I head up the slope. Finn's still in the water.

"I'm headin' back," I say, picking up the iron shooter and two of the water skins.

"Hey, you said you wouldn't peek," he yells all offended and hunkers down behind Cat. Sighing, I turn my back to him.

"Sorry. Don't stay much longer. The snake's probably charred by now. And don't forget your water skin."

I leave him, knowing he'll be fine with the beast guarding him, and head back in the direction of the camp. The smell of the cooking critter is guide enough, and it isn't long until I see the light of our campfire flickering through the trees. Before I reach it however, I get a real strange feeling pounding through my blood. The hair on the back of my neck stands on end, and right away I know somebody is there in our camp. We haven't seen hide nor hair of another person for weeks, yet sure enough I see a shadow moving around our campsite. Stepping softly so as not to make the intruder aware of my presence, I sneak closer.

Shizen. We didn't think twice about leaving all our stuff just laying there for easy picking. I figured for sure there wasn't another living soul in these dead woods. I was wrong. The man, least I think it's a man, is hunched over and pawing through my slingbag. At the sight of that my fear dissipates, and I get red hot mad. Slowly I step into the clearing, the iron shooter aimed straight for the intruder's back. My hand is surprisingly rock steady.

"Mister, if you don't wanna hole in the back of your head, then you best put down my slingbag."

He quickly stops what he's doing and stands straight. At least I think he's standing, but he's still a good two heads shorter than a normal man should be. He turns around still holding my slingbag but smiling like he's just here for a neighborly visit. It's a man for sure; he's got a shock of gray hair sticking out from under a black, bowl-shaped hat, a wrinkly face, and a long, skinny, gray mustache that hangs nearly to his chin. But he's so dang small. I stare. I don't recall ever seeing such a small man. He's no taller than Finn.

"Well, good evening, young lady. This is quite the pleasant surprise, I must say."

His tone is mild and friendly. I don't know what to make of him. I realize my mouth is hanging open, and I shut it with a snap. At a loss for words, I keep staring.

"Er ... do you mind pointing that pistol in another direction? They do tend to make me a bit nervous, you see, especially when pointed directly at me," he says with a little laugh.

His reminding me of the iron shooter brings my senses back, and I wave it at him as my anger starts to bubble.

"No, you put down my slingbag first," I growl.

"Whatever you say, my dear." He lays the bag on the ground and holds his hands up in the air. "There, now will you please put that offending piece of weaponry away?"

I sure as hell got no intention of doing that.

"Are you a mutie?" I blurt out. I need to know because I can't understand why he's so tiny.

He looks back at me kind of offended I think and raises one bushy brow.

"No, I most certainly am not. Are you?" he asks.

"What? No, I ain't a mutie," I say. "I'm normal."

He laughs then, like I said something side-splitting funny.

"Ah, normal. That word is a conundrum, is it not? For surely normal stands in the eye of the beholder. And since we all have our own unique perspectives ... well then, wouldn't we all consider ourselves normal?"

Huh? I hope he's not expecting an answer to that line of gibberish since I don't even know what he's asking. Nope, he isn't expecting me to answer because he goes right on talking.

"I have been called many names in my years, my dear: dwarf, half-man, imp, even jester at times, but never a mutant. You are very amusing." He points to the iron shooter again. "Truly, I mean you no harm."

He talks so peculiar I can't decide if he's a threat or not.

"Why were you lookin' through my slingbag then if you ain't aimin' to rob us?"

"Us? You are not alone? Where is the rest of your party?" he asks.

Shizen. I shouldn't have said that. But it doesn't matter none since right at that time, Finn and Cat come crashing through the trees, full speed. They must have heard the stranger's voice. Finn looks all scared and worried and runs right to my side, but Cat heads straight for what she perceives as the threat before me or Finn can hold her back. But she doesn't hurt the half-man. She doesn't even get close enough to lay a paw on him before he takes one look at the charging beast, lets out this gods-awful shriek, and falls right to the ground in a dead faint. Can't say I've ever seen a man faint before either. Well, I'll be.

"What is he, Tara?" Finn is whispering. Don't know why. The stranger's out cold; he can't hear him. I approach the man on the ground slowly and nudge him with my boot. He groans and stirs a little. I figure if we don't want him passing out again when he does wake up, we'd best get Cat out of his eye view, so I shoo the beast away from the stranger. She doesn't want to go. She's sniffing the man as curious as the rest of us, but Finn calls her over and she obeys. She goes and sits calmly by the boy's side like she never just scared the little man to death. I nudge him again, still pointing the iron shooter at him. I'm not taking any chance that he may be faking. After a bit, he opens his eyes and stares up at me. I back off a pace.

"You're okay," I say. "The beast won't hurt you. Not unless we tell it to."

I watch as his memories come flooding back to him,

and he bolts upright looking around in naked fear. Finn is keeping Cat firmly by his side, but the boy himself is staring all wide-eyed.

"That's a … a devil cat!" the little man says like he doesn't quite believe what he's seeing. I don't know who's more awestruck: him or Finn.

"Yeah, it is," I say in my scariest voice. "And a mighty vicious one at that if you get to thinkin' you can rob us again." I reckon if the iron shooter doesn't scare him away, then Cat would do the trick. The stranger watches Finn keeping Cat calm by scratching her ears. Then a peculiar thing happens; he starts smiling and clapping his hands. No. He's supposed to be running away in fear.

"A tamed devil cat. This is extraordinary. I never would have thought it possible. Oh, my heavens, this is remarkable."

He gets to his feet and brushes past me like I'm holding a feather instead of an iron shooter. Bold as anything now, he walks over to Finn and Cat.

"It belongs to you, boy?" he asks Finn. The boy just nods, still in wonder of the stranger.

"Extraordinary!" He puts his hand out towards Cat then stops. "May I?"

Finn nods again, and the half-man starts rubbing Cat's head and ears. Immediately, Cat responds to the stranger by rolling over for a belly scratch. So much for me trying to scare him away with Cat's viciousness. Not even so much as a growl or baring of the teeth like she had done with me. *Traitor,* I think.

"Hey," I yell at his back. "I ain't forgot I caught you pawin' through my slingbag."

"What?" He looks back at me as if he even forgot I was there. "Oh, yes, yes. Forgive my rudeness, my dear. I was not 'pawing' through anything. I was just analyzing the situation, deciding if you were friend or foe. It was the smell of your delectable meal cooking that drew me to your campsite. You see, I am but a simple traveler such as yourself, just hoping to share of your meal and repay you in kind with a fine tale or two."

Finn exchanges a look with me. I don't trust this odd little man, but Finn is grinning like a fool and I know right away he believes him to be harmless. The stranger notices our hesitation.

"Oh please, allow me to introduce myself. My name is Winston Phillip the Third. But you may call me what my dearly departed mother so affectionately referred to me as: Tater. Tater the trader, the storyteller, the minstrel, at your service."

He removes his hat and takes a little bow. Finn is charmed, but I still don't trust him.

"If you're a trader, then where are your wares?" I stare at him through narrowed eyes.

"Ah, very astute for one so young."

He taps his nose and smiles at me. I don't smile back.

"They are just some ways in the wood, packed onto my very trusted companion, my mule Winnie. Named after my dear mother of course. They share the same temperament. Some might even say the same facial features, but that's a story for another time, yes? I shall fetch her if you like." He heads for the trees but falters after a couple of steps. "Oh, but can I trust that this magnificent beast will not take my

Winnie as a late-night snack? As with my mother, I am very attached to my mule, you see."

Finn finally speaks. "Oh no, Cat won't eat your mule, mister. She listens to me real good."

"Wonderful. Then I shall fetch her. And maybe perhaps share in your evening meal?"

"Aye, you can," says Finn. "There's lots of snake to go around. You can even camp with us for the night if you like."

Tater happily claps his hands again and moves off into the woods.

"Finn. What are you doin'?" I hiss, once the odd little man is out of earshot.

He looks at me, dumbfounded. "What?"

"Inviting him to eat with us ... to camp with us for the night. We don't know who he is or what he is. I don't think he's quite right in the head. He could slit our throats in the night for all we know." I can't believe the boy was foolish enough or stupid enough to do such a thing.

"He could slit our throats in the night whether he's making camp with us or not, Tara. He knows we're here," he says. Okay, so maybe not so stupid. "Besides, Cat won't let no harm come to us. And he says he's a storyteller, and I like him. He's funny."

Tater reappears before I can respond. He leads from the trees a dappled gray mule, laden down with two leather saddle bags on either side. Cat stiffens at the sight of the mule, but Finn gives her a stern, "No, Cat. Winnie is not food. You don't eat Winnie, understand?" And as if the beast does understand, she lays down with her head on her paws and looks the other way as if saying, "It don't interest me none anyways."

"Here we are. This is my Winnie, my most loyal traveling companion. And Winnie, these fine young folks are … well, I do not know, now do I? I'm afraid in all the excitement I didn't get your names."

"I'm Finn," Finn pipes up. "And that's Tara, and this is Cat."

"Finn and Tara and Cat. All excellent names indeed. Are you brother and sister by chance?" he asks.

I snort at him. "Do we look like we're kin?"

"Well, no you do not, but then again, I do not resemble my family at all." He smiles but eyes me strangely.

I didn't get a chance to braid my hair since my wash, and it's now almost dried by the warm, evening air. I know this is what he's looking at.

"You have the most striking hair, Tara. I don't believe I have ever seen such contrast. Black and white is usually a combination reserved for the old folk, but for you, someone so young, rare indeed. And so symmetrical."

I don't like his interest in my hair. I find it very unsettling. As if noticing my unease, he then smiles and rubs his hands together with eagerness. "Now, about that snake."

———

Well, Tater truly wasn't lying about being a storyteller. His storytelling was even better than Thomas', and I wouldn't have ever thought that to be possible. As much as I didn't want to, I fall under his magical spell just as much as Finn does. We listen entranced as Tater speaks of life before the Shift. He tells stories of the settlers with their magic picture boxes and their tall sky buildings with their moving floors that went up and down. He tells us about their great cities that had spread out over leagues and leagues, so full of buildings and people you could hardly move. We listen, and for a while, we forget all of our misery, our troubles, and get pulled into the tall tales. It was real nice. And we'd been so caught up in the stories I hadn't even noticed that between the three of us and Cat, we had eaten the whole snake. I knew we should have saved some for the road, but it was just so damn tasty. Finn hadn't lied. I decided snake was now my favorite thing to eat. Well, next to sweet berry bread. Thinking about the bread makes me think of Miz Emma, and I push it away. Not now.

Our bellies full of snake and our heads full of tales, we lay content around the fire. Tater's gone quiet as he sips something from a flat, tin flask he'd pulled out of his jacket pocket. From the way he screws up his face at every sip, I reckon it's not water. Cat is cleaning herself and occasionally swatting at Finn as he flicks her ears. I'm poking the fire with a stick, stoking the flames when Tater speaks again.

"Now your turn," he says, pointing his tin flask at us. "What are two fine young people such as yourselves doing out in the middle of nowhere with a tame devil cat? Which, by the way, no one is ever going to believe when I tell this fine tale."

Finn looks at me as if he expects me to do the talking. I hesitate. I don't want to tell this story, not again. But then I figure he just maybe might know something about Littlepass or Lily for that matter. He is a traveling trader after all.

"We're travelin' to Littlepass. Do you know of it?" I ask.

"Do I know of it? But of course. And as luck would have it, I, too, am traveling there as well. What a remarkable coincidence indeed." He smiles at us like it's the best news he's heard in years. "And what, pray tell, is your business there?"

"We have to find someone," I say.

He takes another sip and stares at me over the rim. "Well, that's very cryptic. Does this someone have a name?"

I stare back for a bit before I decide to answer. "Lily. She's a healer."

He thinks for a while, then shakes his head. "No. I know many people, but a healer by the name of Lily is not one of them."

Finn is looking all worried. "Maybe she ain't there no more, Tara. Tater says he don't know her; maybe she moved on, and we ain't gonna find her."

Tater laughs. "My dear boy, Littlepass, unlike its name would suggest, is a thriving metropolis. There are a multitude of people living there. I simply do not know them all."

I don't find this funny, not at all. If there are so many people, it's going to be that much harder to find Lily. My heart sinks. Oh, Grada, what were you thinking sending me off on this wild goose chase?

"But you still have not answered my question. Why are you both out here traveling these dangerous lands alone? Where are your parents? Your families?"

"Dead," I respond bluntly.

Tater looks taken aback. "Oh dear, I am sorry. Sickness?"

Finn answers this. "No, was something worse." He looks to me, and I nod. He continues, "They were men who came from the sand lands in metal monsters ... well, machines; we know that's what they were really. There was three of 'em, real big, black, on wheels. They ... they killed all of Tara's kin and my own with their iron shooters. Cat killed one of 'em though, and now we got his shooter." He nods toward the weapon that is lying by my side.

"Ah," Tater says, and I look up real quick. He knows something.

"You know what they are," I accuse. He nods.

"Yes. And that does explain how the two of you have a pistol of the Prezedant's Army."

"The what?" It's like he's talking another language.

"The Prezedant's Army? Surely, you have heard of this force?" He can tell by our faces we haven't. He flashes a slight smile. "I forget how isolated and naïve you sand land young'uns can be."

It kind of feels like he's insulting us, and it makes my skin prickle with irritation.

"Tell me what you know of the metal machines," I demand. "And you can leave out your fancy words, understood?"

My anger seems to surprise him, but he just nods at me. "Very well. What you two seem to be ignorantly and blissfully unaware of is the very big, very populated, and very corrupt world beyond the sand lands ... beyond the mountains. There are places you cannot even begin to comprehend. Some of them cesspools of disease, evil, and darkness."

I shiver at what he's saying; I can't help it.

"Some of them, like Littlepass, are more civilized but all of them are under the control of one man. He calls himself the Prezedant. Ridiculous title if you ask me. King or General would be more suitable, but I digress. He is a very powerful man. He has amassed armies of men. Evil men to do his every bidding. They are his loyal followers, his henchmen, and his executioners."

Fear competes with anger as I repeat the name he's given me under my breath, "The Prezedant." Raising my gaze back to Tater, I ask, "So the metal machines that came through our villages ... they're his? They carry his men?"

He nods. "Apparently so, though last I heard they were in no way able to travel this far into the sand lands or even past the mountains." He rubs at his mustache like he's deep in thought. "His scholars must have come up with some sort of fuel alternative for them to be able to travel such great distance."

There he goes talking his odd language again.

"His what?" I ask.

He shakes his head at me. "Doesn't matter. What matters is why have they come this far into the sand lands? He has never bothered to go beyond the mountains before. Why now?"

"I don't care why," I growl. "All I want to know is why he sent his armies to kill my kin and Finn's. They never did anything to this *Prezedant*." I spit out the word like it's dirt. "And why did he take the young'uns from my village? Where would he have taken them? And how do I get 'em back?"

Tater regards me with such a look of sadness that I drop my eyes. I don't like what that look implies.

"As I've said, child, he is a very evil man. As for the murder of your families, I cannot give you a reason why, only that yours is not the first village to meet this same fate. He controls those who oppose him with fear and death. Some have even gone as far as to call him monster and demon. He knows things, possesses things that could only have come from before the Shift. Some say the man himself lived before the Shift, that he is immortal. That he has walked the land for hundreds of years."

Finn is staring at the half-man in wide-eyed disbelief. "So you're saying those metal machines we saw … they're the real moving veacals from the old folk stories. They're from before the Shift? That the stories are true?"

"Most stories are based on truth, boy," Tater says and takes another sip of his "water."

"How do you know all this?" I ask, still not trusting his words. "How do we know what you're sayin' ain't a bunch of shite? You mean to say this Prezedant is hundreds of years old, and we're supposed to believe that?"

He studies me. His piercing, black eyes watch me for so long I begin to fidget under his gaze.

"You believe what you want, but I think you know I speak the truth. All I'm saying is this: I was born in Skytown, the place the Prezedant calls his home, and I have seen him twice in my lifetime. Once when I was but a lad, no older than Finn here. The second time at a public execution just four years back. Now during that time, I have grown old and weary. My eyes have seen far more than they have wanted to, but the one thing they are sure of is this. The Prezedant has not changed his appearance, not one little bit during those years. He looks exactly the same. How is that possible? You tell me."

"Magic," Finn whispers, and Tater nods his head.

"There ain't no such thing, Finn. Don't be foolish." My words are to Finn, but my anger is directed toward Tater, daring him to argue that with me. "If he's so all-powerful and magical, why's he gotta send out men with iron shooters to kill people? Why don't he just do it with his magic?"

Tater stares at me for a bit then unexpectedly points at me and laughs. "You truly are an irksome child. If I knew all the answers, I could tell you why. I could also tell you why the sun is in the sky or why the birds fly through the air, but I do not know why."

He leans back against a dead log and crosses his short legs.

"Are you sure you are ready to hear of the fate of your young kin?" He doesn't give me a chance to answer, to change my mind; he just goes right on talking. "As I have said, there have been numerous villages in the past that have had the misfortune to fall under his notice, and all have ended up the same: murder, pillaging, and abduction of the children. It is said he takes the children to work his iron mines and to be servants in his residences. But there are whispers of other … uses. Some believe he consumes them, their youth and vitality. Their very souls. They say it's what keeps him immortal, you see."

Tater's eyes gleam at us eerily through the darkness, and a faint shiver passes over me. Finn gives a strangled little yelp, and his face goes pale white, noticeable even by firelight.

"That's enough talk for one night," I say, more so to stop from hearing any more terrible words. Like the boy, I'm terrified at what Tater is telling us, and it's almost like he done it on purpose. Why would he want to scare us like that?

"We need to get some sleep. I want to get an early start in the mornin'."

"I wholeheartedly agree, my dear." Tater is all smiles again now. "And if you don't mind, I would truly love to accompany you to Littlepass. I have done the journey many times. I could show you the way, cut maybe weeks of walking off your journey."

I don't want to, but I agree to Tater's company. I still have a lot of unanswered questions. I want to talk to him some more—alone. I get an uneasy feeling that he knows a lot more than he's letting on to. But for now, we need to sleep.

CHAPTER 3

Mountain Gulch

———◆———

The trees seem to go on forever. Sometimes they're so tangled and snarled I don't think we're ever going to get past them, but Tater always seems to know the way around. Most times when I truly believe we're lost and walking in circles, he assures me he knows exactly where he's going. He says to me, "Not to worry, my dear. I have been traveling these woods for many years, far more than I would care to admit. I will not lead you astray."

He always says it with his toothy smile, but it irritates me some. His constant silly way of talking irritates me most times. And to make matters worse, there are these tiny, flying biters that keep buzzing around our heads and nipping at our skin. Sometimes, they're so damn bothersome I want to scream. Tater calls them "maskeetos," but I just call them annoying. They seem to pester me more so than the others. Tater says it's because my blood is so sweet, but he grins all strange every time he says it, like he's not joking at all. I still don't trust him, not one little bit. But I got to admit, he is a real entertaining storyteller. And real good with the musical flute. Lou used to play too, but he wasn't near as good as Tater. When the little man plays at night while we sit around the campfire, the night doesn't seem to be as dark and scary anymore. And he does make Finn laugh, so I guess he's not all bad.

There hasn't been much chance to talk to Tater alone, and I'm still full of questions. Finn sticks as close to the little man as a berry to its bush. But today's travel had been a hard one, and Finn had immediately fallen asleep the minute we made camp. The ground we'd been walking all day had been sloping down, making it an effort to stay on our feet at times. Well, for me and Finn anyways. Tater seemed to have no trouble. I still think he's more mutie than man. So, with Finn already sleeping on the other side of the fire, I reckoned this was my chance to talk with Tater alone. I push aside my own weariness. There are things I need to know—no time for sleeping just yet. I eyeball Tater, who's lounging against a fallen tree and sipping his usual drink. I stare until he finally raises a shaggy brow.

"Well, as my dear mother used to say, you look as if you have a bee in your bonnet. Spit it out, girlie," he says.

"Who exactly is the Prezedant? Why is he sendin' his men out into the sand lands to kill villagers and take young'uns?

What's he do with them when he takes 'em? Why don't the people of Littlepass and Skytown and every place else just stop him if he's so evil?"

The words just pour out of me; I want to know all the answers. Tater stares at the ground like he's pondering his response before meeting my gaze. He flashes his teeth, his laughter all quiet like so as not to disturb Finn.

"I can see this is going to be a long evening," he sighs. He thinks for a while more, takes a sip of his drink, and then finally speaks. "Who the Prezedant truly is I cannot tell you. That's all he is known as. He has ruled for as long as I can remember and longer than that. He is a very powerful man … magician, immortal, as I have said. He is believed to have done things no human should be capable of doing. While the rest of the world's lands are barren and dead, his lands are prosperous, alive, and fertile. How is that possible? The people, they whisper about his so-called 'powers,' but no one can explain. I've heard many stories in my years. Some say they have witnessed the man bring dead trees to life with a touch of his hand or make a dried-up spring run again with just a breath."

I scoff at Tater's words. That was pure shite if I ever heard it.

"Do not dismiss the stories, girl. As I told the boy, most stories stem from truth. And do not dismiss his power. His armies are massive, and they follow his every command. To them, he is their god. And not just his armies. There are many, I fear, who blindly follow the Prezedant. Lost souls who have become as dark and depraved as the man himself. I warn you, girl, the things you will witness in Littlepass and in Skytown ... they will change you."

He stops talking. His words chill me, but I nod at him to continue.

"As for stopping him, some have tried. There have been a few brave souls who have tried to destroy him over the years. But their efforts have been in vain. He hunts down those who dare oppose him and publicly executes those who disobey. He holds no regard for human life. His lands are cesspools of depravity, debauchery, and unspeakable horrors for most. For others, the scum of mankind, the twisted lowlifes, they are a haven. Children are sold into slavery, put to work in his iron mines, in his residences, and sometimes far worse. I will not lie ... the young kin you are worried for have most likely already met this fate."

Even though he doesn't go into explicit detail, he doesn't need to. I get the gist of what he's saying, and it fills me with utter despair. A lump of ice solidifies in my belly and its coldness starts seeping slowly through my veins. Yet I need to know more.

"There must be some good people ... like this Lily. Surely, Grada wouldn't send me to such an evil place on purpose. Surely, not everyone is this way. Grada said Lily would help me. She cain't be all bad," I say, not wanting to believe everything Tater is telling me.

"Do you not know who this Lily is, girl? I assumed her to be your kin. Your family." Tater truly appears surprised by my words.

I hesitate. I don't want to admit it to him, but finally I shake my head. "No. Grada ... before he died, it's like he knew what was gonna happen, and he told me I had to go to

Littlepass and find her. To tell her who I was, and she would help me."

"Help you to do what?" he asks.

"I … I don't know. I'm hopin' maybe she can help me find Ben and the other young'uns."

Tater ponders this for a bit. "So, your Grada was from Littlepass then? How is it that he knew of the Prezedant and his Army but never warned you of the dangers?"

I shake my head again. "No, Grada and the others, they lived in Rivercross their whole lives, I guess. Same as me. If he had known, he would have told me of this evil."

Tater's "hmph" bothers me.

"What do you mean by that?" My words are sharp.

He shrugs. "I didn't take you for a fool, girl."

"I'm no fool," I growl back.

"Then why are you acting the part?"

I open my mouth to argue, my cheeks burning hot from my anger, but he cuts me off.

"Your Grada sent you to Littlepass for a reason. He knew of the place. He even knew of someone who resides there. It just goes to show that he was very aware of the outside world and of the Prezedant. And any village, no matter how remote, that has had traders pass through would most certainly have been told of the news from the other side of the mountains. No, trust me, your Grada and all the other old folk of your village, they knew of the dangers. They had just fooled themselves into believing they had gone far enough into the sand lands. That they would be unnoticed and passed over. That they would be safe. Seems now, nowhere is safe," he says these last words almost to himself and takes another drink.

I don't want to believe what he's saying. There's no way Grada and the others had known about this danger and not warned us, not prepared us. But in the back of my mind, I hear Molly's words as she was running from the dust cloud.

"They found us," she'd said, and Grada telling me, "They cain't be stopped." I think of all the times us young'uns had been sent away from the campfires while a trader was visiting because the old folk wanted to "talk," and I know deep down in my heart Tater is speaking the truth. They had known.

Anger and resentment grow in my heart along with this new realization. How dare they not warn us, not protect us from this Prezedant? They'd known everything, yet had in no way prepared us, and now, Ben, Jane, and young Thomas were in the hands of a madman. I don't even want to think of what they may be going through right now, what they may be suffering. I take my anger out on Tater.

"Why don't he kill you lot then? You traders? Why do you get to live and travel the sand lands free from his punishment?" My voice gets louder, and Finn stirs in his sleep. I stop talking. I don't want to wake him, but I'm simmering mad. Tater stays quiet for so long I don't think he's ever going to answer me.

Finally, he says, "I'm not proud to admit this, but I assume we provide a service to him. We are his harbingers of death. Nothing creates more fear, more obedience in the populace than tales of the villages and people he has destroyed. Through us, his legend grows, so the people become more afraid of him. They stay. They obey. They serve and give everything they grow and produce to the Prezedant. They live in fear and despair while he and his elite live like kings.

But they live."

I mull his words over in my head, truly speechless at what I've just heard. I never could have imagined such an evil existed. My anger at Grada and the old folk for keeping us in the dark isn't lessening any, but I think I kind of understand what they'd tried to do now. They'd tried to give us a normal life … a happy life, free from the fear that the people on the other side of those mountains seemed to live in constantly. Like Tater said, I guess they figured they would never be looked for or found. They were so wrong and had paid a high price for their ignorance.

"You said the Prezedant has never come on this side of the mountains before. Why now do you think?"

He shrugs. "I could only guess. As far as I know, his armies have never made the trek through the mountains. It is a hard journey indeed, and as you well know, the sand lands do not have much to offer. He has in the past left the exploring of the sand lands to us, the traders. The few brave souls who have decided to try and eke out a living in these barren, desolate lands he has never shown much interest in. But with these vehicles of his apparently more mobile now, he must have a reason for venturing into the sand lands. The man may be evil incarnate, but he never does anything without a reason."

What kind of reason could he have to just up and kill innocent people? And why would Grada send me to Littlepass? Toward this Prezedant? Into his lands? It doesn't make a lick of sense to me.

Grada's words on that day play over in my head. *"Find Lily; tell her she was right."* Right about what? *"Tell her I should have sent word long ago."*

Should have sent word to her, Lily. Tater's words ring with truth the more I think about it. Grada had certainly known of Lily and Littlepass. But why had he never spoke of her until then? And was she able to help me get Ben and the young'uns back?

"When he takes the young folk, where does he keep 'em?" I ask, knowing that this now must be my focus. I'm not prepared for the harsh laughter that comes from the little man. It's so unlike his normal, cheerful sound that I can't help but be shocked by it. He leans over and stares at me so intently it's like he's staring into my very soul. He points a stubby finger my way.

"I'm only going to say this once, girlie, so pay close attention. Forget about finding your young kin ever again. They are as good as dead. As we speak, they have already been sold into slavery, put to work in the iron mines, or a dozen other possibilities, but they are gone, understand? Forget about them. My advice to you: Go find your Lily. Maybe she can keep you and the boy safe and give you a home. Keep you from ending up like your kin."

"Shut. Your. Mouth," I hiss, through gritted teeth. "They ain't dead. Don't you ever say those words to me ever again!"

Fuming mad, my blood pounding through my veins, I want to lash out at the little man for his terrible words. How dare he tell me to forget about them? I want to smack that smug, know-it-all look right from his face. But I don't get a chance to do anything before Tater recoils, and his eyes open wide like I really did hit him. I never touched him. I was only thinking it. Why is he looking at me like that? Are my thoughts that obvious? Angry, confused, and not wanting to look at his face anymore, I turn my back to him and lay down on my bedroll, my blood boiling my innards. I'm done with the conversation. I don't want to hear another word from the half-man. I can feel his eyes boring into my back, but I don't acknowledge him at all. I wrap my hand around my flower, my gift from Ben, hoping to get some comfort from it. I feel such overwhelming hopelessness ... all I want to do is cry. But I don't. I won't give him the satisfaction of hearing me cry. Instead, I focus on the faces of Ben and Jane and young Thomas. I try to picture in my mind what they look like, what they sound like, because as angry as I am at Tater for his terrible words, there's this small, nagging part of me that fears he may be right. If the only way to get them back means going up against this Prezedant and his Army, then I've lost before I've even begun.

⎯◆⎯

It's been days of traveling through these damn strangling woods, but the trees are finally starting to thin out. The tangled web of branches and leaves are giving way to golden beams of sunlight filtering through up ahead. Cat takes off, eager to get back out into the open lands, and I feel the same anticipation. Just knowing we're almost through the woods must put Tater in a jubilant mood, and he starts singing a tune I haven't heard before, but Finn knows of it and soon joins in. Usually, hearing the two of them singing is enough to raise a smile from me, but not this time. My mood is somber, has been since my conversation with Tater. Our arguing hasn't affected him at all. Other than the occasional times I've caught him staring oddly at me, he's been acting like nothing even happened. Me, I haven't done much talking these past few days, but I have done a lot of thinking.

I've decided to keep on going to Littlepass, to try and find Lily like Grada wanted me to do. There must have been a reason for his wanting me to. I need to know at least why. I'm not giving up on the idea of her being able to help me find my kin. I refuse to believe that Tater is right. They were not gone like he says. But he is right about one thing. It's way too dangerous for the boy to be accompanying me. I'm hoping Lily can help me with that. Look after him perhaps, give him a home. Keep him alive. More than I can offer him. As for Cat, well, she's a wild animal after all; she can survive on her own. It will break Finn's heart to let her go, but it's either that or probably have her get killed. Finn doesn't have much of a choice. As for me, well, I won't be staying in Littlepass. I can't. Once Finn is settled, I'll be moving on. As dangerous as Skytown seems, it's where I have to go. I don't care what Tater says; I am going to find Ben or at least die trying.

By mid-morning, we're finally out of the woods. After so many days of dim light, the sun is almost blinding. My eyes aren't used to so much light anymore. I close them to give them time to adjust and just stand there with my face turned up to the sun, enjoying its warmth. I notice right away the absence of rot and decay. The air is fresh smelling, like sunshine and grass and sage. It's real nice, and I breathe it in deep.

"Tara. Look!" Finn's voice is just quivering with excitement, breaking my tranquility. He tugs on my arm, trying to get my attention. I open my eyes to see what has him so riled up.

We're standing in a valley spread out about half a league across. The whole floor of the valley is grassland. It's brown and stubbly, but it's plentiful; not a bit of cracked soil to be seen. Surrounding us on both sides are high, sloping hills dotted with gray trees and big, red boulders creating almost walls through the valley. But it's what's on the other end that has Finn all wide-eyed.

They hover on the horizon like blue-gray giants, so massive it seems like they're actually touching the sky. The tips of them are hidden by puffy, gray clouds, making you believe that if you were to climb to the top, you could just hop on a passing cloud and float away. Like Finn, I'm awestruck at this sight. I never thought I'd see such a thing in my lifetime. They're breathtaking and scary all at the same time.

"That's them ain't it, Tater?" Finn's question is filled with breathless excitement. "The mountains you was talkin' about?"

Tater nods. "Yes. Are they not magnificent? I never tire of seeing their majestic beauty. They truly are some of the gods' most impressive handiwork."

"Do we gotta go over 'em?" Finn is sounding all worried now, but I'm glad he's asking because I'm fearing the same. There's no way we'll be able to climb those giants.

"Oh, dear me, no. No, no silly boy; that would be impossible." Tater slaps Finn on the back, laughing as if that were the funniest thing he had ever heard. "You do amuse me so. No, we will go through them. Yes, indeed. You see, there is a gulch, a pass through them, almost impossible to find unless you are aware of its existence. Which lucky for you both, I am. As my dear mother would have said, our meeting was indeed a most fortunate throw of the dice."

I shake my head. After days of being in Tater's company, I'm starting to believe he speaks just for the sheer joy of hearing himself talk. I can't understand half of what he says, and if his ma truly said all those things he says she did, well, she must have been a real odd one. I guess the branch didn't fall far from the tree.

Winnie by now has gotten the scent of the grass, and she's itching to feed. Tater lets her go, and she wanders off to a particularly tasty-looking patch. Cat is way off on the valley floor, running and jumping. Looks like she's maybe chasing some sort of small critter though she's too far away to tell. The open land, the sun, the fresh air, it fills me with a sense of wellbeing. Something I haven't felt for a long time. I don't know why, but I start smiling. It must be contagious because the others start grinning, too. We're just standing, smiling, looking around like we're a bunch of wide-eyed young'uns.

"It's so pretty here." Finn's quiet observation breaks the silence.

I'm thinking the same. It is pretty ... peaceful almost. Like nothing bad could ever happen here. Like a madman never existed just on the other side of those mountains, but Tater quickly crushes that illusion.

"Indeed," he says. "But do not be lulled into a false sense of security. There are hidden dangers we must be aware of."

He reaches into his jacket and pulls something out. At first, I think it's his musical flute, but then he holds it to his eye. It's made of a shiny, light-colored metal. He pulls on it with his other hand, and it gets longer. He looks through the narrow end, and I can now see there's a circle of glass at the wider end. Finn had been standing hands on his hips and looking out over the valley, but at this new object of Tater's, his eyes grow all big and round.

"Shizen. What is that?" he says in wonder.

"Finn," I scold him. "Stop your cussin'."

But I'm sure as shizen wondering the same. What is it?

"Ah yes, this little beauty is called a spyglass," Tater answers, but he doesn't take it from his eye. He just keeps sweeping the valley. "Got this off of a real friendly lady in the sand lands by the name of Glenalda. She was a lovely lady. Traded her a bottle of whiskey and a silk dress of my mother's." His smile is filled with sadness. "Yes, she was quite the woman indeed." He clears his throat and looks up at us in surprise like he forgot we were even here. "But I'm rambling again, aren't I? This, my young friends, helps you to see far off in the distance. Very handy for scouring the vicinity for any sign of danger or threat."

He does another sweep then takes it down from his eye. "And it appears we are good."

I forget all my hostility and anger towards Tater and nearly run Finn over in my haste to reach the little man and his curious object.

"Let me see!"

"Can I try?"

We're trying to yell over each other, to be the first to get a look at this wonder, but Tater holds the spyglass away from us.

"Careful. It's a very delicate object."

He hesitates for a bit, looks from me to his spyglass. I can tell he doesn't want to part with it, but finally he relents and hands it over.

"You promise to be careful?"

"Aye," I say, taking it eagerly.

I hold it to one eye and squint the other like Tater had done. All of a sudden, the mountains that seemed so far away before loom in front of me, and I can't help but step back in shocked astonishment. I can see every rocky ledge and tree valley perfectly clear like I could reach out and touch them.

"Holy Shizen," I say, pulling it away for a moment just to make sure my eyes aren't playing a trick on me. Nope, the mountains are just as far away as before. I quickly put it back to my eye again. How is this little thing making this possible?

Finn is yanking at my tunic impatiently. "My turn. My turn."

I don't want to let it go. It's one of the most amazing things I've ever seen, but it's not fair not to let Finn try so I reluctantly hand it over. My laughter bubbles when his mouth falls open at what he sees. His hand goes up in front of him, and he's reaching like he thinks he can touch what's in the spyglass. At hearing my laugh, he turns the spyglass to me.

"Hey, Tara, you got a hanger in your nose."

"What?" My hand goes to cover my nose, but Finn cracks up laughing.

"No, there ain't, you arsewipe," I yell at him, but it makes me laugh, too.

Finn hands the spyglass carefully back to Tater. "That was amazin', Tater," he says, bouncing up and down. "You got anything else to show us?"

"Another time perhaps,"Tater says, putting it away. "But I think it is best we head out. A word of advice though before we proceed through the valley, yes?"

His tone is light, but I get the feeling he isn't telling us everything and my gut clenches, chasing away my earlier feeling of peacefulness.

"What is it?" I question. "Did you see something in that spyglass of yours?"

"No, no. Everything was clear. No sign of any threat. But I suggest we move through the valley quickly. Not make camp until we get to the base of the mountains. If we make haste, we should be there before nightfall."

Tater's words are not easing my worries.

"Why? Thought you said everything was clear? Why do we gotta hurry? Are there critters or such we should watch out for?"

He chuckles as if the idea of such a thing is ridiculous. "No, not 'critters' really. But beyond that third rise, there is a village I am familiar with. I have done some trading there in the past. They … tolerate my presence. But they are—how shall I put this—very unfriendly towards strangers of any sort. You two, being so young and … innocent, let's just say you do not want to make their acquaintance. And as for Cat, as extraordinary as she is, they would only see meat and a fur cloak. Do you understand?"

I understand. I understand that the world is a lot darker and dismal than I had ever thought possible. But I just nod.

"Yeah. We need to go through unnoticed. Let's move then," I say.

But Finn, as always, is more concerned about his beast than us.

"So, if we get to the mountains, Tater, will Cat be safe from the villagers then? Won't they just follow us into the mountains?" he says, his face a mask of anxiety.

"Oh no, dear boy, do not worry about your she-devil. The villagers, they do not venture into the mountains. They avoid the mountains at all costs." He grins his toothy smile, and I see Finn visibly relax. "They are too afraid of encountering the raiders, you see."

Finn gasps at this, and Tater's smile dies away.

"Oh, dear, maybe I shouldn't have said that."

This just keeps getting better and better.

———

We don't talk. We don't stop. We walk as fast as we can. Tater don't come right out and say what the villagers would do to us, but my mind keeps filling in the gaps with all kinds of horrible thoughts. I find myself looking over my shoulder every few steps and jumping at every noise. I swear I catch a glimpse of movement behind us at times, like someone is following us, but it never amounts to anything. I know it's just my mind playing tricks on me, but it doesn't ease my rattled nerves none. It only makes me pick up the pace and have Finn and Tater struggle to keep up with me. But by sundown, we make the base of the mountain and without incident. We decide not to attempt the gulch at this late hour but wait for the morning light. A small grove of trees halfway up a side slope looks to be our best bet for a protected campsite though we'll have to do without a fire tonight. After making it through the valley unnoticed, there's no need to draw attention now.

We set up our beds by the early evening moonlight, but I'm not the least bit tired. I feel all on edge, and my blood is strumming through my veins. I lay staring up at the night sky, listening until finally I hear Finn's slight snores and Tater's louder version. Even Cat is sleeping, twitching as she chases some dream prey. But sleep eludes me. I move my blankets to a tree, prop myself up against the trunk, and lay the iron shooter in my lap. I can't rightly say what's bothering me, but I watch the valley floor and the slopes for any sign of movement. I strum my fingers against the long barrel of the shooter. I wait.

The moon is high in the sky now, but it's not much help with all the shadows of the valley. I keep watching, looking for ... I'm not sure what. I don't know how long I sit there. A critter hoots off in the distance, its call eerie in the quiet night. It's getting hard to keep my eyes open now.

I'm being foolish. I should get some sleep.

Then suddenly below me, something moves. Fully awake now, I bolt upright and hold the iron shooter tighter. I wish I had thought to ask Tater for his spyglass. I keep watching the spot. There it is again. I get a brief glimpse of it as it appears from the shadows into a moonlit patch of valley floor. It looks to be hunched over and shuffling like ... like the creature I had seen in the sand lands. I blink my eyes, trying to focus. It disappears into the darkness again, and I can't see it anymore. I keep watching, not blinking until my eyes start to burn, but it doesn't re-emerge. Was I imagining it? I could have sworn something was there. But if there had been something, there's no way it can be the same creature. What I'd seen that night in the sand lands had been weeks and leagues away from here. What were the odds the creature had been traveling in the same direction as us? Following us? Even though I don't see any more movement, I decide I'm not sleeping tonight. Imagination or not, somebody needs to keep watch. I sense something in my gut, and it just don't feel right. I settle back against the tree and level the iron shooter on my knee, pointing it straight ahead. If there is something out there, it isn't getting past me tonight. No way in hell.

———◆———

"Tara. Tara, wake up."

Dazed and confused, I open my eyes. The sun is up. It's morning. Suddenly remembering the moving shadow, I search my lap frantically for the iron shooter. It's not there. Then I realize Tater is standing above me, waving the shooter and grinning down at me.

"Looking for this, oh great protector?" He was obviously aware of my intent last evening and my total failure in staying awake. I yank it out of his hand, ignoring his laugh, and pack it into the slingbag at my feet. Finn walks over to join us and hands me a water skin.

"How come you slept sitting up against that tree, Tara?" he asks.

"No reason," I say. I take a big gulp from the water skin, but he keeps looking at me curiously, waiting for more.

"I was just star gazin', and I fell asleep is all."

He seems to accept this without question and moves on to pack up his bedding, but Tater is eyeballing me. He knows I'm not telling the whole truth.

"Did you witness any unusual constellations during your gazing?" he asks.

"If by that you mean strange stars, then no, just the usual," I say. I reckon it best not mention what I had seen last evening or thought I'd seen. I kind of feel foolish for my fright, and I'm not even sure it was real now in the light of day. No sense worrying them over what could have very well been my imagination. Besides, if something had been here last evening, Cat would have sensed it. She would have warned us. Instead, she had slept sound through the night. Obviously, she hadn't sensed anything amiss. No, best push it out of my mind and blame my jitters on my exhaustion. We got us more pressing matters like some crazy villagers, mountains, and possibly raiders to worry about instead. Just another typical day in the sand lands.

———•———

Mid-afternoon, day five in the mountains. The ground changes the higher we climb. And we are climbing. Not so quickly that you really notice, but the ground is sloping upwards. It's getting rockier and sparser. The loose shale sometimes makes it hard for Winnie to get her footing, but Tater coaxes her along with gentle patience. I believe he truly does love that mule.

It's getting cooler too, especially the nights. I'm real glad I have Thomas' rawhide jacket to keep me warm since the wind that sometimes blows cuts like a knife. I'd made Finn a cloak out of one of my blankets to keep him protected from the biting wind, but Tater, he only seemed to need the warmth of his tin flask, just adding to my belief that he is indeed a mutie.

The half-man assures us it will only take a few more days' travel before we start going down the other side, and then things will get better. Better, he says. I'm not sure about that. Littlepass means closer to Lily and answers to my questions about Ben and the young'uns. But it also means we're getting closer to the Prezedant's lands. To my plan of abandoning Finn. I haven't yet told him of my idea to settle him there. I hope he won't hate me too much, but it's all I can think to do for him. I know it's going to be hard to say goodbye to him. I kind of enjoy having him around. Cat too. Even Tater don't irritate me as much, though the thought of not hearing his voice every day doesn't bother me at all. But the thought of not seeing Finn every day … it doesn't sit well.

I watch him now plodding along after Tater, yammering with a hundred questions.

"How much further, Tater? What does Littlepass look like? What kinda food do they eat there? Do they have sticky buns? Ma used to make those, and they're my favorite."

His hair sticks up like normal, and there's a big streak of mud across his cheek. Don't know how he got that. He sees me watching him, stops talking, and gives me his goofy, gap-toothed grin. It tugs at my heart, but I squash those feelings right away. I don't have time for sentimentality. I can't afford to have any kind of care for anyone right now except for Ben and Jane and young Thomas. They're my only concern.

Besides, I know it's best for him and me to part ways. Some of what I'm thinking must be showing on my face, because his smile fades away.

"You okay, Tara?"

"What? Me? Yeah, I'm fine, you mule turd. Why you askin'?" I say.

"Cause you look … I dunno … sad kinda," he says and starts walking towards me.

I give him my brightest smile and reach out, try to wipe the dirt off his cheek, but it's stuck good. "No, I'm okay. Truly. I … I was just thinkin' about how the sky looks mighty dark up ahead."

I grasp at anything to change the subject. I don't want to have to tell him anything yet. I don't need to be arguing with him the rest of the way.

"Looks like it's gonna rain."

Tater stops at my words and studies the sky.

"Hmm, you're right, Tara. There is definitely a rainstorm up ahead. We should wait it out. It's too dangerous to be walking in the gulch right now."

"What do you mean, Tater? Why is it dangerous?" Just like that, Finn totally forgets about me at the mention of danger. He trots back over to the little man. "Why is a storm comin' dangerous?"

"Rain in the mountains is different from the sand lands. The rains are intense and torrential and can cause the gulch to flood and sweep us away before we even realize it's coming. We need to get out of the gulch now, wait it out on that plateau above us."

I'm not sure what a pla-toe is, but I follow Tater's gaze

and figure he's talking about the mountain ledge up ahead. The ledge is flat and open, but there are a couple of boulders high enough to give us shelter from the rain if it comes this way. It will have to do.

Reaching the ledge, I choose one of the boulders to rest against and ease my slingbag and bow from my shoulder. Tater does the same, easing Winnie's burden by taking off her saddlebags and laying them under the other boulder to keep them as dry as possible. Winnie is enjoying this bit of freedom and takes a happy little romp about the grass, scaring away some sort of mountain bird that had been using the grass as a hiding spot from us. The bird squawks and takes off, Cat following and nipping at its tail feathers. I smile at the chase. I'd be willing to bet we're having mountain bird for our evening meal tonight.

I lay back against the rock and close my eyes. I feel bone-tired, and my shoulder is aching something fierce. The slingbag strap has been irritating me some lately. I'll have to try and get some extra padding on it.

Finn, unlike me or Tater, is showing no signs of weariness. He's not even bothering with sitting down; he's too busy exploring the ledge and continuously yelling my name to get my attention. I crack open one eye. He's at the ledge's drop off, not close enough for worry, but close enough to see how high up we've climbed.

"Tara, you gotta come see this. It's like we're at the top of the world. It's amazing!"

I close my eye again. "I'll take your word on that, Finn," I say, too fatigued to move. "Don't get any closer to that edge."

"Yeah, yeah," he says, brushing aside my warning.

I'm still listening to his yammering about the view below when suddenly, I get a real bad feeling in my gut. Seconds later, Winnie starts braying in fright. I bolt upright and on instinct grab for my bow. The mule rears up on her hind legs, and before Tater can stop her, she runs off towards the gulch.

"What the—?" I duck as a huge, dark shadow sails from the boulder above my head. It lands right in between us, with me and Tater on one side and Finn on the other.

"Holy damnation!" Tater's cussing bursts out of him as he stumbles backward into me, nearly knocking me from my feet.

The creature standing before us is enormous, even bigger than Cat. Definitely a male devil cat. Its light fur is matted and dirty, and the red eyes regarding me and Tater at the moment look wild and hungry.

"Tara!"

At the boy's cry, the creature's head swings toward him, and I can see the powerful jaws on the massive head. It bares its teeth. They look like a mouth full of daggers. Finn sees what I see, and it freezes him in place, his face a mask of fear.

"It's okay, Finn," I yell out to him, sounding a lot calmer than I really am. Slowly, I raise my bow and reach for an arrow only to grab at empty air. Shizen. I'd taken my quiver off with the rest of my things earlier. I see it out of the corner of my eye, laying about four paces from me, and I make a move for it, but the creature's head swings my way. I freeze, waiting for it to pounce on me. Finn must fear the same because he cries my name again, causing the devil cat's attention to shift back to him. It crouches then, finally deciding on the boy as the easier prey. I don't stop to think; I just drop the bow, grab my knife from the sheath, and run at the beast screaming. I can't let it get to Finn. It springs into the air away from me, and I yell in terror, "Finn! Run!"

From out of nowhere Cat flies past me, her teeth bared and snarling like the she-devil she is. She collides with the other beast in midair, and she brings it down. They tumble over and over, a black and golden blur, their claws and teeth ripping at each other's throats.

"Finn, get away from them!"

I yell at him to move, but all he can see is his beloved beast in danger, and it's like he don't even heed me.

"Cat," he screams. "Cat, no!" He runs right into the path of the fighting beasts, and I watch in horror as he's knocked from his feet and disappears over the mountain edge.

———

Once when Ben and me had been real young, he had challenged me to see who could jump from the highest rock ledge above the old swimming hole. Never one to back down from his challenges, I'd climbed straight to the top of the highest ledge possible. I'd jumped, convinced it was going to be my best dive ever. Only when I hit the water, I hit belly first, and it felt like every breath of air was knocked clean out of my lungs. I couldn't breathe, I couldn't move, I couldn't think. This is that same feeling. I watch Finn go over that edge, and my body goes numb ... useless. I can still hear the beasts' shrieking off to the side, but it doesn't matter. Not anymore. Finn is gone.

Distant yelling breaks through the fear-fueled buzzing in

my head, and the realization it's Tater dawns slowly. But his yelling of Finn's name, over and over again, is like a slap to the face and jolts me into action. I push him out of the way as I run to the edge. I have to see with my own eyes before I can believe it. In desperation I scan the ground below, fearing for what I will find. I search for Finn's broken body, my ragged breaths loud in my own ears. I keep searching, but he isn't there. Where is he?

"Tara …"

The voice is weak and terrified, but it fills me with such relief my knees go numb. There he is; I see him. He's sprawled on a narrow ledge, about halfway down the rocky slope. Thank the gods.

"Finn," I yell. "Are you okay? Are you hurt?"

At first there's no answer. He's blacked out, I think.

But then, "My leg hurts some, but I think … I think I'm okay."

Tears well up at his response, but I quickly dash them away. No time for tears.

"Don't move. I'm gonna get you up," I say.

If only I knew how. I glance around wildly, looking for something, anything to help the boy. Tater, in the meanwhile, has retrieved the iron shooter out of my slingbag, but it hangs limply at his side as he stares at me in shock. He doesn't need it. The two beasts have disappeared, which is a good thing. I don't have time to be worried about Cat. My eyes fall onto Winnie's saddlebags.

"Tater, you got rope in those saddlebags?"

"Rope? Yes. Yes! I have a rope," he says and heads for the saddlebags.

He doesn't move quick enough for my liking. By the second yes, I'm already halfway there, knocking him out of my way again. I don't give a care for what else is in the bags; I dump them on the ground spewing the contents everywhere. I just want that damn rope. There. I grab the thick, cotton cord, and a desperate prayer for it to be long enough repeats in my head as I run back to the ledge.

"Finn," I yell down. "I'm gonna make a loop in the rope and lower it down. All you gotta do is put it around you underneath your arms, and we'll pull you up. Can you do that?"

"Yeah … I think so," he yells back, but he sounds so frightened.

"Good boy," I say. As fast as I can I make the loop in the end of the rope and cross it again to make a sturdy knot. The other end I tie around my own waist real tight. I'm not taking a chance of that rope slipping out of my hands. Kneeling over the edge, I start lowering it down.

Please be long enough.

A moment goes by.

"I got it," he yells.

I close my eyes in relief. Thank the gods.

"Okay, good. Now be careful. Don't move too quick. Put the loop over your head and move it down under your arms so it's across your chest."

I wait for him to do as I say, holding my breath. That ledge is so narrow. *Just one wrong move,* I think. I can hear Tater behind me, muttering, "Oh dear, oh dear, oh dear …"

"Okay." I hear Finn's quivering voice from below. So far so good.

"Now, the end of the rope that's sticking out, I want you to pull on it until the rope is tight around your chest. Pull until it's tight, understand?"

I can feel movement of the rope on my end as he does what I tell him to.

"It's tight, Tara. I did it."

"Good boy. Now, hold onto that rope because we're gonna pull you up. Hold it tight, Finn."

I get to my feet. Tater is still aimlessly pacing but runs straight for me as I motion for him to grab the rope. I move back, and he stands in front of me, hanging onto the line and still muttering or praying. I'm not sure which.

"Now, Tater," I say, and we start pulling slowly so as not to hurt Finn.

Little by little we reel the rope in until finally a tuft of red hair comes peeking over the edge, followed by a pair of huge, frantic eyes. He swings wildly to and fro, and one of his skinny arms reaches desperately for the rock ledge trying to grab it.

I yell at Tater, "I got the rope. Go help him."

Tater grabs for the flailing arm while I keep pulling. Once I see Tater has a good grip on the boy, I give one last tug and we get his body onto solid ground. Tater throws an arm around Finn and drags him away from the edge. They both fall to their knees once they've cleared the edge, gasping for air. I join them, grabbing Finn's shoulders real tight. A mixture of emotion courses through me. My relief quickly butts heads with the brewing anger at his not heeding my words to run. Instead he'd been stupid enough to head right into the path of the fighting beasts. He'd almost gotten himself killed. What the hell had he been thinking? Why didn't he listen to me? I want to shake him until his teeth rattle, but lucky for him, the relief wins out.

"Are you hurt?" I ask gruffly, trying not to let my anger show as I run my hands over his arms, feeling for any injuries.

"Don't think so … just my leg is banged up some is all." His answer is shaky, but at least the color is coming back to his face. Tater starts laughing and does his crazy little clap.

"Thank the gods for this glorious miracle, indeed. We rescued the boy. We are true heroes, Tara. Well, us and that magnificent cat of yours, boy, for without her we'd most likely be in the stomach of that other beast right about now."

At the mention of Cat, Finn brushes my probing hands away and looks around with frantic eyes.

"Cat? Is she okay? Where is she?"

Tater tries to calm him down. "No need to worry, my little friend. Last I saw of your she-devil, she was chasing that mountain cat off with its tail between its legs."

"Truly, Tater?" he asks, fighting the tears that threaten to flow.

"Cross my heart," Tater says. "And as my dear mother used to say—"

"Tater, shut up." I don't know why I say it; it just comes out of me. The offended look on the half-man's face at my command starts a fit of hysterical laughter. I can't help it. Not sure if it's relief or shock, maybe a bit of both, but I can't stop laughing. Then Finn starts laughing too, and finally Tater joins in. We're all laughing uncontrollably. Finn laughs so hard he starts hiccupping which makes us laugh even more.

"Well, well boys … seems like we've interrupted a

celebration."

The voice is as rough as gravel and totally unexpected. Instinctively, I push Finn behind me as I whirl around. Who spoke I'm not sure because there's about nine, possibly ten men standing there watching us. Least I suspect they're men. They don't look like anything I've ever seen before. The faces, staring at us with a mixture of curiosity and smug amusement, are painted with stripes of green and black, making the whites of their eyes weirdly stand out. A couple of them have painted bald heads, but the rest have hair decorated with feathers and beads and such. A real peculiar sight. As much as my fear is spiking right now, so is my fascination. What the hell are they? Even their way of dress is so strange. Oh, they're wearing tunics and trousers all right, but their chests and shoulders are covered with an array of weird objects attached to the clothing. Settler relics I'm guessing.

One of them steps in front of me, and my eyes are instantly drawn to the small, rounded pieces of metal covering his tunic. There's so many they make me dizzy, so I focus on the faded red one with the white lettering. I can barely make out the fancy writing. C O L A, I think it says. So odd. What does that mean?

I don't get to figure it out since the weapons they're carrying quickly outweigh my fascination with their clothing. Their shooters are massive, about twice as long as the one we have and are pointing directly at us. In all the hullabaloo of Finn's rescue, we never heard even a footstep of their approach. Tater starts cussing under his breath behind me, and his next words make me shiver in fear.

"Damn the gods' luck. Raiders."

Raiders? Shizen, Ben, the old folk were speaking the truth after all. They are real.

—————

We've been walking for hours feels like. Single file, through the rain. Tater, then Finn, then me. All of us tied together with the same rope we'd used to rescue Finn off the rock ledge. The raiders had thought it hilarious that we were already tied together; they had a good laugh at that. At first Tater tried to reason with them. He'd tried to convince them that we were just poor traders traveling through. How they had no reason to have any interest in us. How we had nothing of value that they could possibly want. They'd listened in silence and then just knocked him off his feet and proceeded to rob him of his flute, his spyglass, and even his hat. The one to the left of me is now wearing it, off to the side of his bald head all cocky-like. I glare at him with all the hatred I'm feeling inside, but he just winks at me. The jackass.

They'd taken everything, gone through every bag. My iron shooter, my bow, my knives, Tater's wares. They'd even found Winnie along the way, and she's now being led along just like the rest of us. Finn is limping something fierce on the muddy trail. He had truly banged up his leg in his fall. I'd pleaded with them to at least let the boy ride on the mule. He's in pain, I'd said. Let him ride the rest of the way. All that had gotten me was a hard slap across the face. Finn had cried out at this.

"I'm okay, Tara," he'd said. "I don't need to ride. Don't

worry about me."

Brave kid, hiding his pain to keep me quiet. He doesn't want to see me get hit again. So, I watch him ahead of me limping and wincing, but not saying a word. Holding it all in. My hatred at these raiders grows inside of me with every painful step he takes.

I have no idea what direction we're moving in. We're way off the mountain pass we'd been traveling through. Obviously, their intention wasn't to take us through the mountains, but deeper into the mountains themselves. I'd tried to ask Tater if he knew where we were heading, but all that had gotten me was another painful whack between my shoulder blades, this time with the butt of an iron shooter. It had taken all my willpower not to spit right in the raider's face. Finn's look of concern was the only thing that stopped me, so I behave. But I keep watching. I need to know which way to go once we escape.

So far there hasn't been any sign of Cat, which is probably a good thing. As brave and strong as she is, she won't stand a chance against so many powerful iron shooters. If she was to attack, she could probably take out a couple of the raiders, maybe more if she wasn't injured too badly from her tangle with the other devil cat. But they would take her down for sure. I know Finn is fearing the same as I'm thinking, because his head swings back and forth, checking the hills and woods for any sign of her. No, it's best she's not around right now, though sooner or later she will pick up on our scent. I'm hoping she's as smart as Finn says she is and knows to stay away, but when it came to protecting Finn, she's like a mama and its cub. I pity the raider who might raise a hand to Finn if she's anywhere near us.

The trail we're walking on now snakes around the edge of a steep slope, and we come out on a rise atop of a rocky valley. My heart drops at the sight lying before us, and the three of us stumble to a stop. It's the raiders' camp. There are canvas-covered shelters and lean-tos scattered everywhere. The valley floor is dotted with campfires and more raiders. They're everywhere. So many of them. There must be about a hundred or more. Finn looks back at me, his eyes wide with fear. I share that same fear, but I don't let it show. I just nod at him like it's going to be okay. The leader of our captors lets out a loud, echoing whoop and there's an answering call from the valley floor.

"Move," we're ordered, and we do as told. Our arrival is starting to draw attention, so by the time we reach the camp the other raiders are lined up to get a good look at us. I'm shocked to see women amongst them, but they're gawking and laughing at us just like their men folk. We get prodded and poked as we're herded through the camp. One of them, I can't see who, snatches my hat from my head, and I can hear her pleased squawking at her new prize.

We're finally stopped in front of a canvas shelter, but it isn't like the others we've seen. This is a full-out canvas shanty with a flap for a door and all. It's not open like the rest of them. We're lined up side by side in front of the flap, and the crowd falls silent all at once like somebody had given them a signal. My heart is thumping in my chest, and without all the hollering and whooping now, I can actually hear it. We stand there, silent, waiting, not sure for what, and I don't know what to expect.

Suddenly the flap is thrown back, and a man emerges. No. Giant is a more apt word. He stands about two heads over me with bare, massive arms and a chest so wide he could probably crush a person to death from just a hug. His hair isn't decorated like the rest of the raiders but hangs around his face in long, odd ropes. On his head he wears a hat unlike anything I've ever seen. It looks to be some sort of black, shiny metal with a tiny spike sticking straight up out of the top. *A settler's relic to be sure.*

His presence is so overwhelming I feel my innards clench. Finn unconsciously moves closer to me so our arms are touching, looking for some form of reassurance. The man silently regards us with hooded eyes. I don't read any emotion from him at all. Finally, he speaks.

"And what have you found here, Toole?" His booming question is directed to the leader of our captors but fans out over the crowd with its sheer forcefulness. I can feel Finn trembling beside me. The man named Toole steps forward.

"We found them in the mountains, Busher. The dwarf says they're traders, but they were carrying this."

He hands the huge man my iron shooter. It looks tiny in his massive hand like he could crush it no problem. He studies it.

"H'm. This is Army issue," he says. He turns his obsidian eyes our way.

"A girl, a boy, and a dwarf. I can see your need to keep them bound, Toole. They are a dangerous bunch indeed."

This is met with much snickering and laughing from the other raiders. Toole reddens at the giant's words, but he doesn't respond.

"Untie them for the gods' sake. That is no way to treat our guests."

Immediately his bidding is done, and our ropes are removed. Finn's skinny wrists are chafed and bleeding, and he rubs them to ease his pain. Mine are about the same, but I refuse to show them any weakness. The giant smiles at us, his teeth a startling white in his sun-bronzed face.

"There, isn't that much better?"

"Yes, thank you, kind sir," Tater says gratefully, and I glare daggers at him. He shrugs at me but falls silent.

"Excellent. Now about this?" he waves the iron shooter. "Would any of you mind telling me the story of how you came about this? For I'm sure it is an interesting one indeed."

None of us speak. The giant waits for a moment, his perusal of us full of expectation. Finally, he sighs.

"Please, don't be like that. I promise no harm will come to you from us. I'm just asking for a simple explanation," he says in a most pleasant manner.

I make a decision. I don't know if he can be trusted, but I see no harm in telling him the truth.

"It was left behind by the Prezedant's Army. They attacked our villages ... mine and the boy's. Killed our kin," I say. My voice breaks a little at those words, but I go on. "They came from the sand lands in big metal machines ... veacals I know them to be now."

I reckon this interests him since he takes a step closer to me. I back up a pace. I can't help myself. He bends over and stares me straight in the eye.

"You saw the Prezedant's trucks? In the sand lands?"

"Yes, if that's what they're called," I say, staring back at him eye to eye. "They're real. As real as you and me."

"And when did this occur?"

I shrug. "I cain't rightly say. I've been travelin' for weeks now I think ... just walkin' the sand lands until I come across Finn and Tater. We're just travelers like Tater told your men."

He's staring at me, but his words are directed more to himself, I think. "I'd heard stories of his machines traveling the sand lands, but I hadn't thought it possible." He brings his attention back to me. "And where would such an unlikely trio as you be traveling to?"

"Littlepass, sir," Tater pipes up. "I have business there, you see. It is a very profitable city for a lowly trader such as myself. The two young folk, well, you've just heard of the misfortune that has befallen them. I've merely taken them under my wing since they have no other kin to look out for them."

The giant laughs. It's so loud it hurts my ears and I wince. "Well, aren't you the magnanimous one," he says to Tater.

Tater nods, smiling himself now. "Indeed. As my dear mother used to say, small in stature ... big in heart."

The giant nods. "A nice sentiment to be sure." He waves the iron shooter again. "So, you came by this by pure misfortune then? You have no associations to the Prezedant or his Army?"

Tater by now has taken to talking to the giant like they are long lost friends. "Oh, dear me, no. No, no, no, we are in no way affiliated with that group of barbarians."

"Ah, good." He studies the three of us standing in front of him and gives us that brilliant white smile again. Then he nods. "Throw them in the cage with the other prisoner," he says to Toole and turns his back to us dismissively.

"Yes, sir."

I watch dumbfounded as our original captors start to advance on us. What the hell just happened here? We'd answered all his questions. Why would he want to lock us up?

"Wait. No." I push away from the raider trying to capture my arms and yell at the giant's retreating back. "You lyin' jackass. You said no harm would come to us."

I can hear Tater hissing at me through the corner of his mouth, "Shut up, girl," but I'm simmering mad and I don't pay heed.

The giant stops at my words, turns on his heel and walks back to me. He looms over me with his sheer size, but I stare back at him in defiance. He looks me up and down, and when he speaks his voice is soft.

"Oh, but I did not lie, girl. No harm will come to you, not while in my possession. You are more valuable to me unscathed." He runs a finger down my cheek, and it takes all my willpower not to shrink from his touch.

"You, I think, will fetch a very high price indeed. I know of a buyer who would be willing to pay a king's treasure in iron for a chance to break that spirit of yours. Oh no, I won't harm any of you. But what happens to you all after you've been sold, well, for that I can make no promises."

Tater unexpectedly escapes from his captor's grip and falls on his knees in front of the giant.

"Sir. Kind sir. I am but an old man. I am of no value in the flesh trade. These young folk, yes, they will fetch you a good price indeed. But me? I will gain you nothing. Please, kind sir, just set me free, and I will be forever in your debt."

I'm not certain who I hate most at this exact moment: the giant for threatening to sell us or Tater for trying to save his own miserable skin. He looks down at Tater kneeling in the dirt at his feet and regards him like he's no more than a pile of mule droppings.

"You're quite right, dwarf," he says, and Tater sags in relief. "You are of no value. Toole, kill the dwarf."

Toole yanks Tater to his feet, and I'm shocked to see the half-man is actually smiling. He has truly gone mad.

"On the other hand, good sir, I am quite the impressive storyteller, musician, and court jester if you like. I'm sure your band of merry men—and women—would enjoy nothing more after a hard day's raiding than an evening of pure entertainment. What do you say, good sir? Keeping me alive can be very beneficial to your wellbeing and that of your entourage."

The raider leader looks confused at this turn of events. He studies Tater like he can't believe his ears. Then unexpectedly, he laughs at Tater's attempt to save his skin.

"You are truly entertaining, dwarf," he says between his bouts of laughter. He looks out over the group and calls to someone. "Meela, come here."

A tall, striking girl about my age joins the giant at his side. She's dressed like the others but wears no paint on her dusky skin. Her hair is laced intricately with beads and hangs straight down her back to her waist. I've never seen a more perfect face; or a colder one.

The giant takes her hand. "I will let you decide the dwarf's fate, my daughter."

She regards us with her stony, flat eyes and then shrugs, apparently not the least bit concerned that a life hangs on her decision. *What kind of people are they to treat a life so casually?* I think.

"I don't care either way, Father. But if he speaks the truth, then maybe I'll let him live to hear his stories and his music. If he can keep me entertained for a while, then he shall live for a while."

"So be it," the giant announces, beaming out at the crowd, and they respond with a roar of approval. "You are truly fortunate, dwarf. My compassionate daughter has spared your life. It would be wise not to disappoint her."

"Thank you! Oh, thank you, kind lady," Tater says, falling at her feet now, but his groveling is making me stomach sick and I don't want to look at him anymore. Instead, I stare at the girl with all the hostility and insolence I can muster at the unfairness of our situation. She stares back, her dark eyes like chips of flint. Then with a half-smile, she steps toward me and starts untying my neck wrapper. Slowly, she removes my gift from Grada and wraps it about her own neck, staring at me, daring me the whole time to do something about it. I feel my cheeks heating up with my anger, and I so desperately want to push her away, but I don't do anything. I let her have it without a fight. Then her eyes travel down my chest and fall on the leather thong. She pulls my flower, my born day gift from Ben, out of my tunic and holds it on the palm of her hand. There's no way in hell I'm letting her have that too, and my anger gets the better of me. Grabbing her wrist, I spit out a defiant, "No."

She looks surprised, like she's not used to not getting her

own way. I push her hand away, but I'm totally unprepared for what happens next. She throws a punch at my face. I feel my lip split at the contact. Before I can react, she punches me in the ribs. I bend over in pain, the breath knocked out of me. I hear the raiders around me all jeering and laughing. They're enjoying the show. She grabs my hair and jerks my head up hard, stares into my face.

"You dare touch me, sand lander?"

She yanks on my hair so hard it brings tears to my eyes. I can hear Finn calling my name, but I can't answer him to let him know I'm okay. She jerks the flower from my neck, snapping the leather. Letting go of my hair, she pushes me back now that she has her prize. I stumble a bit and spit the blood out of my mouth. She holds her prize above her head, victorious, laughing, and reveling in the cheers of her people. I see it in her hands—my one last link to Ben, to Rivercross, to everybody I ever loved—and a red-hot pulsing starts in my blood. It feels like my blood is set aflame, there's a buzzing in my ears, and I know there's no way in hell I'm letting her keep it.

I straighten up and leap at her with a flying kick to the stomach. She's thrown backwards and lands on the ground in a heap, and I'm on top of her before she can get a breath. My fist bashes her in the face and her blood sprays out over my hand, but I don't stop. It's like the sight of it sends me into a frenzy. I bash her again and again, then I get her by the throat, both my hands wrapping around her neck. She's grabbing my arms, trying to get me off her neck, but she can't budge me. I squeeze, my hands possessing strength such as I've never known before. Her eyes are bulging now, and I smell her fear, but I don't stop. I can't stop. I'm aware of other hands grabbing at me, voices yelling, but I focus on the face in front of me. My hatred is so overwhelming it's all I can feel, all that I know. My one and only thought is to snap her damn neck.

I don't know what hits me, but the hard whack to the back of the head stuns me enough for me to loosen my grip. The second whack sends me into complete oblivion.

CHAPTER 4

Raiders Camp

———◆———

"Tara. Can you hear me?" I know the voice is Finn's, but he's yelling so loud. Why's he yelling? His words are echoing around in my head, adding to the drums already beating inside of there. I want to tell him to stop yelling, but I don't say anything because it hurts to even think right now.

Shizen. What happened? But then I remember the raiders.

"She ain't answerin', Tater. I think they've gone and killed her."

"She's not dead, boy. She's too thick-skulled to be taken out by a blow to the head. She'll be fine." This is from Tater.

He doesn't sound the least bit worried, not like Finn. Good to know he's so concerned about me.

"Ain't they killed you yet?" It comes out as a croak, but his answering snort assures me he understood. "You sniveling coward," is what I want to add, but I don't.

"See, Finn, I told you she was fine."

I open my eyes to Finn's anxious face looming above mine. Every freckle seems to stand out against his pale skin in worry, but he smiles at me in relief.

"Tara. Thank the gods, you're okay."

I smile back at his obvious joy to see me alive, but it makes my split lip crack again and that reminds me of the girl and my reaction to her.

"I'm fine," I say. "Help me up, will ya?"

He pulls me up to a sitting position, and right away my head starts spinning. *I gotta stop getting hit in the head,* I think as I reach around to feel the damage this time. The back of my head is real tender, but there's no lump. No blood. I probe a bit more with my fingers, but there's nothing.

"I already checked. You have no injury," Tater says, but his tone is awful strange. I look at him. He regards me with an odd expression. If I had to guess, I would say he looks … pleased?

I'm not hurt. How's that possible? I don't ask though because Finn, happy that I'm okay, is now jumping around like some crazy rabbit.

"Tara, you were amazin'. You took out that raider, gave her a real whoopin'. None of the others could get you offa her. It was like you had the strength of ten of 'em. Took the raider leader two hits with his big iron shooter to knock you out. You showed her real good."

He emphasizes his point by punching at the air, but his words don't please me none. "Is she okay?" I ask, Finn's account of events terrifying me. I remember how I felt at that time. I remember all the hatred, all the anger, and how my only thought was to snap her neck. To kill her. I've never felt that before in my whole life and it scares me.

"She's bruised and battered, and her pride is a little damaged but otherwise she's alive. You didn't kill her if that's what you fear."

Tater's words ease my panic some and I relax. The next words come from a voice I don't recognize, and they fill me with utter dread.

"You're probably going to wish she *had* killed you though."

Still sitting, I spin around on my butt. There's another occupant in the wooden cage that imprisons us. A young man leans against the thick bars of the cage, arms folded, and regarding me with such a hostile look I reckon he must be one of the raiders.

"That's Jax," Finn says, answering my unspoken question. "He was captured just like us."

He's a captive like us? So why's he looking at me like I just stole the last of his berry bread? I struggle to my feet. I don't like having to look up at him.

He's not much taller than me, but he's all sinewy muscle like he's been used to working hard his whole life. He's got short-cropped, spikey black hair, sun-darkened skin, and a smattering of stubble covering his lower jaw. But it's his eyes that capture my attention. They are a sky blue, so light in his dark face that I find it nearly impossible to look away. I know pretty isn't a word you'd associate with a man, but his eyes … they're so damn pretty. If you can get past the fact that they're staring at me right now like I'm his worst enemy.

"I … ah … " I stutter a bit. "Why would you say such a thing?"

"Oh geez, I don't know, let's see. Maybe it has something to do with the fact that you just nearly killed the daughter of our captor and severely pissed him off." His voice is low but filled with fury. "They were planning on taking us to Littlepass to sell and make a few pieces of iron for themselves. That wouldn't have been a problem since any fool can escape from Littlepass. But thanks to your stupid little stunt earlier, I heard the big guy tell the guards they are taking us directly to Skytown. To the Prezedant himself. Apparently, you're more valuable than they first thought."

His words do not make any sense. I look to Tater. "What's he talkin' about? I ain't valuable to nobody." For the first time since I've known him, the half-man remains quiet. He actually drops his eyes from me, and I prompt him again. "Tater? What's he talkin' about? I ain't of no concern to the Prezedant. Why are they takin' us to him?" I say, my alarm making me more insistent this time.

"Tara." It's surprisingly Finn who answers me. "When you attacked the raider girl … something real strange happened to you. Not only were you so strong none of the men could budge you, but your hair … those white stripes … they were glowin' like there was some kinda light inside of you. It scared most of the raiders. They backed off; some of 'em even ran away they were so scared. They were callin' you a name. They were callin' you a New Blood. Least I think that's what they were sayin'."

A what? I don't know what Finn's talking about. It doesn't make a lick of sense.

"Finn, that's just craziness," I say a little harsher than intended. "My hair don't glow with no light. You were scared is all, and you imagined that. Right, Tater? And I don't even know what a ... a New Blood is, but I sure as hell know I ain't no such thing."

A harsh laugh from this "Jax" brings my attention back to him.

"It's bad enough that I'm being included in your group of misfits and herded off to Skytown with virtually no chance of escape, but to be captured with a New Blood who's too stupid to even realize what she is ... that's damn bad luck indeed."

I don't recall moving, but I find myself nose to nose with Jax, my arm pressed tight against his throat and that now familiar, red-hot anger burning through me. "Stop callin' me that. And if you don't want your neck snapped, you better not call me stupid ever again."

If he's scared by me, he doesn't show it. He merely stares back at me with his strange, hostile eyes.

"Tara, let the boy go," Tater says calmly, his hand on my arm.

I ignore him at first, but just as quickly as it came my anger is gone. I drop my arm and step back, suddenly overcome with such weariness I just want to curl up in a ball and cry. What's happening to me? This anger? This hatred? I nearly killed someone, would have killed her if I hadn't been stopped. What am I? I look at Tater, my eyes demanding the truth.

"Is what the boy sayin' true?" I ask.

Tater nods. "It is indeed. It was quite the impressive show. I have never in my life seen a bunch of grown men run off like little maidens wringing their undergarments in their hands. It was quite the amusing sight to behold. Why I—"

"Tater! Did something happen to me like Finn said?" I interrupt the half-man's rambling words. I need to know if this strange occurrence Finn's talking about really happened. I know what I'd felt—the strength and the hatred—and I've never felt that intensity before. The pounding of my blood, the buzzing in my ears. It had been like my body wasn't even my own anymore. Like it had been taken over by some other being. Something real strange had definitely happened to me. I need to know what.

At first he don't want to answer, I can tell, but I prod him some more. "Tater? What happened to me?" I say. "What were they callin' me?"

The half-man rubs his mustache, curling up the ends nervously as if he doesn't want to tell me anything else, but finally he takes a deep breath. "Finn was not mistaken. The raiders, unfortunately for us, did recognize you for what you are and for what I suspected you to be. A New Blood."

I don't understand. "What the hell does that mean? And what do you mean you suspected? You knew something? All this time?" I accuse.

He nods. "As I said, I suspected. The unusual hair coloration is associated with New Bloods but not always. And there have been no reports of true New Bloods for years now. And I never imagined I would ever meet one in person.

I wasn't sure, not until the night of our conversation in the woods. When I told you your kin were gone for good. You became angry, distressed, and your hair, it, well, you had this aura about you, just as Finn said. Then I knew for certain."

I stare at Tater in silence, trying to process what he's saying. I want to believe he's lying to me. Surely none of what they're saying can be true. Can it? But then I remember the look on his face that night in the woods. He'd been truly shocked and surprised, and I know deep down that he's not lying. That he did witness something. That he truly believes I am what he says I am.

"What is a New Blood? What the hell is it? What's happenin' to me?" I know I must sound desperate, pleading with him to ease my fears, but I can't help it. It's how I feel. Desperate and completely terrified. I glance at Finn, who's still regarding me with awe like he'd just watched me turn sand to iron instead of almost kill another person. "Am I dangerous to others?"

"No, no girl … it's a glorious thing, a wonderful thing indeed. New Bloods are a true marvel of the gods." Tater's expression is one of wonder and amazement, and I know he believes his own words.

The fear constricting my chest eases some. If my condition was dangerous or evil, Tater would tell me, wouldn't he? He would be afraid of me. He doesn't look afraid. Maybe it's okay. But then another harsh snort from Jax makes my stomach clench, and I feel like I wanna retch all over again.

"Tell her the truth, old man. Tell her what she truly is."

As if the venom dripping from his words isn't proof enough, I can see the hatred and disgust in his eyes. It seems wrong somehow to see such things of beauty marred by this ugliness. I catch Tater's gasp, and I know I don't want to hear what Jax is about to say, but I can't look away from his eyes.

"A freak of nature. A mutation. A danger to everyone around her. A carrier of death to anybody she's ever come in contact with."

Jax's words are spoken softly, but they cut deeper than any knife could have done for I know in my gut he's speaking the truth. It had already happened, had it not? Rivercross … Grada … everyone gone because of me. Deep down, I'd always suspected it. I'd always felt that I was the reason for the metal machines attacking Rivercross. I just wouldn't admit it to myself.

"Shut your mouth, boy." Tater tries to stop him, but it's too late. The damage has been done. We keep looking at each other, me and Jax, his light eyes staring into mine as if he's looking into my very soul. I can't draw a breath. It's as if all the guilt and grief I've been carrying around inside of me is laid open for him to see. Something shifts in his expression, and he looks away from me as if he can't stand the sight of me anymore. I start gasping for air, like I suddenly remembered to breathe.

Finn comes to my side and grabs my hand.

"You don't know shite about Tara, Jax. She ain't no freak. And she ain't a danger to nobody but the raiders."

Loyal Finn. I squeeze the little hand gripping mine and close my eyes, too overcome for words. Why is all this happening to me? I don't understand what I did to anger the gods so much. And am I truly to blame for the fate of Grada and Rivercross? I'm not given time to ponder everything I'd just learned before the sound of crunching rock underfoot warns us of someone's approach.

"Ah, the New Blood is awake."

I open my eyes to the raider leader. He appears bigger than I remember if that's even possible. He folds his arms across his massive chest and looks me up and down.

"And looking no worse for wear I see. Good. I would hate to have to deliver such precious cargo as damaged goods." He gives me that brilliant smile. "A New Blood in my possession … how fortunate indeed. You, my dear, are going to make me a very rich man."

I try the stupid approach. And since I still really have no freakin' idea what's happening to me, the stupid approach is all I have. "I don't know what you're talkin' about. I ain't no New Blood … don't even know what that is."

"Hah!" His burst of laughter is genuine. "Don't try and lie to me, girl. I just watched you nearly strangle my daughter with your bare hands and scare the life out of a dozen or so of my best men. Men who have faced devil cats and wolflings with nary a blink, but one look at your Chi was enough to send them off screaming like young'uns."

"My what?" I ask, not knowing that word.

He studies me for a bit, frowning at me in puzzlement. "You truly are unaware of what you are. Fascinating. A New Blood's Chi is a sight to behold. Never thought I'd see the day when I would witness such an event again for you and your kind are a dying breed."

Tired of his gibberish and fed up with the whole situation, I lash out. "I ain't a breed of nuthin'. Let us go right now." I shake the bars of the cage in frustration. How dare he keep us locked up like animals? "Let us out now or ... or else I'll use my Chi," I repeat his word. If it was enough to scare his men, but he doesn't fall for my threat. He just laughs even harder.

"A New Blood you may be, but a babe at that. You cannot control your Chi no more than I can control the wind. No, I don't fear you, baby New Blood, but I do respect you. That is the reason I return this."

His hand is too massive to fit through the bars, so he dangles my flower in front of my face on the other side of the cage. Fearing a trick, I reach for it slowly, expecting at any moment to have it yanked away. But he's true to his word, and I snatch it quickly from his grasp before he changes his mind.

"Why?" I ask.

He shrugs. "It's yours. You fought for it valiantly; it must be very important to you. Meela had no right to take it."

This from the leader of a band of thieves. Somehow, it doesn't seem right.

"If you respect me, then let us go," I say again.

"Ah, yes." He sighs deeply. "Regretfully, I cannot do that, for as much as I respect your kind, I respect riches even more. The Prezedant has placed a high bounty on the heads of New Bloods. I cannot resist. If I don't turn you over, then someone else will. So why shouldn't it be me who reaps the rewards?"

He shoots me the toothy grin again. "As we speak, my messenger is on his way to set up a rendezvous with the Prezedant's men. So rest up ... all of you. We have an early start in the morning." He starts to walk away but turns back. "Oh, by the way, if you get to thinking you can escape, my men have been ordered to shoot to kill. Everyone but you of course."

As if to drive his point home, two raiders appear to flank either side of our wooden prison, holding those massive iron shooters. One of them is the same who stole Tater's hat. He's still wearing it, but he's not looking at me all cocky-like anymore. He's regarding me now with almost a look of fear. What did they see? What did I become? Is Jax right? Am I a freak, a monster? I lay my head in misery against the thick bars of the cage, watching him walk away.

"Let us go now or else," Jax's voice is high and shrill in his mimicry of me. "Brilliant plan. Don't know why I didn't think of that."

I've had just about enough of this jackass. Whirling around, I snap at him. "Yeah, well, I can see your plans have worked out great for you so far, you moron. How long have you been captured now? I can tell by your whiskers you been here a few days at least. You must be real good at escape plans."

He takes a couple of paces towards me so we're almost nose to nose. "I did have a great escape plan as a matter of fact, but it's all been ruined because I'm no longer being taken to Littlepass, now am I? Because of you, mutie, I'm being dragged off to Skytown. Do you know what the chances are of escaping from Skytown? Zero. Nil. None. People don't escape from Skytown, freak. They disappear, never to be seen again."

"Stop. Calling. Me. Freak." I punctuate each word with a shove, so by the end of it Jax's back is pressed against the other side of the cage, but I'm not finished. "I hope you do disappear never to be seen again. That would be a blessing to all of us."

"Stop it, the both of you!" Tater worms his way between us and pushes me back, holding us both at arm's length. I'm simmering mad, and I just wanna scratch Jax's eyes out, punch him in the nose, something.

"He started it—" I begin, but Tater's not having any of it.

"And I'm finishing it. Do you really think it's wise to be yelling about escape plans when we have two guards watching our every move? Does that seem like a good idea to either of you?"

I take a couple of deep breaths before realizing Tater is right. Both guards have moved closer to our cage and are watching us with great amusement. I glare at the one with the hat.

"Whadda you lookin' at?" I snarl, and he backs off in a hurry, holding his shooter out in front of him like I'm about to pounce on him. The other merely flicks the twig he's chewing on at the cage and wanders casually back to his post. Seems I don't bother him at all.

Finn approaches me with a quiet, "Tara?"

"What?" I yell, and he takes an involuntary step back at my show of temper. Instantly feeling ashamed, I mutter a contrite, "Sorry," but he only keeps staring at me in uncertainty. Jax by now has decided he's done with all of us and sits in the corner of the cage, legs crossed and his back to us. Which is fine by me. Tater clears his throat.

"Hmph ... yes, well, I suggest we do as the giant says and get some rest. Night has fallen, and we will think much clearer in the morning after we sleep."

Don't know who Tater's trying to fool. None of us are going to get any sleep tonight, and I'm too wound up to rest. Too full of anger and burning with questions. But they are questions I need to ask without Jax around to give his input. So since there's nothing else I can do, I settle against the side of the cage as far away from Jax as I can get. Finn comes to sit hesitantly beside me, and I take off the heavy jacket, motioning him closer so we can both use it as a blanket. At first he don't want to come any closer. I can tell.

"It's okay, Finn," I whisper, giving him a ghost of a smile. "I ain't gonna bite."

Finally deciding I could be trusted again, he scoots closer and I wrap the jacket around the both of us.

We sit in silence, listening to the sounds of the raiders go about their business off in the distance. The smell of an evening meal cooking wafts by us, and Finn squirms a little.

"That smells real good, Tara," he says.

"Aye, it does," I say.

"I'm hungry."

"I know, Finn."

We're quiet for a bit more.

"What's gonna happen to us, Tara?"

I think about lying to the boy. To tell him there's nothing to worry about, and that everything is going to work out just fine. But before I can say a word, a loud wailing not far from the camp interrupts me. Finn bolts upright, and out of the corner of my eye I can see our two guards jump to their feet and grab their weapons.

"That's Cat," he whispers to me. "She found us."

"You sure?" I ask, scared for what that might mean.

Hopefully, she isn't about to attack the camp. We don't need her getting fired on by the raiders.

"Yeah, that's her all right. I know the sound of her bellyachin'. She's lettin' us know she's there, and she's waiting for us."

He settles back underneath the jacket, his scrawny little frame strumming with happiness at the knowledge his beast is okay. I can't help but feel a little relieved myself, although what the cat could do against an army of raiders, I'm not sure. But just knowing she's out there still gives me some measure of comfort. The wailing stops finally, and our guards settle back down, although I notice Hat Head keeps his shooter in his hands. Cat's howling has rattled him. *Good,* I think. I hope he's as scared as we are. Finn stays quiet for so long I think he's asleep, but then he speaks.

"Everything's gonna be okay, Tara. I know it. With Cat watchin' out for us, and you bein' a New Blood and all. Tater says it's a good thing, so it must be. Yup, everything's gonna be okay."

I can't help but smile to myself in the dark. He sounded so sure, so positive. A total turnaround from his earlier outlook. I don't say a word as I move closer to him and rest my chin on the top of his head. *If only I could believe that, Finn,* I think. But how can it be okay? I just found out I was some sort of freak of nature from an idiot who, it seems, would be happier to see my head on a spike than be stuck in a cage with me. And we're on our way to be turned over to a madman. All in all, I've had better days. But I don't burst the boy's bubble. I just sit quietly with his head resting against my shoulder until I hear the deep, even breaths that tell me he's asleep. *Good,* I think. At least one of us should rest.

———◆———

I fall to my knees on the hard ground and grab eagerly for the tin of water dangling in front of my face. I don't even try to fight the raiders tying me to the fallen, dead tree like I did the last evening. There's no use, and I'm just so thirsty. The water is warm and tinny, but I drink deep and it eases my parched throat.

Without warning a body falls on me, sending the tin flying right out of my grip and spilling its precious contents into the dry earth. From the muffled cussing I know it's Jax, and I push at him angrily with my tied hands.

"Get … off … me," I grunt, pushing at his weight, and he falls awkwardly face-first in the dirt beside me. His own tied wrists offer no help in cushioning his fall, and it seems to delight our captors immensely. Their laughter at his misfortune is met with his icy glare, but he stays mute as he struggles to his knees. They watch still laughing until he rights himself, then three of them drag him back to my side and lash him to the same tree I'm tied to. Tater is quickly tied as well, but he manages to reach the water tin before it can be kicked away by any of our numerous guards. I blow the hair that's come loose from my braid out of my eyes and look for Finn. I spot him being lifted off Winnie's back, his hands tied just like the rest of us.

We've been on the move, non-stop, for two days now towards the exchange with the Prezedant's men. Me, Jax, and Tater have been walking, tied behind Busher's horse, but at least the raider leader had taken pity on Finn and his injured leg and let him ride the mule. He's not taking any chances though. There must be at least ten or more of them accompanying us, plus the scouts and guards he had posted in the hills. I don't know if he expects the threat to come from us or the men he's meeting, but I do know one thing. I'm no threat. New Blood. Hah, what a joke. No matter how hard I try to summon this power, this "Chi," it doesn't happen. Oh the anger and hatred are there all right, but there's no fire in my blood or buzzing in my ears. There's nothing I can do except follow along like some trussed-up hog.

Cat has been trailing after us, and a couple of times she's even attempted to attack the camp, but they chase her off with their shooters, much to Finn's dismay. So far she's been lucky. They haven't nicked her since she's still off to the side, wailing and rattling all their nerves. They can't understand why they're being stalked by a devil cat, and I see their glances and hear their whispers about me, about the New Blood and how I must be controlling the she-devil. It makes me smile. *Good Cat,* I think.

"You all right, Finn?" I ask the boy once they have us settled. We're tied together, all in a line along the tree's carcass. Tater, then Finn, then me, and Jax. Even our feet are bound. They obviously don't want any of us getting free and making a run for it during the night. Finn looks up at my question. I can tell the past couple of days have been hard on him; he looks tired. His face is stark white, and there are dark bruises under his eyes, but he gives me a crooked grin.

"Yeah, I'm fine except for my unmentionables. Ridin' on a mule all day ain't easy on a man's parts."

I know our situation doesn't warrant it, and maybe it's just a mixture of exhaustion and shock, but I can't help but laugh. It even draws a low chuckle out of Jax, and my head swivels in disbelief. Did I just hear that? He can actually laugh? If these past few days were any indication, I figured all he knew to do was scowl and cuss and hurl insults. Besides that, we haven't heard a single word come out of his mouth. He catches me staring and raises a dark brow. Embarrassed, I look away and busy myself with fussing with the boy's ropes.

"Well, I'm glad you three can find humor in our situation," Tater huffs, frowning at me from under his bushy brows. He has been unusually quiet over these past two days too, and I realize it's to do with me and my condition. The whole idea of him staying on at the camp for the raider girl's amusement was totally thrown to the wind at my almost killing the girl. Instead, he found himself still a prisoner and on his way to certain death at the hands of a madman along with the rest of us. I can see where his annoyance with me may stem from.

"You're right, Tater, and I'm truly sorry I got you dragged into this mess. You and Finn both," I say, instantly ashamed for my laughter. I ignore Jax's mocking snort at my words. The raiders look over at us talking amongst ourselves, but they don't seem too concerned. After two full days of no sign of any "powers" on my part, they don't jump at my every move anymore. They're paying more attention to setting up their campfire and cooking their evening meal than they are to us. Tied and bound as we are, we don't offer them any threat.

Tater seems a little taken aback at my apology. The look of surprise on his face, coupled with his wild, gray hair blowing around his head, almost makes me want to laugh again. But

I don't. The half-man is right; there's not one thing about our predicament that should be making any of us laugh. And if last night was any indication, we're in for another long and uncomfortable night. I try the best I can with my bound hands and feet to get closer to Finn so as we can prop up against each other's backs for sleeping.

Cat, unfortunately, chooses that moment to start her howling again, and Finn bolts upright, causing me to almost fall over. He can't contain the sharp cry that escapes from his lips when Busher orders two of his men to "Go find that hell cat and get rid of it for good."

"She'll be fine, Finn," I whisper to the boy as we watch the raiders leave in search of Cat. "She's smart, and she'll smell 'em approachin' well before they can get anywhere near her."

"Tara's right, Finn," Tater adds, and Finn's fearful gaze darts back and forth between us until finally he seems to accept our words as truth and settles back uneasily against the tree trunk.

"And no need to apologize, my dear." This is directed to me I think, though he's still looking at Finn. "Maybe a little joviality and whimsy is what we all need at the moment to keep our minds off the severity of our situation. As my dear mother would say, we are indeed between a rock and a hard place. But I have been in many strange predicaments during my years of travel. Sometimes the unexplainable happens when you least expect it, eh?"

As scared as Finn is for his beast, he can't contain his gasp of wonder as Tater's tied hands deftly reach for the boy's ear and pull out a white feather. It truly surprises me that Tater seemed to care enough to distract the boy from his fear.

"How'd you do that, Tater?" Finn asks, mystified.

Tater merely winks and whispers, "Magic," as he tickles the boy's chin with the feather, causing him to snicker.

"Well maybe you can use some of that magic, old man, and get us out of here. Our time is running short. Instead of a feather from the boy's ear, can you pull a knife from thin air?" The amount of talking coming out of our moody companion surprises me. I expect Tater to be upset at his harsh tone, but he merely sighs in defeat.

"Ah, I'm sorry to say that I cannot do."

Jax just grunts at Tater's answer, but his words have unsettled me some.

"What do you mean our time is runnin' short? What do you know that we don't?" For the first time since I've known him, the light blue eyes look at me with more than utter contempt. Worry seems to outweigh his disgust at the moment.

"We're getting close to coming out of the mountains. Closer to his lands. We have at best a day—possibly two—before the Army will be here to collect us," he says.

"How do you know that?" I ask.

"I know this area. It's on route to my own village. Gray Valley is maybe only four- or five-days' ride north of here."

This interests me some. "You came from a village? So there are others ... your family who know you're missin'? Will they be searchin' for you then?" I feel a little hope flicker at his words, but the flat look on his face destroys any expectations of a rescue.

"Nah. No one's gonna come looking anytime soon. I

don't have no other family besides my ma, and she's used to me disappearing for days at a time. I was on a hunting trip. Sometimes, I can be gone for as much as two weeks. She's not gonna start worrying for a bit yet," he says.

We all fall quiet at this, Jax's words extinguishing that tiny spark of hope for a rescue party. If we're going to get away, it will have to be of our own doing. And we have nothing remotely close to an escape plan. Frustrated with myself and the whole situation, I give a hard tug on the ropes binding my hands and bite my lip to stop from crying out at the pain it causes me.

How the hell did we end up in this situation? I think. How the hell did everything go so wrong? Find Lily in Littlepass. That was all I had to do, yet here we were. Prisoners and on our way to see a madman. And Finn ... he doesn't deserve to be involved in this. Why hadn't I left him back where I found him? At least he'd been safe there. What was I thinking dragging him into this mess? As if he can hear what I'm thinking, he looks up at me and smiles that gap-toothed grin of his like he's trying to reassure me, and I feel the guilt envelop me twofold. I'm almost glad for the distraction of our raider guards as they bring us each a tin cup of hot broth, our only meal of the day.

"Broth again," Finn mutters in disgust as soon as the guards walk away, but it doesn't stop him from downing his hungrily, almost in one gulp and then start licking the cup. I take a sip of my own, watching him try to get every last drop, then pass him my cup.

"Here, have mine. I'm not hungry," I say, lying through my teeth, but his obvious hunger bothers me.

"You sure?" he asks with hopeful eyes. My grunted "Aye," is all it takes for him to eagerly lap up mine as well.

"What I wouldn't give for my ma's wolfling stew right now," Jax sighs wistfully as he tosses his own empty cup aside. "Or a big platter of her sweet corn and boiled snips."

My stomach rumbles loudly at Jax's mention of his ma's cooking, and I snap at him. "Really? You suddenly choose to talk to us, and you talk about food to a bunch of starvin' people? Were you dropped on your head as a baby, or were you just born stupid?"

His light blue eyes narrow in anger at me, and I'm sure Finn's muffled snicker doesn't help none, but Tater intervenes smoothly and turns the conversation before he can respond.

"Gray Valley was it you said, Jax? That's where you're from? I have never been there in my travels, surprisingly. What's it like?"

At first, I don't think he's going to answer Tater. His eyes still regard me with hot fury, and I almost welcome his angry outburst. At least it would be something to take my mind off my stomach eating itself. But just like that, he dismisses me and turns to overlook the raider's campfire.

"It was a good place to live … once," he says quietly, almost to himself.

"And it's not anymore?" Tater questions again. "Why is that?"

"Why is any place not a good place to live anymore?" Jax says in contempt. "It belongs to the Prezedant now. What little we are able to grow or hunt, the majority of it goes to him and his lot. Same as anywhere, I guess. We may not live in his strongholds, but we are under his oppression just the same."

Finn, done with his second cup of broth, belches loudly and joins in on the conversation. "Is Gray Valley a big place, Jax? Is it as big as Littlepass? Tater says a multitod ... a multitad ... Tater says a lot of people live there, more than he even knows. Is Gray Valley the same?"

I'm shocked to see the corner of Jax's mouth twitch in almost—but not quite—a smile.

"No, not that many. There are maybe a hundred or so. There were more, but we had ... an incident a few years back and some of our people died, my pa included." Any trace of his earlier smile disappears almost instantly at his own words, and the steely eyes rake over me like it was my fault. Why is he looking at me like that? What did I do?

"I'm real sorry about your pa, Jax. My pa died too ... and so did my ma," Finn trails off, his voice quivering with emotion, and unbelievably, I think I see compassion in Jax's sky blue eyes as he looks at the boy's downcast face. So he did possess a heart after all.

"Everybody I ever knew died except Cat, but then Tara found us, and we found Tater. And now we're on a mission to find Tara's kin."

Jax turns away from the boy and gives his usual scornful snort at this. So much for any compassion, any chink in his shell I thought I'd witnessed.

"The only mission you all are on right now is to survive the Army. And good luck with that. I've never heard of anybody tangling with the Army and living to tell the tale," he says.

"Okay, then. Thanks for that little tidbit, Jax. We all needed to hear that," I growl, angry at him again for the new fear showing on Finn's face at his remark. Why's he always such an ass-wipe?

"I'm just speaking the truth," he grunts. "It's not looking good for any of us."

"Yes, well, as much as I hate to admit it, Tara, Jax is right," Tater intervenes again. "We do have a bit of a problem on our hands. We are indeed in a tight spot. I suggest, girl, if you have any use of your powers whatsoever, this would be the time to use them."

"You think I ain't tried?" I snap back at Tater then clamp my lips shut as a couple of the guards glance over at my heated words. Once they see we're still tied tight, they go back to their meal.

"I got nuthin'," I say, a little lower this time so as not to draw attention. We don't need them watching our every move.

"A useless New Blood, as if there's any other kind," Jax mutters, and the grunt of pain from my kicking him in the shin is not near enough satisfaction.

"If you insist on being a part of this conversation, Jax, then at least make your contribution worthwhile." Even Tater is vexed with his constant insults. It somehow makes me feel better. "And as my dear mother would suggest, 'If you have nothing good to say, then don't say anything at all.' I agree."

Jax rubs his shin and glares daggers at me, but as if he's heeding Tater's words, he doesn't say anything else. I guess we all know where he stood on that wise saying.

We're quiet for a moment, the gravity of our situation saturating our bones like a damp fog. Then, with hesitation, I utter what's in my head. "Do you think y'all could be wrong about me, Tater? I don't think I'm a New Blood. I cain't bring forth no power, no … Chi. Maybe y'all imagined what you thought you saw. Maybe I was just so angry, and that's why I was so strong. Being red-hot mad can do that, you know. Grada used to say sometimes he was so mad he could chew nails. I think now I kind of know what he meant—"

"As much as I know you do not wish to believe it, child, we all saw your incandescence," Tater interrupts me with a half-smile, though I don't believe he finds anything to be funny at all. "There is something special about you; that much is undeniable. I wish I could give you more answers, but I'm afraid I do not know much else about your … uniqueness. Stories of New Bloods, though once abundant, have since been delegated to whispers in the wind. No one dares say those words out loud for fear any of the Prezedant's numerous spies will overhear and then have the Army drag them off for questioning, never to be seen again. You, my dear, are truly a rare commodity. The raider leader is quite right. You will indeed bring him a fortune."

"Right, and our deaths along with it most likely," says Jax with such cold hatred I cringe from his words.

I want to lash out at him, to yell at him, to tell him he's wrong, but his words scare me more than anything. If something happened to Finn … to Tater … hell, even to Jax because of me, I would never be able to forgive myself. Ever. I shake my head, the reality of our situation crashing in on me like some flash flood. How can any of this be happening? All I wanted to do was find Ben. I didn't ask for any of this other stuff.

I pull my knees up and lay my head on them, overwhelmed

with hopelessness. I block the rest of them and everything else around me. I don't want to deal with it or with them. I can't deal with any of it. I just want to be back in Rivercross in my bed, listening to Grada snore and feeling safe.

Maybe that's where I really am, I think. *Maybe I am in my bed and this ain't all nuthin' but a bad dream.* Trying to convince myself that I'm truly dreaming, I bash my head on my knees—hard—in an attempt to wake myself up.

Besides the shooting pain in my head, I also hear Finn's gasp of "Tara!" and I know it's no dream. It's real all right. All of it. And there's no way out of it unless I create one. I've got to get us out of this mess.

Shizen. The thought of me being the only hope of us getting out of here—well, it kinda makes me stomach sick. I can't even make corn biscuits right. How am I ever going to save the four of us from the Prezedant?

I hope you were right, Grada, when you said that the gods will always provide, since the way things are going right now, I need all the help I can get.

——◆——

Day four of our capture is almost over, and we still no closer to any mastermind escape plan from the raiders. All day walking in the merciless heat, my mind had been working overtime trying to come up with a plan. Any sort of plan, but I had nothing. None of us say a word as we're tied and bound again for another long night, but our guards are barely out of earshot before Tater's urgent whisper surrounds us.

"Bad news I'm afraid, my dears. I overheard the colossal

leader speaking with one of his men earlier today. It looks like we have until possibly morning before the Army will be here to collect us. It has, as my dear mother would have said, come to the final countdown. We have but mere hours to make our escape. Have any of you managed to concoct an infallible plan to get us out of our current situation? Please, I encourage you to lay any ideas on the table for consideration."

Did Tater truly have to use so many words to ask if any of us had a plan? But as irritated as I am at him, I don't say what I'm thinking simply because I don't want to admit I've got diddly-squat. None of us speak. Jax eventually breaks our silence.

"Whatever we do, it will have to be soon before the Army gets here. If they get their hands on us, we're done for. But there's no way we're going to be able to take out all these raiders unarmed; that's for sure."

I snort quietly at his words and mutter, "Ya think?" but he chooses to ignore me. Instead he keeps talking to Tater.

"Our best bet would be to wait until nightfall. Until most of them are asleep. I'm an expert shot. If I can get my hands on one of their weapons, we may stand a chance."

I nod my head. "Yup, that should work. Just grab one of their shooters. Oh wait, our hands and feet are tied, and we have guards watchin' our every move. Got a backup plan, genius?"

He doesn't ignore me this time. "Yeah, we just let the Army take you. It's only you they want anyways, freak. Make a deal for the rest of us, see if we can keep ourselves alive," he glares at me. He's no longer whispering, and it catches our guard's attention.

"Hey, what's going on over there?"

"Oh, nothing to concern yourself with, my good man." Tater holds his tied hands up in a gesture of innocence. "It's just that this young fellow is a little perturbed at being around a New Blood. That's all. Nothing to worry about. It's not as if we're making escape plans or anything … Hah!" Tater's nervous burst of laughter makes me roll my eyes and groan inwardly.

Did he really just say that? The guard eyes us suspiciously, pointing his iron shooter. He looks us over trying to notice anything amiss.

"Yeah, well none of us are happy having this mutie around, but you don't hear us all bellyaching about it. Keep it down. And don't try anything funny. We're watching you."

"Certainly, certainly, good sir. We will be as quiet as a mouse." Tater grins at the guard and holds a finger to his lips to enhance his point. The guard gives us one last, hard look before he joins the rest of the raiders at the now roaring campfire. Busher is sitting cross-legged by the fire and watching us intently, so we hold off on any more talk. Once he's satisfied we're behaving, however, he lets his attention be pulled away by the sudden appearance of a whiskey jug. Only then do we dare to continue our conversation.

"Let's get two things straight." Tater jumps right back in. "If we stand any chance of escape, it has to be tonight. Jax is right; once we are under the Army's watch, we will not stand a chance in hell. And if we are to escape, then you both must let go of your annoying idiosyncrasies."

"Idio … wha?" I start to say, but Tater cuts me off impatiently.

"You have to stop fighting and work together. Got it?"

"Well, why couldn't you say that in the first place?" I hate how his way of talk always makes me feel so stupid. He ignores my biting remark and continues on.

"Earlier when I pretended to stumble into one of the guards, I skillfully managed to relieve him of this." One of his tied hands deftly pulls a small dagger down out of his sleeve for a quick perusal before it disappears again. I'm impressed. I'd seen Tater fall into the guard earlier, and it had earned him a hard punch to the back. I had no idea there'd been another motive for his contrived clumsiness.

"Ask and ye shall receive," he says to Jax, grinning from ear to ear. "Now, as you said a moment ago, we wait until most of them are asleep. These past two nights, I've noticed our guards have been taking forty winks at their post. Obviously with Tara's lack of any show of power, they have become a little lax about our threat assessment. We wait until they are asleep tonight, I cut our bindings, and we make a run for it."

I look to Tater, expecting to hear more, but he doesn't say anything else. Jax and Finn look just as expectant, waiting for Tater to go on.

"That's it? That's the plan?" Jax asks finally, not bothering to hide his disbelief.

"Yes, that's it. I said I had a plan. I didn't say it was a good one. Do any of you have a better idea?" Tater asks. "I free us; we run. What else do you expect? As you most astutely pointed out, we cannot go up against so many armed raiders."

He's right. "Sounds good enough to me," I say. "Finn, you make sure you stick to me like a shadow. I don't wanna lose you in the dark." He nods at me in agreement.

"If we get split up, head east into the hills. That will keep you onto the path to Littlepass."

A loud whooping from the group around the campfire interrupts Tater and he clams up, but they're not paying any heed to us. The whiskey jug is being passed around freely, and they're celebrating like they already have their reward. Busher catches my eye and raises the jug to me in a mock toast before taking a big swig of the brew.

"I hope he chokes," I mutter, but it's just wishful thinking. I drop my eyes and look toward the horizon. Not much longer until sunset, I reckon. Tonight will be our only chance. Tater's plan is sound … sorta … but since it's the only plan we have, we'd better make the best of it. For some reason, I have this sinking feeling it just isn't good enough. I'm hoping I'm dead wrong.

The first inkling we get that something isn't right is when Hat Head, back to being his cocky self again now that he's been swigging the whiskey, wobbles our way. He brushes past Tater and Finn to stand directly in front of me. I get to my feet. I don't like having to look up at him, and I'm not sure what he's about to do. He stares at me, swaying back and forth like he downed the whole jug of whiskey himself.

There ain't no way he drank enough to be this wasted.

"You don't look like no freak," he says, least I think that's what he says. His words are all slurred like his tongue is too big for his mouth. He wobbles a bit more as he points his finger at me.

"Ya ... nawe ... bood ..."

Huh? What the hell is wrong with him?

Then suddenly, his eyes roll back in his head and he falls with a loud thud, face first into the ground. I jump back. Shizen. What's happening? Before I can get a word out, there's another thud. Then another. The raiders. They're falling like leaves off a tree in a big wind, one after another.

Busher is the last to be standing. He's wobbling just like Hat Head did, but he's fighting it. He lets out an angry roar, and he kicks the whiskey jug over. His eyes, so full of hot anger, seek me out. He looks like a mountain bearing down on me, and I can't help but back away as far as the rope will allow. But he doesn't get to me. He falls to his knees before he can get more than four paces. Trying in vain to push himself back up, he gives me one more burning look before he also faceplants the ground—hard.

"What the gods ...?" Tater is looking at me, but I'm just as dumbfounded. I shake my head at his unspoken question. This isn't me. I have no idea what's happening.

I look around at all the raiders on the ground lying where they fell. *Are they dead?* I think. Finn's panicked, "Tara!" pulls my attention away from the bodies, and I follow his fearful gaze to a figure approaching us from the trees. It's walking kind of hunched and shuffling, but I recognize it right away. The creature I'd seen that night in the sand lands and again in the valley on the other side of the mountains. I was right. It had been following us.

It comes closer, and I get a better look at its face. Shizen. What the hell is it? It resembles something more out of a night terror than a human face. Its yellowed flesh hangs in loose folds around its neck, and the skin on its odd-shaped head not covered by tufts of hair is dotted with visible veins. There's not much nose to speak of, just a bump with two holes where a nose should have been and a fleshy mouth that looks too wide for the face it's on. I can feel the bile rising in the back of my throat, and I find myself searching the ground, looking for anything that I can use as a weapon. Finn cowers against me, and I hold him close as it approaches. I can hear Tater muttering something, prayers maybe, and Jax starts tugging at his ropes, cussing under his breath. Tied and bound, there's nothing we can do but watch helplessly as it shuffles closer.

The muttering gets louder, and I almost yell at Tater to shut up when I realize the sound isn't coming from him. In fact, Tater doesn't look worried at all. The muttering is coming from the critter. Its mouth is moving all odd-like, like it's not used to forming words, but that's exactly what it's doing. It's talking. Good gods … it's talking! As much as it terrifies me, I find myself straining to hear what it's saying.

"Mus … ove … mus ove …"

I don't understand, but it keeps shuffling towards me like its words are meant for me and me alone. It comes straight for me, and I'm shocked to see its eyes. As strange and wrong as the rest of it is, its eyes are so human-like. It grabs my wrist with a skeletal hand, and the contact sends a tingling up my arm. The dark eyes bore into mine with such fear I shiver. I can't help it.

"Mus … ove!" It speaks with more force this time, and suddenly I understand.

"Move. We must move." I say. It nods in relief, I think.

My fear eases some at the realization that the creature's not trying to harm us, but help us.

"Men ... come." Its long finger points to the trees.

"There are more men coming?" I ask, and it nods again. Tater looks at me in concern.

"The Army," he says, and the creature confirms.

"Ess ... yes ... Must go."

Tater doesn't hesitate. The little blade suddenly appears, and he starts sawing at his bindings. The creature is also prepared. It pulls a wicked-looking blade from the sash around its waist and starts at my ropes. The smell of it so close to me is overwhelming, but I just hold my breath and let it continue sawing my ropes and then Finn's. As soon as we are free, I reach for Hat Head still lying at my feet, pull the shooter out from underneath him and hook it over my shoulder. Tater by now has freed Jax and they get the same idea, grabbing the nearest weapons they can find. Tater even takes the time to scoop up his hat even though the creature is making frantic movements with his hands, trying to hurry us. But there's still something I need to know.

"The raiders." I point at the bodies on the ground. "I'm guessing you did this. Are they dead?"

"No ... dead ... sleep. Po no kill."

"Po?" I say, not knowing what the critter means by this.

It points at itself and says again, "Po ... no kill."

"That's your name? Po?"

It nods a yes, and I find myself amazed that the creature ... that he (I assume it's a he) had the smarts enough to carry out such a plan. Somehow, it had figured out a way to put a sleeping herb or such in the raiders' whiskey. It must have been waiting for its chance for days to do so. Why though? Why was it helping us? I don't get the chance to ask. Tater, hat now planted firmly back on his head, interrupts my line of questioning.

"I hate to interfere with your getting acquainted and all, but as the mutie so accurately pointed out earlier, we must move."

I realize the cause of his growing concern as I hear the dull thumping coming from the ground below us. Horses—a lot of them—and they are coming fast. The Army is here.

"This way," Jax makes a beeline for the closest grove of trees, and we hightail it behind him. We hear shouting and then popping sounds. Iron shooters. Did they see us already? But then we hear more shouting, and I remember the scouts Busher had planted around the campsite. They didn't drink the whiskey. They're still awake. And from the shouting we're overhearing, the Army isn't greeting them with open arms. So much for honor amongst thieves or such. I grab Finn by the front of his tunic and drag him faster, trying to get into the cover of the trees. I don't want to be in view when they reach the campsite.

Stumbling into the trees, I look around wildly, fearing either raiders or Army to be waiting for us, but we're alone. Tater bends over with his hands on his knees and wheezes loudly.

"Tater?" I ask, worried, but he just waves a hand at me and keeps gasping.

"I'm okay," he manages to croak, but Jax grunts with impatience.

"We don't got time for this, old man." He ignores my glare

and paces around. Finally, he jerks a hand over his shoulder.

"This way," he says, but Po puts a restraining hand on his arm much to his obvious disgust.

"No," the creature says and points with his bony finger. "There."

Nestled away in the trees are Winnie, and Busher's much larger horse, grazing contentedly, unaware of the trouble around them.

"Faster," Po says, and I nod in agreement.

"Po's right. Finn, you and Tater on Winnie. You two ain't so heavy; she should be able to carry you both easily. Jax, you, me, and Po on the other beast if we can."

As I speak, I head for the two animals and quickly untie them from the trees. We help Finn and Tater onto Winnie's back before I climb onto Busher's beast and take the reins. Thankfully the horse doesn't resist. Jax leaps nimbly behind me, but the mutie doesn't move.

"Po, come on!" I urge. The shouting is getting louder now, and I know they've found the campsite and the other raiders. The creature shakes his head and says, "Go."

I ignore Jax's muttered, "You don't have to tell me twice. Let's move."

"No, he helped us; we're not leaving him," I hiss at Jax.

But the creature shakes his head. "You go. Po will hide. They look for girl … they no find Po."

"You heard him. They no find Po," Jax hisses back, but the creature is done debating. He smacks the horse's rump, and we bolt off without warning. I struggle with the reins, but finally I get the horse under control and I glance back over my shoulder. Finn and Tater are riding directly alongside us, but Po is as good as his word. He's nowhere to be seen. What I do see; however, is much more frightening. Emerging from the grove of trees we just cleared is a line of riders, all on big, black, powerful-looking beasts.

The Prezedant's Army. My heart pounds in my chest, and I grab the reins tighter for fear they will slip out of my sweat-soaked hands.

"Don't look back, just ride," Jax shouts in my ear, and I know he's right but deep down in my gut I fear we're doomed. We may be able to outride them on Busher's horse, but Winnie doesn't stand a chance against those beasts. And there's no way in hell I'm leaving Finn behind.

Oh gods, why didn't I make Finn ride with me, I think as I look over at him hanging on for dear life to Tater, his eyes closed in fear.

And that's all it takes; that one moment of inattention.

I hear Jax's shout of, "Look out!" an instant before the horse stumbles, and I fly through the air. I hit the ground hard, the breath knocked clean out of me. The loose rocks on the mountain trail bite painfully into my face and hands as I slide across them before coming to a stop. The beast I'd been riding a moment ago gallops past me, rider less and missing my head by a hair. Dazed and breathless, I hear Finn's cry of "Tater, stop!" and I know right away what he and Tater are about to do.

"Don't you dare stop." I try to scream at him. "Keep movin'," but it comes out as a whimper. I have no voice. I push myself to my knees and watch in horror as Finn jumps from Winnie's back and heads straight for me, unaware of the brown-robed rider closing in on him. I watch as the rider leans low in his saddle, arm outstretched, ready to scoop Finn off the ground and take him away. Take him to the madman.

"Finn," I try to warn him, but he can't hear me over the pounding hooves. The rider is on top of him now, the arm encircling his waist, and I see Finn's eyes go big with fear.

"Noooooooooo," The scream is forced from my lungs as I try to push to my feet. I have to do something. The slug whistles over my head, and I duck instinctively. *They're shooting at us,* I think at first, but then I see the rider about to grab Finn fall from his saddle. His foot still entangled in the stirrup, he's dragged by his horse away from Finn and bashed mercilessly about by the rocky terrain. Finn, finally realizing the danger, takes cover behind a large boulder. I whirl around to find Jax standing above me, shooter aimed and ready. The shot had come from Jax. He'd fired on the rider.

"We gotta move," he yells, the noise of the approaching riders almost drowning out his words. I just stare at him, dumbfounded. He grabs my shoulder and shakes me hard.

"Run, you idiot."

I hear him yelling. I do. I can see the men bearing down on us too, but I don't move. It's happening. The blood starts pounding through my veins. The buzzing starts in my ears, and I'm taken over by a dead calm. There's anger and hatred like before, but those feelings lay simmering beneath the overlying quiet. I pull the shooter I'd taken, and focus on my first target.

I zone in, calm and focused, as if the iron shooter is just an extension of my body. With no hesitation I fire, and the soldier falls from his horse. I do it again … and again, each shot finding its target true. I feel no guilt, no remorse. Just this calm. I don't know when they start returning fire, but it galvanizes Tater and Jax out of their shocked stupor and into action. The sound of shooter fire is all around me, but it's no more bothersome to me than a maskeeto buzzing. My focus is intense and concentrated.

I watch a brown-robed rider approach Jax from behind. I watch him lift his shooter and aim. I see all this, but it's like I'm not seeing it with my own eyes. It's like I'm watching from off to the side in total indifference. In response, I aim my own barrel and fire a hole into the middle of the rider's forehead. I witness the bloody debris bloom out, but I feel no repulsion, no disgust at my actions. It's like I'm encased in some deep, freezing cold that not even this horror can penetrate. The rider falls from his horse as his shooter explodes. Almost in slow motion, I push Jax out of harm's way as the slug sucker-punches me in the gut.

The force of the slug's impact is enough to send me stumbling back a couple of steps, but I don't feel any pain. My hand explores the wound at my stomach before I lift it in front of my face. The hand is covered in blood. My blood. I shield the wound again as if doing so will stop the bleeding. I raise my head then and look around.

There's so many of them, I think. So many riders of death. Surrounding us, boxing us in. We're going to die. I know that. Right here, right now. Me, Finn, Tater, Jax … all dead, and there's nothing I can do. We're all going to die just like Grada and Molly and everybody else at the hands of these same madmen.

My calm finally evaporates, and the anger begins to take over. I feel it bubble to the surface like a tapped well and explode into every fiber of my being. It's so big I can't contain it. It overwhelms me, like my whole body is filled with fire. I lift my eyes to the darkening sky, open my mouth, and scream just to release it before it consumes me. A wall of dust and earth starts to rise before my eyes, forming between me and the Army, blinding me to them.

A sand storm! I think frantically. Really? As if the Army isn't threat enough, now we're going to have the very breath stripped from our bodies by the suffocating sands of a dirt devil? I search for the others to warn them, to tell them to run, but I can't see them anymore. They're consumed by swirling sands. I can't see anybody. I'm all alone.

Dying and alone, I think as I fall to my knees, the wall of sand closing in on me. The last thought in my muddled brain as my life's blood seeps through my fingers?

At least I didn't get hit in the head again.

CHAPTER 5

Gray Valley

———◆———

The tall, green stalks ripple and sway in the cool, morning breeze. There's so much corn, as far as the eye can see. I've never seen the fields so full. It's like the stories of the old folk have come to be right in front of me. I stand for a bit just admiring the waves of corn, wishing Ben was here to see it. He never would have believed this possible. Deep down, I think he truly thought the old folks had lied to us with their settlers' stories. That their stories about fields of crops were shite. But here they are, spread out before me plain as day.

A shadowy figure stands in the middle of the field. How did I not see him before? I squint a bit into the sun, but his back is to me; I can't quite tell who it is. I start moving closer. I don't know why, but there's this urgent need to find out who it is. I don't get far however, before familiar whistling reaches my ears, and I stop in my tracks frozen in disbelief. Grada?

He's standing in the middle of the waist-high crops, whistling as he picks the golden harvest, his battered, old hat pushed back on his gray head.

How is this even possible? Is this real?

The sunshine warming the top of my head and the breeze blowing on my face feels real, sure enough. He turns then and sees me, and that familiar smile lights up his face.

"Tara, girl."

"Grada!" I run to him, not giving a care for how it's possible. It just is. I run through the corn, ignoring the stalks slapping at my face and straight into his strong arms. He lifts me up high just like when I was a little girl. I hug him real tight and bury my face in his worn tunic. He smells of earth and root wad and … home. I'm home.

"I thought I'd lost you, Grada, for good." I'm bawling like a baby, my tears soaking his shirt, but I can't help it.

He chuckles quietly, his chest rumbling underneath my cheek. "Don't be foolish, girlie. I'm with you always," he says, and I look up into his wrinkled face.

"But you were dead, Grada. Those men, they killed you. All of you were gone. Molly, Shelly, Miz Emma, all dead."

"Aye, that we are. But that don't mean we ain't with you, girl. Look around."

I do as he says, realizing beyond the field lays Rivercross. But not the Rivercross I remember. The shanties are gone, replaced by new and sturdy-looking wood cabins. The ground isn't no dusty, hard-packed soil like I recall either. Instead green grass sprouts cover the land like a warm blanket. And flowers ... so many flowers, every color you can imagine. And there are people everywhere: Molly, Shelly, Thomas, everybody. They're all there. I stare unbelieving as Lou looks up from his still and waves at me.

"Am I dreamin'?" I ask and Grada chuckles again.

"Maybe you is, maybe you ain't," he says, his eyes twinkling like they always do when he's teasing me.

"It's so beautiful. What happened here?" I say in wonder.

"Nuthin' ... and everything," Grada answers, confusing me even more. "This is your home, Tara. It's how your heart sees it: beautiful, whole, perfect. It's as it was meant to be."

Suddenly, I know he's right. This is how the world was meant to be, how it had been. Alive, green, plentiful. It isn't supposed to be the dusty, barren land that we know it as. The beauty of the land, the fields, of seeing everybody ... it's so overwhelming I just want to cry again. But then that nagging, bitter thought surfaces, and my smile slowly fades away.

"Grada, did you all die because of me? Was I the reason the evil came to Rivercross?" I say, needing to know yet fearing the answer.

He chuckles quietly again and squeezes my shoulders. "Is that what you think, child?" He shakes his head at me. "Evil came to Rivercross because, well, that's what evil does. It spreads like a dark plague and don't give a care for nuthin' or nobody that stands in its way. It would have found Rivercross sooner or later. You couldn't have stopped what happened no more than I could have stopped you from growing up and trust me, I tried."

An intense rush of relief flows over me. It wasn't my fault. Grada said it wasn't my fault, and he would never lie to me about this, would he?

"But things have been happenin' to me, Grada," I say, still not quite believing my innocence. "People are callin' me names, sayin' I'm supposed to be this thing called a New Blood. New Bloods, they draw evil. That's what Jax believes. If it's true, and I am this thing—"

"What will be, will be, Tara," he says, cutting off my words. "Everything has a destiny, whether it be a wild hog or a sand biter or you. And your destiny, my girl, it's a wondrous one indeed. New Blood or not, you are meant to do great things."

I've never known Grada to speak in riddles before. What exactly is he trying to say? Is he saying I'm not a New Blood after all? I close my eyes, just for an instant, trying to make sense of his words. The cool, morning breeze that felt so good on my face earlier changes, just like that, to a hot, scorching heat. I open my eyes again, wishing I hadn't done so. Everything I'd just witnessed is gone. Everything burnt away, nothing left but charred remains. No cornfield, no flowers, no Grada. Only black, smoldering ruins.

"Grada," I scream in frustration, searching the blackened landscape. I just got him back. I can't lose him again. There's so much more I need to say to him. To ask him. It's not fair.

"Tara," the voice that answers me isn't Grada, but it's just as familiar. He's standing at the other end of the burnt field, almost glowing against the blackness of the scorched background.

"Ben." A wave of intense happiness washes over me, my heart almost exploding with sheer joy.

"Ben … everything is burnt. Gone," I say.

"I know, Tar Tar, but you can fix it."

"I don't know how," I cry as I try to walk to him. But with each step I take, he gets further away.

"Ben. Wait." My voice is frantic.

"Found a good patch of berries by the old swimmin' hole," his voice is fading away. "Ma was real pleased …"

"Ben," I yell again, but I can't run after him because now there's hands holding me back. Rooting me in place. "Ben, come back." I struggle, but the hands won't let me go. I can't shake them off no matter how hard I try.

"Let me go!" I try kicking and struggling, but they just seem to hold me tighter.

"Tara. It's okay. Stop fighting."

The familiar voice reaches my consciousness at some level and snaps me awake. My eyes open to faces looming above me. They swim in and out of focus, but I know Finn is there and Jax … and another face, one I don't recognize. It's this face I focus on since the blue eyes that seem so familiar to me aren't filled with the disgust I'm used to seeing in them, but compassion.

"It's okay, dear girl. You're safe." Her voice is soothing and calm, and I know she's speaking the truth. I stop struggling and the hands loosen their grip.

I've been dreaming, I think. Grada and Ben, they weren't real. It was all a dream. My heart swells with pain as I realize that I'm not in Rivercross at all, but laying in a bed. My gut feels like it's been ripped open by a devil cat. I was shot. I remember that. Tentatively, I reach down and feel the cloth bandage wrapped around me.

The blue-eyed lady smiles at me before moving my hand away. "You're going to be fine; you just need to rest."

"Yeah, that's great. She's gonna be fine and all, but I think she broke my nose." Jax's voice is strangely muffled, and I look over at him. He's holding his nose, and there's blood dripping down his arm. Had he been shot too?

"What …" My voice cracks and I clear my throat. "What happened to you?"

"You punched me is what, you crazy freak. All I was doing was trying to hold you down so you wouldn't tear open your wound and you sucker-punched me in the nose," he says, not trying to hide his anger at all.

"Well, I guess you should count yourself lucky I didn't punch any lower," I mutter back, and Finn's bark of laughter holds a tinge of relief.

"Hey Finn," I say, eyeing him as he hovers anxiously in the background. He moves around the still irritable Jax to get to me, and he takes my outstretched hand. It's good to see him. "You okay?"

He nods and settles himself beside me on the canvas mattress. He sniffs and wipes his hand across his nose.

"You almost died." The accusation is heavy in his eyes as well as his words.

His remark scares me like crazy, but I don't show it. Instead, I poke him gently in the chest.

"Now, what did Tater tell you about me while we were in the raiders' cage?"

"That you was too thick-skulled to die."

"Yup, and for once he was right," I say, giving his hand a little squeeze. He gives me his gap-toothed grin and squeezes back. Totally awake now, my dreams fading quickly, I look around the little room we're in, take in my surroundings. It's no shanty; that's for certain.

Besides the bed I'm lying in, there's a tall, wooden chest in the corner painted with all sorts of drawings of flowers. A window covered with real painted shutters, not tin scraps. And what looks to be dolls in every corner. Peg dolls just like the ones Grada used to make me when I was a young'un. There are also carved, wooden dolls and other sorts I don't recognize, but they are plentiful.

"What is this place?" I say in awe. It's so pretty looking and clean. You can smell the freshness. I almost feel guilty about my stinky carcass lying in the fresh bed. Almost. Jax is still busy acting all wounded with his nose, and the blue-eyed lady is doing her best to look at it but he's being difficult, so it's up to Finn to answer me.

"This is Gray Valley. Jax brought us here. This is his cabin, and that's his ma."

His ma. No wonder those blue eyes seemed so familiar. She'd passed them on to her boy. But she seems nice. Kind. Caring even. How is Jax any son of hers?

"How did we get here? The Army," I trail off remembering my last thoughts. Of how we were all going to die. We'd been surrounded—by the Army and a dust storm—with no way out. I was gut shot, but yet here we are; here I am, alive. For the first time since I'd met him, Finn regards me with a look akin almost to fear. Is he scared of me? Shizen. What happened for him to look at me like that? That look on his face, it hurts me more than any shooter wound could ever do.

"Finn?" I say, my voice gentle. "What happened?"

"Was a freak dust storm." Jax interrupts, pushing his ma aside and striding over to Finn. He grips the boy's shoulder and nods to the boy. "Right, Finn? The gods sure were watching over us. Come out of nowhere and gave us perfect cover to escape."

"Aye," Finn agrees, but he don't look at me. He's looking at the floor. "We got away and rode for four days to get here."

Four days? Holy hell. I don't remember riding for four days. I don't remember anything.

"Tater?" I say, but Jax nods.

"He's fine and that mule of his as well. Even that she-devil belonging to Finn here is okay though she's given a few of the villagers a scare or two."

We all made it? "How—"

"Ma, maybe you can go let Tater know of Tara's recovery," Jax cuts me off. "I'm sure between the pints of ale he's been downing, there's a real concern for her well-being there somewhere."

Her eyes are questioning, but all she says is, "Of course, dear," and leaves us, sending me a reassuring smile.

Jax waits for her to be out of earshot before he turns back to me. "Look, I know you're full of questions, but maybe now isn't the right time."

"How did we escape, Jax?" I demand, and my tone leaves no room for argument. I need to know what happened. They fall silent, both him and Finn, and they exchange a look. That look irritates me more so than their silence because it says to me they share a bond and a secret. Jax has no right to have a bond with Finn. No right.

"Tell me," I say through gritted teeth. I know I sound desperate, but that's how I'm feeling. Something's not right.

It's Finn who speaks. "You don't remember nuthin', Tara?"

I shake my head. "I … I recall being surrounded, and I was shot. Then that wall of sand …" Suddenly a memory of a brown-robed rider with a red, gaping wound in his head pops into my brain, and I gasp. "Oh gods! I shot some of 'em. I killed 'em."

I try to sit up, the memory of what I had done so horrifying that I want to get away from it.

"Hey, hey," Jax pushes me back down on the bed none too gently. "Yeah, you killed some of those bastards. So what? Would you rather they have killed Tater, or Finn … or me? And they would have. They would have killed all of us, but you. You were what they wanted. You saved us, Tara. All of us."

It must be a hard admission for him, being saved by a New Blood since he doesn't look too happy about it. His blue eyes are like ice chips, and he runs an irritated hand through his spikey hair. Not much of a thank you, but I figure it's about all I'm gonna get out of him.

"But we were surrounded." I still don't understand. "How did I save any of you?"

I look at Finn, still sitting beside me. He doesn't want to meet my eyes, but I force his chin up.

"Finn, tell me and speak the truth," I say.

He looks to Jax first, who gives him a slight nod as if giving him permission. *Permission for what?*

Finns voice is hesitant, scared. "It ain't like nuthin' I ever seen before. There we were, surrounded. The Army was everywhere. You were shot, Tara. I could see all the blood, and I was so scared. I thought for sure we were all done for. But then you ... you started yellin'. It weren't no words I could understand, but something happened. It was like ... Hells, I don't know. It was like the land itself was being summoned by you, controlled almost. It rose up like a dust devil only bigger. Much bigger. We were in the middle of it. It didn't touch us at all, but the Army ... When it cleared, they were just gone. There weren't nuthin'. No bodies, no horses. Just gone."

He stops talking, but his eyes desperately search my face for an explanation. One I can't give him. How is that even possible? Surely, Finn must be wrong about the whole thing. He'd been scared, terrified. He must have imagined it. But then I look at Jax, and I see the confirmation in his eyes. It's true. All of it. A coldness starts to move over me, and my whole insides feel numb. It's like my brain refuses to process what Finn's just told me, and I stare at him in disbelief. That surely isn't something any normal person should be able to do, raise a dust storm. Jax is right. I am a freak. A mutation. Horrified and overwhelmed at Finn's admission, I try to sink further into the soft bed.

"I wanna be alone," I say dully, turning my head from both pairs of searching eyes. I just want to slip back to unconsciousness, to see Grada and Ben again. To be back in Rivercross where things made sense and I was normal.

"Tara—"

"Get out!" I scream, cutting off Jax's words. I don't want to talk. I don't want their questioning eyes looking at me anymore. I'm grateful they do as I ask because they don't get a chance to see the hot tears that start to flow down my cheeks onto my pillow. I cry and cry. I can't stop. Everything that has been building up over the past few weeks, it lets loose, and I can't control it. I cry for Grada, Rivercross, Ben … for everything that I've lost.

Grada was so wrong. It is all my fault. The sobs rack my body uncontrollably, and my gut feels like it's on fire with every convulsion, but I keep crying. I cry for the lives I've taken—they weren't just Army. I figure they had been someone's son, father, husband, and I killed them. I'm no better than any of them.

The tears flow heavily for a long time. I sob into the pillow, bashing it with my fist. Why did all this happen? Why was everybody I ever loved taken from me? Why in the name of the gods am I being tested so? But no answers come.

Slowly, my sobs subside into deep, shuddering breaths. Exhausted, I lay against my wet pillow too spent to move or to care. I feel numb, emotionless. Like every feeling I had inside of me was now cried out into my pillow. And tired. So tired.

I get no relief in my eventual sleep, however, for then the night terrors come. Filled with images of bloody, gaping head wounds and giant dust storms and burnt crops and bodies. I deserve it, I guess. Evil dreams for an evil soul. It's fitting.

———◆———

For days I refuse to see anyone except Vi, Jax's ma. I'm not up to facing any of them. I don't want to see their questioning looks and to try and give them answers I don't have. They try to visit, especially Finn, but I keep refusing. Vi agrees to my wishes, and every day turns him away with a quiet but firm, "Not today." She's my only connection to the world outside, bringing me food, changing my bandages, and never judging. For the first time in my life I realize what it must be like to be under a mother's care, and I am grateful for her strength. But with each kindness she shows me, I can't help but think about my own ma. Did she abandon me because she knew what sort of monster I would turn out to be? Was the thought of it more than she could bear? I guess I'll never know but thinking about it just sends me spiraling deeper and deeper into despair. I'm in one of those dark moods when Vi brings me my meal.

Without a word to me she lays the soup on the table by my bed and then opens the shutters covering the small window in the room, letting in the bright sun. Wincing, I cover my eyes with my arm.

"Could you close those back up please, Vi?" I mutter.

"I could, but I won't," she says, and I stare at her in surprise. She's never denied me anything since she's been caring for me.

"Enough is enough, child." She stands over me, arms folded. "For days now, I've watched you wallow in self-pity, turning away those who care about you, and for what? Because you found out you're different?"

She sees my shock and nods. "Yes, I know what you are even though Jax tried his best to hide it from me." She sighs. "I swear sometimes that boy thinks I'm an idiot."

"How did you know—"

"That you're a New Blood? Well, if your rapidly healing wound wasn't a dead giveaway, it would have to be your resemblance to her."

I frown at her, puzzled. "Her? Who?"

"Jenna. Jax's sister and my daughter. You remind me of her so much. Oh, not in appearance other than the hair of course, but your temperament and stubbornness and sadness. In that, you are very similar."

I'm surprised by this revelation. "I didn't know Jax had a sister."

Not that he would have told me anyways. We haven't had exactly what you would call civilized conversation in the time we've known each other.

She sighs again and sits by me on the bed. "No, he doesn't talk about her at all anymore. But as children, they were inseparable. He loved her very much."

"This is her room, isn't it?" I say.

Vi just nods and looks around fondly. "All these dolls … Jax made them for her or found them over the years. It was the one thing that made her happy."

"She was … odd? Like me?" Don't know why I'm asking. I already know the answer. At first, I don't think Vi is going to reply, but then she sighs.

"We didn't know. Oh, we'd heard stories, tales of New Bloods and such, but we never imagined. We thought them to be myth. Campfire talk." She gives a harsh little laugh. "There were signs, things I should have seen, but I guess I didn't want to see it. Jenna was always different. We lived a simple life, the four of us, a happy life. We had our hardships; what life doesn't? But basically, we were happy. Gray Valley was pretty much left alone by the Prezedant's Army as long as we paid our taxes, gave them most of our crops. But then it all changed."

Her face hardens, and even though she's sitting next to me on the bed, in her mind's eye she is far, far away.

"*He* came one day. I don't know how he found out about her. Maybe some trader passing through recognized her for what she was. I can't rightly say. But they came, an army of them. He tried to take her from us. They dragged her from the cabin. She was crying, screaming as they tried to lock her in their traveling cage. Why? I wanted to know. What had she done? She was just a little girl ... an innocent little girl. Jax and his father were in the fields with the other men, but they came running at Jenna's cries. Her father, he attacked the guards putting her in the cage. He was a strong man, my husband, but he stood no chance against their weapons. They killed him with no more thought than if they were slaughtering a hog. Jenna, she couldn't handle seeing her father cut down in front of her like that. She ... she ..."

Vi stops speaking, but she doesn't have to say what happened. I know what Jenna must have gone through. I'd already experienced it: Chi. My hand reaches for hers, and she holds it tight.

"She couldn't handle it, my Jenna. She wasn't strong enough, not like you. It overwhelmed her, destroyed her. And even though I was there to see with my own eyes, I can't really explain what happened." I watch Vi struggle to tell me, holding my breath, scared for what I'm about to hear.

"I watched as this light formed around her. The two guards holding her, they fell immediately. Dead from what, I cannot say. Then the light got brighter, and she started screaming as if it were hurting her … burning her. The villagers that had come running at her cries to help, the ones closest to her, they started falling too, just like the guards. I tried to run to her. I needed to reach my little girl, but Jax had ahold of me and he wouldn't let me go. He knew it was too late. That I would die just like the others. That I couldn't help her. I couldn't help my little girl …," her voice trails off, and I think she's done but then she starts talking again.

"By the time it was over, nine other innocent villagers had perished, and my little girl? There was nothing left. It was like she had burnt away on the inside and left an empty, hollow shell."

Tears fall freely down her cheeks, but she doesn't try to stop them. We sit in silence for a bit, me holding her hand while she remembers the horrors. Finally, she speaks again, but this time her voice is hard and unforgiving.

"He watched it all happen—the death, the carnage—from atop his horse. He watched them shoot my husband and my baby girl destroy herself. He ordered his remaining men to take four other children as our punishment for resisting them." Her voice breaks again, but she continues on, "And when it was over, after so many people had died, after he had destroyed so many families, you know what he said? 'Pity, she may have been of use.' I will never forget that as long as I live. *She may have been of use.*" Her eyes harden and a vein pulses in her forehead. She swallows a couple of times like she's trying to swallow her anger, before turning back to me. "So don't you dare feel remorse for what you did to those bastards. You saved my boy's life and the lives of Finn and

Tater." She nods at my questioning look. "Yes, Finn told me what happened, most of it anyway. And I know that's some of what's been keeping you awake at night and causing your grief. Do not shed another tear over any of it. You, my child, have been touched with a special gift. Why you've been able to handle that gift while my Jenna was not, well, that's for the gods to know. You've been chosen for a reason, and what you do with that gift is up to you. But let me tell you this. As long as that evil creature lives, no one is safe."

She stops talking but continues to hold my hand tight. We sit a moment in silence as she struggles to compose herself, to lock those horrible memories away again, and I try to take it all in. What had happened to Jenna scares me. Vi had said it was like she had burnt from the inside out, and I kinda know what she's talking about. The Chi, well, it had felt like my blood ... my whole body was aflame. But why hadn't it killed me like it had done to Jenna? And what must it had been like for Vi? What she must have endured to witness not just her husband, but her child perish in front of her and be so helpless? Kind of like me and Rivercross, I guess. But I don't say that. There was nothing I could say to help take away any of that pain. I know that firsthand. So, I just keep holding her hand as she cries. Finally, she gives my hand a little shake and stands up, wiping the tears from her face. She smooths out her dress, her emotions back under control again.

"I've said my piece; now get up. You've wasted enough time."

I don't want to do that. I'm too full of fear and questions. I don't want to get up, but I also don't dare oppose her. Besides,

I don't think it would have done any good anyways. I kind of can see where Jax got his stubborn streak from, but I wasn't about to tell her that. I stand up tentatively, surprised that the pain I'm expecting doesn't come.

"Don't worry; it's almost healed. One of the advantages of your kind." She taps me on the nose gently as if to take the bite off her words. "And just in time, too. I have a surprise for you." She turns to leave the room, but I grab her arm.

"Wait. There's one more thing I need to know. Jax, he blames Jenna for what happened, doesn't he? For drawing the Prezedant here. For his pa's death. For the villagers. That's why he ... why I disgust him so much," I say.

She nods and gives me a sad little smile. "You have to remember; he was barely past being a child himself when all this happened. He didn't understand. He needed someone to take the blame for his loss, to help him make sense of all that happened. Someday, he will understand. He will forgive her; of that I have no doubt. Now, come with me. Your surprise awaits."

———

Surprise has never been a good word in my opinion. The scrub tub full of hot water she had waiting for me I appreciated since, I'll admit, I was starting to smell pretty ripe. Her washing and braiding my hair with tiny ribbons I tolerated since they did a fine job of hiding my white stripes. But this? This is ridiculous.

"Stop fidgeting, Tara. You look lovely."

"I cain't help it. It's itchin' me something fierce." I skulk along behind Vi, tugging at the constricting, frilly neckband of the stupid dress I'm wearing and fully aware of all the curious onlookers. How she'd talked me into wearing this ridiculous getup is still a mystery. I'd taken one look at the ruffled contraption earlier when she'd showed me and backed away in horror.

"Oh hell no. You ain't gettin' me into that," I'd told her, but she was insistent.

"You don't have much choice, child. Your own tattered, bloodied clothes I burnt, and until I can get a pair of Jax's trousers altered for you, this is your only option."

"Fine then. I'll just wait in bed until you're done the alterin'," I'd said, but she wasn't having none of that.

"You will do no such thing, young lady. Tonight is a grand event, a betrothal celebration. You can't miss this. We've been saving for this all year. There's going to be music, dancing, storytelling, and the food, oh my! Roasted rabbit, meat pies, fresh corn, sweet biscuits. Why, just thinking of it is making my mouth water."

Mine too, but I wasn't going to tell her that.

"I know what you're tryin' to do," I'd said. "And it ain't gonna work."

Shizen. How many villagers lived here anyways? And what are they all looking at? You'd swear they'd never seen a girl in a dress before.

Vi keeps smiling and waving at everybody as we make our way through the village. Why she gotta be calling attention to us like that? I cringe a little bit more every time she calls someone's name, wishing the ground would open up and swallow me. A little dark-haired girl, no more than nine or ten born years, runs right up to us and grabs my dress tail, nearly causing me to trip over it.

"I'm Nina," she says, smiling at me like I was her long-lost kin. "And you're Tara. Finn told me all about you."

"Is that so?" I say, still giving anyone who dares look my way the evil eye. It doesn't work. They're all still staring at me like I'm some weird sand lands critter. I give up and focus on the child's face in front of me just so I don't have to be looking at everybody else.

"Where is Finn?" I say to her. My words come out all breathless and high-pitched since the dress is cinched so damn tight about my waist it's making it hard for me to breath. She just giggles and points.

"Over there at the table. Him and Cat. Cat is so pretty. I just love her. She licks my face all the time, and her tongue is so cold."

"That it is," I say, opting to omit the devouring incident at Finn's village to the girl. Poor kid doesn't need to know where that tongue has been.

I see Finn then, just like she said, propped up against a table so laden with food that my eyes almost bug out of my head. Vi wasn't lying; there's so much food! Finn is stuffing his pie hole so fast I'm scared he's going to choke. Cat is lying under the table, chewing contentedly on a big old bone, but at seeing me she rears up and lunges at me. I brace myself just in time as she rams her big head into my chest, rubbing against me like crazy.

"Okay, okay, calm down, you overgrown lap rat. It's good to see you too," I say, trying to push her away. Finn spots me then, and he's no better than his beast. He comes flying my way, and his scrawny arms circle my waist.

"Tara. I'm so glad you got better. I was so worried. You wouldn't let me see you, and I'm real sorry about before … about bein' scared and all."

"Shush," I say, cutting off his words. "I know you're sorry. Don't say no more about it." Besides, I don't want to talk about that, not here in front of everybody else. He just nods at me in understanding and then slowly looks me up and down as if suddenly realizing something is different about me.

"Tara, are you wearin' a dress?"

"What of it?" I say a little sharper than I intend to. "Ain't no law against wearin' a dress, is there?"

Vi smiles at the boy and tousles his hair. "Doesn't she look lovely, Finn?" she asks, but he just shrugs.

"I guess so," he says, eyeballing me with doubt. Yeah, that really makes me feel a whole lot better.

But he doesn't get time to 'compliment' me more before Tater comes lumbering over to us, a mug of ale in one hand and a huge smile covering his flushed face. It was my first time seeing him since our run-in with the Army. If he's bothered any by what he'd witnessed me do, he's not showing it.

"Ah, the sleeping princess has arisen from her chambers at last. It is truly wonderful to see you, my dear, and in such fine attire. Being in the constant presence of such a lovely lady as our Vi here has most certainly rubbed off on you.

Given a little more time, I have no doubt she could perform the impossible and turn you into a remarkable lady of refinement."

Typical Tater. I'm not sure, but I feel there's an insult amongst those words somehow. But I find I don't care. I'm actually glad to see him, ugly wrinkled face and all. I truly thought he would have abandoned us by now and gone his separate way. He has no loyalty to us. *Why was he even still here?* I wonder. But then my unspoken question is answered as a plump little woman with rosy cheeks yells his name.

"Oh, Winston, I have a fresh mug of ale for you," she says, batting her eyes at him like she got sand in them.

"Coming, my lovely," he answers back then gives me a waggle of his bushy eyebrows. "Don't rush your healing on my account, my dear. Take all the time you need. This is truly an enjoyable village."

I can't help the laughter busting out of me at his retreating back. The laughter feels real good and truly surprises me. I didn't think I had it left in me to laugh. I finally let my guard down and look about at everything happening around me.

The villagers had mostly lost interest in me by now, and they're all talking and eating. Some are dancing to the little band of music makers. It's a celebration of life happening around me, and I'm amazed to find that I very much want to be a part of it. We had been at death's door, but we'd made it through. All of us, alive and whole, and it didn't matter how we'd made it, did it? So I'd performed something totally strange and unexplainable. So I was most undoubtedly a freak. So what? I'd saved them: Jax, Tater, Finn. They are alive and here because of me. It felt good—damn good. Knowing

I'm somewhat responsible for them being alive, well, it makes me feel lighter somehow. Like a weight has been lifted from my shoulders. Like my being able to save them somehow makes up for my failure in saving Rivercross.

Suddenly ravenous, I grin at Finn. "How's the grub table, Finn?"

"Oh gods, Tara, there's everything you could ever want. I still ain't tried it all there's so much."

"Well, whadda you waitin' for? I'm starvin'," I say and hook my arm through his.

⎯⎯•◆•⎯⎯

I don't know where to begin, there's so much food. I've never seen a spread like this, not ever back in Rivercross. Everything looks so delicious, and my mouth waters in anticipation. There are platters of roasted rabbit, meat pies piled high, mountains of golden corn, bowls of greens, and other things I can't even guess what they are. The smell wafting from it all is simply amazing, and my stomach rumbles loudly. Eagerly, I reach for a sweet biscuit the same time as someone behind me, and we try to take the same one.

"Oh, sorry, miss," the voice behind me says, and I stiffen instantly. Gods, not him. I try to move in the other direction, but a dark head pushes past my shoulder to get a look at my face.

"Tara? Is that you?" I can hear the disbelief in his voice, and I turn on my heel to give him a steely look.

"Not a word. Not one word. This dress was your ma's idea, not mine," I say, waiting for the insults to start flying.

Instead, he's looking at me all wide-eyed, like he can't believe what he's seeing.

"By gods … you look like a girl," he says.

"I am a girl, jackass," I say, glaring at him.

"No, I mean without all the dirt and mud and stink, you ain't half-bad."

I truly don't know how to take this. Is it a compliment or an insult? I'm not sure. So I don't say anything and neither does Jax. We kind of stare at each other in silence.

"Tara, I—"

"Listen, Jax—"

We both speak at the same time, interrupting each other. He nods at me. "You first," he says.

"No, go ahead," I say.

"I just wanted to—"

"Jax. There you are." A small wisp of a girl with the loveliest, sun-bleached, curly hair I'd ever seen moves between us and grabs Jax's hand. She throws a smile my way.

"Hello, I'm Sky. Hope you don't mind, but I want to dance and Jax here is the best dancing partner."

"Really?" I blurt out, my eyes opening wide. This dour, sullen stick in the mud is a good dancer? Somehow, I can't picture it.

"Yes, really," he says defensively, like he can see what I'm thinking.

"Well, nice to meet you Sky and by all means, don't let me stop you from havin' the best dancin' partner. This I gotta see." I don't bother to hide my amused grin, and Jax doesn't bother to hide his irritation.

"Look, Sky, I really need to talk to Tara right now," he

says, but I interrupt.

"Nah, it ain't nuthin' that cain't wait. Go dance." I literally push him towards the ever-smiling Sky, and he shoots me a look before he lets her lead him away as if to say, "This ain't finished." I watch them walk away. Jax seems to tower over the impossibly tiny girl. Finn comes to stand next to me, munching loudly on an ear of corn.

"Who's that with Jax?" he mumbles around his mouthful of food.

"Sky," I say.

"She's real pretty," he says.

"Aye, that she is," I say, feeling a bit put out. She did look real pretty in her nice, girly dress. No confusing her with not being a girl. She's not the type of girl you would describe as "ain't half bad." For some reason I can't fathom, it don't sit well with me. *Must be the hunger getting the better of me,* I think. I nudge Finn and grin.

"Did you save me any?"

<hr style="width:15%" />

Shizen. Don't think I can eat another bite even if my life depends on it. I must have tried everything on the table and twice over. And the dress that had been tight before now threatens to cut off my life's breath. But I don't care. I will die full and happy.

We just stood there, me and Finn, eating and grinning at each other as the juices ran down our chins. We'd nod hello or such to anyone who happened to speak to us, but we don't let anything deter us from the food. Cat would occasionally saunter over and gobble up the crumbs we dropped, but she mainly stayed hidden under the table. There were too many people around for her liking. I knew how she felt. If I could have gotten away with it, I would have crawled under there with her. Only when the shouts started of, "A tale, Tater! A tale!" did we let ourselves be pulled away from the food.

Eagerly, we join Vi and Jax and the others gathered around the fire. Vi scoots over on the wooden bench and nods for us to sit. Finn moves real quick and sets himself next to Vi, leaving me no option but to squeeze between him and Jax. For some reason, I hesitate. I don't want to sit that close to Jax and Sky, but at his raised brow I decide I'm being foolish and sit myself down. Or try to at least, but I take one step, and my boot hooks into the tail of my dress, and I go sprawling in the dirt at Jax's feet. Horrified, I stare at Jax's boots, too embarrassed to look any higher.

"Oh my, are you okay, Tara?" I know its Sky's voice asking, but it isn't her hands that help me to my feet and set me straight. I look into the mocking blue eyes and brush his hands angrily from my shoulders.

"She's okay," he says, all the while still snickering at me. "She ain't used to dressing as a girl is all, right Tara?"

"Jackass," I mutter at him and sit myself next to Finn, squishing him almost so as not to have any part of me touch Jax at all. I ignore his sniggering and stare straight ahead at Tater, my cheeks burning hot from my embarrassment. Even Finn is laughing at me, but I give him an angry sideways glare and mutter under my breath, "Don't you even dare."

He stops laughing real quick. Thankfully, everyone's focus soon turns to Tater as he gets himself into his storytelling mode. He clears his throat a couple of times and stares dramatically at the night sky. I recognize the look of intense concentration, and I shiver in anticipation, forgetting about my earlier embarrassment. This is gonna be a good one.

He's as still as a statue, silhouetted against the roaring campfire. A hush falls over the crowd. Even the music makers have stopped playing for this treat. Tater drags the silence out for a bit, building the suspense. It's so quiet you could probably hear a leaf drop. Then suddenly, his voice booms out in a deep, resonating timbre.

"Many, many years ago and in a land far, far away …"

Every soul there is held spellbound as Tater tells us the story of a magical tree planted by the gods that grew up through the clouds right to the sky. And of how a poor boy named Finn (we all laugh at this) came across this tree while hunting for food one day in the woods and climbs to the sky to find a magical kingdom ruled by an evil giant. Now, this giant has kept the kingdom's true, good queen locked away in a gilded cage for many, many years. He tells us of how Finn finds this queen, so sad and lonely in her confinement. She requests of Finn to release her from her prison, and in repayment she gives him her jeweled locket. The problem; however, is the giant keeps the key to the cage on him at all times. Brave Finn waits until the giant falls asleep and then sneaks into the giant's pocket, looking for the key to release the queen, trying desperately not to awaken the giant. All the young'uns sitting at our feet squeal in fright as Tater, who had been pretending to be the sleeping giant, opens his eyes, jumps up on a tree stump, and booms out, "Ahoy! Ahoy! I smell the flesh of a foolish boy!"

Even the real Finn next to me jumps and grabs my arm in fright at this.

Our hero Finn succeeds in getting the key and freeing the queen, but the giant is furious at the boy and tries to stomp him into the ground. Tater builds up the excitement by describing the chase between Finn and the giant. Finn is running for his life, climbing down the tree as fast as he can, but the giant is on his heels. Halfway down, the boy yells to his ma to bring his ax and once on the ground starts hacking at the tree. Tater is by now acting it out, chopping at the air as if his life truly depended on it. The young'uns are all huddled together, terrified. I even find myself on edge a little, holding my breath, he's drawn me into the story so. I steal a sideways glance at Jax and am amazed to see his usual frown replaced by amusement as he watches Tater. Sky is huddled into Jax's arm as if she's terrified by the story. Snorting to myself in disgust, I turn away. Really? She's acting like one of the young'uns.

Finn nearly has the tree chopped through when the weight of the giant topples it the rest of the way, and the giant falls from the sky to the ground, creating a fierce hole so wide and deep into the earth that he disappears, never to be seen again. This hole eventually fills up from the rains and becomes what the settlers of old used to call an "ocean." As for Finn, the locket was a treasure indeed, and it gives him and his ma the means to live the rest of their lives happily, and fruitfully, ever after.

Tater stops talking, followed by a moment of electrified silence, before the whooping and clapping starts. It's so loud it echoes in my ears. Shouts of "Wonderful," and

"Magnificent," and, "Another. Another." Tater is soaking it up, smiling and bowing, but he shakes his head to another tale. Instead, he happily accepts a mug of ale from his rosy-cheeked companion and is content to let the music makers break into a lively dance step. *He is truly where he belongs,* I think as I watch someone supply him with a flute, and he joins in the music making, dancing a little jig as he plays.

I lounge with Vi by the fire, listening to the music and tapping my foot to the rhythm. Finn by now has had enough of sitting and is in among the throng of dancers. I catch glimpses of him every now and then as he swings by on the arm of someone, head tipped back and howling with laughter. It gladdens my heart to see him having so much fun. That's what young'uns were supposed to do, have fun.

Jax is among the many dancers as well. I see him and Sky swing by, hear their laughter. It doesn't seem right hearing that deep laughter coming from him. Definitely not a side of him I'm used to seeing. I've become accustomed to the sullen looks and glares of disgust, but Sky must truly bring out the best in him. I watch in puzzlement as many of the dancers' clap Jax on the back as they pass by or kiss Sky's cheek. It's almost as if they are congratulating them, but for what? Before I can ask Vi about this, the mob of dancers' swoop by and one of them falls out of the line, nearly landing in my lap. Laughingly, the young man gets to his feet and takes a little bow in my direction.

"Why are you not dancing, young miss? Come, dance with me."

"Oh no, I cain't," I say, shaking my head.

"Of course you can," says Vi, and she nudges my shoulder.

"Go. Have some fun."

"No ... no!" I say more insistently as the man yanks me to my feet. Instantly, I am whirled and spun about in every direction. The swarm of dancers crash in on me and then ebb out again like ripples in a pond. I swing from one arm to the next as the magical spell of the music flows over me, stirring my blood, awakening some deep-rooted need to just let loose. It's exhilarating, and the dancing surprisingly makes me feel so alive. My breathless laughter blends with the others as I grab the next person's hand, and I'm pulled into the crook of a strong arm. I look up into familiar blue eyes, and I'm shocked to see them devoid of any disapproval but filled with the pure joy of the moment. For a slight bit, we share in the delight of the dance as Jax holds me tight against his chest, and I stare into his face. I suddenly notice that he's shaved since our escape, and the missing stubble allows me to see the tiny hollow in his chin. Funny, I hadn't noticed that little dent before. I'm stunned at my sudden urge to reach up and touch it, but I fight against it and keep my hands firmly planted on his chest. I can feel his heart thumping through his thin tunic against the palm of my hand. He smiles at me then, a real, full-out smile that reaches his eyes and makes them appear bluer than the summer sky. My breath catches in my throat as a wave of heat spreads over me.

Time seems to stand still for a brief bit as the music and the laughter of the others fade into the background, surrounding us in our own little cocoon of silence. Like at this moment in time, we're the only two people in the world. That nothing else matters. But then the contact is broken, and I'm spun into the arms of the next dancer, surprised by the sharp twinge of loss.

That was it. Just a stupid little smile, but it leaves me more breathless than any dancing. Lightheaded and stumbling, I move away from the dancers and make my way back to the fire. Someone thrusts a mug into my hands, and I drink the foul-tasting ale down in big gulps. What the hell is wrong with me? It was just a stupid dance. Why is my heart doing these crazy little flip flops?

Puzzled by what I'm feeling and not wanting to make conversation with Vi or anybody else for that matter right now, I walk away from the bustling center and head towards the dark outskirts of the village. My head is spinning, and I need to get away and get some air.

I walk the dark path away from the ruckus until the quiet babbling of a little brook beckons me. I settle down beside it, letting the musical sound of its waters soothe me. Pulling my knees up, I cross my arms over them and close my eyes. I can still hear the laughter of the dancers and the music makers from afar and start humming along as they break into a chorus of "Sweet Sally." I tap my foot along with my humming. *Grada used to sing this,* I think as I smile to myself. The knife-sharp pain that always accompanies my thoughts of him comes swiftly, but it doesn't linger as much as it used to. It turns into more of a dull ache now. It kinda scares me because I'm afraid it means I'm starting to forget. I don't want to forget.

"Tara."

As lost in my thoughts as I am, the voice startles me and I jump. I look up as the shadowy figure of Jax approaches and blame my rapidly beating heart on my fright.

"I saw you walk away and figured this would be as good a time as any to talk to you."

He joins me at the brook and plops himself down on the sandy bank. I look at him expectantly as he settles beside me, but he doesn't say anything. I wait for a bit, the only sound between us is the music makers off in the distance and the gurgling waters.

"Well, the whole point of wantin' to talk is to actually say words," I mutter, breaking our silence.

He still doesn't look at me. He keeps staring at the flowing water.

"I know that. I just wanted ... I wanted to say thank you. As much as you don't want to hear about what you did, you saved our lives. You saved my life."

"Jax," I interrupt immediately. I don't want to talk about this right now. I'm not ready. I'm not ready to admit to anything that I supposedly did, but he's not finished.

"Shizen, you took a slug for me. It would have surely killed me, but you saved me. And for that, I am eternally in your debt."

I stare at him wide-eyed and gob-smacked at his admission. Who is this person? The Jax I've come to know would rather tangle with a wolfling than say thank you to me.

"Eternally, huh? That's a frightfully long time," I say finally, making light of his words. "That and a thank you all in the same conversation? You sure you ain't been into the ale, Jax? I mean, this ain't like you at all."

He looks at me then with this hard stare and no trace of the earlier smile.

"Why you gotta be like that?" he says.

"Like what?" I ask, baffled by his abrupt change.

"I'm trying to be serious here, and you're laughing at me."

"I ain't laughin'," I say, smothering my grin so he doesn't see it.

"Whatever, all I'm trying to say is thank you," he says again, and I nod.

"Well, you're welcome I guess," I reply, still trying to hold in my laugh. He truly is pricklier than a prickly bush. Maybe I'd be better off changing the topic of our conversation.

"You know, you never did tell me how you got captured in the first place. How did you end up in that raider's cage anyways?"

He shrugs at my question. "Stupid really. Was out on a hunting trip like I said, alone, and made the bad decision to go further into the mountains than I usually go. Should have known better, but game was so scarce, and I had promised some fresh meat for tonight's celebration. Before I realized it, I was a lot deeper into the mountains than I should have been. Reckoned I may as well spend the night and make my way back at first light. Made camp and settled in for the night. Next thing I know, I'm being awakened by a shooter poking into my gut and those bastards all around me."

I nod at his story. "Yeah, it pretty much happened that quick with us, too. Funny thing is, for the longest time I didn't know if I even believed raiders to be real. Ain't never seen them before. Tell you what though, now I know 'em to be real, I know I sure as hell don't wanna meet 'em again anytime soon," I say.

"Well I can certainly guarantee the raider's daughter

pretty much feels the same way about you," he chuckles, and I can't help but laugh along with his low laughter. Are we actually having a civilized conversation? Weird.

"Why do you think that mutie helped us escape?" he says then, and I shrug my shoulders at him.

"Dunno." I'm not sure if telling him what I think is such a good idea but I say it anyways. "I think … I think maybe it was followin' us. Followin' me. I think I seen it before, back out in the sand lands when I left Rivercross. Though why it was helpin' us I cain't say. Maybe it just felt sorry for us. Maybe it recognized me as a fellow mutie because that's what you believe of me, right?"

Don't know why I added that last part. We'd been talking all pleasant like, and I had to go and throw that up at him. Why'd I do that?

"It is what it is. Can't change the facts," he says, looking away from me like he doesn't want to talk any more.

We both fall quiet then, our moment of camaraderie gone. Jax tosses a few pebbles into the brook, the plops loud in the darkness. I can tell there's more he wants to say, but he doesn't say it.

"Sky seems very nice," I add finally just to break the silence. The uneasy quiet is getting to me.

"That she is," he agrees.

"And pretty, too. Her hair is lovely. I ain't ever seen hair that pretty," I say. I know I'm rambling on now, but I can't think of what else to talk about.

"I suppose so," he says.

"Is she … are you two …," I trail off; I don't know how to word it.

"She is my promised," he says then. My brow wrinkles, not sure what that means.

"Promised?"

"Aye. You know … promised. We'll be wedded someday when we're ready."

"Wedded? Wait," I say, starting to understand now, "your ma told me tonight was a betrothal celebration. Is this all for you and Sky?" He nods in response. "Shizen. Ain't you both a bit young for that?" I say, shocked, and not sure why, but a little put out at what I've just learned.

He looks at me, puzzled. "No. We've been promised since we were babes. Isn't Ben your promised?"

To hear him speak that name is like a punch to the gut. I wasn't expecting it, and I certainly wasn't aware he knew of it.

"How the hell do you know about Ben?" I whisper.

He shrugs and keeps tossing his pebbles. "When you were sick with the fever from your wound, you called out his name over and over again. It's all you would say. Drove us crazy. So I asked Finn. He told me all about it. How the Prezedant's Army took him and the other young folk, and how it was all you could think about was to get him back. I reckoned for you to care so much he must be your promised."

I don't know why, but his belief about Ben adds to my unexplainable irritation.

"Well, he ain't. I ain't got no promised. That's just downright craziness. Ben is my friend, my kin. And I gotta get him back just because."

I don't come right out and say because it was my fault he was taken in the first place, but I don't have to say it. It hangs in the air like a heavy weight between us.

"You know you don't stand a chance of getting him back," he says, finally making eye contact with me.

To hear him say those words aloud, it awakens all my own deep-rooted fears. I don't like it. "You best not say another word about it, Jax," I warn, but he doesn't give up.

"What you're thinking about doing, it's not going to work. Nobody gets away from the Prezedant."

"This really ain't none of your concern, Jax," I warn again, but he still doesn't heed me.

"You're going to end up getting yourself killed, maybe Finn and Tater, too. Is that what you want?"

Now I'm angry. Who's he to be saying stuff like that?

I snort at him, my voice harsh. "Why do you care what's gonna happen to me? I'm just a stinkin' New Blood, remember? A carrier of death just like Jenna. You shouldn't give a damn what happens to me."

I didn't intend to say her name, to throw it in his face, but it just pops out of me and from the look in his eyes, I regret it immediately. I'd gone too far. The kinder, nicer Jax who had smiled at me earlier is nowhere to be seen in the stone-cold glare I'm getting from him right now.

"I'm sorry … I shouldn't have said—"

He cuts me off. "Ma told you about her?" He doesn't give me a chance to answer. "Don't matter. I'm only gonna tell you this once. You know nothing about Jenna—or me for that matter—so you have no right to talk about it."

He gets to his feet as if to walk away, but I'm not done.

"Don't be mad at your ma. She was only tryin' to make me see reason. She knows what I am, what I'm capable of, and she don't care. The same with Jenna. She don't blame her because it wasn't her fault. She couldn't control what happened no more than you can control the sun settin' every day. What happened to the villagers, to your pa, it wasn't her fault."

He whirls on me then, and the anger emanates from him in waves. His hard, blue eyes bore into mine.

"You're right. It wasn't her fault. It was mine. I knew what she was, what she was becoming, and I didn't say anything. I had seen the things she was capable of doing. I knew, but I didn't tell Ma or Pa. I should have said something, anything, and maybe we could have run. We could have hid out in the sand lands so nobody would have known. Nobody would have found us. But I didn't. I stayed quiet, let it happen. Pa, Jenna, the villagers … they were all killed that day because I just didn't want to admit it. I didn't want to admit that my little sister was a mutie … a freak."

I can tell he regrets his words right away. He closes his eyes and sighs, runs a hand through his dark hair. I don't say anything; I just watch as he struggles to get himself back under control. I want to tell him I understand how he feels. I understand because I carry that same kind of guilt around with me every day. But I don't. I stay quiet. Finally, back in control, he looks at me straight on. The anger, the fire, is gone, and his voice is emotionless when he speaks again.

"Look, I'm just going to come right out and say what I came here to say in the first place. Thank you for saving my life. As I've said, it's a debt I can never repay. But you and Finn and Tater … you have to leave Gray Valley as soon as possible. Every moment you stay here, you are putting us all in danger, and I can't … I won't have anything happen to the people I love again because of some New Blood. Ma says you're almost healed. Traveling should be no issue. So, I want you all gone by the morning, before anyone else finds out what you are. There's no place for you here."

Whatever I was expecting him to say, it surely wasn't this. Shocked and hurt, I watch his rigid back walk away from me as he disappears into the shadows. I want to yell after him the few choice words floating around in my head right now, but I don't. I keep quiet. My hands clench at my sides, and I take my frustration out on the nearest object I can find: a rock about the size of a wild rabbit. I kick at it, wanting to release some of the hurt and betrayal I'm feeling inside, but all it does is send shooting pain up my leg and into my gut.

I don't hold back with the cuss words this time. I let them fly at the night sky.

Fine. Good. If that's how he wants it, so be it. We're wasting time here anyways in this stupid village. No big deal. I want to leave anyway, so there. As a matter of fact, I can't wait to leave. What the hell am I doing here anyways in this stupid dress and dancing to that stupid music? I have important things to do. I have to find Ben and the young'uns. I don't have time for this foolishness.

Mind made up, I head for Vi's cabin. I've some things to do first though, like finding me some decent clothes. The least he could do is give me a pair of trousers in exchange for saving his life, the ungrateful jackass. And I need to let Finn and Tater know we're leaving. Good riddance, too. The morning can't get here fast enough. And if I never ever see Jax or Gray Valley again as long as I live, it would still be too soon.

CHAPTER 6

Iron Bones

———◆———

I was real surprised at the lack of arguing on Finn and Tater's part at the news of our leaving. I had expected some resistance to my decision, but they'd just simply nodded and agreed to what I said. Tater had even gone as far to say, "No worries, my dear; our imminent departure is understandable and totally predictable. It was truly fun while it lasted, but I never was one to delay when something had to be done. As my dear mother would say, 'never let the grass grow under your feet.'"

I figured that meant he was okay with it. And as for Finn, well, I reckon I could have told him we were going to the moon and he just would have asked how long it was going to take us to get there. The only one who seemed to have any trouble with us leaving was Vi. She truly seemed upset with my telling her. She had questioned my decision. Didn't I think it was too soon? Shouldn't I take more time to heal completely? Did Jax have anything to do with my decision? As much as that mule turd didn't deserve any loyalty from me, I didn't rat on him to his ma. She needed him, and to know that I had caused any strife between them was not okay by me. So, I had told her the decision was mine and mine alone. She wasn't happy with it, but she did accept it. And being a woman of her word, waiting for me in the morning was a clean pair of trousers and a tunic all fitted for me. She must have worked long into the night to finish it. I'm truly touched by her gesture and find myself wishing I could stay longer, to get to know this remarkable woman better. Quickly, I squash this thought. As much as I hate to admit it to myself, Jax was right. I would never be able to live with myself if any harm came to Vi or anybody in the village because of me. There truly was no place for me here. I ignore the little voice in my head questioning if there was any place for me anywhere and focus on getting dressed.

The sun is barely up yet, but Vi must have already been up for hours getting everything prepared. She has waiting for us slingbags filled with supplies, food, and water, all packed neatly onto Winnie and another horse, one I don't recognize. I question the gifts and the horse. It's too much. We can't take so much from them, but she assures me the trade made for it had been a good one. The villager she'd traded with had gladly taken Busher's hardy beast in exchange for the older nag and the supplies. Hearing that lessens my concern some.

She then hands me a hunting knife in a real leather sheath and all. It was her husband's, she tells me, and to go ahead and take it. I feel real guilty, but since losing all our own stuff to the raiders, I know we're going to need it. I secure it to my leg and try to thank her, but she's not done. Stepping in front of me, she folds a soft cloth over my head, covering my hair, and then loops it loosely around my neck. A neck wrapper. Of all the gifts, this one is my undoing. It reminds me of Grada, and I can feel the tears filling up my eyes as her lips gently brush my forehead.

"Remember what I said, child. You have a great gift, do not waste it. And if you ever find yourself in need of a safe haven, we will always have shelter for you here."

If only that were true, I think, but I know I'll never see her again. I could never put her in any danger, this woman I barely know, but who has touched my heart so deeply. I hug her real tight and whisper a thank you in her ear. The words sound so inadequate for all she's done. I wish I could express to her my gratitude, but as usual, the words don't come. I find I don't have to say anything though, because it's like she can see straight through me, right into my heart and sees what I'm feeling. She just nods at me and smiles. She says her goodbyes to Finn and Tater, and I half-listen but my eyes are seeking, looking for him. Jax is nowhere to be seen though. He doesn't even have the decency to see us off. It doesn't surprise me none, but I can't help but be a little hurt by it. We'd been through a lot in our short time together. I'd even saved his life, but obviously it wasn't enough for him to even wish us a safe journey. Oh, well. Maybe it's a good thing he isn't here. Can't rightly say if I would have just said goodbye or told him to go straight to Hell. Though the way I'm feeling right now, it probably would be the latter. Sky is welcome to the jackass.

Vi keeps waving as she watches us ride off, and I keep looking back until she's nothing but a little speck in the distance. Finally, I can't see her no more, and I stop looking back. *He never came,* the little nagging voice in the back of my head keeps saying. He doesn't care about any of us. I quell the hurt and push it away. It was done.

Gray Valley is way off Tater's usual trading route, so the territory we find ourselves traveling in is unfamiliar to all of us. Vi had told us that Littlepass was likely no further than a couple weeks of riding, but she'd failed to mention anything of the strange lands we would have to pass through. Maybe she was truly unaware, or maybe she had simply forgotten, but after a day of riding through valleys and slopes, we'd come across a much unexpected, strange sort of track cut through the rocky hills.

The path is wide and level … and old. Settler-made to be sure. The parts of it not cracked and overgrown with weeds is a strange combination. It isn't rock nor metal. Nothing I could put a name to. Tater said he believed it had once been called a "highway," and that these highways were how the settlers' veacals had traveled around. He said that the highways went on for leagues and leagues. I find it amazing that the settlers had been able to build such things. They must have had a lot of time on their hands for sure. The track goes on into the horizon as far as the eye can see. I wonder how far it goes. Will it take us all the way to Littlepass? I reckon we'll find out soon enough.

We keep riding; Tater's occasional singing the only sound in the deserted stretch of open ground other than the clip clop of the animals' hooves. We talk some, play a few riddle games to pass the time, but we avoid any mention of New Bloods or our run-in with the Army. It still isn't something I'm willing to talk about.

Sometimes a wolfling or some other creature I can't put a name to picks up our scent, and they follow along with us on the outskirts, tracking us almost. But it only takes a warning growl from Cat or a shot from one of our iron shooters to scare them off. I'm real glad Tater had saved the shooters and had been smart enough to barter for some slugs for them. I've a feeling they're going to be well-needed out here.

We stop only long enough to sleep, making camp in the sandy ditches that run along the sides of the "highway." We don't bother with making campfires. Besides the fact that there's no kindling to be found, I get the uneasy feeling it would just draw attention to us. Like we'd be making ourselves a target. I can't say why I feel this way; other than the critters, we haven't seen anything else moving out here.

We take turns on watch throughout the night, Cat as our companion. Our shooters may scare off the critters during the day, but that doesn't mean they won't try and sneak up on us in the dark. Sometimes when I'm sitting and watching over the others, my blanket covering my shoulders to keep the night's chill at bay, I turn my face into the wind and I swear I can all but smell the creatures that occupy this land. It's a blended odor of dirty fur and fresh shite, and the clarity of it, of my awareness, spooks me. It says to me I'm changing. To what, I'm not sure. But I don't say a word to Tater and

Finn. How can I explain it to them when I don't understand myself?

—•—

Five days we've been traveling. Quiet and uneventful days. Days so full of boredom it's almost an effort at times to keep from falling asleep as we ride and falling off our nags. But on this day, mid-noon of the sixth day, we pass over the top of a rise and see an astonishing sight.

It stands in the distance, a massive shape against the blue, mid-morning sky. I pull my nag up short, and Tater pulls abreast of me on Winnie. Finn, who has been resting quietly against my back, pokes his head around me to see what has stopped our travel.

"What is that?" he whispers, but I don't have an answer since I'm not quite sure what it is. I can make out two sets of tall, metal towers, one set at each end of the structure. Between them hang a few gigantic ropes or wires … some sort of material joining them together though there are mainly just gaps and holes and empty air since most of it has already crumbled away. The broken, fallen pieces are piled high underneath the span in the remains of a dried-up riverbed. Realization of what it is comes from the riverbed— or more so what it *had* been at one time. It's on a much bigger scale, but it's the same kind of structure the old folks had built in Rivercross for crossing the river. It's a bridge. But it hadn't been built by anybody in my lifetime or dozens of lifetimes before mine. It was a true settler's relic and still standing. Amazing.

Tater is the first to speak. "This is not good."

"What is it, Tater? Is it dangerous?" Finn says, showing more interest than he has in days.

"Course it ain't, Finn," I say. "It's just an old bridge the settlers used for crossing the river that used to run here. We can just cross the dry riverbed, Tater. It's not a big deal."

He raises one of his shaggy brows at me. "It's not the bridge, dear girl, that has me worried. It's what's on the other side."

For the first time, I see what Tater is seeing. Off in the distance on the horizon are the rusted, iron skeletons of sky towers. The dead remains of a settler's city. Just like in the old folk tales.

It was vast, bigger than anything I'd ever imagined, spread far into the landscape. Would probably take days to go around, days we can't afford to lose. As amazed as I am at the sight in front of me, I understand what has Tater so concerned. Out here in the open lands, you can at least see the dangers approaching, but in there, in the midst of all those ruins, dangers could be hidden anywhere. Critters, raiders, anything could be waiting for us. But we haven't come this far to stop now. And we're not wasting any more time. We're going through.

"Let's go," I say.

I nudge my horse but don't get far before Tater calls after me.

"Tara, think about this. Trust me; I am just as eager to reach Littlepass as you are, my dear, maybe even more so, but this is foolhardy. We have no idea what to expect in there. I have avoided areas like this my whole life. These dead cities are aptly named for a reason," he warns.

"Maybe Tater is right," Finn joins in hesitantly. "Maybe we should go around—"

"No, Finn, we're not goin' around," I snap at the boy, and I can feel him stiffen behind my back. "I ain't goin' around; I'm goin' through. We've wasted enough time already. The longer I take to get to Littlepass, the colder Ben's trail becomes. You and Tater can do what you want … I won't stop you. But let me remind you; you both hitched yourself onto me and slowed me down, so now this is my decision. I'm goin' through. It's just a bunch of stupid empty ruins. So make your choice. You can go your separate ways or stay with me but decide now."

Finn doesn't speak, but the scrawny arms that encircle my waist give me his answer. Squashing down the guilt I feel at snapping at him, I nudge the horse again and start moving. I don't look back to see if Tater is following, but the incessant muttering and grumbling I hear behind me makes me fully aware of his presence and his feelings about the whole idea. So be it.

We reach the city by late afternoon. It had been a bit of a struggle to get the animals up over the riverbank, but the gods had been on our side and we had stumbled onto a slope leading out of the dry riverbed. Whether it had been the wind or other travelers who had made it, only the gods knew, but it had come in real handy.

The road we've been traveling carries on through the city, overgrown and full of deep craters but still passable. We're going to have to be careful with the animals though. Can't risk having one of them stepping in a hole and breaking its leg. We'll have to lead them through.

The rusted remains of the sky towers line both sides of the road, looming above us like menacing overseers. They're mostly destroyed, just bare bones left really, but it makes me wonder what could have brought down such massive structures. Was it the great war like in the old folks' tales or just the ravages of time? And what happened to all the people that had lived here? Taken down by sickness? Eaten by critters? Dead from drought? Were they all lying here, rotted away under our feet, or had they been forced to move on? Reckon we'll never know, but I can't help but speculate.

Different sized mounds dot the landscape, all that's left of the buildings that had crumbled away ages ago and had been covered by the sand and grass and earth. Once majestic structures now nothing more than rubble under our feet, their secrets long hidden by the passing of time. It was kinda sad, really.

Numerous other roads branch off from the one we're on and weave through the rusted bones, dark and spooky looking, but there's no way in hell we're going to stray from the main road and travel those. We're going to try and stick to the open the best we can. It seems the safest bet.

The city is dead quiet. No sound other than the sighing of the wind through the sky towers and our own terrified wheezing. Cat slinks along beside us, her head twisting in the breeze, catching scents of things we can't—and possibly don't want to—know about. The quiet is nerve-rattling, and I find my hand hovering over the butt of my shooter. I know it's just my imagination, but I can't help but feel we're being watched. Like at this very moment there are countless eyes watching our passage through the dead city. Maybe it's just the ghosts of the settlers long gone, but even that thought doesn't make me feel any better. At least a critter or a mutie you could bring down with an iron shooter.

A loud shrieking erupts to the right, scaring me something fierce, and the shooter is in my hand before I recall moving. I duck instinctively as a black cloud sails past my head and disappears down the path to the other side of us. My heart thumps frantically in my chest, but I'm real glad the scream on my lips doesn't escape because I feel kind of foolish now seeing as it's just a bunch of crows. Our intruding on their territory must have scared them off. Cat takes chase after the birds, but I don't bother to call her back. I know she won't go far. I look up at Finn, who's still riding the nag, and grin at him in relief. He grins back, though I can tell from his eyes his fright had been just as bad as mine. It's good to see his smile. It tells me he's forgiven me for yelling at him earlier. It eases some of my guilt. Tater is holding a hand to his chest, not bothering to hide his fear, his face pale and ashen.

"Oh, dear me, that was rather disconcerting. But as my dear mother would say, 'Fright makes the wolfling appear bigger than he is.' Truer words were never spoken."

I've come to realize that Tater tended to prattle on the more scared he was. Hope we don't come across any more crows; we don't need to hear any more of his "wise sayings."

I grab the nag's reins and give her nose a reassuring rub as she snorts nervously. The crows had startled her, too. These iron bones have put us all on edge. Hope it doesn't take us too long to get through. I give a slight tug to get her moving again, but we don't get more than two paces before a howling pierces the air and roots us all in place.

"Cat!" Finn yells, and just like the boy, I know right away her wailing is one of pain. In the blink of an eye he's down off the horse, and I grab him by the scruff of his tunic before he can run. I know what he's planning. He struggles against me, but I hand him over to Tater.

"Stay here. The both of you. Tater, make sure he doesn't follow me," I call over my shoulder.

Pulling my shooter I run in the direction of the wailing, ignoring the words the boy is hurling at my back. From the sounds of it, Tater had heeded me and is physically containing the boy, and he doesn't like it one bit. But I can't be worrying about Finn trailing me. Something has Cat howling and it probably isn't anything good.

The path between the building husks is dark and narrow. I hesitate and try to adjust to the dim light. I peer into the dark, but all I can see is dirt mounds and empty road. No sign of Cat. I'm going to have to go in deeper. Taking a few deep breaths to steady myself, I step into the darkness, my shooter firmly gripped in my hand.

I make my way between the crumbling relics, looking around swiftly, making sure nothing is trying to sneak up on me. I don't hear Cat no more, but I can still hear Finn's yelling. The boy is going to wake the dead with his fool shouting. Slowly I creep through, pausing every few steps to look around. Still nothing. I make my way to the corner where another road crosses the one I'm on. *It's like a maze,* I think. Roads and tracks everywhere. I peer past the corner, steeling myself for attack. All I find is Cat, lying on her stomach. She looks like she's gnawing on something, but I can't see what it is.

"Cat," I whisper loudly, and she looks back at me, a miserable wail erupting as she spots me. Slowly I approach, still waiting for something to jump out at me. Finding it clear, I hunch over her and push her big head out of the way. Her front paw is caught in some sort of steel snare. A trap. There's blood on her fur, and I can tell the teeth of the trap have sunk in good. I pray there isn't too much damage done to her paw.

"It's okay ... it's okay girl," I keep whispering to her, rubbing her panting side and studying the thing. At first, I don't notice the fresh bird carcass lying just past her head and the rope tying it to the trap. But at seeing it, my blood runs cold. This was no random accident. Someone had laid this trap deliberately and recently. That meant we are not the only souls in amongst these iron bones. This realization hits me at the same time as the silence. Finn's yelling had stopped. The dead quiet scares me more than anything, and I bolt upright.

"I'm sorry, Cat," I whisper urgently. "I'll come back for you. I promise."

It's like she understands my fear for the boy, and she licks my hand giving me permission to leave her. I high tail it back the way I'd come, berating myself for falling for their ploy. Whoever had done this had split us up on purpose, and I'd fallen for it like a fool. Fearing for what I will find, I emerge onto the main road, and my fears are painfully justified.

I take it all in in an instant. There are two of them waiting for my return, and another two holding wicked-looking knives to my companions' throats to keep them from yelling out a warning. But I don't fall into their hands as easily as they would like. At the sight of the iron shooter rock steady in my hand and pointing straight at their chests, the two hurrying my way bring up short and we eyeball each other for a bit.

I can't quite tell if they're men or muties. The one closest to me is wearing a filthy, red wrapper tied around his head, and the ends hang down his back like a braid. Tiny, white bones dangle from holes in his ears, and what appears to be an actual small skull hangs around his neck. His tunic and trousers are a filthy patchwork of different colors and cloths like he had sewn together the remnants of others' clothing. There are reddish, crusted sores covering his face and arms, some of them open and festering, running with pus. He smiles at me then, and I can see his blackened gums and rotted teeth. He could be twenty, thirty, or fifty born years. I can't tell. But the blade he holds in his hand could probably rip me open from belly to breastbone in a flash; I can tell that much.

"Well, whadda we got 'ere? A lovely little ducky … wot? Look at the ducky, Beanie. Ain't she a lovely ducky?" he calls over his shoulder.

"Aye, Talbert. A lovely ducky … lovely ducky," the other answers in a singsong tone and then starts howling with laughter like it's the funniest thing he's ever said. That laughter echoes with madness and adds to my growing fear. Dangerous I can handle, but crazy is a whole other story.

I gulp hard a couple of times, trying to swallow the huge lump blocking my throat.

"Let my companions go," I say finally, finding my voice.

I'm amazed it only cracks slightly. "And I promise not to shoot you."

The one called Talbert takes an exaggerated step back from me and looks around in fake wonder.

"Wot? Ya 'ear that, Beanie? She ain't gonna shoot us if we let the others go. I think the ducky is threatenin' us, Beanie. Wot you think?"

"Aye, sounds like a threat to me alright, Talbert," he says and snickers some more like he's enjoying himself.

My fear threatens to overtake me, but I push it down. I can't afford to show them any fear. Finn and Tater's lives probably depend on my actions right now; I'm going to have to play this smart.

"I'm only gonna say this once more. Let us go. You can have some of our supplies. But let all three of us pass without harm, and I will let you live," I say.

The Talbert creature grins at me again and rubs his thumb along the sharp edge of his blade. I don't know if the cut is on purpose or not, but he doesn't show any flicker of pain. He merely puts the bleeding thumb to his mouth and licks away the blood, never taking his eyes off me for a second.

"The ducky does 'ave a big shooter fer certain. Could even be a threat to us, Beanie. Wot's to stop us from killin' the two yonder then the ducky an' takin' everthing fer ourselves, eh?"

"What's to stop us?" Beanie echoes then puts a fist to his mouth to stop his maniacal laughter.

I shrug my shoulders at him, keeping the rock-hard lump of fear in my gut hidden.

"I suppose you could kill those two," I say.

I hear Tater's indignant, "Here now!" but I don't look his

way.

"And between the four of you, you may be able to take me down, but not before I can put a slug between your eyes and blow your ugly head from your shoulders. You wanna take that chance … Talbert?"

I pray he don't heed my bluff. My insides are shaking something fierce and feels like I'm going to retch any second, but my hand holding the shooter doesn't waver, not a bit. He studies me for a moment, assessing how much of a threat I may be. Then his grave face turns to cackling laughter, making him sound just as crazy as the other one.

"She's a lively ducky, wot, Beanie? Lotta spirit. I like that. I do. Tell ya wot, ducky. Me an' Bean 'ere, we's reasonable chaps. We'll make ya a trade, we will. We'll let ya pass. Aye, we will. Just give us yer supplies an' yer nags, an' ya can go on yer merry way. No trouble, no fuss. Ya won't 'ave to worry about us."

Beanie's high-pitched howl makes me jump some, and I tense for him to attack, but he's just laughing uncontrollably and whacking himself in the head.

"No fuss … no worrying 'bout us. Yer a poet you is, Talbert. A poet!" he says, wheezing between whacks.

Shizen. How much more crazy can I take? I shake my head no, hoping they don't notice the sweat beading my forehead.

"You can take the horse and two bags of supplies. We keep the mule and the water skins, and the two of you get to keep your heads," I say, hoping my threat is as forceful as I mean it to be. The Talbert one tosses his knife a couple of times, thinking hard and ignoring his companion's impatient, "Tell her, Talbert … tell her!"

The silence seems to stretch on. No sound comes from Finn or Tater, but I don't dare look to see if they're okay. I get the feeling one moment of inattention is all Talbert would need to pounce on me.

"You drive a 'ard bargain, ducky. Tell ya wot. I'll let ya keep the mule, but in exchange, ya leave us the boyo. You see, Beanie 'ere … well, he likes the young'uns, an 'e ain't 'ad a playmate fer quite some time now. 'E may look full grown, but 'e ain't quite grown in the 'ead. Know wot I mean?"

I hear Finn's gasp at the offer before Beanie's howling laughter drowns him out. Just knowing the boy is so scared starts the anger flowing. How dare these lowlifes, these horrible wretches, try and barter for Finn! The evilness of the situation, of these creatures, it surrounds us like a dark cloud … smothering, suffocating. I suddenly understand again what Grada and the old folk of Rivercross had tried to do: protect us from this all-consuming evil that seemed to cover the lands on this side of the mountains. How did creatures like this standing in front of me come to be? What had made them this way? And how dare they even suggest I leave Finn in their vile hands? There's no way in hell that's going to happen.

The coldness of the iron shooter in my hand that used to scare me comforts me now, like it's a part of me. I realize we're not going to come to an agreement. This is a game to them. They're playing with me, and it's going to end badly. I raise the shooter so that it's aimed straight for Talbert's head, confident I will not miss when the time comes.

"Bargainin' is over, jackass. This is how it's gonna be. You let my companions go right now, and you walk away with nuthin' but your lives, and that's bein' damn generous on my part."

All traces of humor disappear from their faces now at knowing I'm onto them. I didn't think it possible, but the sneer on the creature's black lips makes his face even uglier. But it's his eyes that scare me more so. They're no more human than the wolflings or other creatures we had chased off these past few days. They're no different. They are predators, and we are their prey. Only I'm not going down without a fight.

Then the Talbert one winks at me cheekily, all smiles again, distracting me from the wicked blade he's holding out in front of his chest in a fighting stance.

"'Ave it yer way, ducky, but choose wisely. You gonna save the boy? The old man? Or yerself? Ya cain't get us all. Yer shooter cain't—"

"Er … Talbert …," Beanie interrupts, but the other man ignores him and goes right on talking.

"My men, they're gonna kill yer companions the minute ya move at—"

"Talbert," Beanie says again, and I watch in astonishment as the ugly creature drops his knife and turns to him, totally disregarding me.

"Really, Beanie? Wot is so important that you 'ave to interrupt me eh? Wot? Cain't ya see I 'ave business with the ducky 'ere? Wot 'ave I told ya 'bout interruptin' me, eh?"

Beanie looks terrified at Talbert's outburst, but he points tentatively with one of his purplish fingers, and we both turn to look in the intended direction. I'm not prepared for what I see. Talbert's men are now the ones kneeling on the ground, Finn and Tater holding their own knives on them. But that's not all. Talbert finds himself looking down the barrel of another shooter, only this one is held steadily by none other than Jax.

What the hell is Jax doing here?

"If I were you, freak show, I'd take the girl up on her offer and walk away with your lives since it's a damn better offer than you'll get from me."

Unlike me, Talbert don't show any sign of surprise at Jax's unexpected presence. He merely looks from Jax, to me then back to Jax and then, surprisingly, gives a little bow and puts his knife back into his sheath. He smiles at us like he never just threatened our lives.

"Looks like I 'ave been outsmarted, now, 'aven't I? But we're not simple chaps, are we, Beanie? We know when the jig is up an' when to walk away. Come along, boys. Our little adventure is over."

The two on the ground don't need to be told twice. They scramble to their feet and scurry away like rats to disappear amongst the dark ruins. Talbert, however, takes his time, ambling away from us and whistling cheerfully into the wind. He don't even bother to look back at us, not the least bit concerned we might just shoot him in the back. Beanie follows, but not as trusting. He doesn't take his eyes off of us, still laughing like a maniac until they, too, disappear into the darkness of the rusted bones. We stand there for a bit, the four of us, sweeping the area, making sure they're not about to double back on us and try to attack again. I don't even notice I'm holding my breath until it comes out in one big sigh of relief. It's over.

"Jax!" Tater's yell startles me so fierce that I nearly drop my shooter. "My dear boy. I have never been so relieved to see anyone in my life." He does his strange little clap and then smacks Jax on the back so hard he causes him to stumble.

"I must admit I truly did see my life flash before my eyes, but your timely arrival and ensuing heroics have certainly saved the day. Just like one of my tales. As a matter of fact, this will indeed become one of my tales and one of my finest to be sure."

Don't know why Tater is gushing on so. I had everything under control. We didn't need saving by Jax. And what the hell is he doing here anyways? Last I seen of him, he couldn't wait to be rid of us. Why had he followed us? I ignore Tater's withering comment of, "Hmph. Stupid empty ruins indeed. Famous last words." I want to know why Jax is here. But before I can ask anything, Finn's tortured question of, "Cat?" draws my attention.

"She's okay, Finn. No need to fuss. Got herself caught in a little trap is all." The boy's face sags with relief at hearing his beast is in no immediate danger.

"We need to go get her, but we're gonna all have to stick together. I don't trust those creatures, not one little bit. Finn, Tater, follow me with the nags. I ain't leavin' them behind for the taking. Jax, since you're here, you can make yourself useful and bring up the rear, watch our backs. I got a feelin' we haven't seen the last of those crazies."

Cat is just as I left her. Seeing her lying there, hurt, Finn runs to her and wraps his arms around her furry neck. She rubs her head against the boy, mewling a little but doesn't resist when I go to work on prying the teeth of the trap open with my knife. I release it enough so as Finn can pull her paw out. The steel teeth had broken the skin some, and her fur is matted with blood. Gingerly, I probe her paw a bit, but I can tell there's no bones broken.

"Her injuries can easily be treated with some maloe leaves," I tell Finn, easing the worry on his face. Lucky for her, the trap had been meant for a much smaller animal. She gets to her feet and takes a few test steps. She limps some, but at least it looks like she's still able to walk. She hobbles to Finn and starts licking his face, and the boy's laughter is tinged with relief.

"Enough with the reunion, people. We have to move. It's going to be dark soon, and I don't want to be in crazy territory when the sun goes down."

Jax is right. We'd best move, get through the city as quick as we can. My questions at Jax's presence are going to have to wait.

The city is still as quiet and calm as when we first entered it, but I know now that there are indeed eyes watching our progress, and it's no ghosts. We walk single file, me at point, Finn and Tater following with Winnie and the horses, and Jax bringing up the rear. We can't see them, but occasionally Cat catches a scent and raises her head to snarl at the darkened building husks. They're there all right, following us, just waiting for their chance. I keep my shooter in my hand, ready and waiting for the slightest movement.

Sometimes we walk for a bit, and Cat doesn't seem to sense them any more, and I think they've finally given up. But then I hear the faint laughter coming out of the dark ruins or a low, singsong "lovely ducky," and I know they are torturing us. It's like some game to them, and I can't help but wonder how many other poor souls had been stalked through this place of death, frightened and terrified. I grip my shooter tighter and keep walking, trying to see into the ever-growing shadows. I don't want to think about what will happen if we're trapped in here after dark. Those crazy bastards know this city like the back of their hand, I reckon. They will truly have the advantage over us in the darkness.

We walk until the sun is nothing but a red glow settling over the city, but still we're not through. My worst fears are coming true; we're going to be in here after nightfall. I peer ahead, trying to see if there is any end to this stretch of road, but all I see is a seemingly endless line of iron skeletons. Hiding places for our pursuers. I stop walking, and Finn brings up short behind me. He's quickly joined by Tater and Jax. Jax don't take his ever-searching eyes off the ruins around us, but his question is directed at me.

"Why are you stopping? What's wrong?"

"We're not gonna make it through before dark," I say. "I don't think it's a good idea to be travelin' this road after nightfall. We're too exposed. Maybe we should take shelter in one of the ruins. You know, get some walls around us, so they cain't jump us unawares."

He still doesn't look at me, but he shakes his head, disagreeing. "No, we can't risk it. There isn't anywhere we can hide that they won't find us."

"I don't think they're followin' us no more, Jax," says Finn. "I ain't heard 'em for a while now, and Cat ain't been growlin'. I think they gave up. And 'sides, I think Cat needs to rest. She's limpin' real bad."

"No, we aren't stopping, Finn. Now, keep moving." Jax snapping at Finn only reminds me that I'd already done so earlier in the day, and it adds to my agitation.

"That wasn't called for, Jax. There's no need to yell at the boy. Besides, I agree with him. And who made you leader anyways? Nobody asked for you to follow us and get involved. We were doin' fine on our own. We didn't need your help," I say.

"You didn't need my help? You didn't need …?" he breaks off like his surprise is too much to even express. "Well, excuse me for saving your miserable hides back there. If it weren't for me, you'd all be carved up like roasted hogs right about now," he says, finally looking at me even if it is just a stone-cold glare.

I shake my head in disbelief at his words. That's what he thinks? He actually thinks he saved us?

"If it weren't for you, we wouldn't be in this predicament in the first place." I growl. "You were the one who dragged us off to your gods-forsaken village and then drove us out to travel unprepared through this awful place."

"Ahem, actually, Tara, it was you who insisted we go through—"

"Shut up, Tater." I yell at the half-man, but I don't bother to look his way. My anger stays focused on Jax.

"And what the hell you doin' followin' us, anyways? You wanted us as far away from you and your precious villagers as soon as possible, but then you followed us. You ask me, I think you're as bat shite crazy as the rest of 'em here." I know I'm shouting, and it probably isn't the smartest thing but I can't help myself.

"Er … perhaps this is not the appropriate time for this conversation,"Tater interjects again with a nervous fluttering of his hands, but Jax merely brushes past him, almost knocking him over.

He stares down his nose at me. But he don't scare me none with his frosty glare. "I followed you because as much as it irks me to admit it, I am in your debt. Since I always repay my debts, I have decided to make sure you make it safely to Littlepass … all of you. Then, I will no longer owe you anything, and what you decide after that is up to you. You can all run off and get yourselves captured by the Army or killed by the Prezedant or whatever, but I at least will have a clear conscience."

Shizen. I can't believe he just said that. He really doesn't give a damn what happens to any of us. His only reason for following after us was so he could have a clear conscience? He truly was a mule turd of the worst kind. All the anger and bitterness I've been feeling ever since he kicked us out of Gray Valley comes bubbling up.

"We don't need your help, Jax." My words are pure ice. "And if there's any imagined debt you think you owe me, then as of this moment, I release you from it. You don't owe me anything, so go. We don't need or want you with us."

"Tara." Finn objects to my words, and I can tell I'm scaring him, but I don't care.

"We don't need him, Finn. We're fine on our own. Besides, we've had nuthin' but trouble ever since we met him," I say to the boy, but my eyes don't leave the object of my anger.

"Stop your squabbling, the both of you!" I've never heard Tater so angry and to hear that booming voice come out of that little body is real surprising. Whatever Jax is about to say dies on his lips as we both turn to the little man in astonishment.

"What the hell is wrong with you two? Don't you think we have much more pressing matters than your exasperation with each other? In case you two halfwits haven't noticed, the sun has gone down. We're standing in the middle of the road in pitch black, and you two have been making so much noise that a herd of elephants could sneak up on us and we would never hear them. Now, I for one do not wish to be captured again by that foul-smelling, putrid little gang of degenerates, so make a decision. What are we doing? Moving on or making camp but decide at least."

As much as I'm itchin' to yell more at the moron standing in front of me, Tater is right. And I hadn't even noticed the sun had finally set. This is not good. As Tater said, we need to make a decision and fast. Before any decision is agreed upon, that maniacal laughter starts up again, sending chills down my spine. We had dropped our guard, and no doubt the crazies had taken advantage to sneak up on us. Stupid! Angry at myself for being distracted, I make a call.

"Head for that buildin' on the right. If we can get—"

Thunk.

At first, I can't tell where the noise has come from, and I spin around in a circle. What was that? Then I see Jax's wide-eyed look of stunned confusion as blood starts seeping from the side of his head. He raises his hand and touches his temple where the rock had hit him, wobbles a bit, and then falls hard to his knees. He loses his grip on his shooter as he needs both hands to hold himself up from sprawling in the dirt. A whizzing sound past my right ear warns me that I'm pretty close to meeting Jax's fate, so I duck. They're attacking us with rocks? What the hell?

"Finn, Tater, get behind that wall now." I yell, heading for Jax, who by now has lost his battle with consciousness, and is out cold on the ground. Grabbing his arms, I start dragging him but don't get no more than two paces when I hear Finn's panicked cry of, "Let me go!"

My heart leaps into my throat as I see the boy kicking and struggling against Beanie, who has him pulled tight to his chest with one arm, trying to drag him off. Cat makes a run for the boy, her growling louder than the boy's screaming, but from out of nowhere two more of the creatures appear holding long, wickedly sharp spears. She tries to get past them, but they're too quick, and one of them manages to jab her in her side. She howls in pain but don't give up. She goes after the boy again, but they block her at every turn.

"Sorry, Jax," I mutter as I drop him back in the dirt, abandoning him for now. I pull my shooter as I run, knowing it's the only hope of saving Finn. But by now, the horses and mule are panicked and running in front of me, blocking my view. Where are they? I can still hear his screaming, but I can't see him. I dodge between the animals just in time to see the Beanie creature dragging him into one of the ruins. My panic is almost overwhelming. I have to get to him because I somehow know if Beanie manages to get him deep into that maze of ruins, I won't stand a chance in hell of finding him again.

I run, so intent on getting to them I don't even see the Talbert creature tackling me from the side. He rams into me with the force of a rockslide, taking me completely off my feet before we come crashing down into the unforgiving, hard ground. I land on my back, my breath knocked clean out of me, the weight of the creature pressing down on my chest. His hate-filled face hovers above mine, and I can smell the rotted meat stench of his breath causing the bile to rise in the back of my throat.

My clawed hands reach for his eyes, ready to tear his festering skin from its bones, but he is stronger than I think, and he quickly pins both my hands above my head.

"Did ya really think ya wuz gonna beat me at my own game now, ducky? Wot? Ya think ya's smarter than ol' Talbert? Ducky none and Talbert one. Tra la la la la."

His black lips stretch wide in a smiling grimace, and I realize at that moment I am staring into the face of true madness.

"Aarrgh!" The scream that bursts out of me is pure frustration. I need to get to Finn. I need to get this crazy bastard off me. I lift my head, smacking it hard into his face, causing a ringing to reverberate in my ears. Blood spurts from his damaged nose, but he doesn't loosen his grip on me. He don't even stop smiling. That grinning skull above me … Finn's cries for help … It infuriates me. Almost with relief, I feel the hot fire starting to flow through my veins and the buzzing starting in my ears. It's happening. The Chi enhances my anger, increasing my strength. I pull my arms out of Talbert's grasp with ease and shove my hands against his chest. He flies off me, and the look of pure astonishment on his face pleases me immensely. I don't recall getting to my feet, but I find myself looming over the now crouching creature, shooter aimed straight for his temple. The anger is replaced by the dead calm, and I know what I should do now. Just squeeze that trigger, take care of the problem. But then his words somehow make it past the buzzing in my head, and I hesitate. I realize he's pleading with me. But it's not just the pleading. The words he's crying stop me from scattering his brains all over the road.

"Forgive me, mistress of light. Forgive me. I did not know wot you was. 'Ave mercy, mistress New Blood!"

He falls at my feet, cowering like a child. I can still hear the others tangling with Cat and Finn's cries getting fainter and fainter.

"Call them off," I demand urgently, my shooter still at his temple. "Tell him to bring the boy back."

"Stop! Stop in the name of the light!" His voice rings out loud and clear, and just like that, all sounds of battle cease. "Beanie bring back the boy. The mistress of light 'as decreed it so."

I don't understand why he's talking like that, but I watch in relief as Beanie comes back into view. At seeing Talbert on the other end of my shooter, he releases the boy. Finn turns and aims a hard kick at Beanie's shin before running to my side and leaving his captor howling in pain. I do a quick scan. Tater is helping a woozy Jax to his feet, and Cat comes slinking to Finn, blood oozing out of a couple of nicks on her side, but nothing too major don't look like. But it's the diseased creatures that hold my attention. There are more now than before, all creeping out of the darkness around us.

I hadn't realized there were so many of them. Even through the gloom, I can see all their pale faces, feel their eyes silently staring.

"Get up," I say to the one kneeling at my feet. Talbert does as I ask, but I hold my shooter firm, still not trusting him. The look of hatred I'd seen on his face earlier when he'd been on top of me, it's gone now, replaced by ... well, I'm not sure what. An overhead break in the clouds allows a sliver of moonlight through, and I can see a peculiar shine to the creature's eyes. It takes a moment for it to register, but I suddenly realize it's tears. He's crying?

"By all that is 'oly, I'd never thought I'd live to see the day when the light would shine again. It's a miracle; that's wot it is. A miracle."

"Stop talkin' like that," I growl, his words irritating me. Having all their eyes on me, staring like that, it's making me a might touchy. Beanie slowly approaches and reaches out to me. I flinch, ready to defend myself, but he merely touches my hair. I had somehow lost my wrapper in the tussle with Talbert, and my hair is now hanging in tangles around my shoulders.

"Did ya see it, Beanie? 'Tis the light, no doubt. A true New Blood. Someone run an' tell the others the light 'as come."

Talbert still stares in awe, but his words set the others all to murmuring. It quickly turns into an echoing chant.

"The light. The light."

It spooks me something fierce. I wave my shooter at Talbert.

"Tell 'em to shut up."

"You 'eard the mistress. Shut yer traps," and just like that they fall silent.

What the hell new kind of craziness is this? Tater and Jax finally reach my side, but Jax is still holding onto the little man like he's going to topple over any second.

"You all right?" I ask. As much as I hate to admit it, the flow of blood down his face has me worried some. He nods at me, but his attention, like mine, is on the creatures in front of us. They're all standing motionless. Still. Like they're awaiting some command. Why are they acting so strangely? It doesn't look like fear or hatred. Awed is the only thing that comes to mind. Jax looks at me with glazed, questioning eyes, but I can only shrug. I have no idea what's happening.

"You," I say to Talbert, and he steps forward eagerly. I pull my shooter up, expecting another attack, but he just smiles his ugly, black smile at me. "What's happenin'? Why aren't they attackin' no more?" I say.

"Attackin'? No no, beggin' forgiveness fer that, mistress. Wuz a misunderstandin' that wuz. We saw yer shooters an' thought ya's to be Army. We woulda never 'armed an 'air on yer 'ead if we 'ad known," he says.

"Known what?" I ask, but I already know the answer. I just don't understand why it's so important to them.

"That ya were a New Blood! Yer a mistress of the light. We ain't seen one of yer kind fer years now. We 'ad lost faith," he says, still smiling that horrible smile.

"Faith? Faith in what?" I say, rubbing my forehead. It's throbbing something fierce from smashing it into Talbert's face earlier, and his confusing words right now are not making it any better.

Talbert looks at me like he can't even believe I'm asking such a thing. "Why, the prophecy of course. Ain't ya 'eard of the prophecy?"

"Humor me," I say, still trying to get to the bottom of this.

"The prophecy, mistress," Beanie says, stepping forward and talking louder like if he raised his voice I would understand better. "Everybody knows of the prophecy. It is said that one day, the New Bloods would return and reclaim the earth and heal all that has been broken and bring hope from the darkness. It is foretold."

Talbert elbows Beanie out of the way angrily. "I was gonna tell 'er that, Beanie! She weren't askin' you. 'Ow many times I gotta tell ya 'bout interruptin' me, eh?"

Yup. Bat shite crazy, all of them. And what the hell was this prophecy talk? This is just getting stranger and stranger.

"Let me get this straight," I say, shaking my head and hoping to clarify the situation. "You stopped wantin' to kill us because you think I'm a New Blood, and I'm supposed to heal and reclaim … something?"

"Aye, that is so," says Talbert, still shooting Beanie a dirty look as if daring him to answer me again.

None of this makes a lick of sense. I look at Tater, hoping that he at least can make some reason out of this.

"Tater, what are they talkin' about? Have you ever heard of this so-called prophecy? And why are they all starin' at me like that?" I whisper.

Tater studies them for a bit before he answers back in a hushed tone so they can't overhear. "If I would have to guess, girl, I would say they are looking at you in reverence. Every clan, every pocket of humanity, has amassed their own doctrines over time. This group has obviously built a belief system on the basis of New Blood stories, passed down through the years no doubt. I, for one, have not heard of this prophecy per se, but New Bloods have long been associated with healing properties as well as their great strength, that much I do know. These simple ... people ... have probably taken those stories and expanded on them over time so that your kind has been elevated in status. In other words, my dear, to them, you are as near to the gods as they will ever get."

Unbelievable. These creatures think I'm some sort of what? Healer? God? Why would they believe such a thing? As much as I didn't want to, I was going to have to look into this New Blood thing, find out what exactly they think me to be. And why are they calling me the light? I need answers.

"A suspected New Blood in our midst, and this is how you treat her? Imbeciles, all of you."

This new voice blasts out of the darkness, and we're not the only ones to be startled. Talbert and Beanie shrink visibly as the owner of the voice walks into view from the shadows. Well, hobbles is probably a better word. She is old. Older than Grada or anybody else I'd ever seen, so shrunken and wrinkly and bony she looks like a long-dead carcass that has been left to dry out in the sun. Her sparse, gray hair is woven tightly into a bun atop her head, and her dress hangs loosely about her withered frame.

She leans heavily on a wooden walking stick as she makes her way to us, two others following her closely, ready to catch her at any moment should she fall. But she doesn't fall. She brushes past all the others and yanks the lit torch from one of her companion's hands and comes to stand directly in front of me, studying me with fierce intensity in the torchlight. I wince at the close flame and try to shield my eyes, but she yells at me.

"Stand still!"

It shocks me enough that I do as she says. She studies me a bit more like she's trying to peer into my soul, lays her wrinkled hand on my hair, and then leans back on her heels and cackles so loudly I jump. I think she's about to fall over she's leaning so badly. The two others fear the same and try to hold her elbows, but she shoos them away impatiently.

"It is true. By all that is holy, a New Blood stands in front of us."

Talbert slides in eagerly. "It was me, Orakel. I found 'er I did."

Whack.

She hits him in the gut with her walking stick, and his breath leaves him with a loud "Oomph," as he doubles over from the impact.

"You buffoons nearly killed this child from what I have been told." She gives a hard look at Beanie who is trying real hard to hold in his laughter. At her glare his grin falls away and he backs up and out of the reach of the walking stick. She certainly is an overpowering presence. She turns her attention back to me, and I find myself under her piercing gaze once again.

"My apologies, child. These idiots make for quite capable lookouts but truly have shite where their brains should be. Allow me to introduce myself. I am Orakel, and I have been awaiting your arrival for a very long time."

Against Tater and Jax's very vocal objections, I agree to accompany Orakel back to their camp. For some reason I can't explain to them, I know she's true to her word and will not harm any of us regardless of what her people had tried to do to us earlier. Besides, my burning questions far outweigh any fear I might have for our safety. They don't like it, but they follow along with me; Jax mutters the whole time under his breath and his hand rests on his shooter.

I try to keep track of our progress, but it isn't long before I'm lost in the maze of paths and ruins we pass through. If their intent was to remain hidden and unseen in these iron bones, then they had truly succeeded. I'm not even aware we're at our destination until Orakel steps aside and says very mannerly, "After you."

It looks like we're just standing at a pile of rubbish and debris until I notice an entryway and steps leading down into darkness. Her companion holding the lit torch goes first to light the way, and I quickly follow, ignoring Jax's loud whispers behind me. I chuckle quietly to myself as I hear Orakel berate him.

"Oh, for the gods' sakes, boy, if we wanted to harm you, we would have done it long ago. I wouldn't have brought you to my home just to bloody it up. Now, stop your braying and move."

He doesn't say anything back. I suddenly decide I like this strange old woman.

We descend the steep steps, and I find myself wondering how that crippled old woman is able to handle doing so when she passes by me, hanging piggyback on the larger of her two companions. My unbelieving stare is met by her loud cackling as it echoes down the wide tunnel we now find ourselves in. The tunnel is massive, its walls smooth and rounded, definitely no storm cellar. Settler-made to be sure, but no idea what it could have possibly been used for. Maybe Tater knew. I will have to ask.

At the far end of the tunnel, we find ourselves facing a large, metal door with a long arm on it. The man carrying Orakel lifts the arm and slides the door open, and it seems to disappear right into the wall. I stop in amazement, touching the wall and trying to find the hidden door, but Orakel shoos me into the next room. It takes a moment for my eyes to adjust since the cavernous room is so lit up by torches it's almost like stepping into the daylight, but the sight below us only makes my amazement double two-fold. It isn't the huge room or the dozens of lit torches or the other people waiting down below that has me and Finn staring with our mouths hanging wide. It's the *stuff*. I can't think of no other word to describe it. Settler relics everywhere, as far as the eye can see.

There are chairs and tables and boxes and plenty of other shite, all piled on top of each other, towered so high I fear it's going to topple at any moment. They had used it to partition off the large room, creating walls and rooms and pathways. The word of our arrival is spreading fast because more people seem to appear out of the numerous nooks and crannies, eager to get a look at us.

"Come on then," Orakel urges and we follow her down the few metal steps to the floor below. Once we hit the bottom, the companion places the old woman on her own two feet, and she begins making her way through the piles, not the least bit concerned about it toppling on top of her. I reckon it must be safe enough. We follow directly behind her, me and Finn and Cat, and the boy's eyes are opened so wide I fear they may just pop from his head. I can still hear Jax and Tater behind me, bellyaching with every step we take further into the overflowing room, but I don't heed them; I'm so entranced by our surroundings.

I gasp out loud and cover Finn's eyes as we turn a corner and I suddenly see what I believe to be a naked woman standing at the bottom of one of the piles. I ignore Finn's indignant "Hey!" as I quickly realize she isn't a real woman at all. She's some kinda statue, made from plastic or such. Finn pulls my hand away and laughs as I rap on her solid, bent arm with my knuckle, causing it to fall from her body. What the hell? What kinda uses could the settlers have had for a plastic woman? I want to pick up the arm and examine it, but Orakel quickly kicks it out of the way and continues walking.

We pass a couple of thin, flat, metal boxes, their glass fronts shattered with dozens of spider web cracks. I hear Tater's amazed, "Moving picture boxes," and I stop to look. No matter how hard we stare however, we see no moving pictures. I glance over at Tater in disappointment. He must be wrong about that.

We move on past another pile, and I spot some rubber wheels poking out of this one. They kinda look like the ones Grada had got from the pickin' grounds once. His he'd attached to his hand cart, but these seem to be joined together with strange metal rods and a set of handles as if it's meant to be steered. I can't even begin to imagine what it was used for. My eyes are drawn to a strange, multi-sided, faded red piece of metal standing at the corner of another pile, and in big white lettering, it spells S T O P.

Why the hell would you need a piece of metal to tell you

to stop? Stop for what? Curious. I'd never seen so much stuff, not even at the pickin' grounds, and I'm just as bad as Finn. My eyes are wide, trying to take it all in. A brightly colored ball grabs my attention now, and I stop to pick this up. Its heavy weight surprises me, and I study the three perfectly formed holes in its smooth surface but don't dare put my fingers in, since I'm not sure what it would do. Finn just grins at my questioning look, but I put it back down and hurry to keep up with Orakel, who is moving at a speed that amazes me for someone so old.

I'm aware of the curious onlookers trailing behind us and how the number keeps growing so that by the time we finally stop in the middle of the huge room, there are at least twenty or thirty other people besides me, Finn, Jax, and Tater. The braver ones walk up to me and touch my hair or take my hand, but most hold off, scared by Cat's presence I'm assuming. Some of them are like Talbert, covered in the sores with blackened lips while others appear to be disease-free. *Why?* I wonder. *What happened to them?* Orakel shoos them away, and they listen immediately like they were used to obeying her every command. I'm grateful for that. I'm uncomfortable with all the eyes and hands on me. She then points to the darkly stained table surrounded by eight high-backed chairs sitting in the center of the clearing. There is a big, stone hearth behind the table, and the crackling fire burning in it almost makes the huge room feel homey.

"Sit," she says. "You must be hungry." She gives a slight nod to someone in the mass of people. A very tall, very thin woman with a long, hooked nose steps out of the assembled crowd. She gathers up a stack of clay bowls from the table and wordlessly starts spooning up some sort of broth from the cauldron sitting in the hearth. The smell of it makes my mouth water, but none of us sit as asked. It's like we're all of the same mind and hesitate at the thought of taking food from them. As if Orakel can read our thoughts, her cackling laughter fills the room.

"Do not worry. What they have is not catching."

The smell of it is too hard to resist, however, and with an unspoken agreement we all sit on the strangely padded, soft chairs while the tall woman serves us the stew. I hate to admit it, but I'm relieved she shows no signs of the sores on her skin.

The broth is hot and tasty and filled with chunks of meat I think is wolfling, but I can't be sure. Orakel enjoys hers as much as we do, though, so I'm not too worried about the meat's origin. Even Cat is treated with a charred bone though Finn has to take it to her. None of the others will go anywhere near her. Even the woman serving us goes out of her way to avoid Cat at all costs. Can't understand why she's so afraid. The devil cat isn't going to bother with her. Cat would probably get more enjoyment out of chewing on a chair leg than that scrawny carcass.

After she serves all of us, she then approaches Jax again with another bowl, and he flashes her an eager grin. I reckon he's thinking he's getting a second helping. Without speaking a word, she knocks his hands away from reaching for the bowl and pulls a cloth from it. None too gently, she starts cleaning his head wound.

"Ouch. That hurts,' he whines, but she don't heed him; she just goes right on cleaning. I can't hide my grin as she stares in disdain down her long nose at Jax's complaining, and when she's finally done, she motions for him to hold the cloth to his head while she takes the bloodied bowl away. I raise my eyebrow at his exaggerated winces of pain.

"What?" he says crossly at my look. "She didn't have to be so rough."

"Cry baby," I taunt softly, but he chooses to ignore me.

Orakel waits patiently while we finish eating, but her shrewd eyes don't leave my face. I can tell she's eager to talk, but she lets me finish my stew before the questions start.

"Tell me, child; how is it a New Blood is in our presence right now? What is your name? Where do you come from?" she says.

"I think we should be the ones asking the questions," Jax answers before I can, throwing the bloodied cloth on the table. "Like why the hell did your people try to kill me?"

She sends him a withering look. "Please, if they had wanted you dead, then dead you would be. My people were merely … defending their territory. We are quite used to strangers trespassing through our city and having to protect ourselves and our property."

"Hah," Jax snorts at her. "Attacking and robbing poor, innocent people unfortunate enough to find themselves in your crazy town is more like it."

"My name is Tara," I say, cutting short whatever the old lady is about to say to Jax. I have questions as well. We don't have time for arguing. "I come from the sand lands—a place called Rivercross. Have you heard of it?"

She tilts her head, thinking for a bit. "Mayhap … it feels to be a distant memory," she says finally. "The sand lands, a harsh place indeed. You must be very resourceful, young Tara, to have traveled so far and for so long and have not been killed or captured. The gods truly must be watching over you."

I smile at her, but there's no humor in it. "Rivercross was attacked by the Prezedant's Army. My kin either all killed or taken. I don't think the gods give a damn about what happens to me," I say.

She gives me a slight nod. "My condolences on your loss, child, but you couldn't be more wrong. The gods have guided you here to us. They have sent us a New Blood. That is indeed divine intervention whether you believe it to be or not."

"I believe that to be pure shite," I say shortly and ignore the gasp of Orakel's two companions, who are still hovering behind her chair. Not sure if they aren't used to hearing someone speak to her this way or if they're just scared the gods will smite us where we sit. Orakel don't seem to take no offense though, just nods at me some more.

"I think otherwise. So, what do you believe has brought you to us then?" she says.

"Coincidence, happenstance, bad luck?" Tater is the one who answers. "We were on our way to Littlepass when we encountered raiders and … Well, long story short, here we are, guests in your charming abode. Which by the way, I must say I find a little disconcerting to be underground. Does anyone else find that bothersome?" he asks, looking around the table and tugging at the neck of his tunic like he can't breathe.

Orakel gives a loud snort at this. "It is a necessary precaution, little man. The only way we can avoid his ever-searching eyes. You grow accustomed."

The tall woman starts circling the table again, this time with tin cups of tea. I pick mine up and sip it. I can't quite place the taste, maybe dandy weed, but it is hot and tasty. Jax eyes her suspiciously as she sets a cup in front of him, but she passes on without incident.

"What did you mean, Orakel, when you said you have been waitin' for me to arrive?" I ask the burning question that's been bothering me. "How did you know I would come here? Are you some sort of seer?"

"I have been called that, among other things." She laughs again like what she said is side-splitting funny, but I don't get it. "I didn't know it would be you per se. The prophecy just said *a* New Blood would return, and we have waited very patiently. And now, here you are."

"Ya 'ave graced us with yer light, mistress." The voice comes out of the crowd hovering in the background, and I recognize it from our earlier entanglement. Orakel also notices, and her piercing eyes search the crowd.

"Talbert, step forward."

He does as she asks, Beanie bringing up the rear. The look on their faces clearly saying they both wished he'd kept his mouth shut.

"The watch?" Her question is curt, but he bobs his head up and down.

"It's covered, but we need to be 'ere, Orakel. Please. It's the light …," he trails off as if pleading with her to understand. She finally gives him a slight nod, and I can see him sag with relief at her approval. She is definitely the one in charge here. Hopefully, she's also the one able to answer my questions.

"What does he mean by 'the light'? When we had our earlier … disagreement with your people, they were callin' me that, the light. What does that mean?" I ask.

"It's obvious, is it not? A New Blood's power comes from the light, the aura that shines when your powers are at their peak. Talbert and the others, they witnessed your light, your life force, or Chi as some call it," she says.

"But you didn't. All you did was stare into my eyes, and yet you have yourself convinced I am this New Blood, this thing you been waitin' for. I think you're wrong. I think you've been waitin' so long that you have yourselves convinced on the wrong person. I ain't nuthin' like Beanie said the prophecy spoke of. I'm no healer, no mistress of light …," I stop talking, not knowing what else to say. She leans forward and studies me with those piercing eyes again.

"Are you trying to convince me or yourself, child? You are what you are. There is no denying it."

Before I can respond to her puzzling words, we're interrupted by a young girl, maybe my own age, as she starts gathering the stew bowls. I hand her mine, and she bows her head as she takes the offering. I notice the reddish sores on her skin. Once she is out of earshot, I ask because I need to know.

"What's wrong with them? What sickness do they carry?"

Orakel shakes her head. "It is no sickness that comes naturally, child. They were given those pox marks on purpose-like."

Her words shock me.

"Who would do such a thing?" I say, horrified, but it's surprisingly Tater who answers.

"They are refugees from Skytown, are they not?" he says.

Orakel leans back in her chair and studies Tater with shrewd eyes. She's trying not to show it, but I can tell she's taken aback by his question.

"Aye, that they are. And what do you know of this, little man?"

He shrugs and takes a sip of his tea. "I have heard things. Rumors about experimentation being carried out by the Prezedant. Experiments that end badly and leave his subjects strangely marked," Tater says, answering Orakel.

Her loud, "Hah," rattles us all, and the fist she slams on the table makes the tin cups all wobble, but they don't fall. "Marked? Is that what they call it? Try deformed and diseased and minds so damaged that madness is all they know. And they are the lucky ones. Marked." She snorts the last word with derision.

"The Prezedant did this to them? But why?" I can't even comprehend the reasoning for something so cruel.

"Because he is the maddest of them all," Orakel says. "His whole life he has been obsessed with hunting your kind, New Bloods. Why? No one can say. Once he has found one, though, they are never seen again, that we do know. He has brought your kind to the point of extinction, I'm afraid. There haven't been any true New Bloods for years now, not any possessing Chi anyway. So, what do you do if you can no longer find the object of your burning desire? You try to create it yourself. His ... experiments, as your friend refers to them number in the hundreds, maybe more. Most end in death for the fortunate ones. Some end up like the ones you see here, deformed and disfigured. But none yet have ended in what he is so desperately searching for or so I have been told."

"Is it true what they say about him, Orakel? Is he really magical and hundreds of years old?" Finn, who had been real quiet up until now, speaks, and his question makes her cackle again.

"Mayhap it is, boy. Mayhap it ain't. I could say the little man over there has a boil on his arse the size of a toadie. That don't make it so."

This gets a chuckle from Jax and Finn, but Tater doesn't find it so funny.

I'm still too full of questions to get any amusement out of this either.

"Why, Orakel? Why does he need New Bloods so badly?" I say. "And why seemingly wipe them out on one hand and then try to create his own on the other? It doesn't make a lick of sense."

She shrugs. "Like I said, child, no one knows what he does with them, but I'm guessing it isn't anything pleasant. And he's a madman, as crazy as they come. He don't need no reason."

This coming from the queen of the crazies is kind of funny.

"So you give shelter to the ones that get away?" I say.

She nods and shoos the tall woman away who's trying to refill her cup.

"The ones we can help. If they are lucky enough to escape, to find their way to us. They are mostly always young'uns that much we do know. Most of the time, there isn't anything we can do for them. They pass on quickly to meet their gods.

But sometimes, if they're strong enough, we can nurse them back to health, physically anyways. Mentally, well, we aren't sure if they can't remember what's happened to them, or they choose not to remember the horrors they've endured."

It's starting to make sense to me now—some of it anyways. Why he sent his men into the sand lands. He was looking for New Bloods. And he takes the young'uns on the off chance they may be what he is looking for or at least more fodder for his experiments. I desperately hope Tater is right, and my kin were sold off as slaves or put to work in the iron mines. It would be a much better fate than becoming a diseased, mad creature. Just that thought alone fills me with despair, but I push it down deep. I can't think of that—not now, not with everything else I've heard. What the old woman is saying, what she's telling me, it's overwhelming, and the weight of it crushes me. But there's one more thing I need to know.

"What exactly is a New Blood? What exactly do you believe I am?" I whisper to her, and all my fears, my frustrations, my anxieties, it all comes out in that one burning question. It's like she understands my inner turmoil, my need to know, and she leaves her chair and hobbles to my side. Taking my hand in her wrinkled one, she stares at me fiercely.

"You, my child, are hope. A New Blood, born of the land, chosen by the gods, able to heal and purify and repair all that has been destroyed. Our world—what the settlers did to it with their wars and their plagues—it was left in ruins. Our kind nearly wiped out, unable to survive in what was left after The Shift. But then the gods made the New Bloods. Stronger, better beings than us, able to withstand this harsh world, to thrive in it almost. You and your kind are the reason we still exist. It is said that your Chi, the power that comes from within, it is a part of the gods themselves. You are a symbol of all that is pure and good, and that is why the Prezedant fears and reveres your kind so. You can heal this world and bring back the light to everything he has worked so hard to keep in darkness, for in that lies his power over the people."

I stare into her feverish eyes, and for a moment, she has me truly convinced I am something special. That I could be the one to bear truth to their prophecy. Then a harsh laugh from Jax breaks her spell.

"That's a load of mule shite if I ever heard it. Tara may be a New Blood, but she's just a mutie with a different name. A bit stronger than most and a lot more irritating, but a mutie all the same. She's no earth healer and no symbol of 'pure goodness' any more than I am."

"And yet you follow her willingly and without coercion." She doesn't take her eyes off me, but her words are directed towards Jax. "That, in itself, speaks volumes, boy. You are a true believer; you just don't know it yet."

"I know that you are one crazy old bitc—"

"Jax," Tater interjects smoothly. "I think it's time we thanked Orakel for her hospitality and her words of wisdom, but I think we should be on our way. Get back aboveground. I think it would make us all feel much better."

I can hear Jax whispering to Tater about Orakel's sanity, but like her, I pay no heed. I still have questions, and this old lady standing in front of me is the only one right now who has the answers I seek.

"Jax is right," I say to her. "I'm not any healer. I have done things, things I cain't explain … things that terrify me to no end, but I've got no control over them. How am I supposed to do these things you people believe I am capable of? I don't know how to fix or heal anything. I don't think I'm the one you're waitin' for, Orakel."

She smiles at me then, and in her eyes, I see the sparkling reflection of the dozens of lit torches surrounding us, and it gives them an almost unearthly glow.

"Don't rush it, child. It will come. We have been awaiting the arrival of a true New Blood for many years. Some had even given up believing that your kind would ever appear again, yet here you are in the flesh. The prophecy will be fulfilled, and the darkness will be defeated of that I have no doubt." She stops talking and looks over at my companions, studying them with her piercing eyes, her head tilted to the side as if she's listening to something that the rest of us can't hear. Finally, she gives a slight nod and leans in to whisper in my ear words that make my stomach drop. A numbness seeps over me, and a foul taste fills my mouth.

"True followers they may be, child, but be careful with whom you share your secrets. One of the three will betray you greatly. It will be so."

CHAPTER 7

Littlepass

———◆———

Betrayal. That's all I've been able to think about, all that's occupied my mind ever since we'd left the city of iron bones and Orakel's whispered words. Days of watching my companions, wondering if her warning of betrayal was true. Wondering if any of what she said had been true. Sometimes, I feel more confused than ever from what Orakel had told me. Her explanation of what I was expected to be, of what I was expected to do ... Well, it left me with more questions than answers. Did she truly believe I could do as their prophecy said? Or was it all just a bunch of hokum like Jax believed? Talbert and Beanie seemed to think there was truth to it. They had wanted to accompany us on our travel to Littlepass, insisting that the mistress of light needed their protection, much to the dismay of the others. I don't know who had protested the loudest—Finn, Jax, or Tater—but I had politely refused their protection and said our goodbyes. They had been truly disappointed at my refusal, but thankfully, they had heeded me. The one thing I do not need is more craziness in my life.

I sit staring at our campfire, keeping watch over the others as they sleep, Cat at my side. She purrs with pleasure as I scratch her ears and head, her fur still holding the warmth of the day's heat. I lift her paw to have a look at her injuries. They are healing quite nicely. Whatever Orakel had given us to treat them had worked well. I have that to thank her for at least.

I drop Cat's paw and turn my attention back to staring at the low campfire, my mind wandering again. If Orakel's calculations were correct, we would be upon Littlepass in the early morning. I'm not quite sure how I feel about that. Littlepass meant finding Lily, and Lily meant answers, and by the gods, I had a lot of questions. But it also meant the end of the journey for them at least. No more Finn or Cat or Tater ... or Jax. I would have to say my goodbyes to this motley little crew of travelers. It doesn't sit well.

And do I truly want to hear those answers Lily supposedly has for me? Am I ready to hear what she has to say? Maybe the only question I need to ask—the only question that I need to know the answer to—is how do I find Ben? That's the most important thing right now, isn't it? That's the whole point of my journey, the whole point of finding Lily, to help me get my kin back. The rest of it ... of them ... doesn't matter. And if Orakel is to be believed, one of them will betray me anyway, so why should I worry about any of this?

More confused than ever, I lift my flower from inside my tunic and hold its warmth to my lips. Shizen, Ben. If there's ever a time when I needed to talk to you, for you to tell me everything's going to be okay, well, now's that time.

"I will find you, Ben," I whisper against my flower as if doing so will help my promise to reach his ears across the distance separating us, wherever he may be. Tears prickle at the corners of my eyes as a wave of loneliness and self-pity threatens to overwhelm me.

"You okay?" The unexpected voice confuses me, and for a split second, I believe it to be Ben. Then the shadowy figure moves into the firelight, and I drop my flower back inside my tunic and turn my head so Jax doesn't see my moment of weakness.

"Yeah," I say gruffly as he sits cross-legged on the other side of Cat.

"Well, why you talking to yourself then?" he says.

"I wasn't talkin'—" I start to protest but realize he'd caught me red-handed, so I change the subject, snapping at him in irritation. "Why are you up? It ain't time for your watch yet."

He shrugs, staring into the low flames of the fire and running his hand through Cat's fur like I'd been doing. Cat arches her back with pleasure, accepting his touch. Accepting him. When did this happen? When did Cat accept him as one of us?

"Can't sleep," he says, not seeming to notice my displeasure at Cat's behavior. "I keep dreaming about those crazy bastards we just left behind. Especially that tall, thin one." He gives an exaggerated shiver. "I'll have night terrors for years."

I don't want to, but I find my lips twitching in amusement at his words.

"Really? *She* was the one who scared you? I kinda think she was sweet on you. I think Sky maybe has some competition," I say.

"Ha ha, not funny, New Blood, not at all," he says, scowling at me. "Besides, you're one to talk. The way Talbert was following you around like a lovesick young'un, I thought he was gonna cry when you turned down his offer to take us to Littlepass. I think you broke his heart."

Is Jax actually teasing me? Did he actually have a sense of humor?

"You wanna hear something weirder?" I say, going with it and grinning at him. "Just before we left, he gave me that creepy skull from his neck. Said it would bring me good luck. I was gonna throw it away, but who knows? Maybe it will."

Jax arches his brows and stares at me in disgust. "You kept it?"

"Aye, it's in my slingbag," I say.

"Well, that's just creepy as hell. Sure wasn't good luck for the poor animal it came from. Best be careful about that though. Some may take that sort of thing to be a betrothal gift. Missus Talbert. Has a nice ring to it, don't you think?"

"Bite your tongue," I say, giving a mock shudder of horror. "Now, *I'm* gonna have night terrors."

He gives a low chuckle as I hand him a tin cup of the root tea I have hanging over the fire.

"Here. Even though it serves you right now to have night

terrors, this will help you sleep."

He nods a thanks and sips carefully at the hot liquid. We sit in silence for a bit, just enjoying the tea and the peacefulness of the night. It's almost nice. But then Orakel's words snake their way into my thoughts again. Is Jax the one Orakel spoke of? Would he be the one to betray me? *Stop it!* I scold myself. Stop raising doubt. She is just a crazy old lady. Besides, Jax is about to part ways with us. Didn't matter. I would never see him again, so how could he betray me?

"Why are you here, Jax?" I ask the question that has been eating at me ever since his unexpected arrival in the dead city.

He looks at me, confused. "I told you, I can't sleep—"

"No, I mean why did you follow us? Why are you takin' us to Littlepass? And don't give me the story about an owed debt. You should be home in Gray Valley with your ma and Sky, gettin' ready for your wedded ceremony. Livin' a normal life. Why are you here with us?"

After his earlier teasing, I wasn't expecting the harsh snort he gives me at my question.

"Normal life? Is that what you think we have in Gray Valley? No such thing. Breaking our backs working the dead soil, praying to the gods to get enough harvest to pay our taxes so the Army doesn't punish us. Hiding the extra meat or grain we have managed to hoard away so our families can make it through to the next season without starving. Living in fear for the children, wondering if at any moment they will be taken away from us by that madman. Fearing to have children of your own. Is that what you call normal?"

He runs a hand through his hair, a gesture I've come to

realize he did when most agitated. I want to tell him I'm sorry. I'm sorry to have brought it up. I hadn't realized. But he goes on talking.

"Hell, I don't know. Maybe I just wanted to get away from that. To get away from Sky, her talk of our betrothal, her talk of a family. How can I disappoint her?" he sighs a little. "Maybe I'm here because of Finn. I kinda see a little bit of me in him: a lost, lonely little kid wondering why things had to happen but trying to deal in the best way he can. You know what he asked me the other day?" I shake my head at his question. "He wanted to know did I think my pa and his pa were hunting and fishing together in the afterlife. Having adventures … friends like him and me."

I laugh a little at this. That was such a Finn thing to say. Jax looks up at my laughter, his eyes burning feverishly from the firelight, and the laughter dies on my lips.

"Or maybe I'm here because of you. Ma was right. You remind me of Jenna so much. Maybe in some strange way, I believe that by helping you, I can make it up to my sister, make up for failing her. I stood aside and let her die. I watched it all happen, and I didn't do anything. Maybe I don't want the same thing to happen to you. I owe you that much …," he trails off and drops his gaze back to the fire.

However I'd expected Jax to answer my question, it was not with such brutal honesty. I'm speechless at his words. Tongue-tied as always, unable to express how I feel at his admission. Is he saying that he cares about us? That he truly cares what happens to us? To me? I should be thanking him for his honest answers, telling him how grateful I am for his help, but all I do is show how uncomfortable I am by saying,

"I ain't Jenna, Jax."

He laughs, but it's void of humor. "No, you are much more irritating and annoying and a damn sight more mule-headed. Trust me, that much I do know."

I shake my head at him. "No. You don't get it. I don't want you helpin' us because you think you owe me something. What happened was out of your control. You don't owe it to Jenna, and you sure as hell don't owe it to me. Your debt is paid, Jax."

He looks at me, confused.

"Your debt is paid," I say again. "Not only did you help us back at the iron city, but we made it to Littlepass alive and well, just like you promised. Thank you for all you've done, but you may as well make your way back to Gray Valley in the mornin'. Gods speed on your safe return home."

For some reason, his admission is scaring me, and I respond in the only way I know how. Change the subject and make it less personal. The old expression passes my lips automatically, and I hold my hand out to him in a goodwill gesture. He looks down at my outstretched hand, ignoring it as his eyes come to rest on my face again, and I can see the disbelief in them.

"Really? That's how it's going to be? You ask me a question, and I answer it in the most soul-bearing way I can, and you want to shake my hand? You're a real waterfall of emotion, you know that, Tara?" he says, and I know sarcasm when I hear it.

"Why you gotta be such a jackass?" I pull my hand back in embarrassment. "Why cain't you just accept my thanks graciously and be on your way in the mornin'?"

"Okay, fine. If it makes you feel any better, then I graciously accept your thanks," he says, but I snort at him.

"Too late. You cain't say that now because I know you don't mean it."

"Aye, I do," he says.

"No, you don't," I say. "You're just repeatin' what I said."

He shakes his head like he doesn't quite understand me. "Whatever. And just to be clear, I won't be leaving for Gray Valley tomorrow."

This catches me off guard. I was not expecting that. "Why not?"

"Because I promised Finn I would stay with you all until you found Lily." His answer is flat and emotionless.

I stare at him over Cat's head, ignoring her grinding against my hand to get me to scratch her ears again.

"Why would you do such a thing? I don't know how long it's gonna take us to find Lily. Could be days ... weeks."

"I'm aware of that," he says, taking a sip of his tea.

"Well, why would you promise the boy such a thing?" I say.

"Because he asked me to," Jax says.

Jax was staying with us because Finn asked him to? When did the boy ask such a thing from him? And more importantly, why? Why would he want Jax to stay around? We don't need Jax around. All he did was cause confusion, especially as far as I'm concerned. I can't even believe Finn would ask him to do such a thing.

"There ain't no need for you to stay," I insist.

He gives a harsh little laugh at my words. "Do you even realize what you're asking the boy to do tomorrow? Have you even discussed how he feels about leaving Cat?" At the mention of her name, the beast looks up at Jax and licks his hand.

"He loves this beast more than anything else he has left in the world, and you are asking him to just desert her and who knows for how long. Do you even know how he feels about that? Do you even care? Because I do. Or is the thought of Ben the only thing that occupies that selfish mind of yours?"

Now he's gone too far.

"Of course I know what I'm askin' him to do, but it ain't like he's got a choice," I hiss at him. "He knows he cain't take Cat into Littlepass. I told him that from the start, and he still insisted on comin' with me. She's a devil cat for cryin' out loud. A wild animal. It's not like she don't know how to fend for herself. He'll get over her eventually …," I trail off, realizing that I said too much. Jax is looking at me through narrowed eyes.

"What do you mean eventually? Why would he need to … Ahhhh, you're leaving him behind, aren't you? You're deserting him here in Littlepass. So you are going to continue with your foolhardy plan then. You are going to still look for your kin even though it will undoubtedly end in your death. I didn't think even you would be that stupid. Guess I was wrong."

"You think you know it all, don't you?" I snarl at him. "Well, you don't. Finn will be better off stayin' here in Littlepass. Tater will be better off goin' his own merry way. You would be better off goin' back to Gray Valley, and I will be better, much better, once I find Ben. He is all I care about. He's all that matters, him and Jane and Thomas. They are my only family, and I will do anything to get them back. If that's being stupid, then I don't care!"

He stares at me silently for a bit and then finally says, "No, I guess you don't give a damn about breaking that poor kid's heart." He throws his remaining tea into the flames before he gets up and walks away from me, adding coldly over his shoulder, "I'll be back when it's time for my watch."

We reach Littlepass shortly after sunrise. Jax had roused the others just before dawn like I had asked him to, but he hadn't needed to wake me. I couldn't sleep. His words from the night before had been crawling around in my brain all night, my guilt gnawing at my gut like some festering wound.

Of course I know how much Finn loves Cat, and I know it's going to break his heart to leave her. Does he truly think I'm so unfeeling? But I have to do this. I have to make a hard choice. It's in Finn's best interest. Why can't Jax see that?

I look over at him now riding beside me, Finn sitting behind him and yammering his ear off. The boy had chosen to ride with Jax this morning. Don't know why. It had miffed me some at first, but then I figured it was maybe for the best. At least I wouldn't have to try to keep my feelings and guilt hidden from Finn and pretend everything was going to be okay. Jax glances up suddenly and catches me staring, and the light blue eyes regard me with such accusation that I look away. *To hell with him*, I think angrily. I don't need his approval. I snap the reins, and the nag bolts forward, leaving the others trailing behind. We ride this way, me way ahead of the others and fuming the whole time until we reach our destination.

—————

The city lays below us, overwhelming in its entirety. I've never seen so many buildings all at once. All of them squished together like they're fighting for room. They are so packed tight it's hard to tell where one ends, and the other begins. Never in my wildest imagination could I have ever dreamed of something like this. They cover every bit of open ground and even halfways up the sides of the mountains surrounding the city. Not as vastly spread as the dead city we had just passed through but made more imposing by the number of people I see occupying the roads and pathways cut through the buildings. They swarm the city like the maskeetos in the woods, and I can feel my heart drop as I view the sight from atop the hill we are sitting on. So many people. How am I supposed to find Lily?

I squat low, hands on my knees, studying the wall surrounding the city and trying to ignore the nagging little voices in the back of my head. As mad as I am at Jax, the thought of what I'm about to do today still almost makes me wanna retch, and it's with relief I hear Tater's approach. He joins me at the top of the rise and quietly studies the sight below us.

"Tater, are those guard towers?" I say, shutting off my thoughts and referring to the wooden structures flanking the open gate of the stone barrier.

"They are indeed, but no worries, child. They are usually

manned by drunkards, too tired or intoxicated to care who passes through. The best of the Army in Littlepass is used to guard the iron mines there to the left of the city."

I look to where he is pointing, and I can see structures on the horizon past the city and a flurry of activity. My heart beats a little faster with a faint hope that maybe I will find some of my kin there. I'm definitely going to have to check it out somehow. If it's guarded as heavily as Tater said, though, it's going to be a challenge.

I rise from my squatting position and turn towards the others. Finn and Cat are playing some sort of fetching game with a dried-out twig, but Jax is leaning against a boulder, watching me intently. There's no expression on his face this time, but his eyes are as sharp as always. I find myself wondering what he's thinking. Will he tell Finn of my plan, or will he keep my confidence?

"You sure there's nuthin' I can say to make you head back to Gray Valley?" I ask rudely as I walk past him towards the nags, and he kind of grins at me.

"No, when I make a promise, I don't go back on it," he says, and I can hear the accusation back in his voice.

A retort pops into my head, but I don't say what I'm thinking since outta the corner of my eye I can see Finn watching us, listening to our conversation. He comes sauntering up to us then, his face all red from his running around with Cat.

"Jax ain't leaving us yet, Tara. He told me he wouldn't leave us until we found Lily. Ain't that right, Jax?"

"Right you are," he says to Finn, but his eyes don't leave my face. Is he waiting for my reaction to that? I don't fall for his bait.

"Whatever. We've put up with you for this long. A few more days ain't gonna make much difference. Just don't expect any more thanks when you finally do leave. I've said my piece."

I turn away from him to hide my confusion. As angry as I am at him for being such a jackass, there's this tiny part of me actually pleased that he isn't leaving us yet. What the hell is wrong with me? Angry at him and at myself, I focus my attention on Tater, who's smiling at me like something is amusing him greatly.

"What?" I say crossly, but he just shrugs.

"Nothing, my dear. I was just thinking we should get a move on. It's early morning; the guards are probably still snoring from their night's partaking. There is no better time to enter the city."

"Fine. Let's go then," I say, grabbing the horse's reins. "Finn, say your goodbyes."

He looks at me then back at Cat, and his whole face drops like he's about to cry. I sigh loudly and rub the back of my neck, dreading the next few minutes.

"Finn, we talked about this. You know Cat cain't go. She will be fine. She's a wild animal for cryin' out loud."

"But I ain't ever left her on purpose like before," he says, trying to be strong, but his quivering lip gives him away. I can feel the little patience I have left slipping, but before I can say anything else, Jax walks over to the boy and lays a gentle hand on his shoulder.

"She'll be fine, Finn. This whole area is covered in caves and wildlife. She'll have a place to sleep, plenty to eat, and it'll only be for a little while. And if it makes you feel any better, until we find Lily, we'll come out and check on her every day. It's safer for her that way. She can't be in the city; you know that."

He looks up at Jax and nods. "I know," he says. "You're right, Jax. Will you come out with me to check on her, truly?"

Jax nods, and the boy wraps his skinny arms around his waist, causing me to feel like my heart is being ripped out of my chest. What am I doing to him? He's leaving his beast that he loves more than anything in the world, and instead of comforting him, I'd lost patience with him. Hating this whole situation, I watch as Finn goes to Cat, hugs her, and whispers in her ear. He then straightens up and says quietly, "Now you know what to do, so go on ... get outta here."

She yowls a couple of times and licks his face, but as if she understands, she shuffles slowly off as we ride away from her. Finn keeps looking back, and I can hear him stifle a couple of sobs, but he doesn't cry. Finally, he says, "I cain't see her no more. She must be gone to find a cave like Jax said to wait for us. You think so, Tara? She's gonna wait for us until we're ready to leave the city."

"Aye," I say, agreeing with the boy, but I don't dare turn around to face him. I'm scared he will see the deceit written all over my face. That he will know I'm lying to him and that when I did leave the city, it would be without him. Instead, I stare straight ahead at the growing city wall and push Cat and the thought of never seeing her again from my mind. *I have more important things to worry about than the animal,* I tell myself. I try to ignore the sick rot in the pit of my stomach and the tears pricking at my eyes and instead focus my thoughts on Ben and Jane and young Thomas. They need to be my only concern now. There's no other choice.

We pass through the arched stone gate in silence, past the guard towers, and I let out my pent-up breath in relief that no one tries to stop us. I almost feel safe when suddenly, we hear a loud, "Oi! Halt! Who goes there?"

My heartrate spikes in my chest, and I pull my wrapper further down over my hair as a brown-robed soldier approaches us. We do as he asks and stop, not wanting to draw any attention to ourselves. He is dressed a little different than the army that had chased us from the raiders, but the long shooter hanging at his side is the same. I'm glad we had taken Tater's advice and hidden our own shooters in one of the saddle bags on Jax's nag. I don't think the soldier would have taken too kindly to seeing them.

"Hello, Doyle. And how goes it my friend?"

I am surprised to hear Tater call him by name. He smiles at the soldier and removes his hat in a friendly gesture. The soldier peers at him for a bit before breaking into a toothless grin of recognition.

"Tater? Is that you? By the gods, I thought you had been killed out in the sand lands long ago."

He gives a hearty laugh like the thought of that is truly amusing, causing his gigantic stomach to jiggle up and down. Tater don't take no offense; he merely laughs along with the man like it's the funniest thing he's ever heard.

"Ah, no such luck, old chap. I'm afraid those two bits of iron you owe me will indeed have to be repaid."

The soldier laughs again, showing his toothless gums, and starts scratching himself in several undignified places.

"That's damn bad luck ... for me. I'll have to buy you an ale at the Two Heads as payback. You here on trading business?"

"Unfortunately not. Met with some rather nasty business in the mountains. Got robbed by a bunch of raiders and lost all my wares. Have nothing to trade at the moment. Was rather hoping to pick up some coin in town, maybe do a bit of storytelling at the Two Heads, earn some iron."

"Raiders!' the man says in disgust and spits on the ground. "Bunch of worthless shite heads. Don't know why The Prezedant don't just order for them all to be killed. I'd gladly go on that hunt."

Tater nods as if agreeing wholeheartedly, but I can feel the sweat beading on my upper lip. Why don't he cut this conversation short and get moving? Why is he talking to this soldier like they're long-lost friends? We don't need him paying any attention to the rest of us.

As if suddenly reading my thoughts, the man in question turns and peers at me and Finn and Jax.

"And who you have with you then, eh? Didn't think you had this many friends, half-man."

Tater laughs again like he doesn't have a care in the world. "Not friends, apprentices. Orphans whose parents died out in the sand lands. Had no one else to look after them, so I took them under my wing, thought I'd train them in the way of the entertainments. Why do all the work myself when I can get paid thrice over?"

The soldier almost bends over with his laughter and points a dirt-encrusted finger at Tater.

"You ain't changed a bit, old man. Always looking to make the most iron in the quickest time possible," he says, taking his gaze off us. I suck in a ragged breath.

"It has been a pleasure, my friend, but it was a long journey indeed, and I am very thirsty. The Two Heads awaits," Tater says and nods a farewell to the soldier, and with relief we start to ride away. I don't look back, but I can feel the soldier's eyes following us. Did he suspect anything? I don't think so. It seemed like normal conversation. We follow Tater slowly through the crowded streets. Don't seem like anyone is paying any attention to us. We're just another group of dirty, tired travelers as far as they're concerned.

The sharp fear at being stopped by the soldier is quickly replaced by the wonder at our surroundings. So many people all crowded together in one place. The noise is ear-splitting.

There are people yelling back and forth, gesturing wildly with their arms, and I finally realize they are bartering, trying to sell or buy the many wares hanging all around us. The whole road is awash with stalls of goods. Amazing.

I see bolts of hanging cloths, every color of the rainbow. Animal carcasses picked and clean, just waiting to be cooked. Baskets of taters and corn and things I don't recognize. Trinkets and beads and bangles and objects of trade. There is so much! Where did they get all this stuff? I am baffled at the abundance of it all. A young boy, probably no older than Finn, runs right up to Tater and starts yelling at him, thrusting a basket of round, orange-colored balls up at him. I don't know what they are, but Tater shakes his head at the boy, refusing his wares. At Tater's rejection, he turns to me, but Tater kicks at him like he's a rabid dog, and he scampers off, cussing at the half-man over his shoulder.

The smell of freshly baked bread suddenly hits my nose,

and my stomach lurches violently. Oh gods, my mouth is watering. Where's that coming from? Finn squirms behind me, and I know the smell is affecting him, too.

The crowd is becoming almost impassable the further in we go, and the nag is getting skittish. Just like me, she's unnerved by the throng of people. The noise of it all, it vibrates in my ears, and a pain starts blossoming in the middle of my forehead. How can people live like this? So crowded and on top of each other? I find myself longing for the openness of the sand lands, and I'm very relieved when Tater finally turns out of the crowd and down a narrow alleyway carved out between two stone buildings. Away from the crowded street, the noise level drops as we go deeper in.

But the noise is the least of our worries in here seems like. An overpowering, sickening stench hits us, and I gag reflexively before I get a chance to cover my nose with my wrapper. Finn's, "Ugh!" hits my ears a second before he buries his nose in my back. And at Jax's cussing, I know the smell has hit him, too. Shizen. What is that? Then, I see the piles of half-rotted debris … and other things. Things that out in the sand lands would have been buried if you had any decency. Ugh. Disgusting. This is what Tater called civilized? The half-man doesn't seem to be the least affected by any of it though; he keeps ambling on ahead of us on Winnie, and I swear I can hear him singing to himself.

Seems like forever, but we finally emerge out of the narrow pathway into an open courtyard. The buildings surrounding us are worn and old, their exteriors mostly crumbling away, but at least the stench is gone. Or maybe my nose was so burnt by it I couldn't smell it anymore. Either way, I was glad to be out of that disgusting tunnel of filth.

Tater dismounts, and we quickly follow suit. I stretch my tense back and look around, wondering where Tater has brought us. Jax is the first to ask.

"What is this place?"

"This, my dears, is my home away from home, my utopia, my oasis, my shining beacon in the darkness. This will be our haven," he says, smiling from ear to ear.

Loud, rowdy laughter reaches our ears at that moment, and the door closest to us in the courtyard flies open with a bang. A man falls out into the road at our feet. He is quickly followed by a woman, scantily dressed, her face painted with such colors I fear for a split second she must be a raider. She stares at us with bleary eyes then quickly dismisses us to help the man to his feet. They stumble away into the narrow alley, obviously under the influence of the whiskey.

"You can't be serious?" Jax says, staring at Tater like he had lost his mind. I don't understand, and I look from Jax to Tater as the little man shrugs.

"A safer place in all of Littlepass you will not find. Trust me, many a soul has hidden here, and the occupants ... they know how to be tight-lipped. As my dear mother would say, 'What happens here stays here.' Besides, the proprietor is a friend of mine."

"Tater, we can't. Finn can't stay here."

I don't understand why Jax is protesting so. If it's a friend of Tater's, then what's the problem? And Tater says it is safe enough. Jax looks over at me and Finn, and I can swear he is flushed with embarrassment.

"What's the problem, Jax?" I ask.

"This place is … it's … it's a service den." He almost whispers the last words but don't make no matter. He could have yelled them, and I still wouldn't have known what he's talking about. He must see the look of confusion on my face since he tries again.

"A service den. A brothel. A house of ill fame." I can tell he's getting frustrated with me, but I still don't understand.

An ill house? Did that mean the house is sick? Maybe Jax is right. We shouldn't be staying in no sickly house. Before I can voice my objections, Tater jumps in.

"What our prudish friend is trying to say, Tara, very ineloquently I might add, is that the ladies who reside in this residence are visited quite frequently by men. Many men. And that they treat those men as a wife would treat her wedded husband. Sometimes much better." He smiles at his words then continues on, "And in return, they get paid for their unique … services. Do you understand?"

I do understand. Somewhat. I mean, I'm not a complete idiot. I've seen animals mating before, and I kinda know that people aren't much different. But Jax seems to be real put off by the whole idea, so of course I, on the other hand, don't mind it at all.

"Can we go in? I'd like to meet those women." I'm bursting with curiosity about what Tater is telling me. What kinda women are they to do that sort of thing for payment? I want to know.

"Oh, for the gods' sake, Tara," Jax mutters at me, and I just stare back, confused.

"What?" I say, still not getting what his problem was. Was it really that big of a deal?

"Trust me, Jax. Finn will be in no way affected by our little side trip. I grew up in a house like this, and I turned out just fine. But if it troubles you so, you all can stay here with the animals while I procure a room for us. I'm sure my friend can provide us with one that is somewhat out of the way of the main … clientele."

Jax seems to be okay with what Tater is suggesting, but I sure as hell am not going to stay out here. I want to see what has Jax so riled up. It can't be that bad. So I leave Finn with Jax and the nags. I can hear Finn's rapid-fire questions as I walk away.

"What's an ill house, Jax? What kinda women did Tater say they are? How does a woman treat her wedded husband? How come I cain't go in? What's an elephant?"

And Jax responds with, "Drop it, Finn … never you mind. Finn, I'm not telling you that! Elephant…what the hell?"

It makes me snicker. Good luck trying to shut Finn up on this one. Once something got stuck in that boy's craw, he don't give up on it easily. Tater looks back at me trailing him with raised brows, but just shrugs as I accompany him into the dim interior of the ill house.

The first thing I notice is the smell. It's an odd combination. It's like sickeningly sweet berries and stale smoke and unwashed bodies all rolled into one. I wrinkle my nose and pull my wrapper up a little higher, but Tater doesn't seem to be bothered at all. In fact, he's smiling, looking around the little room with affection, like he's home.

The room is oddly furnished. There's nothing in it but cushioned seats and pillows and layers of silky-looking cloths hanging from the ceiling. I don't even notice the door behind the cloths until a woman walks through unexpectedly, making me jump. Her appearance is very similar to the woman we'd seen earlier, face heavily painted and her dress barely there, so low cut that I'm afraid her chest is gonna fall right out in front of us. Tater don't seem to be afraid of any of this since he's smiling at her like she's a vision from the gods. Unlike the other woman, however, it seems to work for this one. She walks with grace and dignity, her look almost … queenly. That's the word that pops into my head. At seeing us, her eyes open wide with surprise.

"Why, I'll be … Tater? I haven't seen you in forever, my friend. Where have you been?"

"Hello, Duchess. I hope we find you well?" He goes to her, and they embrace with the familiarity of long-lost friends.

"As well as the gods will allow," she responds, bending slightly and dropping a kiss on his wrinkled cheek. "Are you here as a paying customer?"

"Regretfully no," he says and sighs in disappointment.

She notices me then, her gaze sharp and whatever else she's about to say cut short by my presence. She looks me up and down, sizing me up. "And what have you brought me here, old friend? A new girl perhaps?"

Tater looks back at me in surprise, like he almost forgot I was there. "Oh, dear me, no. No, not this one. I'm afraid she's too … prickly for your establishment. She would chase all your customers away."

They laugh, and I'm not quite sure, but I think I've just been insulted. Again. She keeps eyeing me and then shrugs her slim shoulders. "Pity. With a little work, she would have made for a very profitable investment."

"No, I wouldn't waste your time on this one, Duchess. She is just a poor, orphaned child I found in the sand lands. I escorted her to Littlepass for she has family in the city … somewhere. But I am in need of a great favor, Duchess. We had a rather unfortunate encounter with some raiders in the mountains—barely escaped with our lives."

At her sharp gasp, he continues. "Indeed! They have robbed me of everything, and I'm afraid I am now rather down on my luck. Until I am able to earn some coin, I was wondering if you would be generous enough to offer me a room. I would pay you back of course. Maybe something out of the way … back alley so we do not interfere with your daily business?"

Loud laughter comes from the room the "duchess" just came out of, and I find myself itching to see what was going on back there. I stand on my toes, trying to peer past her shoulder, but all I can see are the gauzy curtains. Suddenly, the curtains are pushed aside, and a man and woman emerge. Eagerly, they make their way to a staircase built alongside the back wall. If there's any doubt in my mind of what Tater was trying to tell me earlier, it's cleared up by the way the man gropes the woman as they make their way up the stairs. Oh, my! Cheeks flaming with embarrassment, I look away, back at Tater and the duchess. They don't seem to be the least put out at all, like they didn't even notice. No wonder Jax doesn't want Finn in here. I hate to admit it to myself, and I sure as hell wasn't going to admit it to him, but he's right.

The duchess smiles at Tater, and it surprises me how that smile makes her painted face look so much younger.

"Of course, my dear. I could never say no to you, Tater;

you know that." She reaches into an unseen pocket and pulls out a ring of keys. I didn't even think that dress could hide a pocket let alone the key ring. Sorting through, she pulls one out and hands it over.

"Here, it's the room above the stable. Rarely gets used anyway, so may as well make some coin for it."

Tater bows to her regally. "Thank you, Duchess. You truly are a generous and noble woman," he says.

"Yeah, yeah, I will expect my full payment. And just make sure you and your ... orphan girl leave it the way you found it."

They exchange a bit more conversation, but it's cut short by some ruckus from the mystery room. The duchess quickly excuses herself, and I follow Tater back out into the courtyard, eager to get away from that cloying smell. I breathe in deep the moment we are outside, trying to cleanse my nose. I wouldn't exactly call it "fresh" air, but it's much better than inside.

Finn and Jax are still standing by the nags like we'd left them, but Jax isn't wearing the "I told you so" look like I was expecting to see. Instead, he looks angry and anxious. *Why?* I think. I take a couple of steps toward them, wondering what it is this time that has him looking like his innards are tied in a knot. Out of the corner of my eye, I catch a quick glimpse of movement. Before I can turn around, something hard and cold is driven into my back, and a voice speaks almost directly into my ear.

"Do not move."

I watch as the courtyard fills up with brown-robed Army. They move real quick, shooters drawn and held on us from all directions.

No! Not now, I think. *Not after we have come so far.*

They encompass us, cutting off any exit, any chance of escape. What's happening here? I thought Tater said we had nothing to worry about? Why is the Army here? And how had they found us so fast?

Jax catches my eye, and his gaze slides to the saddle bag on his horse. Our shooters are in there.

I know right away what he's thinking. Before I can shake my head no at the idea, he moves for it. As quick as he is, he's not quick enough. One of the soldiers whacks him across the back of his knees, and he goes down hard.

"Jax!" Finn cries, but he doesn't run to him. The soldiers between him and Jax prevent him from doing so. Jax struggles back to his feet, not bothering to hide the anger on his face.

"Try that again, boy, and the next time, you won't get back up." The sneer on the soldier's face as he stares down at Jax is full of arrogance, and I can tell Jax is just itching to wipe that smug look right off of his face, but he doesn't move. He may be angry, but he's not totally stupid. Tater steps out in front of us all, his hands held up in surrender.

"Calm down, gentlemen. This is all a misunderstanding. I think you have us mistaken for someone else. We are nothing but a group of travelers, minstrels, and traders just looking to do some business," he says, a disarming smile on his face.

"Is that so, old man?" This from the same soldier who'd spoke to Jax. "A dwarf, two boys, and a girl. A very distinct group, is it not? The exact same sort of group an Army squadron was sent out to pick up weeks ago and from which only two survivors returned. You can see why such a group entering our city walls has raised our suspicions."

Tater nods. "Yes, yes, I can see where you may think that, but really, we are just travelers. Harmless, entertaining travelers. As a matter of fact, if you know of anyone looking for our services—"

The soldier rolls his eyes impatiently and interrupts Tater. "Enough talk old man." He turns to his men. "Take them all."

"Wait." He stops and turns back to us at Tater's command. Tater drops his hands and steps boldly up to the young man, and I tense. What the hell is he doing?

"Where is your commanding officer?" he asks.

The young man looks taken aback. "I am—"

"No, you are just a trainee." This time it is Tater who interrupts the soldier. I'm shocked at Tater's words, his tone. What is he playing at?

"You are just a little boy playing soldier. Who is actually in charge here today?"

"That would be me." The voice is mild, pleasant, and comes from the shadowed alleyway. He steps into view, and I'm surprised to see a potbellied, squat little man with a balding head and round, silver spectacles sitting low on his nose. If it weren't for the Army getup, you would believe he was just a neighborly sort. He ambles over to Tater, his chins wobbling from his effort.

"Hello, Naryz. I thought it would be you," the half-man says.

"Tater." The fat man nods, and I feel a huge wave of relief washing over me. Tater knew him just like the other guard. It's going to be okay.

"I have information for you," Tater says.

"Is that so?" The fat man sounds dubious.

Tater nods. "Indeed. First thing's first though, in anticipation of what may occur, I have to inquire about your diligence. Are you equipped with serum today?"

"As you well know, Tater, we are always prepared. Why do you ask?"

"And the reward still stands?" Tater's words are puzzling me. Where's he going with this?

"It does." The fat man nods again, making his chins wobble some more.

"Then *he* will be very pleased for I have brought him a wonderful gift indeed. This girl standing before you is probably one of the most powerful New Bloods to come into his possession for a very long time."

Wait! What? What is Tater saying? Shizen. Why's he telling them I'm a New Blood?

"And you are sure, Tater? He has been disappointed before, and trust me, old man, you do not want to disappoint him." The fat man's words are meant for Tater, but he is eyeballing me like I'm suddenly a piece of meat on his dinner plate. I'm stunned, unsure of what's going on. Did Tater truly just say those words, or is my mind playing tricks on me?

"I am sure. I've seen it with my own eyes. She is a true New Blood in every sense of the word. And the two with her are her willing accomplices."

Jax's "Bastard," shocks me, as he lunges for Tater, snarling like an animal. He is immediately taken down by half a dozen soldiers before he can get anywhere near him and disappears under the barrage of bodies.

Jax's yelling brings me out of my stupor, and I finally realize what's happening. I stare at Tater with uncertainty. "Tater? What are you doin'?" I whisper.

He ignores me entirely and turns back to the fat man. "I shall expect my payment to be prompt."

The impact of what is happening hits me like a punch to the gut. "You bastard!" I echo Jax, only this time, it doesn't come out as no whisper. "You lyin', traitorous bastard!" I move at him quick, my intent to wrap my hands round his scrawny neck. But like Jax, I'm instantly restrained by numerous hands. Struggling against them, I stare at Tater's back with hate-filled eyes. "How could you do this? We trusted you. I trusted you. Look at me, Tater. Dammit ... look at me. You betrayed us all."

I can hear Jax still struggling against his captors and Finn's quiet sobbing, but my focus is solely on the half-man in front of me. I need to understand. I need to know why he would do such a thing to us. He turns then, and his eyes are cold and ruthless, not like the man I had come to know at all.

"I warned you, girl, of the evil and corruption. I said you would see things that would change you forever." He shrugs. "This is merely one of those things. Only the strong survive in this world, and when you have riches, that's when you are the most powerful."

That's why he did this? For the reward? We meant so little to him that he turned us in for iron? He turns his back to me again and starts to walk away with Winnie in tow, but I'm not done.

"I'm gonna make you regret you ever crossed us, Tater." I'm screaming now, but I don't care. I'm pulling at my captors, nearly dragging them as I try to follow Tater. "Mark my words, half-man. I will kill you!"

Hurt, anger, betrayal. The emotions all boil over, and the buzzing starts out of nowhere. I welcome it with open arms. I welcome my Chi. I embrace it. The hands that seemed so strong holding me back I now shake off like swatting away maskeetos. I almost laugh out loud as the fat man backs up in fear, his eyes almost bugging out of his head, and yells at someone behind me, "For gods' sake man, take her down already."

I feel a small prick of pain as something jabs me in the neck. I whirl around, hand on my neck, and come face to face with my attacker. His eyes open wide as I grab him by the throat, and he drops a small white chamber with a sharply pointed end. He'd stuck me with that? What the hell?

An icy coldness starts at the spot on my neck. I can feel it quickly working its way through my enflamed blood, cooling me down, making me weak. The hand holding the soldier's throat goes limp and falls away on its own, like I can't control it. What is happening? The coldness works its way down into my legs, and I wobble a bit. What is this? Magic? I try to step away from the soldiers approaching me, but I fall into their hands instead. Jax by now is back on his feet, and I can see his bloodied face peering at me, calling my name. Finn too, but they sound strange ... distant ... distorted. I shake my head, trying to clear it, but it doesn't work.

I'm dragged helplessly through the narrow alleyway and tossed roughly into some kind of boxed wagon. I land in a heap on the floor, but I'm too weak to even make myself sit up. I hear the others being herded in, then gentle hands grab me, move me to a sitting position, and I stare up into angry, blue eyes. One of Jax's cheekbones is already turning purple, and he's bleeding from his lip and the old injury on his temple.

"You're bleeding," I try to say, but it feels like my tongue is swollen twice its normal size and all that comes out is gibberish. But he understands, and he shakes his head.

"I'm fine. Finn, too." He sounds so strange, like he's talking real slow. Finn sits on my other side, staring at me with worried eyes. I want to tell him I'm okay, but I can't seem to form the words. What is happening to me? I can't move, can't speak. I'm so scared. Is this what it feels like to die? A single tear escapes the corner of my eye. I can feel its wetness trail down my face, but Jax gently wipes it away.

"You're going to be okay. We're here with you. I won't let anything happen to you, Tara. I promise." Somehow, I know he actually means it. Jax always keeps his promises. I find it eases my fear some, and I relax in his arms.

I drift in and out of consciousness. I know we're moving. I can feel the bumps and ruts in the road, but time has no meaning to me. Can't rightly say how long we are on the move. I wake occasionally, panicked, but Jax is right there soothing me, keeping me calm, and I quickly drift off again.

I wake once more when they move me outside, but whatever magic they had attacked me with is still very much in control of me. My body is useless, and I'm shifted from the wagon to a sturdier metal cage like a sack of taters. I watch, immobilized, as Jax and Finn are forced in as well, and the clanging of the metal door as it locks behind them resonates in my ears. Finn immediately runs to me, but Jax starts shaking the cage door and yelling cuss words that would have embarrassed the most bad-ass raider at their retreating backs. They ignore him. I, on the other hand, for some reason find it extremely funny, and I start laughing uncontrollably. Jax whirls and stares at me in disbelief. I don't know what's wrong with me, but I can't stop laughing. It's like their magic has affected me in some other way now.

Finally, Jax's lips twitch, and he joins me and Finn at the other side of the cage.

"That's it … you have truly gone mad," he says as he slides down the wall to sit at my head, running his hands through his hair.

I nod, amazed that I am able to do so. "I think you're right," I whisper.

Ah. I can speak. Whatever they had used on me must be starting to wear off. I raise my hand slowly and try flexing my fist. I manage to do it once before the hand falls useless at my side again. But at least I had done it.

"Can you help me up?" I whisper, and Jax pulls me up in a sitting position against the wall.

I peer through the bars of the metal cage trying to figure out where they've brought us. I was expecting to be in some dank, underground cell, but we're not inside. We are definitely still outside, and amazingly, there are people milling about everywhere. And no one, not one single soul, is paying any attention to us prisoners in the cage. Then again, if there is a prison cage around, I guess they're very well used to seeing prisoners in it. Then I notice that these aren't just normal, everyday people walking around. These people were dressed in filthy rags, dirty, unkempt like they hadn't seen a bath in years. Not at all like the people we'd seen in the city. Soldiers are herding them along like cattle, and they rattle and clang as they pass by the cage. The noise is coming from chains around their ankles, and I suddenly understand why they're not bothering with us. They are prisoners just like we are.

"Where are we?" I ask, and my words come out a little stronger this time. I try moving my legs; I'm happy when they respond.

"I'm not sure, but I think we are being held in the iron mines," Jax answers, and I can feel my heart skip a beat.

Really? There may be a silver lining here after all. If that's where we were, then I don't have to worry about finding my way in to search for my kin. No, seems like I just have to worry about finding my way out.

I look around the cage, and my eyes come to rest on Finn. He's staring at the floor, head hanging on his chest, and I realize I haven't heard him speak since the courtyard.

"Finn?" I say, and when he looks up, his eyes are shiny with his tears.

"Why, Tara? Why would Tater do that to us? I thought he was my friend. And what about Cat? She ain't gonna know what happened to me. I promised her I was gonna come out and check on her every day. She's gonna think I deserted her. Why would he do that to us?"

I don't know how to answer the boy. I don't know because I'm feeling the same kinda hurt and betrayal and loss. "Finn—" I say, but he grabs my hand tight and cuts me off.

"Promise me you won't kill him, Tara." he says, staring at me fiercely.

"Finn, what are you talkin' about?" I say, bewildered. He was just bellyaching about Tater, now he's afraid I'm going to hurt him?

"You said you was gonna kill him. You cain't do that, Tara, no matter what he's done. He's still Tater. You cain't kill him. It ain't right."

"Finn, he turned us in—"

"Promise me," he says again with more urgency.

"Okay. All right, I promise not to kill him," I say, but more so just to shut the boy up. I've got no intention in hell of keeping that promise. I instantly feel ashamed for lying since the boy hugs me real tight in relief. Shizen. This is not going to be easy. I awkwardly pat his head, still not in full control of my muscles. "Cat will be fine," I say to him, and he nods even though I know he don't believe me. He's just desperate to accept any form of reassurance right now. I stare at Jax over the boy's head. "Any idea what they did to me back there, Jax?" I say, my brain and tongue apparently working together again. He shrugs at me.

"I was hoping you could tell me. After Tater sold us out, I spent the rest of the time at the bottom of a pile of soldiers. By the time I managed to climb my way out, you were nothing but a wobbly wreck."

Hearing Jax mention Tater's betrayal makes my hurt and anger come rushing back, but I push it away. "I got a glimpse of the weapon they stuck me with ... ain't never seen the likes before. The Prezedant may not be able to create his own New Bloods, but he definitely knows how to take 'em down. It was damn powerful magic."

Neither of us comes right out and says it, but that's

definitely not good, not at all. My one and only defense against this so-called Prezedant, my Chi, and he's able to take it away from me that easily and make me as helpless as a babe. It scares me.

"Why are they keepin' us here you think? Why ain't we on our way to Skytown right now?" I say.

"Oh, you will be, bright and early in the morning, I assure you." The round little man moved quietly for someone his size. I didn't even hear him approach our prison. He stands just out of arm's reach on the other side of the cage like he doesn't trust what I would do, two more soldiers at his back. Smart man. I glare at him as an idea unfolds in my head. We need to know some things, and I wonder if he had the answers. I struggle to my feet and walk on wobbly legs to face him. I hold onto the bars to keep myself upright, but he involuntarily backs up a pace. It pleases me to know I scare him.

"Naryz, if I remember correctly," I say, and he nods at me. "Why wait for the mornin'? If I am so important to the Prezedant, why keep him waitin'?"

He studies me through his little round spectacles. "I shouldn't think you would be so eager to meet him. He is not what you would describe as the most pleasant of men."

"Oh, trust me. I ain't eager to meet him at all. I'm just curious," I say. "You seem like a true soldier eager to please and all that. I just find it strange that you would make your master wait for his prize."

"He is not my master, and it takes a lot of preparation for a prisoner transport. Things someone like you could not even begin to understand," he says with more than a hint of smugness and superiority. My fingers itch to get at his throat, but all I do is nod at him all serious-like.

"I'm sure. But you know what I think, Naryz? I think he doesn't trust you to be able to take me to him. I think he thinks you lot are a bunch of idiots, drunkards, and dimwit soldiers. Why else would he stick you out in this shite hole instead of Skytown?"

He puckers his lips at me like he doesn't like what he's hearing. "Say what you will, mutie, but the overseeing of the iron mines is a very important business. I cannot afford to lose any of my men to take you on your little journey, so the Prezedant, well, he is sending his own elite group of men to handle you. You will be under their watchful eye in the morning. They have been well-trained in dealing with your kind."

I nod at him like I'm agreeing wholeheartedly and then give him my brightest smile. "Thank you, Naryz. You've been most helpful."

His look of confusion is almost comical. "I have told you nothing."

"Ah, but that's where you're wrong. I now know that we're bein' kept in the iron mines and that the few soldiers you have here are all there is to be had in Littlepass, and that we have until the mornin' to make our escape before more soldiers arrive. Good info, indeed."

The open-mouthed look on his puffy face kind of reminds me of the fish we used to catch as young'uns back in Rivercross, and I fight to hold back my laughter at the ridiculous sight. But then a disbelieving, "Tara?" reaches my ears, and I spin around to Jax and Finn to see what has them yelling so. But it's not them yelling. The voice is coming from the other side of the cage bars, and I follow it to its source.

I see him. Dirty, dressed in rags, and much thinner than I remember, but I know him right away.

Ben.

My shock roots me in place. Is it really him, or are my eyes playing a trick on me?

He's in a line with a bunch of other prisoners, all chained together, but it's him all right. He stares at me, and the brown eyes that have haunted my nightly dreams search my face like he can't believe what he's seeing. He tries to move closer to our prison, but a soldier walks by and gives him a fierce shove, sending him and the poor young'un chained to him sprawling in the dirt. He helps the child back to her feet, glaring daggers at the soldier the whole time. The young girl is crying, and there is blood splattered on her torn, yellow tunic.

"Get back in line."

They shuffle away from me, dragged by the others, and too late I stumble to the end of the cage.

"Ben!" I scream his name, and he tries to look back, but the soldier prodding him with the shooter keeps him from doing so. My heart is beating wildly, and the emotions coursing through me are almost overwhelming. Disbelief, shock, happiness, anger. How is it possible to feel all this at once?

It's him. Ben. He's here. I'd found him.

I had forgotten about the fat man. He waddles into view and his gaze wavers from Ben's departing back and back to me. A smug smile spreads across his face, causing his eyes to almost disappear into the surrounding folds of flesh, and he says, "Good info, indeed."

He turns and walks away from me, content in the knowledge that he has the upper hand. I bite my lip to stop from yelling every cuss word I can think of at his retreating back, but I don't want to give him the satisfaction of knowing he's rattled me.

I turn away, running a hand through my hair in frustration. "Dammit."

Why did I react like that, yelling Ben's name? I probably put him in more danger than ever now because of what I'd just done. Stupid. It's bad enough Finn and Jax are in this predicament because of me, but now I've done the same thing to Ben.

Finn comes to join me, his eyes wide. "That was your Ben, Tara? He's alive?"

I nod yes, still too overcome with emotion to answer.

"Then why are you so upset? I don't get it?" he says.

Jax does the explaining for me. "Because, Finn, Tara believes by showing her connection to Ben, Naryz will somehow use him to get at her in some way, hurt him to control her."

I stare at Jax, amazed that he understands exactly what I'm thinking. Then he flashes me a crooked grin. "What do you think he's going to do to him? Keep him prisoner? Starve him? Chain him up? No wait, I know, he's going to put him to work in the iron mines. Yeah, that's it." He snorts. "He's already been through all that, Tara. There's not much else they can do to him."

Relief washes over me. "You're right, Jax," I say.

"Damn right, I'm right. It's us you should be worried about. We're the ones stuck in a cage with you. And on our way to being carted off to Skytown in the morning." He shakes his head. "How the hell did I end up in this same situation with you again? Must be a sucker for a pretty face, I guess."

I start laughing; I can't help myself. I throw my head back and laugh until it brings tears to my eyes. Finn's gaze says it all; he thinks I've lost my mind, and he's probably right. Here we are, captured again like Jax said, being shipped off to the Prezedant in the morning to be most likely experimented on and turned into crazy, diseased creatures, but it all doesn't matter to me. Not at this moment. Ben is alive. That is enough for now.

<hr>

I'm not sure what awakens me. I can't even believe that I fell asleep in the first place, but something has pulled me from my slumber, and I wake with a start, listening. At first, there's nothing other than Finn's quiet snoring. I peer through the cage bars, trying to adjust my eyes to the moonlight. I see the two guards that had accompanied Naryz earlier and hear their quiet murmurings. They don't seem to find anything out of sorts. Maybe there isn't anything, and I'd just been dreaming.

I settle back against Finn, trying to get some warmth from him, when a slight thump occurs above my head. I don't move, but my eyes seek out the guards once more. They still seem to be unaware of anything amiss. Silence follows again.

I start to think I imagined the sounds when suddenly both guards are jerked off their feet at the same time and seem to dangle in midair. I watch in confusion as they struggle, their legs thrashing wildly about. What the hell is this? It's probably only for a few seconds, but it seems like forever before their thrashing stops and they crumple to the ground in a heap. Something leaps from the top of the cage. I can't tell what it is—it's just a black blur to me—but it appears to be now crouching over the soldiers. I shake Finn and Jax, holding a finger to my lips as both sets of eyes pop open. Much to their credit, they don't make a peep as I point to the black shape outside of our cage. Shapes. There's two of them; I can see that now. A quick glint in the moonlight just before I hear scraping as the key is put into the locked door. Someone is trying to get us out.

We're on our feet in an instant. The rusted cage door squeals as it opens, and I suck in my breath. The shapes stop and stand still for a moment, but no alarm sounds. Pushing the door all the way open now, they motion for us to move. We don't hesitate. Brushing past them, we're directed with an upward point before they form a boosting step with their joined hands. They want us to get on top of the cage. I go first, and I'm hoisted over the top before turning to help Finn, who's right behind me. Jax comes next, and the three of us help pull our rescuers up over the ledge.

Once on top, and bathed in moonlight, the shapes become people dressed entirely in black right down to the hoods covering their heads. We follow them across the top of the metal cage that sits underneath a rocky overhang. How the hell did they get here? Then I see the ropes they'd used to lower themselves down. One of the rescuers grabs a rope and hands it to me.

"Put this around you and tug; our friends at the top will pull you up," a voice whispers in my ear. I push the rope away and shake my head no.

"Take Finn and Jax, but I cain't go."

Jax, who is in the process of hitching a rope to Finn, turns to me in amazement. "Tara, what the—go up the damn rope," he hisses at me.

"No," I whisper back. "You both go. I gotta go after Ben."

All I can see are the whites of Jax's eyes as he glares at me in disbelief. "Are you crazy? You can't do that by yourself."

"Tara. You cain't," Finn whispers, his worry evident, but by now he is being lifted, and whatever else he says gets whisked away.

"We don't have time for this," one of the black robes hisses at me. "Take the rope, girl."

I shake my head again and turn to Jax. "I cain't leave him, not again. I am his only chance, Jax," I say, begging him to understand.

"If you get captured again, then he has no chance. Tara let's get out of here. We'll figure out a way to come back for Ben, but if you are sent off to Skytown in the morning, who will help him then? At least if we are free, we can come up with a way to help him, too."

I know what he's saying makes sense, but it feels wrong, so wrong. How can I leave Ben here to endure any more suffering? How can I leave him when I have just found him? The memory of him and the young girl with the bloody tunic pops into my head, and I know I can't go.

One of the black robes grabs my arm so tightly it hurts. "Listen to me, girl. We don't have much time. The soldiers are due for their rounds any minute now. Soon, somebody is either going to find those two down there or our friends at the top. Now, do what your boyfriend is telling you and move."

I yank my arm out of his grasp and hiss at him angrily, "He ain't my boyfriend," but my eyes are focused on Jax.

"I cain't go without him, Jax. The Gods only know what Naryz will do to him …," I trail off, not wanting to think of that possibility.

"Go up that damn rope and I will come back and get Ben myself," he whispers at me and shoving the rope in my hands. "But there is nothing we can do tonight. Use your head, Tara. If we get captured again, he won't have anyone to help free him."

Jax is right. Dammit! I know he's right, but I still don't want to admit it.

"You promise to help me get him out of here?" My whisper is fierce and demanding.

"I promise. Now go, dammit."

Hoping that I'm not making a mistake, I believe him. Fitting the rope under my arms, I give a little tug and suddenly feel myself being lifted. Immediately, once I hit the top, arms pull me onto solid ground, and the rope is yanked off me and sent down again. Finn stands at my side as we wait anxiously for Jax to join us. I look around at these people helping us. There must be at least five or six of them, plus the two still below. Who are they? And why are they helping us? There's no time for questions though. As soon as the three of us are together again, we are ushered quickly down the hill and through a grove of trees by a woman in a large hood. I can't tell any more than that. The trees are thick and don't allow much moonlight to filter through, so we stumble more often than not in the darkness. I hold fiercely onto Finn and Jax as we are hurried through, not taking any chance of losing them.

It's not long until we come out on the other side. A covered wagon attached to two nags waits in the clearing. They snort with nervousness at our sudden appearance. Standing by the wagon are three others: a girl about my age and two young men, one not much bigger than Finn. They, unlike the others that had just helped us, wear no hoods. It's like they're not trying to hide their faces at all.

"Go now," the woman says to them. "And make sure you're seen as you ride out of town. We want them to believe the fugitives have clearly left Littlepass. Make haste for the safe house. Ride swift and safe, my friends."

They nod and scurry away. The rest of the hoods blend into the shadows of the night now that they have secured the last of their people and disappear. The woman ushers us into the wagon just as a loud shouting comes from below us. The Army. They must have found their men and seen that we were gone. The woman leaps in behind us and shouts, "Go!" at the driver, and the wagon takes off so violently I fall over from the sudden jolt.

The wagon ride is fierce. We must hit every rut and hole possible. Feels like my bones are going to shatter they're jarred so much. But no one dares to utter a sound or complaint. We travel in complete silence, our eyes wide, fearing at any moment to hear the shouts of the Army telling us to halt. But it doesn't happen; the ride is uneventful, and we reach our destination, whatever it may be, without incident. To my relief, the wagon finally grinds to a halt, and we are herded out.

Wherever we are, we're no longer outside. Stone walls surround us. The circular room we stand in is full of hay and mud, and from the smell, I would say more than a few animals had called this place home. Are we in a barn? Where the hell has she brought us? No chance to ask a single question before the woman moves us again.

"This way," she says, and we follow her through a little door cut into the rock wall of the room.

As dirty and foul-smelling as the stone room was, the room we now find ourselves in is the complete opposite. Walls and floors so blindingly white it hurts my eyes just to look at them. I blink for a bit, trying to let my eyes adjust. It's so bright in here it's almost like daylight, yet it's the middle of the night. My confused brain is telling me the light is coming from the torches on the walls, but there's no fire from what I can see. Torches without flame, what the hell? I look at Finn and Jax in amazement, but they're also standing and staring with the same gaping, fish mouth at this curious oddity. I want to ask a hundred questions, but like the woman knows what is about to spew outta my mouth, she pulls her hood off and just glares at me, startling me into silence.

"Come," she says abruptly and starts walking down the white hall. Dumbfounded as we are, we follow meekly. Every step we take on the shiny, smooth stone floor echoes back at us from the bare white walls. We don't talk; it's like the room demands silence and to break it would be committing a sacrilege. She leads us to two massive black doors, the only bit of color in this otherwise white hall. She knocks once, then turns the handles, and pushes them open.

The room we step into is completely different yet again. If the other room had been cold and barren, this one is warm and inviting. A fire burns in a huge stone hearth at the center of the room, and chairs flank it on both sides, sitting on a nice, thick rug. The walls of the room are made up of shelves, filled to overflowing with colorful objects of varying sizes. Big and small, the items occupy every space, and it takes a moment for my brain to register what they are. Books. So many of them. I've only ever seen a few in my lifetime, shown to us as a rare find by some trader who had been passing through. Only ever held one, which was the ratty, torn one Grada used to have when I was real young. The one he had taught me to read and write with, but that one had rotted away long ago. There's so many of them here and in such good shape. I never could have imagined so many existed. So entranced am I with my surroundings that I don't even notice the woman standing in front of the fire until she speaks, making us all jump.

"Welcome."

She is tall; I notice that right away. Her hair is black, black as mine and hangs long and straight down her back. She is dressed in a long, gray robe, and her hands are tucked away in the voluminous sleeves. But she is smiling, and that smile says she is very glad to see us, easing the knot in my gut. She walks towards us, right up to me, and the hands that come out to cradle my face are covered in puckered, raised scars. At the contact, I can feel a tingling shoot straight through me, and I startle.

"Tara, you have grown up. It is so good to see you again, child."

Again? I'd never seen this woman before in my life. Why would she say that? I grab her hands and pull them away, finally finding my voice.

"Where are we? Who are you? And why did your people save us? What do you want from us?" I say.

She chuckles then, a soft, tinkling sound, and squeezes my hands in hers. "So curious and so full of bravado. Just like your mother. I shouldn't have expected any different. This is Sanctuary. And I am Lily."

CHAPTER 8

Sanctuary

———◆———

I awake from my sleep disoriented and confused, and for a brief moment, I don't know where I am. Then the previous evening's events come slowly back to me and I remember. Lily had found us. Rescued us. And we were now in a place called Sanctuary. That's still all I know. As full of questions as we had been last evening, she had taken one look at us all and refused to answer anything coming out of our mouths.

"Look at you." She had clucked her tongue worriedly. "Tired, exhausted, and probably scared witless I'm sure. You need to rest … all of you. Zoe, take them to their rooms."

Our rooms? She had rooms prepared for us? Like she

knew we were coming? I had ignored the stern woman trying to usher us back out into the white hall and tried to question Lily again. There was so much I needed to know.

How had she found us? How did she know Grada? Why was I told to find her? But she had laid a finger to my lips and smiled that kind, but firm, smile at me again.

"Shush, child. There will be time to ask all your questions in the morning, after you are all well-rested. You have been through an enormously terrifying ordeal ... things that would have broken even the strongest of soldiers. You need to sleep. The boy needs to sleep."

I had looked at Finn then, and I knew she was right. His eyes had been huge in his pale, drawn face, and he looked befuddled, shocked, like someone had punched him hard in the head. *Did we all look like that?* I wondered.

She must have seen the stubbornness on my face as well though, because she added, "Tara, all your questions I will answer in the morning. I promise, child."

I must have been more tired than I realized since without so much as a peep of protest, I'd let the strange woman lead us back through the white hall to a bunch of doors I hadn't noticed the first time around. She'd opened three doors, one for each of us, and I had nodded at Finn that it was okay before I headed into mine. I didn't take much stock of the room at the time, just the fact that it held a bed and that I had collapsed onto it without even bothering to undress or even take off my boots. I'd immediately fallen into an exhausted sleep.

This morning; however, I take more notice. The room is simple enough. It contains a bed, a chest, and a small, wooden table and chair sitting on the same smooth, stone floor as found in the white hall. The late morning sunlight filtering through the high window above the bed falls onto a neatly folded pile of clean clothes sitting on the chair and a basin of water on the table. Those were not here last night; I'm sure of that. Are these things meant for me?

I unfold them. There's a pair of dark cloth trousers and a white tunic, both of them looking to be my fit. Deciding it must be, I take off the dirty things I'm wearing, give myself a quick wash from the basin, and dress myself in the clean things. It feels real good to have the clean cloth against my skin, and I can't help but smile at how it makes me feel so normal just to be clean. Or maybe this happiness has more to do with the fact that the sun is reflecting off my born day gift, and that the person who had given it to me is alive and here in Littlepass, in arm's reach.

I will get you out of there, Ben, I think. *I promise you that.*

Voices filter through from the hall, and I open my door to find Finn and Jax standing there. They're dressed in the same kind of clothing as I am, though from the dirt still on Finn's face, I don't think he bothered with the basin of water. Jax, however, looks clean, but the huge bruise on his cheek and the cut on his lip tells the tale of Tater's betrayal. I nod at his cheek, trying not to let my anger take root.

"Does it hurt bad?" I ask.

"Only when I smile," he says, making me laugh.

"Well, you should be fine then since smilin' ain't one of your better habits," I say, and he surprises me with his own deep laughter.

From out of nowhere seems like, the woman from the

night before appears in the hall and I jump in startled surprise. Zoe, I think Lily had called her. How the hell does someone not make any noise when they walk?

"Good morning. I trust you all slept well?" I don't think she was truly concerned about that though since she doesn't give us a chance to answer before she speaks again. "If you would follow me, Lily is waiting for you all at the breakfast table."

Breakfast? Now, we're talking. My stomach rumbles at the thought of food, and all three of us eagerly follow the woman. She leads us down the hall, through the room full of books, down a flight of steps, and into yet another hall. I look around all the while, overwhelmed at the vastness of each room we pass through. What the hell kind of place is this Sanctuary, and how big is it really? This second hall is much smaller than the first though, and we pass under an archway into a room containing a long, wooden table.

The table is huge. Must be at least ten chairs sitting on either side of it. Lily occupies the one at the end, and she rises as we enter, gesturing for us to join her. I still got the same barrel of questions from the night before bouncing around in my head, but the sight of the food on the table takes priority right now.

"Please," she says. "Sit. Eat."

She doesn't have to tell us twice. We promptly fill the chairs on either side of her, and I make a grab for the fresh bread I could smell as soon as we entered the room. It's still warm. And is that—oh, gods, it is. Butter. I haven't seen butter since our goat died about four years back. Wasn't all bad; the goat meat had kept us fed real good for quite a while, but I sure did miss that butter. Grabbing the closest knife I can find, I cut off a chunk of the white stuff and start smothering my bread with it. My mouth is watering something fierce as I watch it melt on my bread and ooze down over my fingers. I take a huge bite and close my eyes in pure pleasure.

The only noise for the next little while is our lips smacking and our sighs of satisfaction. Zoe pops up at my elbow at one point, replenishing the bread, and I nearly jump from my chair in fright. I almost yell at her "Stop doin' that," but I didn't wanna be ill mannered. Especially to Lily who surely had every right to be horrified at our lack of table manners, but she doesn't say a word as we stuff our gullets. After about my fifth or sixth slice of butter-soaked bread (I'd lost count), I look up to find her watching me, a sad little smile on her face. She must see my questioning look because she raises a brow in apology.

"I'm sorry, it's just you look so much like her, Rease, your mother," she says, and at the mention of my ma, my appetite dies just like that. The bread that I'd been enjoying so much earlier now tastes like dust in my mouth. I lay it down, about to wipe my greasy lips on my sleeve, but Lily hands me a folded white cloth from the table with a little smile.

My ma's name was Rease. I never knew that. I mull this over for a bit, trying it out in my head.

"You knew her well?" I say finally.

"Very much so. She was a great friend and a powerful New Blood."

At hearing those words, my heart skips a beat. My ma was a New Blood, too? Did Lily know about me? I raise my eyes to her, and as if she can read what I'm thinking, she nods at me.

"Yes, I'm very aware that you follow in her footsteps, Tara. I was hoping you would. Praying really. That was the reason I took you away to the other side of the mountains, so he wouldn't get his hands on you. So you wouldn't end up with the same fate as your mother."

This is it. What I want to know—what I need to know—but now that I'm finally about to get some answers, I don't know if I'm truly ready to hear them.

"You were the one who left me in the sand lands?" I ask. "So my ma didn't abandon me?"

"No," she whispers gently, and that simple word causes me to grip the edge of the table. "Leaving you was not her choice."

Hearing what Lily just said, it's like some huge weight lifts from my chest ... like I can suddenly breathe again.

"What happened to my ma then?" I'm pretty sure I already know, but when the answer passes from Lily's lips, I'm a little surprised at the sharp pain in my chest that accompanies it.

"She died at his hands. Just like every other New Blood that has ever had the misfortune to cross paths with him," she says, and I drop my eyes to hide the tears that suddenly well up.

I can't rightly explain why I'm tearing up. It's not like I didn't know she was already dead. Maybe there was this tiny little part of me that had been hoping I was wrong. I take a couple of breaths, get myself back under control, and when I speak again, my voice doesn't waver.

"How did you know that I would be like her? That I would carry the same curse?" I say.

"Curse?" Lily looks at me in shock, like she can't believe what she'd just heard. "Is that what you think, child? That you are cursed? You are blessed! You have been touched, chosen by the gods to do their bidding here on this Earth."

The unexpected anger comes over me like some rogue wave. "What the hell is that supposed to mean? Why cain't people talk plain enough when describin' what a New Blood is? Is it because I am a mutie, a freak, and you don't want to come right out and say it? Touched by the gods ... fulfiller of prophecy ... what a bunch of shite. I just want to know what I am and where I came from. Is that too much to ask?"

This is met by silence. Finn regards me with wide-eyed surprise, the slab of hog he had been devouring sitting precariously on his fork halfway to his mouth. Jax is quiet as well, but his blue eyes convey silent understanding. To my surprise, Lily is smiling at my outburst.

"So much like your mother." She motions to Zoe, who has been hovering creepily at the end of the table. At Lily's request, she picks up a cloth-covered tray and joins us at our end.

"I cannot tell you how New Bloods came to be because I do not know for certain. There may have once been a few souls who knew this answer, but I am afraid those people have long since passed. There are some who believe that New Bloods descended from the gods, brought about to heal our destroyed world. Others believe that they were created by man. The same men who brought about the Shift and now needed a stronger breed to be able to rebuild and repopulate the dead lands. I do not know which version is the truth. What I do know to be true, however, is that New Bloods' gifts are very rare and vary in strength. I, for example, can heal others from life-threatening wounds if I get to care for them quick enough. But that is the extent of my ability, I'm afraid."

Was Lily admitting to being a New Blood as well? But her hair, she didn't have white stripes. She notices what I'm looking at and nods.

"I am not of the light. That sort of Chi only occurs in the most powerful of our kind. I hear you have experienced it a few times."

She heard? From who? Who had she been talking to? I look to Jax and Finn, but they are both shaking their heads at my unspoken question.

"I have experienced … somethin' … and I've done things I cain't explain, but I got no control over any of it," I say.

"You will. It takes time to know your Chi and learn to control it. It took your mother years to know hers. Let me show you something."

She pulls the cloth off of the tray and sitting there is what looks like a little bowl of silver-colored water and a wilted weed sitting in a pot full of dirt. Okay, is this supposed to mean something to me?

"Give me your hand."

I do as she asks, and before I realize what she's up to, she pricks the tip of my finger with her knife, causing the blood to flow.

"Ow," I cry and try to pull away from her, but she holds on tight. What the hell is she doing?

"Trust me," she says in her calm voice.

Trust her? The crazy bird just cut open my finger. But

against my better judgment, I don't pull away. She holds my bleeding finger over the water, and a few drops fall into the bowl. Gently, she wraps my finger in the folded piece of cloth. She picks up the bowl and swirls it around so that the red blood looks pinkish mixed with the odd-colored water. She then pours the water into the pot. I wait expectantly for…something. Nothing happens.

Shizen. I think to myself. *She is just as bat shite crazy as the others we had met.* I don't say it out loud though because I don't want her pricking me with the knife again.

"How did you know Grada?" I say to her, pulling my hand to my chest and thinking I should take her mind off New Blood talk for a bit. "And why did you take me to him? Why didn't you just keep me here with you?"

"Is that what you called him? Grada?" She smiles to herself. "He must have been pleased with that name. Your 'grada' was my friend, my ally. He was once one of the Army himself until they found him out of course. He was lucky enough to escape into the sand lands before he could be dealt with. And I took you to him because he was the only one at the time that I could trust with keeping you safe. After your mother died … the Prezedant looked high and low for you. He questioned everyone, tortured many, executed some. He wanted to find you very badly. I needed to get you as far away from him as possible."

"Why? Why did he need to find me so badly? And how did he know I would become what I've become?" I say.

"He didn't. No one did. We hoped and prayed that you would take after your mother. That you would be as strong as her. And from what I have been told, it appears we have been right. He wanted you badly because he wanted to kill you. We needed you badly to stay alive because we want you to kill him. Just like your mother was attempting to do and would have done had she not fallen herself." She says the words calm and offhand like it was just normal conversation, like we were just talking about the weather.

"Are you crazy?" Jax hasn't said a word up until now, but he's looking back and forth between me and Lily. I can't be certain, but I think his words are directed at her.

"You want Tara to go up against a powerful, immortal being that's protected night and day by his Army and kill him? Just like that? She's just a girl. She may be a mutie, but she doesn't have the ability to take on someone like that. She would just get herself killed."

Lily doesn't seem to take offense. In fact, she nods like she's agreeing with Jax's words. "You are quite right; she doesn't have the ability, not yet. But she will. That is why her Grada sent her back to me. That is why he protected her to the end. He knew she had to stay alive."

Her words confuse me. How did she know so much? How did she know what Grada had done for me that day? Before I can ask, though, I hear Finn whisper, "Tara," and I look at him across the table. His eyes have gone all big, and he is pointing towards Lily. But it's not Lily he's looking at. It's the flower. The bright yellow flower rising from the pot, which only a moment ago had been a wilted stem. Shizen. What kinda magic is this?

Lily sees what we are looking at, and her smile grows wider. "You asked me what you are, child? This is what you are. All your power comes from within. There are no limits to it. This Chi, or bio-energy as it is truly known, is said to exist in everyone. A gift from the gods? Maybe. But in New Bloods, it is immensely powerful. While others can only use their Chi within their own bodies, New Bloods can use it externally. Apply it to others or objects as we desire. Our Chi flows freely through our energy field. Some never learn how to use it, while others have enormous Chi. It overflows, crying to be released. Ours is abundant and until you learn to control it, it can overwhelm you. Through us, it has the ability to impact anything it comes into contact with. We are able to control and manipulate, well, life energy itself."

"How is that possible?" I whisper, still not believing what I'm seeing. "It was almost dead. I cain't do something like that ...," I trail off, but then another question pops into my head. "Why didn't I know I had this energy? I didn't have a clue about this Chi until the attack on Rivercross. Why did it wait for then?"

"It has always been a part of you, Tara. Your hair—those white stripes—they are a result of this massive energy trying to manifest itself. Your ability to heal quickly, to feel the lands, to control the sands is all bio-energy. Your Chi was always there; it was just brought to the surface by the stress and grief you suffered. And it flows strongly through you, Tara. I can sense it. It flows through your blood. That's where your energy is the most powerful. When you learn to control it, you can awaken new possibilities of strength and influence. That is why he needs you so badly. He takes New Bloods and drains them of their power, their blood, and uses it for himself. Our bio-energy carries the ability to heal this Earth and make it livable again for all mankind, yet he chooses to keep us from doing so. Instead, he depletes us to make his own life prosperous while the rest of the people live in despair. Starving. Sickly. Why should such a callous, ruthless creature continue to live? You have to be the one to finish what your mother started, Tara. It is your destiny."

None of us speaks for a moment. It's like what we're hearing and seeing is just too unbelievable for words to even express. I can't even pretend to begin to understand what Lily has just told me, but I do know one thing for certain. If the Prezedant is looking for me so badly, then I can't put the two sitting across the table from me in any more danger. I can't expect them to follow me anymore. They need to get as far away from me as possible. Maybe Jax would find it in his heart to let Finn go with him back to Gray Valley, him and Cat. Keep them safe. But I also can't expect to do what Lily is asking me to do. It's just craziness. How does she expect me to go up against the Prezedant and his Army?

"No," I say simply, but she looks at me like she doesn't understand. "I cain't do what you're expectin' of me. I'm sorry, Lily, but I'm not who you expect me to be. I'm just … Tara from Rivercross. I cain't do the things you think I'm capable of. I don't know nuthin' about bio-energy, whatever the hell that is. Like Jax said, I'm just another mutie who can pull off a couple of tricks, and I cain't even control those. The only thing I want to do right now is find my kin and go as far away from this Prezedant as we can. You're a New Blood. You found me. There's probably a hundred more out there somewhere; you just gotta find the right one."

She doesn't react at all like I expect. Instead of getting angry at my refusal, she merely smiles and takes my hand, causing that tingling again. "I'm sorry. I have rushed this. This is not at all the way I wanted this conversation to go." She sighs and gives my hand a little shake. "I know this is a lot to take in right now, child, and that you are scared, but—"

"Hah," I say, cutting her off and pulling my hand away. "Scared? I'm terrified beyond words to have a madman breathin' down my neck wantin' to kill me, accordin' to you. I'm afraid for my kin, for what they may be sufferin' right now. For my friends and their safety even to just be around me. I'm so angry at what he did to Grada and to everybody I ever loved. They died because of me. Nah, scared is not exactly the word I would use to describe how I feel at the moment."

"You are feeling doubt, Tara, and questioning your abilities. That's normal. But we will help you with that. We will help you learn and grow into your powers. Trust me. You are the one. We have been waiting for you for a very long time," she says.

"Who exactly are 'we'?" I'm getting a little frustrated now that she's not taking no for an answer. "And what exactly is this place? And how is it that the Prezedant hasn't come for you already? It's not like you're exactly hidin' here."

She shrugs. "I have found the best way to hide is to stay in plain view. This is Sanctuary, a place of healing and recovery. We are well-known for our treatments and get paid quite handsomely for our services. The Army bring their wounded here quite often."

"You heal the Army? The same men you want me to defeat?" I'm starting to think she's even crazier than Orakel.

"The best way to fight is from the inside, Tara. Over the

years, I have gained their trust, their respect. They have no idea what I am. In this way, I have been able to plant many of my own people—spies, if you will—into his elite circle. It is the only way we are able to stay ahead of him at times."

"Yeah, well your spies didn't help with savin' Rivercross, now did they?" I say, and my words are bitter. For the first time, she drops her gaze from me.

"No, and for that, I am truly sorry. We tried to get warning to you when we heard of his men traveling to the sand lands, but my messenger … he was too late. He did, however, save you all from the raiders and the Army. At least it was some form of redemption," she says.

"You mean the mutie-Po—he's one of yours?" I say surprised, and she nods.

"He's one of us, Tara. A New Blood in his own right. We all share a connection, a blood bond if you will. He tracked you across the sand lands, following you. Protecting you."

It makes sense now, the feeling of being followed. Of sensing something … something I just couldn't put my finger on. I look up sharply. "We lost track of him at the attack. Is he …?" I can't finish, but Lily knows what I am about to ask, and she eases my fear.

"He is well. They did not capture him." It makes me feel better. He did save our lives after all.

"So all the people that rescued us last night. They work with you? What are you, some kinda little army yourselves?" I say.

She laughs at this. "I guess you could call us that. We are in our own right a rebellion. We try to warn as many people as we can when we get word he is on the move. We provide shelter to those attempting to flee his oppression and help them with their journey into the sand lands. We try to save the mutants from the games."

At my questioning look, she explains, and her voice hardens with each word. "Oh yes, he is very fond of his 'mutie games' as he calls them. He captures these poor, innocent, altered souls from the outlying areas and forces them to fight each other in arenas just for the sheer enjoyment of watching them fight to the death. Many of them are women and even children at times. But it all ends with the same result. You are given the choice to beat your opponent to the death or a wild, starved wolfling is let loose in the arena with you, and you are both torn to shreds anyway. It is quite the popular pastime among his elite."

Jax and Finn's faces both mirror my own horror. Is there anything this madman isn't capable of? It makes my fear for my kin and the two sitting across from me grow twofold. It's like Lily knows what she's saying is terrifying us, and the hardness in her voice drops away.

"You can see why it is crucial we stop him, Tara. With each passing year, his madness grows and spreads to those around him. And it is the innocent, the mutated, the righteous that suffer from it. Your mother knew this, and she gave her life in her attempt to stop it. Will you let that go unpunished?"

I hold onto my flower, clutch it in my hand tight, as if expecting an answer to come from it, telling me what to do. The things Lily's telling me ... they are horrible and savage indeed, and I admire this little band of rebels for trying to fight back. But it's not my fight. There's nothing I can do about the Prezedant or his Army. My concern, my only focus, is to free Ben and find Jane and Thomas. Find them and run, hide far enough in the sand lands so that he would never find us. Besides, they had that magical weapon that made me weak as a newborn babe. How am I supposed to go up against that? I look up to find Jax's eyes on me, silently asking what my decision will be. Surely, he will understand. The Prezedant had killed his pa and his sister. He never went looking for revenge because he knew it would be just asking for his own death.

"I'm sorry, Lily. But I ain't the right person to help you with this. All I'm aimin' to do is find my kin and go far away. Somewhere safe," I say. I tense, waiting for her response to my words, but at that moment a voice I never expected to hear again interrupts what she's about to say.

"Ah, so the rebels were able to free you successfully. That is good news, indeed. It is wonderful to see you safe and sound, my friends."

I think I would have been less surprised to see the Prezedant himself standing there in front of us than the half-man. He's smiling that toothy grin of his, looking not the least bit ashamed for what he did to us. I don't even stop to think what I'm about to do. My chair flies out from underneath me, and I tackle the little man, the knife I had used earlier to butter my bread pressed threateningly into his throat. His eyes pop from his head in surprise, and he claws at my hands, trying to get them off his neck.

"Tara … stop … for the … gods' sake …," he gasps words at me, and I can hear Lily yelling from behind. Finn too. But I don't take no heed. All I know is that Tater will pay for his betrayal. I press harder on the knife, and a drop of blood appears on Tater's neck.

"Tara, stop. He hasn't betrayed you."

I hear Lily's words, I do. But just like every time before, my anger is so overwhelming it's like I can't control what I'm doing. I watch as the drop of blood turns into a bead and trickles down his neck.

"Tara, you promised."

Finn's plea is what stops me. I look up into his beseeching brown eyes, and I know I can't do it. I can't go back on my promise to him. I can't betray his trust like Tater had done to me. I push myself away from the little man in disgust as Lily helps him to his feet. His hand clutches his neck, but his eyes watch me warily as if afraid I will attack him again. Lily examines the wound.

"He's fine. It's just a flesh wound," I say coldly, indicating that he's very lucky it isn't much worse.

"I take it you have not imparted to them—to the girl— how their miraculous escape came to be then?" he says to Lily, but he's still watching me with cautious eyes.

She bows her head. "My apologies, Tater. In all the excitement, I'm afraid I have forgotten to tell them who their savior was."

What are they talking about? I look at Jax who seems just as confused as I am.

"Do you two know each other?" Jax asks.

"Only as of yesterday." Lily is the one to answer. Tater by now is, I'm assuming, realizing how much of a close call he just had and is making his way to the nearest chair on wobbly legs.

"Imagine my shock and dismay when this gentleman

shows up on my doorstep yesterday with information of your capture. I had no idea you were so close. When Po lost track of you after your escape from the raiders, we searched high and low for you. But it was like you had disappeared from the face of the Earth. Po couldn't sense you at all."

Tater had come to Lily?

"But you said you didn't know Lily. You lied to us about that too?" I growl, my anger still very real.

"I did not," the half-man answers in a haughty tone, picking up the cloth Lily had wrapped my finger in earlier and holding it at his neck. "I did not know of your Lily, but I did know of Sanctuary. You told me Lily was a healer. I just put two and two together. Imagine my surprise when this lovely lady here had already heard of me and my association with you from the mutie. And my even greater surprise at learning she was the brains behind the much-rumored rebellion."

"But you turned us over to the Army." I'm glad Jax is questioning all this since I still can't wrap my head around what they're saying. "Why would you turn us in then get us rescued?"

"Ah, yes, well, that move was born out of necessity, I'm afraid. We were surrounded, captured, with no chance of escape. If I had not done what I did, we would all be on our way to Skytown right now under the watchful eyes of the Prezedant's elite guard. I saw a chance for one of us to be free, and I made my choice. Luckily for us all, it worked."

Lily picks up the story. "Tater informed us of your capture and of the location where you were being kept. If it wasn't for him, we would have never known to rescue you."

"You are quite welcome by the way," he says sarcastically as he dabs at his bleeding neck. "However, my reward for my heroism has definitely been a disappointment, I must say. Especially now that your escape ensures I won't see a single piece of iron from said reward." He keeps dabbing at his neck and staring daggers at me like I was the one who'd done the betraying.

"I knew it! I knew you wouldn't betray us, Tater," Finn says, grinning from ear to ear. "Tara, Tater saved us. Ain't you glad you didn't kill him?"

"I haven't decided yet," I say, torn between what I'm hearing and the hurt I'd been carrying around since yesterday. I keep staring at him, still not convinced of his innocence. Yesterday at our capture, he'd been so cold, so callous. Had he just been pretending, or was that really his true colors?

"Why did you help us?" I ask. "You ain't got no loyalty to us. You could have taken your reward and walked away, washed your hands of us. Why did you come here lookin' for Lily?"

He sighs and drops the cloth back on the table. An awkward silence follows, like he doesn't have an answer for me. Finally he says, "To be quite honest, I'm not sure myself. The reward was indeed enticing. Riches like that … they can indubitably turn a man's head. Maybe I'm just as crazy as those poor wretches we left back in the dead city, but I think there is hope yet." Disbelief tinges his voice like he can't believe he's actually saying these words. "I think that maybe you *are* the one they've all been waiting for, and that these dark days will indeed come to an end. Maybe it's just the wishful thinking of an old man who's soon to meet his gods, but I think I have regained my faith."

Whatever I expected to hear Tater say, it surely isn't that. Is he being truthful? Or is this just another act?

"Well, I hate to disappoint you old man, but your faith is put in the wrong person," I say. "Ain't nuthin' I can do about the Prezedant. All I'm fixin' on doin' is freein' Ben from the iron mines, findin' my other kin, and gettin' the hell away from Littlepass and Skytown. Hell, I don't even wanna speak those two names ever again."

I can tell Tater is genuinely surprised by this. "Your young man, he's here? In the iron mines? Are you certain?"

"Aye, we seen him while we were bein' held there," I say.

"Well, that is wonderful news indeed! To find him alive and well, that has to be of prophetic significance," Tater says. "It is a good omen, Tara. It is destiny telling you that you are where you should be in Littlepass with Lily and her rebels."

Did Tater get dropped on his head since the last time we'd seen him? Or had he been in the ale already this morning?

"What if we can help you free your kin, Tara?" Lily picks up on what Tater is saying. "Would you be willing to listen to us then? To at least listen to what we have planned, what we believe you can be capable of?"

I know she's just using Ben as bait for her own purposes, but at the thought of them helping to free him, I can't resist the offer.

"Can your people do that? Can they help me get him out of there?" I say, fearing to raise too much hope.

She gives a slight nod. "It will not be easy. Zoe informs me that our ruse has worked, and that our decoys seen leaving the city walls were indeed believed to be the three of you, but they will not be as easily fooled the second time around. Security will be tightened. You will probably have to go into hiding for quite a while—"

"I don't care," I say, cutting off her words. "I will do whatever it takes to free Ben. I will listen to you until I turn blue in the face if you help me get him out of there."

"So be it. I will send the word, gather our forces together. Develop a plan."

She waves her hand, and Zoe gives a curt little nod and quickly leaves the room.

I can feel my heart fluttering with excitement. They were going to help me get Ben out of that hell hole. I was going to see him soon, possibly tonight. I can't contain the smile spreading across my face. I look up to find Finn and Jax watching me, and the smile drops right away. Shizen. I'd forgotten about them. They can't be here when all this happens. They can't be caught in the city with me, hiding with me and Ben. They need to get out of here. I need to know they are somewhere safe. I take a deep breath.

"Jax, I'm gonna ask you for a great favor," I say. "I need you to take Finn and Cat with you when you leave today. Take them back to Gray Valley. Keep them safe. They won't be no trouble to you. Cat is a real good hunter, Finn too. They'll earn their keep."

I ignore Finn's cry of protest. I was expecting that. It's Jax who surprises me.

"I didn't realize I was going back to Gray Valley today," he says matter-of-factly, and I look at him in confusion.

"But we found Lily. She's gonna help me get Ben back. Your job is done. Just promise me you will keep Finn safe,"

I say.

"And what good is my promise if I don't keep it?" he says.

"I don't get it. Wha—?"

"I promised you I would help you free Ben. Last night when you were too mule-headed to take the damn rope, I made a promise to you, and I'm aiming to keep it."

"But you don't have to," I say slowly, like he's too dimwitted to understand. "Lily and the others … they're gonna help me now. I just need you to look after Finn. The two of you cain't be here in the city when this happens; it's too dangerous."

"I ain't going nowhere," says Finn and sits his butt down on a chair, arms folded and staring me down all defiant-like.

Oh gods, not now, I think.

"Look, I know you want to help, but I cain't have anythin' happen to you. The both of you need to get out of the city while you still can. Don't worry about me; I'll be fine with Lily's people. We'll be in and out of that iron mine in a split second. They won't know what hit 'em," I say, smiling at Finn, trying to assure him everything would be okay.

"Tara is right," Lily says, and I nod, happy she's agreeing with me. "You should take the boy and leave. I will have one of my men take you out the back way just to be safe. And if it's Tara you are worried about, have no fear. She will not be accompanying my people into the mines. It is far too dangerous."

"What?" I'm not sure I heard her right.

"My people will do this without you. We cannot risk you being captured again."

I can only stare at her and blink stupidly. "Dangerous? You want me to go up against the Prezedant, yet you call this dangerous?"

"You need proper training; you are not ready for battle yet. My people know what they're doing," she says in her serene voice, but it irritates me to no end.

"Really? And do they know who to look for when they go in? What are they gonna do, take the time to go around and ask every poor soul in there if their name is Ben?" I snap.

"She has a point there," Tater interjects, leaning over on his chair. He quickly shuts up at Lily's withering look.

"I can go with them," Jax says, and I groan in frustration. Not him, too. Good gods, why are they all being so mule-headed?

"I saw him yesterday. I know who to look for. And Tara gets to stay here out of harm's way."

"Well, if Jax gets to stay, so do I." Finn says stubbornly. "I can help too."

"Stop it. All of you. I will be the one to go, and that's that. Ain't no use in arguin'. Jax, you take Finn and go back to Gray Valley. I thank you, but I don't need your help no more." My tone is firm. This conversation is done, and my decision is final.

"Tara," Lily's voice is calming, like she's talking to an irate young'un. "Think about what you are saying. My people can't be worried about protecting you from the Army. If you wish Ben to be free, then you have to let them do their part. Jax is right; he can go. He's seen Ben's face; he knows who to look for. You would just be a liability and endanger them all."

Dammit. I know what she's saying makes sense, but I can't stand the thought of not going. Of not being there to make sure it all goes right and they get Ben out of there safe.

"Fine," I huff because I don't like it, not one little bit. But if it means seeing Ben in front of me safe and sound, then I will do whatever it takes.

———————

Over the course of the evening, Lily's people began showing up. Not all at once so as to draw attention, but one or two, spaced apart like they were just people coming to seek treatment from the healer. I had to admit it was a real smart setup she had going on to avoid suspicion. And I'm real surprised to see what her little band of rebels consisted of. There were men, women, young'uns not even as old as me, and even muties who'd arrived, faces covered with wrappers so as not to be detected. But whether man, woman, or mutie, every one of them greets me warmly. Like they're all so happy to see me. I ask Lily about their strange behavior, but she says it isn't strange at all. I was a true New Blood of the light; they were honored to meet me. I don't like it.

I'm happy to see Po in amongst them though, to see that he's alive and well after having saved us. He greets me with hands on my forearms, and I feel that tingling again, which Lily informs me is a common response between our kind. We are blood connected, she says. I will get used to it, she says. She seems to be forgetting that I'm not sticking around long enough to get used to anything. I don't remind her.

They gather at the huge table we had breakfast on earlier, so many of them that there aren't even enough chairs for them all to sit. I watch from off to the side, partly because I can't stand all their curious looks and touching, but mostly because I'm still mad that I'm not going on the mission. Even Jax gets to sit among them and help plan. Seems funny that I'm some all important New Blood but I have no say in the matter.

After confirming with Zoe that the guards were in place around Sanctuary to stop any unwelcome guests from walking in, Lily begins talking in earnest. She does most of the talking, well, her and one other.

A tall, brick wall of a man with close cropped, gray hair seems to be just as important to these rebels as Lily. I study him curiously. He wears a patch on his right eye, covering the eye but not the jagged, raised scar that runs from his eyebrow down his cheek. I find myself wondering who he is and what had happened to him. As if suddenly aware of my scrutiny, he looks up and catches my gaze. The heated blush rises in my face at being caught staring, but he doesn't take offence. He merely grins at me and winks his good eye before turning his attention back to the group. I hear Lily call him Mack. The name is fitting somehow.

I listen intently as they plan. The talking goes on for quite some time, long into the night. Finn had been keeping me company earlier, but at his stifled yawns I send him off to bed with the promise I would wake him if they came back with Ben. Tater had wandered off, too. I figure there had to be an ale room somewhere nearby that needed attending to, so I watch the rebels plan on my own.

They eventually arrive at a good strategy. A sound proposal that just may work. As I listen to Lily outline it, I realize how much of a natural leader she really is. She skirts around the issue of me only agreeing to stay here based on them being able to free Ben. Instead, she plays it off as rescuing my kin would free me up to be able to concentrate on their cause, their rebellion. That they would be doing me a great honor. I'm amazed to see not one person protest this escape plan. As a matter of fact, they are all arguing over who should be in the select few able to go. They finally decide on the chosen eight, Jax and the man Mack being two of the eight. I'm still put out at not being included in the rescue group and watch in simmering anger as the chosen group is divvied out the black gear, right down to the black hoods, same as our rescue group from the previous evening. I still can't believe they are going after Ben without me.

Zoe lays the remaining dark clothes on a smaller table back against the wall and leaves them unattended as she disappears into thin air again. I do a double take. Where the hell did she go? As I search for her in the room, my gaze falls on the clothes. They're just sitting there, calling to me almost, and all of a sudden an idea starts forming in my head. I'm still listening to Lily, but I stroll almost casually to the table, trying not to draw any attention to myself. The group is arguing now over who should be the ones to go in and who should be the diversions. I take advantage of their inattention to quickly swipe a hood and black tunic and shove it under my own. Before anyone can see the telltale bump, I scurry out of the room up the hall and straight to the room with all the books. A quick perusal tells me I'm alone, so I hide the clothes under one of the tall, backed chairs, and I'm back in the kitchen before the argument is even over. I'm relieved to see that no one seems to have been aware of my absence except Jax who looks up as I enter, but I just smile brightly at him and give him two thumbs-up. His brow furrows in puzzlement at my behavior, but he just shakes his head at me and turns his attention back to the tall man.

"It is decided then. Jax, Krowell, Riven, and I will be the four to go in. Our inside man assures me he will get himself assigned to the prisoners' quarters tonight, so he can give us access with no problem. You other four will create the diversion we need to get in. It won't be easy. I have heard the Prezedant's men arrived this morning, and they were very upset at hearing Naryz had lost the three prisoners. Security is at high alert right now; no one wants to be the next one to screw up."

Lily speaks again, "Mack is right. This will not be easy. It will, however, be very dangerous. Some of you … may not come back. Are you all willing to take that chance?"

Hearing those words being spoken aloud and the reality of it all suddenly hits me like a punch to the gut. It is a dangerous thing they are doing, and they're doing it for me. I'd asked them to do this. Why would they do such a thing for a stranger? I look, waiting to see if anyone wanted to change their mind. I wouldn't blame them if they did, but no one backs down. The one called Riven slams his meaty fist on the table and grins out over the crowd.

"I'd be willing to chop off me own arm if it meant a chance to take out a few of that evil bastard's men."

This is followed by a round of howling laughter and a few shouts of, "Aye!"

I'm truly astounded. I can't even begin to understand why they are doing this. Why would they wanna help me? Then another realization hits me. Shizen. Jax is going, too. He's going to put himself in grave danger to help rescue someone he's never even met. Just because he promised me. I can't believe that I've been so selfish, so intent on Ben's rescue that I haven't even thought about the danger the others and Jax would be in. I look at him with this fresh awareness only to find those light blue eyes already on me. It's like he knows what I'm thinking in my head, and he smiles at me. A real, full-out smile like the night of the dancing and my heart does that same crazy flip flop, only this time, I've got no excuse that it's dancing causing it. Right then and there, I know. I know my anger at not being allowed to go isn't just from my fear they're going to mess up rescuing Ben, but also because I won't be there to watch Jax's back. I had to go. Jax needed me there, and I know I made the right choice by swiping those clothes. There's really no other option.

I glance up again to see him crossing the room and heading straight for me, like he wants to talk to me. Panic starts building in my chest and I turn tail and run out of the room. I can't talk to him right now. I'm too full of confusion and guilt and fear.

Back in the book room, I do another check to make sure I'm alone before dressing in the clothes and covering my head and face with the hood. The plan is to take the covered wagon that had brought us here last evening, back out to the mines, so *my* plan is to hitch a ride. Once dressed in the stolen gear, I make my way to the smelly stone room off the white hall, hoping I don't run into anyone and have to explain what I'm doing. Thankfully, I don't meet nobody. Not even creepy Zoe who seemed to haunt these halls and pop up when you least expect her. One of Lily's rebels or not, she truly does gives me the willies.

The stone room is still empty as well, so I choose a nice, big pile of hay at the back of the wagon as my hiding spot. I don't wait long before the rescue team start showing up. I watch from my hiding place as they pile into the wagon. I need to time this perfectly.

Jax is the last in line but he lingers, looking at the stone door hopefully. *Is he waiting for me?* I wonder. Is he expecting me to see them off? Finally, he shrugs, runs a hand through his hair and pulls on the hood before joining the others in the back. I'm not sure, but I think I see disappointment on his face.

Zoe shuts the door to the wagon behind them, but pauses and cocks her head, looking around the room like she senses something. I don't dare to even breathe as I sink lower into the pile of hay. She can't find me. I need to be on that wagon. I reckon she finally decides all is good as she gives up on her inspection. Opening up the two massive doors to let in the night's cool air, she climbs up into the driver's seat behind the two horses. I wait for my chance and then run at the wagon, jumping onto the back step just as it begins to move. I get a firm grip on the metal bar at the top of the wagon cover and hang on for dear life, since if I remember correctly from last night, this is gonna be a bumpy ride.

Thankfully at this late hour, there's hardly a soul traveling the roads, but Zoe don't take any chances. She sticks to all the winding back roads and alleyways. The few stragglers we do come upon are either too drunk or too involved in their own transgressions to care what we're up to. They don't pay no heed to the wagon or to the bouncing madwoman hanging off the back. We don't meet no resistance at the back gates leading out of the city either since Po had been sent ahead earlier in the evening to "take care of" the guards. Not quite sure what that entailed, whether it was the same trick he had pulled on the raiders or not. I don't want to know. Whatever he'd done, it worked. There isn't a guard to be seen.

Once we get through the gates, the light of the city fades behind me, and it takes a while for my eyes to adjust to the inky darkness of the outer lands. I'm surprised at how Zoe can maneuver the wagon so easily through the sand mounds, but she doesn't slow her pace at all. I simply hang on tighter and grit my teeth so as not to bite my tongue as the wagon jerks and bounces.

Finally, we pull to a stop in the shadows of a high sand dune, concealed from any watching eyes of guards that may be lurking in the area. I can see the iron mines off in the distance. It's hard not to. As dark and shadowed as the rest of the outer lands are, the iron mines are lit up like it's the middle of the day.

There are blazing fires burning everywhere, surrounding the perimeter. They definitely aren't taking any chances. Shizen. Those fires will surely make it that much harder to sneak in. Why are they taking so many precautions, I wonder? It isn't like they know we're coming to break Ben out. I don't get no time to wonder about it, though, before I hear Zoe make her way down from the driver's seat and start coming around back. I hop down from my perch and sneak to the other side of the wagon. Only after she opens the door and the rebels are all standing outside do I casually make my way into the pack under cover of darkness. They don't even realize I'm there; they're all looking at the lit-up sky surrounding the mines and wondering the same as me.

"No matter. We knew they would increase the security. The plan still stands," Mack whispers loudly, and the uneasy murmuring ceases at his commanding words. "You four, up the ridge. Get ready but wait for my signal."

They slink away and disappear into the night without a sound.

"Let's go," he whispers again, and I fall to the back of the line as we head out. Following their stealthy approach, my heart beats wildly as I fear they will notice their number is five, not four like originally planned. But I don't have to worry for long. As we get nearer to the mine, we can tell something isn't right. The fires burning all around the mines are done on purpose-like, a light show to enhance what is put on display. At first, I think my eyes are deceiving me. But at Mack's, "Holy mother of gods!" I know what I'm seeing is real sure enough.

Bodies. At least fifteen or twenty of them, all hanging by their necks from a long platform built across the entrance to the mine. They sway quietly in the night air, a blood-curdling sight to behold. My stomach lurches and it feels like I'm gonna retch, but as much as I want to, I can't tear my eyes away.

The first I see is Naryz, his bloated body made even more so by death. The two next to him are also soldiers; I can tell by their uniforms. But then I see something that almost brings me to my knees. A frail body in a ragged yellow tunic. The young girl Ben had helped get back on her feet yesterday after the soldier had knocked her down. No. That can't be her … can it? Why would they do such a thing to her? Not even the Prezedant could be this brutal. This evil. But even as my heart argues with my brain, I see the chains circling her ankles linking her to the next body hanging beside her and the next. The rest of them hanging there … they're all prisoners.

"No!" I cry, unable to bear the horror of it any longer. It can't be. Ben can't be there, too.

My cry is enough to rouse Jax from his shocked stupor, and he whirls. "Tara?" he says in disbelief.

"What are you doing here, girl?" Mack's voice is an angry whisper, but I'm way beyond caring about getting caught.

I want to run. I don't want to look. Please, he can't be there. He can't be one of the bodies.

"Jax … they're prisoners," I whisper, grabbing at his arms to keep from falling, and he understands right away. His eyes do what mine refuse to, and they search the faces of the people hanging there.

"He's not there, Tara," he says finally, and my knees actually wobble in relief.

"You sure?" I whisper, and he grabs my shoulders as if he fears I'm gonna fall.

"He's not there." His answer is firmer this time and I'm glad for his hands supporting me because I'm too weak to stand on my own.

"Mack." The urgent whisper comes from the darkness as a brown-robed soldier steps outta the shadows and into the light. Already rattled by the gruesome sight in front of us, the rebels' shooters go up in alarm at the soldier's sudden appearance, but then Mack relaxes and puts up his hand.

"It's okay, he's one of us. Stand down. What the hell happened here, Stein?"

The young man looks around in fear like he believes at any moment we're going to be attacked.

"The Prezedant ... he came for the New Blood," he says, and my relief at knowing Ben isn't there is quickly replaced by panic again.

"You mean, he was here? In person?" I say.

The soldier nods. "He arrived this morning to the news that they had escaped ... that they had fled Littlepass. He blamed Naryz. Naryz, he tried to atone; he gave up the boy you were coming to rescue. He said that they knew each other, him and the New Blood."

"What do you mean gave him up?" I'm glad Mack is asking since I can't form the words right now. I'm too busy trying to swallow the lump in my throat that must surely be my heart. "What did he do with him?"

The soldier shrugs. "He took him when they left. He took him with them and left this as a message for the New Blood."

"A message?" I say, but it comes out as a croak.

The young man wipes his face like he's still in shock at what he'd witnessed.

"He killed all these people like it was nothing and then those of us he left alive, we were given a very specific message to pass along." He closes his eyes like he's trying to remember or trying to forget; I'm not sure. "Tell the New Blood if she returns, this is on her hands. But she can save the boy if she wishes. Turn herself in, and she can save his life. A life for a life. That's what he said."

I shake my head at his words. The Prezedant, he did this.

He killed all these people, that innocent young'un, because of me? What have I done? And Ben. Now he has Ben. That's my fault, too. We'd been so close. Ben was here ... I'd seen him. I could have gone back and helped him. I should have, but I didn't because I'd chosen to listen to Jax. And now he's snatched away again. It's not fair.

"Tara," Jax says, still grasping my shoulders, but as grateful as I'd been earlier for his support, his touch now feels as if it's making my skin crawl. Ben is gone again, taken away from me because I'd been stupid enough to believe in Jax's empty promises. I lay my hands flat against his chest and shove him away from me. He staggers backward, but he doesn't fall.

"This is your fault," I hiss at him, lashing out with my anger. Needing to blame someone for the crippling pain that's squeezing my heart right now, Jax becomes the target. His eyes open wide in wounded shock at my words, but I don't stop. "We were so close last night. I wanted to go back. I wanted to go get him. But you talked me outta it. I let you talk me out of it. Now, the Prezedant has him, and I ain't ever gonna see him again!" I shove him again, wanting so badly to hurt him. But he doesn't even try to defend himself; he just keeps staring at me.

"This is your fault, Jax." I whisper, my words filled with despair.

I turn and run. I can't be around them anymore. I ignore the voices calling my name because the anger is rising and my blood catching fire, and I'm scared to be around them. I'm scared for what I'll do to Jax or the rest of them. So I run into the darkness, away from the mine and Littlepass. I run and run until I have no breath left, and I finally fall to my knees in the dirt.

On my hands and knees, gasping for air as sobs wrack my body, the soldier's words bounce around in my head. *A life for a life. A life for a life.* I say the words over and over again like a chant until my anger disappears and my blood cools down. *A life for a life.*

I suck in a couple ragged breaths and release them, giving myself a mental shake. Calmness overtakes me, and my next breath is even and controlled. All the fear and anxiety I feel for Ben, it solidifies around the chant in my head, forming one rational thought. The knowledge of what I have to do now strikes me with intense clarity. A life for a life. If that's how it has to be. If it's a life the Prezedant requires then let it be his own, because it sure as hell isn't going to be mine.

I hear the voices off in the distance still calling for me. Jax and Mack. I know I should answer them. I should go back. I have to go back. Ben is depending on me. His life depends on me, and if the only way to get him back means becoming what so many believe the gods have decreed, then so be it.

I get to my feet and turn into the wind toward the voices, truly ready to accept what I must do now. It's time to live up to their expectations: Orakel's, Lily's, and Grada's. It's time to face the truth and become what they already believe me to be. It's time to stop being afraid and to live up to my destiny. It's time to awaken the New Blood.

About the Author

I wish I could tell you I've climbed Mt. Everest or taken a hot air balloon ride around the world, but alas I lead a very quiet life in Nova Scotia, Canada. The only adventures I go on are in books. But what adventures they are! When I'm not reading or writing, I manage a chocolate shop. That's right; I work with both books and chocolate. Living the dream. The rest of my time is spent with my three favourite guys; my hubby, my son, and my crazy fur baby. We are a family of geeks. Fans of Game of Thrones and The Walking Dead, lovers of books of any genre, and players of video games. And I wouldn't have it any other way.

Other books by Michelle Bryan

Crimson Legacy series
Crimson Legacy
Scarlet Oath
Blood Desstiny
Bood Hunt (a short story)
The Waystation (a novella)

The Bixby series
Grand Escape (Prequel)
Strain of Resistance
Strain of Defiance
Strain of Vengeance

Legacy of Light series
A War for Magic
A War for Truth
A War for Love

Printed in Great Britain
by Amazon